Guardian of Power

Guardian *of* Power

David Rose

Matador
9 Priory Business Park,
Wistow Road, Kibworth Beauchamp,
Leicestershire. LE8 0RX
Tel: 0116 279 2299
Email: books@troubador.co.uk
Web: www.troubador.co.uk/matador
Twitter: @matadorbooks

ISBN 978 1789017 632

British Library Cataloguing in Publication Data.
A catalogue record for this book is available from the British Library.

Printed and bound by CPI Group (UK) Ltd, Croydon, CR0 4YY
Typeset in 11pt Aldine401 BT by Troubador Publishing Ltd, Leicester, UK

Matador is an imprint of Troubador Publishing Ltd

For all my family

PART ONE

I

There was just a little bit of tidying up to do and then he would be finished for the weekend. His young, green eyes flashed around the room, giving everything a final check before it was time to head for the heavily secured, glass doors. Through one of the Lab's small side-windows, he caught sight of a farmhouse light teasing from a distant hill, calling like an isolated amber beacon. For an instant the familiarity reminded him of his home in the Cheviot Hills and brought back a cherished memory of his childhood days before he forced himself to return to the matters in hand. Although it was the end of the working week, there were still another seven more days to go before his summer break, when he planned to revel in some well-earned rest and enjoy the company and unwavering love of his family.

Leaning over the work-bench he caught his security tag in the folds of his stomach, causing him to mumble at its irritation, before he adjusted the plastic label. The white name tag was worn beside the silver-star buckle on his belt rather than on his chest or lapel as a minor gesture of individuality. He was not sure whether this frequent inconvenience to his personal comfort was worth the statement. The black bar-code printed along the top of the synthetic badge enabled him to access those parts of the complex relevant to his work. Ben Moyles was one of the highly skilled physicists and computer whizz-kids working on the Puissance Project, a major international research programme based in France, aimed at finding a clean and sustainable source of energy for the modern world.

There was general agreement among his peers that a breakthrough was possible, a solution could even be within their grasp at some point during the next two years. The thought allowed Ben to feel superior as he pinched the bridge of his nose to edge out the tiredness that was beginning to impact on his body. The other workers in his section had already left their stations so he could afford to take his time and indulge his ego in silent isolation: his control of the normally busy environment was now total in the relative peace of his clinical workplace. Stroking his chin, he felt some relaxed comfort and turned to explore his working world totally unchallenged. While silence echoed down the modern, glass hallways, Ben was omnipotent, perusing his prestigious surroundings in complete control.

He rolled his tongue around the inside of his mouth, sensing the impending taste of coffee at the end of his shift. By chance, he caught sight of his own reflection as he walked past a trio of blank computer screens. After five years of dedicated focus on the international research mission, he was surprised at his mirrored image and thought he looked older than he felt. He straightened his back and extended his arms to cosset a wide yawn, turning away from his unwanted self.

It had been a challenging time as one of the small cogs within the Puissance Project, especially working under Professor Ian Thompkins, who was a demanding task master. Thompkins made sure all his research huskies were constantly driven forward and several of Ben's younger colleagues had already been left behind to be picked-off, after experiencing too much of the boss's supercilious bullying. All things considered, Ben thought his own time working for the Australian, prize-winning physicist had been a success. He had even impressed on a couple of occasions, providing some fresh insight into the research. Now Ben was looking forward to flying home and seeing his father and brother. It had been a while since he had been able to enjoy the peace and seclusion of their isolated farm. Only one more week to go before he could truly relax. However, there were more pressing immediate needs as that waiting time was to be filled by a review of the research project and it was going to be conducted by the top man himself.

Ben's hard-earned status would enable him to attend all Thompkins' seminar groups during the seven days, albeit in a supporting role. With the thought of being part of something special, he slowly lowered a clenched fist onto the work bench and knocked twice for luck. He then swung a small bunch of keys around his thumb and pondered whether his own tasks had been completed as he looked around the Lab for some inspiration. Ben spotted a wall-cabinet underneath the old, white Timex clock. The cupboard's sliding, glass doors were open, so reaching his six-foot frame to its maximum, his index finger pushed the panels together to close the cupboard. His fastidious attention to detail was something Ben's brother Richard had often teased him about during their childhood. *'You sure you haven't got OCD?'* was the taunting voice inside Ben's head as the clock's minute hand jerked forward with a click. The sound caught his attention and he stared at the pristine Roman numerals, without paying attention to the time. The clock was something of an anachronism in this high-tech location but it added character to an otherwise sterile environment.

After ensuring all was perfect with the cabinet, Ben returned to his key-turning exercise, while whistling silently under his breath and giving his private world a final perusal. There was only one thing left to do: it involved closing-down his computer and then initiating the programme to run the elaborate security codes, before his pc could finally be switched-off. The loading process in the morning normally took about ten-minutes to boot-up and a similar period was needed to close down the system when he had finished for the day. Given the fact that his pc was connected to the main-frame, which contained very important, highly sensitive information, the procedure was a necessary safeguard. There was no latitude for mistakes and forgetting to switch it off would almost certainly lead to dismissal, no matter how much of an impression he had made.

Ben put down his keys on an adjacent table and sat in front of his computer screen. Without looking down at the keyboard, his dancing fingers initiated the necessary programme that comprised his final task. After a few seconds, a myriad of screens of white text on a dark blue background produced a rolling slide-show of apparent chaos as each programme was closed in sequence. While the dark screens appeared intermittently in front of him, Ben could see his reflection staring back and this time he gave his image more scrutiny.

Although he was not a vain individual, Ben took pride in his appearance. While his emerald eyes glazed-over to another place and allowed his mind to wander to a state of tired neutrality, the familiar routine of words on the computer screen appeared before him in a futile attempt to gain his attention. Ben's prestigious job was due in no small part to his father's encouragement to leave the family business and spread his wings after university. Once he had graduated from Imperial College with a double-first in Physics and Computer Science, Ben had initially worked with his father and brother on the family farm but Graham Moyles was astute enough to realise that the younger of his twin sons was destined for bigger things. After six months of wasting his talent on the land, Graham and his other son Richard nagged Ben into applying for a research position.

Finally, he relented and eventually progressed onto the prestigious Puissance Project. After proving his value and impressing his bosses during an assessment year in London, Ben moved on to their research headquarters in France. A further rigorous selection process saw more than eighty-per-cent of the top graduates fall by the way-side before the remainder were taken on by Bosson International, the corporation responsible for running the Puissance Project. Ben was now into his fifth year, working near the small settlement of Sergy, at the foot of the French Jura Mountains, close to the Swiss border, about ten miles from Geneva.

Ben's glazed state of hypnotic self-admiration was suddenly broken as the computer's concerto signalled the software's closing-down process was complete. He picked up his keys from the table and slipped them into the pocket of his brown, leather jerkin as he was getting ready to leave. Scooping-up his briefcase in a well-practised motion, Ben finally headed for the door, satisfied with a job well done. His hand shadowed over the white control panel by the exit, before returning to his side. There was no requirement to switch-off the light system because the security staff needed to ensure the cleaners were closely scrutinised as they went about their daily routines.

The automatic lock was engaged when Ben closed the door and strolled down the pristine corridor, satisfied with his contribution for the day. After progressing through three more security codes, the last doorway saw him arrive at a swish elevator, which would take him to the main archway in front of the reception desk. In a scene reminiscent of an airport departure desk, Ben placed the metallic contents of his pockets and his briefcase into the large plastic tray on the conveyor belt. After being scrutinised on the security monitor by Bastien, who was into the second hour of his night-shift, the items were reclaimed by their owner. '*Bonne nuit*, Monsieur Moyles. Ave a good week-end.' Bastien touched the peak of his cap, with a mock salute.

'*Merci, Bastien. Et vous aussi.*' Ben's reflex response involved no eye contact as he turned away and headed for the exit.

Stepping out into the fresh, crisp, evening air, Ben devoured the tranquil evening and looked upward to absorb the beautiful, silhouette view of the Alps in the distance, just beyond Lake Geneva. It was an inspiring moment as he felt an upsurge of morale, almost skipping towards the wire-fenced car compound, where his red Peugeot was waiting.

Ben's feeling of tranquil optimism was misplaced: he was not the only employee working on Puissance to be unaware that the Project's security had been seriously compromised. Although he did not know it at the time, his fastidious attention to detail when closing down the team's computer system half-an-hour earlier had been a complete waste of effort. Information and data on the system's mainframe was already known to a third party. They were not interested in the contents of a pathetic little desktop computer being worked on by of one of the Bosson's minions. Fifteen miles away, across the border in Switzerland, in a factory that was not all it seemed, the image of Ben's laboratory was showing on a monitor screen and being viewed by contemptuous eyes.

The factory was privately-owned but manufactured nothing that could be bought on the open market. The stacked pallets outside the large, sliding double-doors served only to deceive any nosy onlooker. Operating anonymously under Swiss legislation, a foreign State was secretly operating to ensure the Puissance Project failed in its mission. Investment in oil had gone too far down the pipeline to be threatened by the discovery of a new source of power. There was no way that any research project was going to be allowed to establish a rival alternative and nothing was going to be permitted to upset the status quo. Whatever the factory needed to do its job would be provided. This secret complex had the highest authority to use anything in its mission to subvert Puissance. Oil's position as king of energy had its protectors who were prepared to be proactive in crushing any threat.

While Ben Moyles made his way back to his bijou flat, he was blissfully unaware that the secrets of his work were known to a group of people who did not have his best interests at heart. The sinister click of a mouse closed the scene on a monitor screen in the secret Geneva factory – for now.

II

The morning alarm rang out at six o'clock and it was all Ben needed to wake from his deep slumber. As he lay in indulgent semi-hibernation, he gave a thought to his plans. Although Saturday was not a work day, it was not going to be a *Samedi sans travail* either. Ben never liked to simply lounge around the apartment, hence the early rallying call on his mobile phone. Years of growing up on a farm had given him the appetite to appreciate the innocence of mornings.

His mind soon programmed his schedule before he friskily kicked-off the duvet. The first task was obvious: his vest, shorts, socks and trainers were restless for exercise. Soon Ben was in full kit and looking forward to his run. He acknowledged another early-riser, who was more appropriately dressed while waiting for the lift doors to open. Deciding not only to curtail his embarrassment but also keep moving rather than share the elevator, Ben self-consciously made his way to the stairwell and exited the building, before quickly picking-up his pace.

He jogged out of Sergy, towards the minor farm roads, which paralleled the base of the Jura Mountains lower down. It was a beautiful day, not yet hot and ideal for running. The hedgerows were low enough to observe a small herd of Friesian cows, grazing in a paddock, as he ran past. He thought for a moment that he could so easily have been in the UK, although the comfortable developing warmth of the bright morning and the pristine detached houses, with their thirty-degree roofs, suggested he was somewhere rather more continental. Developing a regular, comfortable rhythm he glanced to his right, where the Alps stood proud against the wakening sky.

There was usually a very simple analysis to Ben's jogging sessions: half-an-hour out and half-an-hour back. The main variable was the direction he would take, although the Saturday run was nearly always the same, running out of Sergy into the countryside and towards his favourite market village of Villeneuve. Following the spring-line of the Jura escarpment, he would switch to the cycle track into Crozet and head for Avouzon, before returning on a similar loop back to his apartment block. The run enabled him to absorb the beauty of this region of France, his peace only disturbed by the isolated mooing of curious dairy and beef cattle. His route along the side of the Jura Mountains was a surprisingly flat circuit that allowed him to enjoy the wonderful views from an elevated position.

As he approached the thirty-minute mark, he glanced at his watch to check progress. A grimace was followed by a smile as he recognised the run was going well, giving him the confidence to lift his head and look around at the view. There was a black Renault Clio parked just inside the rubble track beside the Water Treatment Plant, facing towards a red '*Entrée Interdite*' sign. Ben thought it odd that a car would park like that and risk the possibility of a ticket from the local *Gendarmerie*. Soon the notion evaporated and he was gliding around the perimeter of the Avouzon roundabout, heading back to Sergy.

The dark red stain on his scarlet running vest indicated an intense level of perspiration as his legs continued to pound. Just before the Sergy road sign, Ben had to leave the convenience of the cycle track and briefly run across the road, against the general direction of traffic. As he was running he did not bother to look over his shoulder and consequently failed to spot a speeding black car. A piercing honk came too close for comfort and the shock caused him to outwardly curse and raise a middle finger to the disappearing vehicle. '*Vous branleur*!'

He soon arrived back at his apartment, where he dumped his running kit on the bedroom floor before fleeting into a warm shower. Once dried and dressed, he was ready for the next part of his weekend routine. Popping his lips together before looking around the kitchen to give himself time for one last thought, Ben left his apartment and headed for the local shops. He always enjoyed fresh croissants from *Renoir's Patisserie* on a Saturday and he knew his neighbour Antoine Moreau looked forward to receiving a surprise pastry from his friend, along with his weekly copy of *Charlie Hebdo*. Antoine was in his seventies and since a tricky fall he relied heavily on the help of friends. The legacy of a dislocated knee still caused him some mobility problems and although past his prime Antoine retained his wicked sense of humour. Ben appreciated the paternal qualities shown towards him whenever they were engaged in meaningless banter about the world at large. It was no trouble to help out the old man who lived on the downstairs floor and if Ben ever needed a favour in return, he knew he only had to ask.

Antoine's door opened as soon as Ben entered the apartment block. It was Ben who spoke first, 'How long have you been waiting for me, *mon ami*. I am sorry if I am a bit late this morning but my run was longer than usual.'

'Ahh – feeling fit today are you *mon jeune stud frisky* ?' was Antoine's teasing retort.

'Never mind me – that little red-head in *Renoir's* was asking about you this morning, you old goat !'

'You're never too old – I have told you before, once you have it and you are French, you never lose it, my English *novice*.'

Handing the folded magazine to Antoine, after slapping it onto the old man's stomach Ben explained, ' I have brought you a *carac* this morning but be careful the chocolate does not spoil your figure.' Antoine spotted another paper bag in Ben's hand and raised his chin with curiosity

Ben realised what his greedy friend wanted. 'Oh no you don't. That is *my* breakfast and you are not having any. Just go and enjoy your pastry and I will see you later, *d'accord* ?'

'Oui – à plus tard, Ben, et merci une fois de plus.' Antoine's saluted, raising the rolled-up copy of *Charlie Hebdo* to his temple, while Ben skipped upstairs.

Ben was soon enjoying the isolation of his galley kitchen, with a strong coffee and a couple of still-warm croissants. While the endorphins were kicking into his system, he appreciated the sacred minutes of self-indulgence before his mobile phone vibrated on the glass-top table and he responded with reluctance. It was Camille, calling about the dinner party later that evening. Ben knew why she was calling and had almost expected her to ring. Looking up at the kitchen ceiling, he needed to curtail the conversation, otherwise she would be talking for the next half-an-hour. 'Yes, don't worry I'll be there …I hope you are not going to try and … I'm perfectly capable of … So who is going ? …Ok, I'll bring a nice bottle of Bordeaux … ok, ok, see you there. Bye.'

Placing the phone next to his half-eaten croissant, Ben's ironic smile said it all. He knew Camille would not take a blind bit of notice of his attempt to fend her off. Crossing to the sink from his high kitchen stool, he placed his used breakfast remnants on the workspace and moved his keys onto their hook. He was still buzzing with the morning glow: the hour was early, he had been on a run, eaten breakfast and abated his evening host's enthusiasm to find him a partner. It was obvious that Camille would not let the opportunity of a party pass without trying to fix him up with a date, she had done it several times before. Although Ben had been out with a few girls while living in France, he was not looking for a relationship, not that Camille would be deterred.

Ben had first met Camille at a science conference in Geneva, a couple of years earlier. He had noticed her arrive in a bright green Peugeot 406 Coupe and during dinner they found themselves sitting next to each other by chance at one of the large circular tables. While the meal was being served Camille reached across for a serviette and inadvertently knocked over a glass of Bordeaux which spilled onto Ben's lap. To make matters worse, the shock caused her to suddenly jump out of her chair and add some sauce to the mix. While this would not normally have caused too much fuss, her piercing shriek of embarrassment did trigger a measure of curiosity from some people sitting nearby. The comical scene was concluded when Ben left the dining room with a grovelling Camille following behind, trying to wipe him down with a clean serviette, which she had pilfered from a neighbouring table. In the lobby of the conference's hotel Camille tried desperately to apologise for her *faux pas*. This only caused Ben to convulse in laughter at the ludicrousness of the situation, which was more like a scene from a Shakespearean comedy than a convention for scientists.

The missed speech on self-charging batteries turned out to be a stroke of luck because the whole thing was a mega-yawn and Ben later learned he was better-off for not attending. When Camille phoned him the day after the conference to reinforce her apology, she offered dinner by way of compensation. Ben visited her house the following weekend, where he was also able to meet her husband Gaston. Following a lovely evening together when the conversation flowed naturally, Ben subsequently became close friends with Camille and Gaston Dubois, who lived in a neighbouring village, just a few kilometres away from his apartment.

After pausing all thoughts of Camille, Ben left the kitchen and returned to a corner in his bedroom, where he lifted several carpet tiles beside a house plant, to reveal a couple of laptops and a box of flash-drives, hidden next to one of the joists. Although he was not allowed to remove any data from the Lab at work, no one could prevent him from transporting his knowledge and ideas. Using his computer skills and his natural ability for total recall, he had been able to replicate the essence of his research onto his own laptops. When they were connected to his desk-top computer via the Dark Net, the set-up was almost as good as the hardware he had at work.

Ben had cut a lonely figure out of the Lab during the years he had been living in Sergy. Camille and Gaston along with Antoine were the only people he truly regarded as friends so settling into some undirected activity to explore his own ideas on sustainable energy was a labour of love that he relished. He eagerly assembled the leads and the keyboards which allowed the hardware components to function as one unit. Ben enjoyed the opportunity to break from the research constraints imposed by his boss at work and explore his own theories, in total secrecy. He knew it was dangerous to operate with such subterfuge, not just a threat to his employment but also his own safety. If any foreign power became aware of what he was up to, there would almost certainly be an attempt to steal the data. However, he found this risk intensely stimulating and the deception gave him a buzz.

Casually, he booted-up the system and loaded the confidential data. Ben reckoned he could indulge himself for about five hours in the apartment, before he would need to get ready and face what Camille had in store. Tapping his fingers lightly onto the keyboard he sat mesmerised as prancing on-screen icons played out a ballet before his eyes, while he plotted the directions of a seemingly infinite number of atoms, protons and neutrons, shooting across the screens like falling stars in the firmament. Their movement and power were being choreographed by a dazzling scientific mind, with his dancing hands conducting the instruments of his brilliance. Ben hoped that one day, he could show Professor Ian Thompson that the direction of the Puissance Project needed to alter course and follow *his* theories.

The Puissance Research Project (PRP) had been established in 2010 by the European Union, following an international symposium on climate change, where all the world's great super-powers were represented at the highest level. It was one of three global, mega-endeavours trying to explore the possibility of limitless clean power, harnessing the same nuclear reactions that keep the Sun burning. The Puissance strategy focussed on nuclear fusion, where atoms collide in an extremely hot, pressurised, hydrogen environment to produce enormous amounts of energy. The biggest conundrum for the scientists engaged with the research was how to make the hydrogen sufficiently hot and dense to generate sustained, continuous reactions. Ian Thompson was targeting temperature control as the way forward but all Ben's research persuaded him that the solution lay with pressure management. He had spent just about every spare weekend for four years exploring his own theories on how to generate such intense pressures in a safe environment.

Working in the apartment obviously had its shortcomings. For a start, he had only two computer screens, four at a push, if he included his old laptops. There was a need to constantly dart his eyes back and fore on the monitors to see how the different graphs were responding to the ever changing input of data. In the Lab at work, he could rely on about ten screens, each pulsating to accommodate fresh statistics. Ben was never deterred by the constant dive-bombing of virtual protons, neutrons and electrons as they buzzed around like a huge fireworks display. Each failed trial told him something new, helping to build a pattern of evidence. Eventually, stinging eyes told him it was time to finish and get ready for the dinner party to celebrate Gaston's fortieth birthday.

III

Ben hoped the bell would work because he hated knocking on doors like an expectant brush salesman. The last time he visited Camille and Gaston's place, the master of the house promised the chime would be fixed and to Ben's surprise, a resonating ding-dong called out. He thought to himself that perhaps he needed to be kinder to Gaston and cut him some slack, after all it *was* his birthday. Feeling a little self-conscious with a bunch of flowers in one hand and a bottle of best Bordeaux in the other, he waited for someone to arrive at the door and let him in.

'Hello darling, good of you to come.' Camille was her usual charming, coquettish self.

Leaning forward to *faire la bise*, Ben could not help himself and he responded to her remark. 'Ok, no need to be like that *Madame Sarcastique*, I know I'm late.'

'Again, you mean !' she laughed as she returned *la bise* . Camille then turned into the hallway and headed for the throng of other guests, while beckoning with her arm, 'You know I'm only teasing. Come on in and meet everyone.'

As Ben prepared to enter the large elegant room, Camille relieved him of his hospitality donations with a perfunctory, 'You didn't have to bring anything darling, but thank you'. Looking out towards the patio doors, he felt momentarily threatened by all the faces turning in his direction, realising that apart from Gaston, he hardly recognised anyone. The host approached and offered his hand. '*Bon anniversaire, mon ami,*' submitted Ben, sounding just a little like a schoolboy repeating a well-worn, classroom phrase.

Gaston was genuinely pleased to see him. 'Ah, there you are, Ben. Camille was beginning to get a little worried.' Turning to the group, he announced Ben's arrival and the nearest couple gathered around to offer their greeting. 'Ben, this is Sabine and Léo. They live in Villeneuve. I'm sure you'd like to tell them about your love of their village market. Let me get you a drink.' Gaston made his way to the temporary bar, leaving his guest to flounder in unfamiliar company.

Camille soon re-entered the room and immediately recognised Ben's uncomfortable collar adjustment. She crossed the polished wooden floor and broke into their conversation, in an attempt to rescue her friend. 'Ah, Ben there is someone here I'd like you to meet. I'm sure Sabine and Leo won't mind if I steal you away for a minute?' Leo stood back to accept his host's wishes and allowed Ben to make his escape. As Ben was being saved, the thought that crossed his mind was *'Of course there is someone you would like me to meet – and not for the first time.'* He was a little worried that Camille's attempt to find an acceptable partner for him was beginning to become something of a crusade. 'Ben, this is Veronique. She is new to the area and has just started working for Gaston in his bank in Geneva. I'm sure that you can help her feel at home.' Smiling his most sincere expression and raising his eyebrows only slightly, Ben tried to *faire la bise* while lightly taking her hand and was a little surprised at the manner in which she teasingly returned his kiss.

During their inevitable exchanges of initial niceties, Ben tried as surreptitiously as possible to assess the potential prize being offered by Camille. Veronique rated quite highly on the scale of possibilities, although the bright green nail varnish gave him some cause for doubt. Her hair was shaped in the local style of a Geneva-bob, ideal for office work. She had beautiful eyes and clearly worked-out in the gym, judging by the muscle tone in her legs. At the very moment when Ben was beginning to enjoy their chat, Gaston chinked his whisky tumbler with a knife and announced that everyone should retreat to the adjacent dining room, where dinner would be served.

It was no surprise that Ben and Veronique found themselves sitting next to each other during the meal, particularly as everyone else was either married or in a long-term relationship. After the initial kerfuffle, while Camille directed everyone to their seats, a member of the hired catering staff began to place the starting dishes in front of the assembled gathering. The food looked delicious and Ben began to relax as he took a sip from his second glass of wine. When he eventually looked up, averting Veronique's eyes, he caught sight of Camille's gaze from the end of the table. She raised her empty glass and gave an ironic, dry toast in his direction accompanied by a smile of victory.

Veronique was becoming more captivating with each sip of wine and Ben could sense his resistance begin to wane as he was drawn into her casual charm. He learned that Veronique had started working for Gaston about three weeks earlier, when his friend's personal assistant suddenly left her position for pastures new elsewhere. Gaston had needed someone with the appropriate skills at very short notice. The job, albeit temporary, offered opportunities to Veronique's career in banking. She had moved from her home in Lugano, on the Swiss-Italian border and came with excellent references. Veronique informed Ben that she saw the job as a stepping stone, Gaston's position as Chief Executive of the *Schtern Banking Group* could enhance her possibilities if she could make an impression.

Mademoiselle Veronique Perrin had registered on Camille's radar during a visit to see Gaston at work. Camille thought that she should consult with him about who to invite to the party as Ben's consort. Whenever she raised the topic at home, Gaston was always too tired to talk about something that was beyond his interest. However, Camille knew she would quickly get an answer at his office because he would want to get rid of her in order to get back to his responsibilities. On the day of her visit she had bumped into Veronique in the ladies' toilet where both engaged in a brief but friendly exchange. When Camille left her iphone beside the sink, she was swiftly followed by Veronique, who was able to return the valuable item. Suddenly, Camille could see the perfect solution to her conundrum right in front of her eyes. She was delighted when Veronique accepted the couple's invitation to the party.

When the meal was over, chatting guests sauntered through the patio doors and onto the terrace to enjoy the still, warm air. The sounds of Montbeliarde cattle wafted across the countryside and the Alpine peaks pierced the lilac sky, while the guests relaxed into casual conversations. Ben and Veronique strolled along the tiled pathway towards the gazebo at the bottom of the garden. They were being scrutinised by their matchmaker, who was standing with her arm on her husband's shoulder. 'Make a nice couple, don't you think, my old, *old* husband ?' Camille followed her question with a smacking kiss on Gaston's cheek.

'Do you think so ? I'm not so sure.' Raising his brandy glass in their direction, Gaston pondered, 'You're sure he's not gay ? I've sometimes wondered, you know'.

'Believe me darling he's not gay.' Her affirmation was sealed with another kiss as she turned away and headed to her guests, wearing an unseen cheeky grin.

'How do you kn…. ?' Gaston shrugged a smile of his own, admiring his wife's teasing, before his eyes followed her into a group of guests.

Ben thought that he must have been drinking too much and was aware that he could not drive home. He would either have to get a taxi or scrounge a lift back to his apartment from a willing guest, someone else was bound to be going his way. Most people seemed to live in the cluster of small villages along the French-Swiss border. Ben was now resting his elbow on the gazebo table for more support than he cared to admit. 'So what's Lugano like, Veronique ? I've heard it's supposed to be beautiful, despite the Mafia banks clogging up the centre.'

If Veronique had known him better she might easily have been offended by Ben's remark but she recognised that his empathy was being attacked by too much wine, so she played along. 'Lugano is a stunning city. Some of the views from the funicular railway on the way to the top of Mt. Sighignola are breath-taking. I know Geneva is lovely too but it does not compare with Lugano.'

'You'll have to take me there some day.' It was the best line Ben could muster under the circumstances.

Veronique bounced the flirtation back in his direction, making deliberate eye-contact. 'Perhaps,' she teased with equal coyness. However, the Bordeaux was fuelling Ben's bravado, so she decided to make a semi-retreat. 'We should be getting back to the party, otherwise Gaston and Camille will be talking about us.' Ben scraped his chair clumsily as he stumbled to an upright position and gave himself an inward rebuke, ordering his body to take control of itself. 'I'll be surprised if they're not,' he said, cuttingly. The pair started to walk back slowly along the path but Ben's gait was clumsy and he was feeling strangely drunk. Veronique thought she had better hang on to his arm, to save him from falling over and potential embarrassment.

As they merged into the gathering, the hired staff were busy laying after-dinner coffee cups onto the tables of the semi-lit terrace. A few people glanced in Ben's direction as he sighed up the large step from the garden lawn. Camille handed Veronique a strong espresso and she took the saucer in one hand, while hanging on to Ben with the other. Ben drank the caffeine in two large gulps. 'Thanks, Veronique – I needed that.' Camille and Veronique exchanged a knowing look. The hostess took the initiative, 'You stay there Ben and I'll go and order you a taxi. It's probably best if you don't drive home tonight. Leave your car here and phone me to make arrangements about collecting it in the morning.'

Veronique saw an opportunity, 'It's ok, Camille. I have my car with me and I can take him home. I'm sure Ben can show me where he lives.' Within ten minutes Veronique was driving her sleeping suitor back to his apartment.

IV

A heavy arm rolled onto the empty space beside the waking body. The warm sensation of the sheet under his elbow suggested that someone had only recently risen from the bed. Ben felt depressingly ill as he raked his stiff fingers over a face that was waking from an unusually deep sleep. It had been a long time since he felt this bad after a night's drinking and he did not think he had drunk any more than normal. The feeling was so unusual that he thought he must be going down with a bug or something, yet there had been no other signs of sickness prior to last night's debacle. His limbs felt heavy and stiff and his re-call of the previous evening was sketchy. The last thing he remembered was Veronique's gorgeously naked body on top of him, with her well-toned legs straddling his thighs. Then – nothing. He was not even sure if he had been able to complete the deed, although the sensation in his loins told him that he must have done. He contemplated Veronique's whereabouts until a chinking noise from the kitchen told him she was still be in his apartment. It was definitely time to get up.

Ben stumbled into the *en suite* bathroom, still unsteady on his feet. While splashing cold water frantically into his sleep-stuck eyes, he suddenly felt nauseous and turning away from the sink, he vomited into the toilet bowl. Surely he could not be this hung-over after a night with friends? Completing a one-eighty he returned to gaze at himself in the bathroom mirror. After wiping the detritus from his lips, he leant on the sink with both arms and examined himself more thoroughly, but his reflection simply confirmed what he already knew. Completing his cold water, wake-up routine and quickly swilling some mouthwash, it was time to engage his brain.

Ben's thoughts turned to his guest and as he sat on the edge of the bed, preparing to enter his boxer-shorts, the smell of coffee wafting into the room indicated Veronique was still in the kitchen. Semi-dressed, he tracked her down beside the percolator, where she was standing with her back to the door. She was fully clothed and much more alert than her sloppy host. Veronique did not hear Ben approach from behind as he placed his arms around her waist before kissing the back of her neck. She jumped slightly and turned into his embrace, before they both kissed passionately, with Ben hoping that the mouthwash was doing its job. Breaking from their clinch, Veronique interrupted the silence. 'There you are sleepy-head. You alright, you look a bit washed out?'

Ben felt the need to defend himself. 'Yeah, I don't feel too clever, either. Didn't realise I was so drunk last night. I didn't embarrass myself did I?'

Veronique offered some genuine reassurance. 'No, you were fine and in any case, everyone was a bit merry, it was a party after all. I think you had a good enough excuse don't you. Certainly if you have been working the hours you were telling me about, it's no wonder the wine and tiredness did that to you.' She shot her fingers into his chest, firing in rapid succession. Grabbing her into another embrace more forcibly this time, he could smell the gorgeousness of her hair as she nestled under his chin. Veronique eventually broke his hold and turned away to fill two cups with espresso. 'There, you'd better drink this. It will soon bring you around.' The first sip told Ben the coffee was cool enough to be swallowed easily so he drank the rest as if it was medicine, before he reached across to pour a second cup.

'What are your plans today ?' asked Veronique, hoping to extend their time together.

Replacing the cup onto a work surface Ben responded, 'Not sure … I really need to do some work. I've got a busy week coming up, before I go back to England. Thing is, I don't feel like working right now. Certainly can't get my head around anything demanding …. and there's my car. I should really ring Camille and arrange to pick it up.'

Camille offered some help in that direction. 'I can give you a lift over there … if you would like, that is.'

He pulled her close. 'Thanks, that would be great if you could. Then perhaps we could have lunch or something.'

As Veronique placed both arms gently around Ben's neck she said, 'Tell you what. Let's go and get some fresh air first – it will probably help you to get over your hangover – then we could go and have something light to eat and I can drop you off at Camille's place mid-afternoon. I should really return to Geneva tonight. I've got some work to do, too.'

'Sounds like a plan, let's do it !' With that, Ben became more animated, rubbing his hands together as if spinning a straw. 'Just give me a chance to put the rest of my clothes on and I'll be with you.'

Soon, Ben and Veronique were motoring out of Sergy and heading for the open countryside, in her black, convertible Mini Cooper with its roof down. The refreshing breeze washed over his face and felt better than any medicine. Too soon for Ben, Veronique pulled-over into the village of Avouzon where a few street-side tables outside a small café proved to be irresistible for some reason. They walked from her car to the white plastic chairs and sat quietly while Veronique swirled her sunglasses around her fingers. Somewhat surprised about having stopped at such an isolated spot, Ben was not really bothered about ordering anything to eat or drink, preferring to absorb the beautiful views and the tranquillity of the Jura Mountains. Conversation between them was restricted to eye contact and then Veronique reached across the table. Her blatant invitation to kiss was accepted gratefully and Ben was neither aware nor concerned about any passing villagers commenting on their behaviour at such an early hour. Nobody came outside from the café to take their order so after fifteen minutes of French indifference, they got up and ambled away from the tables.

They strolled down a side-street, through a lane and towards a small area of woodland. Veronique took Ben's hand and pulled him towards an isolated patch of sun flickering through the branches of a large birch tree. Giggling together, they collapsed to their knees where Veronique made her intention obvious. This time Ben was conscious of creating a memory that he *would* be able to recall and he took her in his arms once more. Their open-air lovemaking was passionate and intense, with Veronique taking the lead, trying to remind him of her skills the night before. She was making more noise than was sensible but she was also capturing Ben's emotions with each impassioned sigh.

All too soon their union had climaxed and the coupled turned onto their backs, to gaze at the sky and recover their composure. Ben wriggled to adjust his trousers, while his partner searched for her shoe with her foot. It was Veronique who started to laugh first but she was soon joined by Ben and before long, their snorting became synchronised. Veronique rolled on top of Ben once more, with her skirt creased up to her waist and her bare buttocks facing the clouds. By now Ben was aware that she was a woman with few inhibitions. 'Where are we going with this?' she asked with some seriousness.

For once, Ben was in a carefree mood. 'I don't know and right now, I don't care.' He was happy to lie in a state of contented post-coital bliss. Eventually, he scrambled to his feet, simultaneously tucking-in his shirt and adjusting his hair. Veronique picked up her thong, which was lying on the grass beside her feet, and pushed it purposefully into her handbag, before she tried to make herself as respectable as she could in the circumstances.

Their energy spent, the walk back to the car was silent as their minds contemplated what had just taken place. They drove out through Avouzon , unsure about another destination until Ben took the initiative. 'Now might be a good time to take me over to Camille's place so I can pick-up my car.'

'Of course – if you're sure.' Veronique sounded vulnerable, something Ben found attractive.

He made a suggestion, 'Perhaps we could meet up again, later in the week ?' Veronique smiled and her nod of approval was all the confirmation he needed. Before long, the Mini Cooper was pulling into the driveway of Monsieur Gaston Dubois before the couple gave each other one more final kiss.

Ben walked towards the front door and pressed the button but this time he could not hear the bell ring. He wondered if the damn thing had already stopped working after Gaston's attempt to repair its chime so he was forced to knock on the rapper. Fortunately Camille had seen Veronique's car arrive from her bedroom and was already on her way to the front of the house. She greeted Ben with a hug and gave *la bise* with three kisses before standing back to admire her pupil. 'Well how did your date go ? Don't tell me – let me guess. No… I can tell because you look absolutely exhausted. Come on in. I want to hear all about it.' Taking his arm she virtually pulled him onto the terrace.

'Where's Gaston ?' inquired Ben. I hope he enjoyed his party. He seemed to be having a good time from what I can remember.'

'He's gone to his golf club. Nothing will stop him from going there on a Sunday morning. He claims it's where he does his best business but I think that's just an excuse to visit his pals and have a boozy lunch. He should be back soon.' Pouring her guest his fifth coffee of the day, she did not break eye contact. 'Well, I'm waiting. How did it go with Veronique ? Do you like her. Oh, please say you do *mon cher*.'

Ben and Camille nestled into an intimate conversation about his exploits after leaving Gaston's party. There was not that much to say because he could not remember most of what had happened. A lot of his account was fictional bravado, motivated by what he believed Camille wanted to hear. She was more pleased about her own success as a matchmaker than Ben's enjoyment of Veronique. When his tale was almost done, the slamming of Gaston's car door indicated he had returned from the golf club and it was Ben's signal to leave. Gaston entered by the side-gate and bumped into Ben who expressed his gratitude for having been invited to the party. After their brief hello-goodbye moment, Ben started his car and headed home.

During the isolation of his short drive back to his apartment Ben reflected on the previous twenty-four hours. There had been significantly more social interaction than he was used to and he was not sure how he felt about the experience. Sure, the sex was good but it seemed like Veronique had been parachuted into his life from nowhere. He knew very little about her. Ben preferred changes in his life to be organic rather than volcanic and this was taking him out of his comfort zone. At least he still had his work. It was now mid-afternoon and he had to decide whether to work or go for a run and rid himself of the toxins that still remained in his system. Given that work tomorrow was going to be the start of an important week and he needed to be on top form, he decided to park his research and go for another light jog.

V

The brilliance of the Monday morning sun shining through the glass-wall into the conference room on the third floor was too strong for comfort as Ben's eyes assessed the scientists in the room. A body count suggested that in terms of contribution to the Puissance Project Ben ranked about eleventh out of fourteen team leaders present. There was not much small-talk within their gathering, the high level of secrecy involved with their work meant that no-one wanted to risk being compromised by saying something out-of-turn. Since it was solely their research that had brought this collection of scientists together, social niceties were unnecessary.

The impressive place cards on the conference table were an ostentatious gesture intended to massage the egos of those physicists who wanted to feel important. The long table had a glass top, presumably to ensure nothing untoward took place below waist level. Everyone had been scanned on entry to ensure the room was 'bug free,' while mobile phones were barred from the meeting. Ben was sitting at the end of the row by the door, at the furthest point from the singular name at the head of the table, which belonged to Professor Ian Thompkins. At two-minutes-to eight, the leader of the Puissance Project entered and before anyone had a chance to react, he issued his first instruction. 'Good morning ladies and gentlemen, please don't get up.' Although this directive helped Ben to avoid any *faux pas*, it was also irrelevant because he never had any intention of standing. He certainly admired and respected Thompkins' incredibly brilliant scientific mind but he did not like the man whose arrogance hindered any recognition of his positive attributes. Ben wondered how many others were thinking the same thing as the supremo made his way to the top of the table.

Thompkins wasted no time getting down to business. Standing upright like a commanding officer and self-consciously turning the distinctive signature ring on his left index finger, he began his delivery. 'The work in my Alpha Lab is continuing to make good progress and I have made significant advances since the beginning of the year. The lasers my team are directing towards the hydrogen isotopes are bringing enormous energy yields and the helium waste is manageable. However, the difficulty of sustaining the fusion reaction is proving problematic. I need a state-of-play update from all Research Leaders, in order to assess my next step.'

The leaders of each of the eight laboratories gave their reports in turn, including Jonas Brandli who led Ben's team in Eta Lab . All the scientists in the room listened with interest to their colleagues' findings, each member gaining further insight into the overall progress of the research. However, in Ben's opinion the reports did not reveal anything particularly significant or new. Nothing he heard dissuaded him from his view that producing intense pressures at the core of an electricity generator was a safer and cleaner route to producing a sustainable source of energy than raising temperatures.

Just before the end of the seminar, with lunchtime approaching Thompkins invited open questions from the floor. Ben decided he had nothing to lose and raised his pen. Thompkins waggled the ring-finger at his minion in response. 'Yes, Dr. Moyles – you have a question ?'

'Thank you, Professor Thompkins. Yes, I do have a question relating to our work in Eta Lab. We have been working with magnetic pressures in toroidal machines for some time now.' Thompkins was nodding and staring intently as his inquisitor. 'Using this intense pressure we believe we have been able to create the state where hydrogen behaves like a metal, which could in theory cause it to act as a zero-resistance superconductor. This could help to harness helium waste and would mean greater laser-temperature efficiency, rather than focussing on increasing temperatures *per se*. Have you considered developing this further in Puissance?' As soon as he had finished his question, Ben wondered if he had gone too far in challenging Thompkins' approach. He soon found out.

'I'm sure you're aware of similar work in Washington University, which has recently been mocked within the world's scientific community. I have no desire to be a laughing stock in any work I lead so the short answer to your question is no.' Looking around the room and standing even more upright he continued, 'Now do I have any serious points from a senior colleague ?' Ben tried to fight-off the instinct to blush with embarrassment and anger after such a patronising response. He sensed stinging smirks from some of his so-called colleagues sitting just out of his vision to his left. More importantly, he was not sure how his line manager, Jonas Brandli would respond to what was seemingly being perceived as a challenge to Thompkins' ability.

'Who is that joker ?' asked the voice in the darkened factory room. His accent along with his dark, swarthy complexion suggested he was not a Swiss national.

'He's English… Miles or Moles or something. Supposed to be a rising star,' responded the co-worker.

His superior enjoyed the moment. 'Looks like he might have just exploded on entry.' They both laughed mockingly, enjoying their hidden power.

The camera that had been recording Thompkins' meeting was secreted in the thermostat on the wall of the conference room, completely unseen and unnoticed. Its fixed position gave a clear view of everyone involved in the room, allowing unsympathetic eyes to revel in authority over the enemy. It had not taken long to infiltrate Puissance and circumvent its security system. The process was easy once the maintenance contract for the buildings had been secured. Authority had been approved at such a high level that it was relatively simple to dupe Puissance staff on a daily basis. The affable servitude of the maintenance workforce was the perfect cloak to fool those looking for breaches in security. No matter how sophisticated the anti-bug screening was, those attempting to protect the Project's secrets had no chance of success. There had been a huge investment in monitoring the labs, buildings and offices of the internationally important mission. The source of the surveillance was closely linked to rich men who had too much invested in oil to allow anything to usurp their position.

Ben made his way to the on-site cafeteria, where he found himself standing in the queue next to Jonas Brandli – it was not a coincidence. About to take one step forward and release a ham and cheese sandwich from its clear-plastic compartment, Ben felt the waft of warm air from a smoker's whisper in his ear.

'We need to talk,' suggested Brandli, quietly enough to go unheard by others but still sufficiently authoritative to ensure the directive was going to be followed.

'I agree,' said Ben, only half-turning around. 'Here now or later somewhere else?'

'Give it half-an-hour and I'll see you back in my office, ok ? Have your lunch first.'

After an unedifying break, Ben found himself in a chair opposite his line-manager's desk. Brandli was more sympathetic than Ben was expecting but it was still a reprimand, nonetheless. 'What were you thinking about?' asked Brandli. 'You should know better by now. Nobody challenges Thompkins and gets away with it scot-free. Especially when everyone else is there to see it happen. You'll be lucky to keep your job after this and one thing's for certain – from now on you'd better watch your back.'

Ben tried to defend himself. 'I know I should not have antagonised him by asking that question but we are close with *our own* work here. Wouldn't you agree ?'

Brandli turned his palms upwards in support. 'I agree we are close but what's the point if you're not around to see it happen ?' was a question posed with more sympathy than accuracy.

'I'm sorry Jonas but Thompkins just hasn't seemed to want to consider the pressure route. He seems fixated on lasers and heat. Can you imagine what our work could mean ? If we are right we could generate enough energy to cover the needs of every European home using the equivalent of only one bath of water per year for every household. Just imagine it – a clean source of sustainable, cheap electricity using what is all around us. We would no longer have to rely on oil and be at the behest of other countries governed by regimes we don't like.'

Brandli had some words of caution. 'I understand everything you are saying, just be careful that's all. Believe me, I hope you are right. It would make all our hard work worthwhile and would represent a breakthrough of immense proportions.'

'So, we're good ?'asked Ben, seeking reassurance about his position, at least with his line manager.

'Yes, Ben *we* are good but make it right with Thompkins and we will be even better.'

Ben got up to leave and turned before closing the office door, blowing out one of his cheeks with a sense of relief as he walked away. It seemed the fall-out from the seminar would amount to nothing more than a slap on the wrists but it could easily have been worse. Ben accepted the consequences of his transgression, knowing that it was highly unlikely he would be fired at this stage of the research because his work was too important to be side-lined, even by Thompkins.

One or two heads turned as Ben's walked down the glass-walled corridor past the laboratories. Arriving at his place of sanctuary, he began to continue his research in isolation. There were four days left before his return home and he believed that would be long enough to set-up an experiment which he could leave to run during the time he would be away. After punching data for the remainder of his working day, he drove home that evening feeling bruised and isolated.

Entering his apartment block around seven o'clock, Ben noticed a light under the doorway of Antoine's flat. Just before placing a stride onto the stairs, Ben hit his neighbour's door with a single blow that he knew his friend would hear, simultaneously shouting, *'Bonne soirée à mon ami, tu vas bien là-dedans?'* A deep Gaelic murmur was enough to reassure Ben that indeed, all *was* well with his neighbour. This was a strategy that both men had come to accept as an unseen form of affection. The friends were of different age, from different countries with different interests, yet they shared an unspoken common bond. Neither tried too hard to analyse their friendship, it was much less complicated to simply enjoy the experience. Ben skipped up the remaining flight of stairs with a smile, wondering if Antoine was enjoying the television, magazine or something else: knowing Antoine, it was probably something else.

Ben rustled-up a potato omelette, which did not take long. Cooking for himself was the last thing on his mind and he was too tired to go out for a drink or start more work. He felt that an evening in front of the television might not do him any harm and perhaps an early night was in order. Just as he was wiping the frying pan with a dishcloth, his mobile started to spin around on the smooth work-surface as it reacted to an incoming call. He shook the suds from his hands, wiping them in the nearby tea-towel before looking at the screen to see if he should accept the call. If it was a sales pitch trying to entice him to buy something, his intention was to hang-up. After gazing at the phone for a few seconds, curiosity got the better of him and he pressed the 'Accept' icon, even though there was no name on the screen and he did not recognise the number. He was surprised to hear Veronique's voice.

'Is that you, Ben ?' was the hushed question, asked in a seductive voice.

He hesitated. 'Oh, hello – Veronique ? Hi, yes, it is me..... I didn't recognise your number when it came up on the screen. Where are you calling from ? I almost didn't accept the call.'

'Ah yes ... this is another mobile I have. I use this one for work sometimes. Gaston doesn't seem to mind if I use it for personal calls. It's not as if the Bank can't afford it.'

It was Ben's turn to be on the defensive. 'Oh, right. Where are you? I wasn't expecting you to call and was going to contact you later in the week. I was going to suggest that perhaps we could meet up and go out for a meal or something.'

Veronique tried to capitalise on the offer. 'I'm just in my place right now and could be with you in less than half-an-hour if you would like me to pop over ?'

Ben contemplated what she was saying and thought, *'Christ, she's a bit keen. I know we did the deed a couple of times but I wasn't prepared for this onslaught.'* Feeling he should err on the side of caution, he deflected the offer. 'I can't tonight, I'm afraid Veronique, I'm in the middle of working on something at the moment and I have to finish it for tomorrow. I'm running a bit low on time, given that I won't be here next week I'd better do it now. How about Wednesday, I could book a table at that Italian bistro in Geneva.... you know the place I mean – that Luigi's Restaurant in Rue Chapponière?' Ben considered this rebuff would be a little less obvious than saying that he was just about to collapse and watch television.

This allowed Veronique to take the lead once more. 'Yes, that would be very nice. What time shall we say ? .... about eight?'

Ben would have accepted any suggestion. 'Ok, good. Sorry about tonight but I will go ahead and book a table and I'll see you there on Wednesday at eight.'

Veronique was making her feelings clear and they appeared to be stronger than Ben had anticipated. She continued, 'I shall look forward to it, darling. Until then ....bye.'

Placing his mobile back onto the work surface, Ben was uncertain about his emotions following the call. He seemed to have made quite an impression on Veronique, who was significantly keener than some other partners he had known. A smile crossed his lips as he recalled their two previous amorous encounters. Nevertheless, he knew he had made the right decision to decline her offer. Although feeling a little perkier because of the call, he still felt tired after his stressful day. He wondered perhaps if this was the beginning of the increasing years starting to take its toll on his body, although at thirty-five he was still a fit young man. A knock at the door announced the arrival of the one person who could always cheer him up in such circumstances – his neighbour Antoine. Beaming the sort of irrepressible smile that was his trademark, Antoine stood with a bottle of his favourite French brandy in one hand, his arms wide apart.

'How about it *mon ami*, would you like to discuss with me why *La France* is better than *L'Angleterre* ?'

Ben waived his arm to gesture an invitation to enter, wearing his own grin of surrender. 'I shall do my best, Antoine but after the day I've had, I'm already prepared to admit defeat. Come on in.'

Ben realised that a good laugh and a tasty nightcap was the perfect antidote for his malaise and Antoine gave him the nicest two hours of a day best forgotten.

VI

For the next forty-eight hours Ben confined himself to Eta Lab, assembling the mini-reactor that would test his ideas. The apparatus being constructed in the middle of the laboratory was as big as a normal household gas boiler and stood beside a meal of wires and cathode tubes. There was some danger attached to what he was planning and like all significant experiments at Puissance, authorisation by Professor Thompkins was needed before it could be activated. In the past, Thompkins had usually expressed a professional interest in what Ben was attempting to prove or disprove. However, on this occasion it was his second-in-command, Dr Sebastian Thiroud who rode shotgun on Ben's project. Ben was concerned that if the outcome did not produce something positive he might be spending a lot more time in the Cheviot Hills than he had originally planned.

On Wednesday afternoon Thiroud's inspection lasted only twenty minutes before he scurried back to report to his master. Ben watched him leave, content with his own progress on the generator's assembly. One more day should be enough and then he could move the whole unit into the safety cell in the Radioactive Zone and allow his theories to be tested. Once the process was activated there was no going back. There were only three more key components to be assembled and then the system would be monitored by computers in Eta Lab, where only a few people would have the access needed to decipher the pulsating graphs and flickering amber digits. If the experiment went badly and the reactor exploded in the safety cell, at least no one would be injured – in theory.

Knowing that he was going out to dinner with Veronique later that evening, Ben decided to do no more preparatory work than was necessary. He left his masterpiece with all the nonchalance of a mechanic abandoning a dismantled car engine and reconciled to leave the Puissance complex promptly at five o'clock. There was a perplexed look on the leathery face of the dark-skinned observer as he examined the unfolding drama on his monitor screen in the Geneva factory. While Ben made his exit through the usual security checkouts, the spectator signalled to a senior figure, who soon appeared at his shoulder. Speaking in a Middle Eastern accent he asked, 'Is there a problem my friend ?' The foreigner leaned over and scrutinised the scene more closely, squinting unnecessarily. 'What's he up to – figured it out yet ?'

'Not really sure. I think I'm going to have to send a recording of this upstairs so the specialists can find out what he's putting together. Whatever it is, it's certainly got his attention. He's been working on it solidly for nearly three days now. Didn't even go to lunch today – and now suddenly he's leaving ?'

'He must have a date tonight.' They both smirked as the sitter's shoulder was squeezed in a gesture of mutual understanding.

There were no barriers at the border crossing that evening as Ben entered Switzerland. Only the hat of a seated policeman jutting over the top of a low window in one of the booths indicated any semblance of security. Sometimes if there was an active alert both security cabins were fully manned and even the cars of regular commuters were searched. Not today. Ben smoothed along the *Route de Meyrin* and headed for the centre of Geneva, most of the traffic at that time was heading in the opposite direction. Parking would normally have been a problem but he was lucky, as he spotted a car pull out of a space in a side-street. In the narrow roadway there were so many idle motor bikes and scooters that at first sight the street looked like the scene of a major accident. The quick availability of his parking space meant Ben was now earlier than expected. Alighting from the vehicle he contemplated how Veronique would interpret his apparent eagerness to get to the restaurant as he was now bound to get there first.

After checking-in with the head waiter, Ben sauntered over to a corner table and settled into his seat, before ordering a small beer. He had a good view of the street and just for a moment in the fading light, he thought he saw Veronique in the distance talking to someone who was getting out of a taxi. A passing van momentarily blocked his view, causing him to doubt his double-take, before both figures disappeared.

About ten minutes later, Veronique arrived and Ben gave a polite wave which was warmly acknowledged as she responded with a beaming smile.

Ben got out of his seat to give *faire la bise* and while she settled into the unfamiliar chair he took the initiative. 'Hi – was that you I could see a few minutes ago ? ….talking to someone getting out of a taxi ?'

Veronique seemed flustered at first but then realised what he was talking about, 'No, I don't think that could have been me ……. oh, yes wait a minute ….. it may have been. I was just giving some papers to someone from another bank. We have a big contract running at the moment and I wanted to show Gaston that I am prepared to go the extra kilometre and can be trusted with clients. I'd arranged to meet their bank's representative here when I knew we would be dining nearby. I wanted to make sure there were no last minute glitches. It is important that I make a good impression if there is to be any chance that Gaston may keep me on.' Veronique moved the cutlery around unnecessarily before placing her serviette onto her side-plate. She seemed unusually coy. 'How are you? … have you had a good day ?' she asked. Before Ben had time to give an answer she looked around and continued, 'It's nice here, isn't it.' At that moment their flow was further interrupted by a waiter inquiring about a drink for Veronique.

During the course of their meal the conversation was strangely stilted. Ben wondered if his question to Veronique had unnerved her and she was hiding something, although he had no reason to treat the thought with any credibility. While on his year of assessment with the company in London, he had been coached in various techniques on how to avoid giving away secrets about the people he worked for and about himself. The main focus of the training had been related to the importance and confidentiality of his research but there was still an awareness about giving away personal details to people who may try to probe. It had been different at Gaston's party, where everyone was more relaxed and the focus of most of the chat was on the host. The different atmosphere in the restaurant seemed to evoke more caution. Taking a final forkful of cheesecake he wondered for a moment if their physical relationship was really enough. Veronique turned to the side and glanced out of the window to observe events in the street, allowing Ben to size up the question as he undressed her with his eyes. Slightly embarrassed when she returned to his gaze, he smiled uncomfortably.

The restaurant was becoming busy with two or three new customers standing near the main entrance, trying to attract someone to come to their assistance. A waiter arrived speedily at Ben and Veronique's table to inquire about coffee and liqueurs. He did not look at either of the couple directly and seemed more concerned about clearing the dessert dishes. Ben thought he was being rather rude so raised his hand to gesture that nothing further was required and simply responded, *'Non merci, juste la facture s'il vous plaît.'* As the waiter retreated to retrieve the bill, Ben's mind raced while he pondered where to go next ? He knew Veronique worked for Gaston in Geneva and that she had a flat somewhere in the city but he did not want to go to her place and he doubted that she would be prepared to drive the thirty minutes back to his flat. Perhaps it had not been such a good idea to have booked dinner at this particular restaurant after all.

While they waited for the waiter to return, Veronique made her intentions clear. 'My place is only ten minutes away. Shall we have coffee there ?'

Ben thought quickly and came up with a solution, 'I need to go back to check on my friend Antoine. He has recently had a fall and I said I would pop in to see him before the end of the night. It's a bit of a longer drive but if you wanted to follow me back to Sergy we could … you know.' Ben did not feel guilty about telling Veronique a lie about his neighbour nor about making his intentions clear. It was the perfect solution for him and it would certainly test Veronique's resolve about their relationship. She seemed to be keen on him, this would assess just how much. To Ben's surprise, she did not hesitate, 'If that's ok with you ?' she purred.

Forty minutes later, they were entering Ben's apartment block in Sergy, where he switched on the lights before turning to Veronique, 'I'm just going to pop down to see Antoine. There should still be some coffee in the percolator if you would like to pour us both a cup. I'll only take a couple of ticks.' Ben left Veronique in the kitchen while he acted out his role. He went to his neighbour's downstairs flat but did not knock on the door. After watching a minute count down on his watch, he returned upstairs, where a cup of coffee was on the kitchen worktop. Veronique was sitting on one of the high stools, cupping her drink with both hands. 'That was quick,' she quipped.

'Yes, I think he must be asleep. I couldn't see any lights on and it was all quiet inside. You manage to find everything you needed while I was out ?' Veronique nodded as she sipped her coffee. Ben ignored his own drink and kissed her once more, this time with genuine sexual passion and intent. Leading Veronique to the bedroom, he sensed her stunning body was beginning to affect his thinking.

The following morning his alarm sounded its familiar early call. This time the adjacent bed-space was cold and there were no familiar sounds coming from the kitchen. Ben thought Veronique must have returned to her own place at some point during the night, while he slept. After completing his morning routine, including a short but enjoyable mid-week run, he was back in his kitchen. As he poured a bowl of cereal, he could see that pasted onto the door of his refrigerator was a yellow stick-note and on it was scribbled a heart containing a large letter 'V' with three kisses denoted underneath, causing him to smile.

He left for work and was soon at his station in Eta Lab. While at his busiest and engrossed in a particular delicate manipulation, Dr Sebastian Thiroud decided to call and make a final check on progress. Although Puissance was a scientific institution and Thiroud was one of the leading physicists, there were no indications from his attire that he was involved in anything technical. In fact, he could have just stepped out of the boardroom of any Geneva executive's office. However, Thiroud was no fool either and was quite happy to leave the dirty work to others. After examining aspects of the wiring and the generator's connections, he broke the stony silence. 'I understand from the technician's reports that all the main safety checks have been carried out so I can see no reason to cancel this experiment. How long are you going away for?' he asked with some indignation.

'Just two weeks,' replied Ben, totally indifferent.

Thompkins' gofer ended the conversation with a sting, 'Well, let's hope this experiment produces something positive. It's about time Eta Lab had something to crow about, instead of sniping at those making real progress.'

This annoyed Ben. 'What do you mean by that ?'

'I don't mean anything by it, Dr Moyles.' Turning away the lackey added, 'Have a nice holiday – I look forward to assessing the progress of your project when you return. Good day to you.'

There was a drop on the 'smug-meter' as Thiroud left the laboratory. Ben was past caring about the snipes being made in his direction. If he was going to get the bullet, at least he had done the best he could, given the level of support he had received from the top and he was already toying with other career options. In the world of physics Ben had earned a good reputation and if he was to put his name into the market place, he was confident that something more lucrative would come along. However, the potential for real glory could only come from being associated with an international project the size of Puissance, and there were only two others that were on a similar scale: one was in the southern state of Louisiana in the USA, the other just outside Dubai, in the United Arab Emirates. Both mega-enterprises had a vested interest in finding an alternative power source to oil.

The preparation work on Ben's experiment was now complete and he had been given a green light to proceed so he planned to arrive promptly the following morning to start the fusion process. When all was running smoothly he would pack his suitcase and prepare for his flight, which was very early on Saturday morning. Veronique had suggested getting together one more time before he left, but Ben decided to shelve that idea. Despite losing himself in his work, Ben's ego had taken a bit of a pummelling after the confrontation with his boss and he needed the reassurance that only his family could provide.

The dark blue suitcase was open on Ben's bed as he made shuttle strides from his wardrobe, choosing only practical clothes. It was summer in Northern England but this was sometimes omitted from the July calendar in the Cheviot Hills. Neither was there much call for fashion statements on Moyles Farm, where brown was the colour of choice. Just as Ben was padding down two pairs of socks into a corner of his luggage, he heard someone at the door. He was not expecting any visitors and was surprised to see Camille standing there, looking a little embarrassed. She quickly crossed into the apartment to give him her usual, generous *la bise* and Ben responded in kind.

'Hello, I was not expecting to see you tonight. Everything alright ?' asked Ben, in a very casual, unassuming manner.

'Yes, everything is fine – just thought I'd call in for a chat before you head-off home for your holiday. I'm off to our new ski lodge near

Interlaken with Gaston this weekend so won't be able to catch you tomorrow, before you go. I've not heard from you for a few days, now that you're all loved-up.' Ben gave her a contemptuous shrug of the shoulders.

'Come on in anyway,' he suggested. 'I'm just doing some packing. Want a glass of wine or something ?' As they made their way into the apartment, their conversation continued. 'New ski lodge, eh? I didn't know you had a second home. Must have cost a fortune if it's near Interlaken.'

'Just a coffee will be fine, thanks. It's still a bit too early for alcohol...... Yes, we've not long had the lodge. Gaston bought it as a surprise for me. Said he'd just had a big bonus off a grateful client and rather than lose tax on the windfall, he decided to invest in another property. You must come and see it sometime, it's absolutely beautiful.'

Ben was impressed by his friends' new-found wealth but did not want to show just how much. 'Mmm ... very nice. Tell you what. I'll finish off what I'm doing and then I'll be with you. I'll only be a couple of minutes, if you can stick the kettle on that would be great. The coffee in the percolator needs replacing so it'll have to be instant, I'm afraid.' While Ben frantically threw his clothes into the remnant space of his suitcase, he left Camille alone in his kitchen to tackle the coffee. Before long, he returned to pick-up on his duties as host.

He raised his cup to his lips and asked the question he had been pondering while in the bedroom. 'Right, you've got my attention so now you can tell me why you're really here.'

Camille looked surprised. 'What do you mean ? I've already told you – to see you before you go.'

Ben was having none of it. 'That's only part of the reason. You forget, I know you... there's something else.'

Camille gave a smile of defeat. 'It's just that I heard what happened at your meeting the other day. Gaston called into his golf club for a drink on the way back home after work and he ran into that friend of his, who I can't stand. I believe you know him too – Sebastian Thiroud?' Ben raised his chin to the sky and resisted the temptation to swear. 'For someone who should know better, Thiroud wasn't very discreet. He was telling Gaston that Thompkins had been foul to him all day, the product of his backlash with someone who dared to challenge his so-called professional integrity. Thiroud let it slip that it was you who he'd had the disagreement with. Thought I'd come over to warn you that you won't get any support there and see that you're alright before you catch your flight.'

'Thanks. That's really kind of you but what you have just told me is not really a surprise. I've not liked the way the project has been heading for quite a while and I couldn't resist the temptation to tell Thompkins what I thought needed to change. I'm my own worst enemy I suppose. Still, it's do or die time and if things don't work out after I come back I'll probably just return to the farm. Either that or get another job over here somewhere. There should be opportunities with some of Thompkins' rivals. I bet I'm not the only one who can't stand him.'

Camille had cleared her conscience. 'Anyway – as long as I've told you. I didn't want you to find out that I knew what was happening and I hadn't said anything.' She was now standing, preparing to abandon her half-finished cup and return home. 'I'd better go now, it was only a flying visit and Gaston will be wondering where I am.' As Ben opened the door for her she approached to *faire la bise* once more, before brushing past to make her exit. Ben pondered the consequences of what Camille had told him, while his glazed stare was without focus. The realisation of what he had done was beginning to strike home. Pride was one thing, professional suicide was something else altogether.

A few minutes later, just as he set about swishing out the dirty cups, there was another knock on the door and Ben allowed himself an inaudible mumble of annoyance. This time it was a sound Ben recognised and he was not surprised to see Antoine standing there, bottle in hand once again. '*Allo mon ami*. I have my old friend, Napoleon with me again tonight. May we enter ?' Ben opened his arms in defeat.

'Of course my old friend,' he said while looking at the bottle of brandy. There was a belly laugh of gusto, as over-the-top Antoine patted Ben's back and entered the apartment.

'I thought we could 'ave a final drink before you 'ead off to *L'Angleterre* tomorrow. Two weeks is a long time without my drinking companion.'

Ben admitted defeat and set about humouring his friend by covering old ground in their anecdotes of *entente cordiale*. After making a slight difference to the level of Napoleon brandy in Antoine's bottle it was eventually time to say *bonne nuit*. 'Ave a good journey and an enjoyable time with your family my English friend. I hope you return soon,' were the words of endorsement Ben heard as Antoine stumbled out of his flat and limped his way downstairs. Checking the stairwell light was switched on, Ben leaned over the bannister rail as he supervised his friends departure, calling down to him, 'Be careful and make sure you do not fall over again. I do not want to take you to the hospital at this late hour.'

As quickly as he arrived, Antoine was gone, leaving Ben with swirling thoughts and regretting that he had allowed self-indulgence to cloud his judgement, although the brandy was enjoyable. Tomorrow was an important day and he needed to be alert before setting up the experiment that could well decide his future. Antoine had not helped.

VII

Ben cruised into the compound as the sun began to peek over the Alps. There were only a few people on site at such an early hour so the usual driving around the parking bays looking for an empty space was not necessary. It was just as well because he had a lot to do. Parking closer to the main building than usual, he hoped that his regular check-in routine would also be quicker. As Ben approached the main building, his thoughts were racing about what he needed to do. He entered the security-check area just as some of the cleaning and security staff were leaving the building. There were pockets of workers sauntering and chatting, before lighting-up that longed-for cigarette just outside the main building. After some meaningless drivel with the guard on the detector archway, Ben collected his briefcase from the end of the conveyor belt and made his way to Eta Lab.

Every sound seemed to echo along the empty corridors, from the clicking of his footsteps on the grey tiles to the spinning locks on the security doors. Although vaguely aware of one or two other workers in adjacent laboratory areas, Ben was focussed on his own preparation. It was always necessary to put on distinctive bright yellow overalls before entering the practical area, something that was more than a gesture towards health and safety. The distinctive colour of the uniform was a signal to other colleagues that the wearer was engaged in potentially dangerous work and should not be approached. In this case, there was an outside chance of some radioactive particles being released during the set-up and it was a time to ensure zero risk. Finally, raising the goggles over his eyes and with a surgeon-like dust mask over his nose and mouth and an elasticated plastic hat covering his hair, he looked more like a terrorist than a scientist. Nevertheless, he was ready and he left the changing area via the exit displaying the imposing sign, 'Danger – Radioactive Area'.

This sensitive area of the Puissance complex looked like a giant garage workshop, with hoists, pulleys and trolleys seemingly everywhere. There was a supply area with a counter manned by willing technicians, even at six o'clock in the morning. Ben entered the radio-active scanning zone and was given the once-over by a magician waving a Geiger counter around his yellowness. After recording audible bleeps at an acceptable volume and frequency, approval from the supervisor was enough to allow Ben to enter the restricted area so he could begin his task.

Ben's two assistants had already arrived, no doubt keen to impress. They made their way to the blast-cells and he punched in a seven-digit code before the lead-lined electronic door opened slowly. Entering the eerie darkness of the cell before the automatic light engaged was always a nervous moment. Ben wheeled out his half-assembled mini-reactor and pushed it into the centre of the zone marked-off by red lines. The whole ensemble had been constructed to scale and to the uninformed observer it looked like an ordinary large gas-boiler, the sort of object that could be found in any airing cupboard in any home in Western Europe. Returning into the stronger light with his accomplices, Ben supervised the men as they carried out their tasks on the remaining *ménage* of wires, panels, lights and switches.

Ben walked around the culmination of his ideas like a matador baiting the bull, preparing to pounce with the final *estocada.* Satisfied that everything was present and conscious that all the necessary safety checks and preparation had been completed, Ben was ready to assemble the work. He stood motionless, arms folded and staring at the entrails of his task, while his co-workers looked on slightly bemused. It was the gaze of a man confronting his foe in the final challenge of a stand-off, before the end game.

This visit to the restricted area was only one of a few when Ben had been allowed to translate his own ideas into practice. The previous prototype had offered some encouragement but not enough to invest more of the company's resources. He had assisted in the projects of other senior colleagues during his time at Puissance and knew his way around the Radioactive Zone well enough but this new attempt at trying to generate energy represented a turning point. He suspected that Thompkins had only granted him permission to set up the scheme in the hope that the test would be a dismal failure, then he could be given his marching orders. Thompkins really was a hard-hearted individual but Ben was determined to get enough from this research prototype to steady the ship. If he was able to offer constructive data from the experiment and possibly get a paper published in a respected scientific journal, it should be enough of a contribution… even for Thompkins.

The trio of scientists was more nimble than their spacemen appearance suggested and their co-ordinated movements had been well-rehearsed. Although this was taking place in the live area, they had practised in the safety of Eta Lab on at least five occasions. The reactor could have even been set-up in the dark, if necessary. After two-and-a-half hours, which was slightly longer than Ben had expected, everything seemed to be in place. The red lights on the console located in front of the reactor indicated that it had not yet been activated but after one final check, that would change.

Ben presented an iPad to one of his co-workers who already knew what to do. His fingerprint was evidence that he agreed with the way the reactor had been set-up and he was supporting the activation process. After replacing his glove he handed the sheet to his colleague, who did the same. Now all that was required was to flip the master switch and isolate the reactor, once all the digits indicated satisfactory engagement. Ben looked at the other two men who smiled simultaneously in support, then he flicked a switch and there was an illumination of digits on the three consoles attached to reactor. After an eternity of thirty seconds, the red digits and integers rapidly flicked through a waterfall of activity before the trio of display panels all showed a green light on their master switches. There was no turning back now, the fusion process had begun.

The men wrapped a synthetic cocoon around the reactor and then proceeded to slowly push the masterpiece and its trolley into the graphite and lead chamber within the blast cell that would be its home for at least the next two weeks. If the worst happened, any explosion would be minimised because of the protective jacket. The men closed the heavy duty doorway and Ben punched the cell's code into the panel once more. Stepping back from the wall, Ben almost stood on the toes of one his colleagues who was positioned right behind him and they laughed together. The smiling workers shook hands, recognising they might be on the brink of something important. They made their way out of the Radioactive Zone, towards the shower and changing areas. Ben could not resist one last look before leaving his baby in the hands of either destiny or disaster.

Ben's absence from Eta Lab that morning had been monitored elsewhere. 'Where's the golden boy this morning ?' one of them asked.

'Cameras show him arriving at 5.46 am and then heading to his Lab before our cameras lost him entering the Radioactive Zone.'

'Hmm…that's unusual. How many times has he been in there before?'

'According to the log, he has led just one project and assisted in six, before today. What do you reckon he's up to?'

'Not sure. Get hold of Zenib and get him in here. It's about time we put Dr Ben Moyles under the microscope. You can imagine what he'd say if he was doing something important and we missed it. Whatever Moyles is up to, Zenib will want to know about it.'

It had been a long day and Ben had to get up at three o'clock in the morning to catch his early flight. Even if he went straight to bed, he would only get six hours sleep. During the drive back he played out every possible scenario in his mind as speeding headlights flickered past in the gloom. If things went badly the safety cell would be in darkness when he returned from the UK, indicating the fusion process had failed. This outcome would present Thompkins with all the ammunition he needed to destroy Ben's reputation. However if the green lights were shining and the fusion was still running, it would prove Ben's theories were correct. He allowed himself an indulgent smile at the thought, while he removed one hand from the steering wheel to rub the back of his neck and ease a minor cramp. Ben's eyes were focussed on the road but he was dreaming about the fame that would come with a successful outcome. A positive result would bring untold credibility within the science community and worldwide renown, while a Nobel Prize would be a certainty. The smile morphed into a self-mocking laugh at the thought of such a fantasy as he leaned forward to engage the car's heater switch.

After the shortest of sleeps, Ben woke before the alarm sounded. Pleased that he had completed his packing earlier, he decided not to bother with breakfast at the apartment, choosing to eat at the airport instead. After a quick splash he was soon dressed, and then he started to check the flat to ensure everything was in order before he left for the UK. In particular, he checked the security of the secret laptops but had some difficulty replacing the floorboards afterwards. Something appeared to have slipped in the grooving of the wood and the floor did not look right. It took longer than anticipated to ensure they were replaced properly and he lost track of time. Suddenly his schedule was under pressure and it was not helped by his lack of sleep. Stepping out quickly into the darkness he threw the suitcase into the boot and started the car. Then he realised he still had his work keys on him so darted back up the stairs and opened his flat. He strode quickly to the kitchen doorway and launched the keys towards the hooks on the wall. They bounced off the micro-wave and ricocheted onto the work surface. Slamming the door behind him, he returned to his car and began his journey to Geneva. Ben finally settled into the drive to the airport. Realising he was over-tired he turned on the radio for company as his demeanour began to stabilise. The music was something he recognised and he decided to join in the chorus, tapping his fingers lightly along the steering wheel. His high spirits were returning despite the pressure he was now under and he started to look forward to seeing his father and brother once again.

When the music stopped, a radio jingle heralded the announcement of the early morning traffic news. At first, Ben did not pay any attention to the mundane jabber that was filling the spaces between the songs. Then the presenter could be heard talking to a political correspondent who was reporting a security alert in Geneva. After finishing the report by stressing there was nothing to be worried about, he handed back to the studio where the male host suggested that traffic was now building-up at the border crossing into the City. Ben's skipping fingers wrapped tightly around the steering wheel before his right fist thumped down onto his thigh. He could not contain his frustration and growled out an expletive. In an instant, his good mood changed to fluster and getting to the airport on time was now a problem.

The accelerator saw some action and the absence of heavy local traffic offered some encouragement. When he reached the last major roundabout at the crossing of the main road into Meyrin, there was only the main five mile stretch into Geneva to be negotiated. He passed through the traffic lights and was about to sigh with relief at breaking the back of the journey, when he was left deflated by the long queue of traffic which stretched out in front of him. Changing into a first gear crawl, the car was moving painfully slowly. Ben turned up the radio once more, hoping to hear some good news. It did not take long before the familiar voice informed the station's listeners that the alert was still active and the tailback of traffic was lengthening. The driver of a car in front tried to seize some initiative by giving a loud blast of the horn in frustration. It looked like Ben was not the only one worried about catching an aeroplane on time. Ever-so-slowly, the cars droned towards the check-point at the border crossing. Finally, with about five hundred metres to go, he could see the long white over-gloves of one of the border guards wind-milling towards oncoming vehicles. It seemed as if cars were no longer being stopped but simply waved through. He glanced at his watch, holding his wrist to eye level out of respect for time. If the cars continued to pass through like this, he might be ok.

In a more dishevelled state than he intended, Ben puffed out both cheeks as he left the bag-drop area and made his way to the Departures Lounge with his travel bag and lap-top strung over his shoulder. Glancing up at the orange digits on a large black screen he could see that the gate number for the Newcastle flight would be displayed within the next ten minutes. Although there was no chance for the breakfast he had promised himself, he had just made it in time for his flight home. In what seemed like a continuous flow of people, he progressed to the Departure Gate and was soon fastening his safety belt in Business Class. Just as the sun was rising, Ben sat watching through the cabin window as a worker in a blue jump-suit detached the giant fuel pump from the aeroplane, while a uniformed stewardess sauntered up the aisle ensuring everyone was suitably prepared for the flight. Once in the air he would treat himself to some much needed food and sleep. Although Ben was feeling pretty good about life, he was innocently unaware there was a maelstrom heading his way and his life was about to change forever.

PART TWO

I

While other passengers had family members and taxis waiting at Newcastle Airport, Ben headed straight for the bright orange neon sign that indicated the car hire area. The online booking showed his four-wheel SUV was ready for collection and all the attendant needed was for Ben to provide a signature and proof of identity. Once she was satisfied with his paperwork the slightly dumpy, uniformed helper escorted Ben to the car-hire compound where the black Range Rover was ready. Cheryl photographed the vehicle from all sides using her iPad, and handed the keys to Ben who was left to familiarise himself with its gadgets and panels before leaving the compound.

Moyles Farm was about an hour-and-a-half drive away. The homestead nestled in the lee of hills around Hubbleton, lying between a clear mountain stream and a copse of trees. Its elevated position meant the views were spectacular and the nearest neighbours were about two miles away. The all-male inhabitants could go for days without seeing anyone else or speaking to another living soul. That is certainly how it seemed to Ben when he was growing up with his younger brother Richard.

There were only fifteen minutes between the birth of the two boys and Ben considered himself lucky to have avoided the health issues that had dogged his brother during their youth. Richard's weak heart prevented him from enjoying most of what Ben could remember doing on the farm. Many of the chores fell on the shoulders of the younger brother, who never minded doing the lion's share of the work. Richard was often at home beside a fire with his mother when she was alive, while Ben and his father Graham were either feeding the herd of thirty Galloway beef cattle or rounding up the fifteen-hundred Cheviot ewes. Despite feeling guilty about not being able to do more than his younger brother, Richard felt no resentment and the two boys were very close.

After Ben had driven for about twenty minutes, the SUV was gritting its way over country roads and making progress homeward. The falling temperature gauge informed him that he was no longer in France but somewhere near the Scottish border. Ben reached forward and pressed what he hoped was the heater button on the cosmic dashboard, although the feeling of returning home also gave some extra warmth while he focussed on the road. The imminent prospect of seeing his father and brother within the next hour gave him a glow of excitement. The power of the new car was stimulating and Ben was beginning to enjoy the way it ate the miles. None of the landmarks were yet familiar, only their suggestion indicated he was close to the area where he was born.

Soon he was at the entrance of the track to Moyles Farm. The name sign was still missing from the time it was knocked over during the severe winters of the late 1950s. Ben's father, Graham had intended to replace the signpost but then his thirty-six-year-old wife Eva died, leaving her boys without a mother and her husband with a heavy load to carry. Replacing a sign that had collapsed under the strain of the wind seemed the least of his worries and over the years he did not have the heart to try and put things back to normal.

The SUV pulled into the farm yard and a few chickens fluttered and clucked a welcome as they attempted to avoid the vehicle's approaching wheels. There was a splash of liquid mush when the car came to a sudden stop. Ben deliberately slammed the door to herald his return before giving a shepherd's whistle but the absence of a response suggested that the farm's workforce were in the fields. Leaving his bags in the boot of the Range Rover, he walked around desperately hoping to see a friendly face but was greeted only by silence. He gave a self-mocking laugh with the frustration of the anti-climax.

Ben walked along the short path to the farmhouse and lifted the large metal slat on the heavy wooden door. It was always left unlocked as there was no need to mistrust any calling neighbour. A draining board displaying the aftermath of a heavy load of washing-up suggested that something had overtaken the daily routine in the house that morning. Ben picked up a sleeping tea-towel hanging on the back of an old kitchen chair and instinctively started to wipe the cutlery, pots and plates as he looked around the room trying to spot any changes that had taken place since his last visit. He was pleased to be unable to record anything new and his silent shrug of satisfaction indicated a level of comfort that finally declared he was home.

A stirring came from the adjacent lounge where the sounds suggested someone was sleeping. Ben eased off his shoes by toe-ending each heel in turn. He did not want to be accused of tracking mud into the tidiest room in the house within minutes of returning. Gently, he pushed open the lounge door which creaked alarmingly as it struggled to reveal someone submerged in work-clothes fast asleep. It was his brother Richard who was sitting on a large leather chair, his heavily socked feet resting on a small foot-rest. Ben explored the worn-out image that was resting before him. The harshness of Richard's illnesses over the years had made the brothers clearly distinguishable. Their mother used to dress them in similar clothes up to the age of eight to enjoy the unity of their identity. However, it was then that Richard began to display signs of the illness that marred the remainder of his youth. Now the weathered, sleeping face showed only glimpses of the expression that Ben used to see every day. He took his brother's dangling arm and gently replaced it to a resting position on his chest. Richard did not stir while Ben walked gently backwards towards the exit, this time leaving the door open in case its noisy movement alarmed his brother.

In the kitchen Ben stepped back into his shoes and decided to go and look for his father. At this time of year he would probably be in the upper *shiel*, where the herd of Cheviot Blackface would be grazing in the summer pastures. These areas were a harsh environment in winter but offered lush feeding grounds during the short summers. Ben crossed the yard in front of the sheds where he could see a mud-strewn quad-bike. No doubt Richard had returned from tending the sheep to crash into an armchair exhausted from his toils. Ben resisted the temptation to jump on the bike and head out in search of his father. It was a pleasant late afternoon heading into evening and Ben's long journey had made his body yearn for a good loosening walk in place of his daily run. About to enter his home pastures, Ben raised his head and drank the refreshing Northern air, almost hoping for rain to invigorate him still further. He made his way out of the farm compound and headed upward where he could see for miles and hopefully spot his father at work. With both hands pushing down into the pockets of his Swiss-made top-coat to trap any warmth, his level of comfort grew into tangible reassurance.

Slowly, Ben headed along the well-worn track towards Hedgehope Edge, the highest point on the farm. The mud on the soles of his shoes soon crept over the laces and masked any memory of style. Ben did not care, he was enjoying being on home soil. About three-quarters of the way up the track he turned along a spur and suddenly heard a familiar sound echo from the valley below. The noise was coming from his father Graham who was whistling instructions to Archie, his trusty ten year-old border collie. It looked like a dry stone wall had partially collapsed and some sheep had got out of the mid-pastures. His father was working in a manner his sons had seen many times before, in command and giving instructions to his most faithful servant. Archie was totally focussed on rounding up the dozen or so sheep, concentrating intently with crouching rounded shoulders, acting like a hunting cheetah ready to pounce on its prey. Every high pitch whistle was followed by the collie darting and circling the sheep and feigning a nip at any disobedient Blackface. Master and dog were in unison, with one purpose, to return the sheep to their rightful fold.

As Ben left the pathway and made his way down the grassy slope towards the action, his father did not notice his son approaching. When the sheep were safely back in the fold, Graham rewarded Archie with a heavy pat and an exaggerated stroking, reinforced by calls of *'Good boy Archie, you got 'em there boy!'* Then the weather-worn face turned inward, towards the paddock and widening his arms like a biblical shepherd, Moyles Senior ensured all the miscreant sheep were ushered well into the enclosure before he turned his attention to repairing the damage of the wall. Crouching down to lift one of the misplaced lumps of granite, Graham paid no attention as Archie brushed past him, no doubt assuming that the dog was returning to his favourite spot behind the driver's seat on the quad bike. However, Archie had sensed the upwind presence of a familiar scent and silently made an arrow for the approaching figure which he recognised immediately. Ben bent down to receive the affectionate wag-tailing welcome before continuing towards his father. The collie vigorously weaved in and out of Ben's legs in his enthusiasm to greet the absent family member, causing his master's son to almost trip over. The air was finally broken by the sound of excited barking and the farm owner glanced over his shoulder to trace the source of the disturbance. Graham's body filled with a joy of its own and after dropping the final stone into place, he allowed himself an overdue indulgence as he turned away to give an unseen smile.

Rising from a crouched position, the old man watched as the younger of his twin boys advanced further. Neither showed any sign of outward emotion as Ben arrived in front of his father. Graham removed his thick leather work gloves and simply let them drop to the grass, before wiping his palms down the front of his crumpled Gore-Tex jacket. He was the first to speak, 'So you're home then?'

'Yes, sir – I'm home.' Stretching out his hand, Ben simultaneously offered, 'You look well.'

This was not enough for Graham Moyles, regarded within the local community as one of the hardest men in the Cheviot Hills. He took his son in a bear hug and squeezed him close, communicating as much love as he was able to without saying a word. The length of the embrace told Ben more than any words, before he was allowed to break from the hold. Ben gazed at the ground and bent down to recover his Dad's gloves so did not see Graham dislodge a tear with his index finger.

The older man quickly changed the mood and turned to address his wayward collie. 'Archie – get on boy !' With this, the border collie darted toward the quad bike and jumped up to lie behind the two seats, snuggling under the comfortable shelter made by the vacant space. A smiling Graham laughed out aloud before smacking his son on the back so hard it would have sent most men reeling. Ben had felt this familiar clout many times before and was almost prepared for the shock of the hit. The two of them mounted the quad simultaneously and Graham asked his son before starting the engine, 'Been in the house yet ?'

Ben knew what his Dad was getting at, 'Just had a quick look around. Richard was in the lounge fast asleep so I just left him.' His father offered no further comment and turned the key before violently revving the engine. The quad shot off in the direction of the farmhouse leaving further conversation impossible and unnecessary.

The journey back to the farmhouse was short but enjoyable. Ben always liked it when his father drove the quad too quickly. The wind rushed past his hair like an old friend in a hurry, the cold freshness all the more invigorating because of the induced thrill of the ride. Grabbing the passenger bar with white knuckles, Ben looked around trying to spot any unwanted changes in the landscape. It was all good, everything displayed a reassuring sameness. Even the gate leading up to the stile connecting with Cuthbert's Way was still leaning at a dangerous angle. With a bit of luck it had at least two more years' life before surgery would be needed. He glanced sideways at his father who was focussing on the route ahead. Graham could have driven blindfolded if necessary, even when the slope of the track required him to lean across to maintain balance. Dusk was calling and the dirty headlights were illuminating their way ahead.

A few of the chickens headed for the safety of the wall as the quad revved noisily into the farmyard. It would soon be time to bring all the poultry inside before any fox came calling. The bike was brought to a shuddering halt beside the other quad. Turning to call over his shoulder in the fresh silence Graham then commanded, 'Home Archie, good boy !' At this instruction, the previously disinterested collie jumped instantly at the command and headed for his kennel just inside the barn. Although Archie was a member of the family, he was still a working animal and was not allowed into the house unless the situation called for a change in routine. Ben's return home did not yet warrant this favour and Graham did not want his best worker to turn soft on him. With a bit of luck Archie had another five working years left before being retired. After that he could come inside the house and be comforted beside a warm stove to his heart's content. In truth he had already earned that right but Moyles Farm was a business and it was hard enough to make a profit without losing such a good worker.

Ben eased himself off the quad and walked around the bike where a blast of the engine's warmth provided a pleasant bonus in the cooling air. The two men arrived at the front door more or less together. Graham scraped off the mud from his thick-soled work boots on the low horizontal bar beside the entrance. He raised the latch and entered the shelter of the porch where he removed his shoes to allow his feet to regain their senses. It took Ben less time to remove his designer shoes which he knew would need his attention in the morning. They were placed next to the other pairs of redundant footwear which surrounded the porch's sheltered perimeter.

Before removing his work jacket, Graham walked over to the kitchen where a large pot was lying on the draining board. Raising the container with half a grunt, he carried it a couple of yards to the stove. A wood fire was rendered more active by the addition of a couple of logs. 'There – that just needs to be warmed up. I cooked it yesterday and expect you're more than a bit hungry after your journey. It should be ready to eat in about twenty minutes.'

Already knowing the answer, Ben asked the obvious question. 'Thanks Dad. What is it ?'

Graham announced the menu with less formality than any Swiss *maitre-d'* might do in a Geneva restaurant. 'I thought you might like some of my rabbit stew – unless you've become too *lardy-da* living in that place they call civilisation these days.'

Ben's accurate prediction about the meal was genuinely appreciated. 'No Dad, that's what I was hoping it was, although I thought I could already smell it earlier. You know I always enjoy your rabbit stew. I was actually thinking about it in the plane on the way over, funnily enough. Lovely !'

Removing his coat and hanging it up in one movement, Graham informed his son, 'I'm just going to look in on Richard and then have a shower. Keep half an eye on the stew and give it a stir if you think it needs it. I won't be long. Don't have to tell you to make yourself at home I hope.'

Ben smiled with uninhibited affection which was returned in style. 'No problem Dad. I'll bring the chickens in as well if you want.' Graham gave a thumbs up before disappearing upstairs after poking his head into the lounge to see that Richard was still asleep in the armchair.

Looking around the kitchen for inspiration, Ben decided to abandon any hope of immediate company and after slipping back into his expensive, muddy shoes in the porch he made his way into the farmyard, where some curious chickens gave him a glance of interest. He lifted the cover from a metal bucket containing some grains of feed and began to spray the tasty morsels around the gathering poultry, calling out to them as he had done in his youth but still feeling a bit self-conscious nevertheless. 'Here chick, chick, chick … come on, chick, chick, chick….' Soon Ben had their interest and a spray of feed in the appropriate direction led the chickens towards their coop. Once they were all inside the henhouse he dusted off his hands to remove the remains of any feed before closing the wired pen to ensure any wayward fowl did not provide Mr Fox with an easy meal that evening. Feeling proud of himself, Ben returned to the farmhouse.

At the door, he turned to face the chicken coop and could see the sun setting over Hedgehope Edge. It was a comforting reminder that he was in trustworthy territory. Without thinking, he bent down to pick up a wayward twig, before returning to the porch. There he leant with one hand resting on the door frame before attempting to scrape away the mud from his shoes, banging the stick against the side of each one to remove any excess detritus. Once satisfied the heavy stuff had been removed, he knew that he only needed to wipe the expensive footwear with a wet rag and a generous portion of polish to make them respectable once more.

Entering the kitchen he was caught by the enticing aroma of rabbit stew which now dominated the farmhouse. He could almost feel himself salivating as he picked up the large wooden ladle to mix the thick cloudy broth. Standing with his back to the doorway he did not see his brother enter the kitchen, although he felt a stirring when he heard his voice. 'Got you working already has he, young 'un ?' Ben's face lit-up into a huge grin before he turned around to share the joy.

'Not quite – but then he knew that stirring his famous rabbit stew would not only be a labour of love, it would be like killing the fatted calf.' Ben walked into a brotherly embrace, before stepping out of the hold and inspecting Richard's appearance with intimate scrutiny. He could see that his twin showed all the signs of having just woken from an intense sleep that had not abated his fatigue. In a repeat of the scene with his father, Ben reversed the roles as he took his brother in another loving hug, while issuing a castigation of sorts. 'Who are you calling young 'un ? Fifteen minutes is all you've got on me, remember.'

'It's still enough to make me your big brother, and don't you forget it!' Richard warned.

Ben took the lead from his brother as he had done all his life, despite the quarter-of-an-hour deficit that he would never be able to change. 'How you doin', Rich ? You're looking well,' he lied.

'Not doin' too bad, I have my moments but I'm still here where I belong – helping the old man.'

Ben ignored the dig, 'How's he doing anyway. Still looks as if he could wrestle the farm's bull for a cow.'

Richard spoke of his father with equal admiration. 'You know what he's like – indestructible and still thinks he can take on the world. Mind you, he's probably right. Where is he anyway ?'

Ben did not have a chance to answer the question. 'He's right behind you and just for your information, I could wrestle the bull for *all* the cows if you must know.' Ben and Rich looked at each before the three of them laughed, sharing a unique moment of family closeness.

Few words were spoken during the meal as each member of the family tucked into the mixture of tender rabbit, fresh vegetables and crusty bread with an accompanying bottle of local beer. After a second helping Ben leaned back in his seat and patted his stomach like a drum before declaring, 'I'm stuffed. Dad, that was absolutely superb and boy how I have missed good old fashioned home cooking. I've not tasted anything as good as that since the last time I was home. You go and sit down and I'll do the washing up.'

Graham was obeying none of his younger son's orders. 'No, you won't. I'll see to these plates. There's not much and it won't take me long. You must be tired after a long day travelling. Go and sit in the lounge with your brother. You should have a lot to catch up on, if I'm not mistaken.'

Ben was grateful and relieved in equal measures. 'If you're sure. I've got to say I *am* a bit tired. It's been a long day and I think an early night is called for, even by the standards of Moyles Farm. Come on then, Rich, let's go in the other room and you can update me on all the local gossip.'

The two boys took the remainder of their glasses of beer into the lounge and during their conversation Ben addressed the elephant in the room. 'So, how are you bro'? Dad has told me you've been having a bit of a rough time recently.'

'It's the same old thing young 'un. This bloody heart of mind is neither use nor ornament. I just get so tired all the time. I've got my name down for a transplant but there's no real sign of anything happening. It seems to be getting harder to keep up with Dad with all the jobs that need doing around here.'

'Do you want me to have a talk with him about taking on some help. It's too much for just the two of you, anyway.'

'There's no need. He's already done it. He's taken on Joe Setherton more or less full time and Eric helps out when we need him during the lambing season at round-up time.' Eric Setherton was the less reliable of the two brothers. The Sethertons both lived in the village with their mother and Joe Senior, their drunkard of a father. 'So I'm really surplus to requirements anyway. I think he just lets me do something to make me think I'm of some use but we both know what the score is.'

Ben did not mind being referred to as 'young 'un' by his brother. One of the few ways that Rich could convince himself he held some superiority over his younger twin was to acknowledge at every opportunity that he was the elder of the two. There may have only been a short time difference between their births but it was an important difference as far as Richard was concerned. During their childhood and the days of their youth, it was Ben who was the stronger, the cleverer and the more able of the twin boys. Rich had little he could use to assuage his inferiority complex.

The uniqueness of the occasion overcame their intentions. Ben had become even more exhausted after eating a good meal and drinking a bottle of the local beer. He decided to take time-out on their intended catch-up simply because he was too tired after such a demanding day. Richard did not seem to object, offering little resistance and he even rose from his armchair to head for his bedroom first. While Ben insisted on helping his father to finalise the clearing up in the kitchen, his twin was in the bathroom to complete his evening ablutions before hitting the hay. As his father put away the clean dishes and returned them to their former home, Ben recovered his travel bag from the hallway. Without saying a word he lifted an expensive bottle of the best Remy Martin brandy from inside the bag and placed it on the draining board while his father stared in silence. Ben affectionately squeezed a hand onto his Dad's shoulder and pointed at the bottle to indicate who now owned the gift from France. Taking a glass from a cupboard, Ben noisily placed it beside the brandy before leaving Graham to indulge in its excellence. While his son made his way upstairs, Graham sat alone and poured himself a glass in front of the stove's orange glow to recover from another hard day in the fields. There was nothing extravagant in their evening ritual, its beauty was in its natural comfort as the three men needed no reassurance about their love for each other.

II

Sunday mornings were always different to the rest of the week on Moyles Farm. Jobs still needed doing but there were fewer of them at this time of the week. Graham Moyles always rose very early and rode around the farm on his quad bike to check there was nothing untoward with the livestock or any of the buildings on his land. Once satisfied that all was well he would return to cook a big breakfast accompanied by several steaming pots of hot, sweet tea. Sometimes the brunch would have to wait, if any of the sheep were caught up in the wire fencing or a fox had been at the chickens but usually it was the time of rest that the Lord intended. A visit to the local village of Hubbleton to collect the newspapers before it closed at noon usually preceded a call into the Black Bull for a couple of pints and a chat with neighbours. The afternoon was spent either sleeping off the effects of the local brown ale or reading about the rest of the world in the Sunday tabloids, or both.

Ben and Richard were part of the weekly ritual and like their father, they quietly enjoyed the assurance of the routine's regularity. However, there was to be one change this week: while Graham was touring his domain, Ben decided he would cook the breakfast and give his Dad a break. Ben did not have to wake his brother, the smell of the bacon dancing on the grill pan did that job. As Rich entered the kitchen he acknowledged his twin with a simple, 'Morning, Ben.' The younger sibling did not respond directly but waving a spatula in the direction of the kettle offered, 'There's some tea in the pot if you want a cup. That should help bring you round a bit.'

Half yawning a grunt of appreciation and one hand pressing on the back of his neck, Richard poured himself a strong cuppa. The first mouthful convinced him that Ben was right and he could feel his morning senses returning as the sweet heat descended through his body. Rich inquired after his father. 'Dad back yet, Ben or is he still out and about ?'

'I heard him leave about six. What is it now ?' Ben then answered his own question after looking at the wall clock. 'About quarter to nine. Something must have held him up. He should be back any time soon.' No sooner had Ben summarised the situation when the roar of a quad's engine from the farmyard announced the imminent arrival of the patriarch. 'That sounds like him now. Boil the kettle again Rich and I'll start frying the eggs. Breakfast should be ready by the time the old man comes in.'

'Something smells good,' boomed the deep voice that heralded Graham's entry. 'Who's done the cooking this morning then ?' Richard, still swallowing a mouthful of tea simply pointed his index finger at his brother like a little boy shooting an imaginary gun. 'I hope he's not picked up any fancy ways in France and we're having croissants or some such rubbish.' Ben had his back to Graham and was busy spooning hot fat over the sizzling panful of fried eggs. He could not resist a response.

'Not today Dad. Today it's nothing but bacon, eggs, sausages, baked beans, fried bread and black pudding. A veritable feast of high octane cholesterol – if that's ok with you? I couldn't get the cream cakes past the guards at Newcastle Airport.' Graham could not resist a stifled laugh as Ben gave the orders 'Sit yer-sels down you two. It's just about ready for serving.' Graham plonked himself onto his chair at the head of the table and Ben immediately placed a huge plate of breakfast food in front of him. When Rich received a similar plateful Graham offered some words of appreciation.

'Thanks son. This looks champion. Should set us up for the rest of the morning. Thought we might go down the village after this and see who's in the Bull.' Richard did not look up from severing a sausage and scooping some accompanying beans, aware that Ben was the target of this special invitation and for a little while at least, he was prepared to play second fiddle. Rich recognised it was a reflection of Ben's return home rather than an expression of favouritism.

The dark green Defender Land Rover was soon booming along the minor road which served as a back lane from the farm to Hubbleton. Driving past the rear gate Rich gave Ben a nudge and nodded in the direction of a collection of stones which marked the site of a Roman relic, just inside a neighbouring field by a small copse. The spot was a reminder to Ben of the last time he ever deliberately frightened his brother during a game of hide-and-seek. Richard reacted not just in fear but with a chest-clutching seizure that caused him to fall to the floor gasping for breath. The incident marked the beginning of the elder twin's heart problems and although Ben knew in reality that he was not the cause of his brother's ill-health, he was aware that it could not have helped either. His regret was compounded by his father's angry response at his stupidity and it remained the worst telling-off that Ben ever received from his father, something Richard liked to prey on whenever they passed the stones.

The trio was squeezed into the front seats like three wise monkeys, each with their eyes transfixed on the road. Graham was driving at speed as usual and Ben was indulging in the familiar scenes of home and the smell of his father's Land Rover. As the 'Green Goddess' entered the village there were only one or two people on the main street and Graham turned left to arrive at the whitewashed walls and black-painted beams that marked the spot of the Black Bull, while the huge swinging sign was another unmistakable give-away. There was a second pub in the village, the Red Lion but this tavern was part of a pub chain and served the sort of food found anywhere in the country. When the Bull included the word 'homemade' on the blackboard inside the bar, the term was genuine. The landlord's wife Jessie Willbourghly was a great cook and her lamb stew was to die for.

Turning off the engine and alighting from the driver's side in one movement Graham barked out the orders. 'You get them in Ben lad, I'm just popping down to the *Backy Palace* to get the newspapers.'

'What do you ...?' Ben tried to ask his Dad what he wanted to drink but by the time he his feet had hit the ground his father was out of earshot. 'I suppose he's still drinking that Ordinary gut-rot ?' asked Ben, causing Richard to smile. 'Thought he might. Still not bothering to lock the Rover either.'

'At least he's taking the keys with him these days,' added his brother. 'Every time I remind him about locking the car doors, all he says is that nobody's gonna take his Land Rover because they know who owns it and they know what will happen to them if they try to steal it from him. He still thinks he's indestructible.'

As they arrived at the pub door together Rich stepped aside and pushed his brother through adding, 'Ho'way young'un. You heard what he said. You get them in and mine's a pint of Lockhead's Best.'

They turned left into the Bar where farmers and locals in urgent need of sustenance were usually the only ones found drinking just after twelve on a Sunday afternoon. The brothers were greeted by turning heads as the door opened. Curious expressions welcomed Ben but as soon as his twin entered they relaxed and were offered a familiar greeting by a man standing at far end of the bar. 'Well, well look who it is – hello Ben, I wondered if I'd see you in here this morning,' said the elder of the two Sethertons. 'Your old man mentioned you were coming home this weekend. Where is he anyway ? Don't tell me he's turned down the chance of a free pint. I don't believe it.'

Ben walked further along the counter to shake hands with the farm's only full-time employee. 'He's just popped into the newsagents to get the Sunday papers. He'll be in here in a minute, now.' As he stepped forward, Ben could see that Joe was with his father, Joe Senior. Rather than brush past, Ben simply nodded a greeting followed up with, 'Hello Mr Setherton. Almost didn't see you there. You keeping well ?' A grunt was all he got in response. Ben could see that the older man's red eyes and blue-veined nose indicated the consequences of years of hard drinking. Although the son was alright and a good worker, his father and younger brother Eric were cut from a different and inferior cloth. There was no doubt that Joe Setherton Senior did not approve of Ben, nor indeed anyone from the Hubbleton area who sought to better themselves beyond the reaches of their parents' farm. The lack of a courteous response came as no surprise to anyone who knew this particular member of the local community.

Ben asked for three pints and although he would have preferred to have drunk lager, he ordered a pint of Lockhead's Best for himself as well as Rich. He was aware of being assessed as he had been on the previous occasions when he had returned home. Manliness was a key aspect of the male culture on Cheviot Hills' farms and Ben knew that there was an ongoing price that needed to be paid. After the first sip of Best, Graham Moyles entered the Bar and Ben dutifully picked up the dark brown pint of Ordinary beer that had only just ceased foaming. 'There you are Dad, get that one down yer.' Graham took one swig equivalent to three mouthfuls from lesser mortals and in the process his eyes circled the room as he assessed who was standing around him. He nodded to everyone he wanted to acknowledge before replacing his depleted glass back onto the counter and within an instant the trio had been assimilated into the culture of the pub. In some ways it seemed as if it had been only a week since Ben had been propping up the bar.

The antiquated wall-clock with its Roman numerals clicked around onto one o'clock and at that precise moment the door opened and a young woman made her way to the bar, lifting the counter hinge to access the servers' side of the pub. While removing her coat she acknowledged the landlord before turning to face her public. Her long red hair was tied into a ponytail for the purposes of work while her tight skirt and figure-hugging blouse was accepted as a necessary part of her barmaid's uniform. Sue Wallace was still a stunner and all the men wanted her to accept their eyes as she addressed them with her first words, 'Right who's next? Is anyone waiting to be served?' The silent response was more an indication of their appreciation of her beauty than whether their glass was empty or not. This was one asset the Black Bull had over the Red Lion that could not be bettered. Sue was surprised at the absence of a response and sensed this particular Sunday drinking session was somehow different. Then she spotted a former boyfriend sipping on a pint of Lockhead's Best bitter. 'Ah, so that's what's going on. I thought there was something different in here this morning. I didn't see our guest from France standing there.' Stepping a little closer to the edge of the counter she added, 'Hello, Ben – how are you?' The men in the Bar turned to cast an envious eye in his direction.

Ben felt his voice hesitate and stumble, 'Hello Sue … yes, fine thanks. How are you?' Before waiting for an answer, he followed up with, 'How's Donny … and the kids ?'

Sue knew she had him on the defensive, 'Oh they're all fine, thanks. Donny will be coming in here in a minute now, though he'd probably have been in here already if he'd known you were back home.' The barbed comment was an indication that her wounds were not completely healed. Ben doubted they ever would be.

After University, Ben and Sue had dated for a while until one night they had a stupid row about settling down together. Ben had not been as keen as Sue to remain in Hubbleton for the rest of his life, preferring to see a bit of the world first. They broke-up after that argument and in order to get back at him, Sue had a relationship with Ben's former best friend Donny almost immediately afterwards. One night when Ben was not around, Donny succumbed to drunken temptation and offered to take Sue home after bumping into her during an evening out. In an angry gesture of stupidity, Sue allowed Donny to have sex with her after he made a clumsy, drunken pass and they ended up in a field near the edge of the village. The sordid encounter ended with Sue crying over Donny's shoulder and wishing to turn back the clock. Donny was so taken aback at her reaction he had no thoughts about guilt or plunging an emotional knife into the back of his best mate. No one could have predicted the pace of her regret when six weeks later in her bathroom, a blue line appeared on a conception indicator. She knew then that all chances of a reconciliation had evaporated.

It was after the pregnancy became public knowledge that Graham and Richard Moyles persuaded Ben to move away as his presence in Hubbleton would only make matters worse. Ben agreed and applied for a post which took him to London and subsequently he never returned to the village – or to Sue. Eventually another child came along after Sue and Donny got married. Sue's mother Janice now did the babysitting while her daughter earned some pin money in the Black Bull. For Sue, bar-work was just an excuse to get out of the house as Donny could drink her income faster than she was earning. Both were now in the early stages of enduring rather than enjoying their marriage together. Once Donny had done the decent thing there was nowhere else to go with their relationship because love was missing. Ben knew they would both eventually have affairs and by his estimation the marriage would fold when the kids reached adolescence – if it got *that* far. Judging by the way she looked and behaved behind the bar and how willing customers responded to her flirting, the process may even have already started.

'How old are they now ?' asked a slightly embarrassed Ben, more for the benefit of intruding ears than out of genuine interest. One or two of the men returned to drinking their pints, once they realised the conversation was on the road to mundanity.

'Thomas is nine and Jessica is almost two now.' responded Sue, as if she was firing bullets at him, still trying to wound and retaliate.

All Ben could offer in response was, 'Good.' It came as a great relief when a regular drinker interrupted with, 'Same again, please Sue…when you've got a minute, like.'

Sue heard the order and taking a pint glass she moved it downwards towards the beer pump. The majority of unoccupied drinkers turned to explore two gorgeous breasts as she pulled the large black handle towards her body. Suddenly all interest in Ben Moyles disappeared and he was able to return to drinking his pint.

By this time, Graham and Rich's pints glasses were in need of a refill. The three of them were standing in one corner of the room under the dartboard and Ben turned inward to ask if they were ready for another pint. At the same time as he moved away to head for the bar, the saloon door opened and he almost collided with the new entrant. Ben could not see who it was, almost losing his balance in the process of trying to remain upright. Donny got as far as saying 'Sor….' before he recognised the identity of his innocent assailant. Initially, Ben did not recognise Donny, who had grown a beard since they last met. However, the black hair could not disguise the piercing blue eyes of his former best friend and Ben felt a mixture of emotions once his brain had assimilated what had just happened. Donny took the initiative, 'Oh it's you is it? I might have known the great *I am* is home. Well you'll just have to wait and get in line behind me' Others turned to see the source of the commotion as Donny called to his wife, 'The usual please Sue, pet.'

Ben was not sure what to do or say. He wanted to knock Donny's head off, or at least break his nose. Sure, a lot of water had passed under the bridge since the birth of Thomas Wallace but there were still too many bruised egos to let it go. Sue was angry at herself for having destroyed any chance of ever getting together with Ben through one moment of madness, while Donny was angry because he was not Ben and never would be. Throughout it all the youngest of the Moyles' twins had attempted to maintain a respectful level of silence. Ben was the only one who had not done anything wrong and he wanted to keep it that way but emotionally he wanted a catharsis – a fight, man-to-man with the former friend who had wronged him and a straight-talking shouting match with his ex-lover who had hurt him even more. Instead, he simply offered 'Be my guest, if it means that much to you, Donny. I can wait.' This was greeted with a dismissive wave over his shoulder by his former friend. Rich could see what was happening and was about to head over to help his brother, when Moyles Senior simply raised a horizontal arm and said, 'Just leave it son.

He's ok.' As ever, realising he could do nothing more than anyone else in the Bar, Rich accepted his Dad's advice.

The cabaret was finally over and the dozen or so men who were in the bar of the Black Bull were able to pretend that it was like any other Sunday lunchtime. They returned to their drinks and continued their banal conversations. Sue handed over a foamy pint to her husband and as she leaned forward to take his money she warned him, 'Don't show me up in front of this lot, Donny. Not if you know what's good for you. Just remember that it's you I'm married to and you I'll be sleeping with tonight.' Ben could not discern what she had said but he knew her well enough to make an accurate guess. Donny lifted his glass and took a sip, before turning away from the counter and deliberately pushing into Ben who had been standing directly behind him. 'Whoah there *monsieur*, I almost did it again and spilled some beer over you. That would have been terrible, a thousand apologies.' Ben said nothing while Donny slipped further into the room to talk to someone else.

Ben placed the two glasses onto the bar counter and ordered drinks for his brother and father, 'One Ordinary, one Best please, Sue.' As she pulled the pumps to release the foam into the glass Sue offered some conciliatory words. 'Take no notice of Donny, Ben. He doesn't mean it but I think he's a bit jealous of your success. You know what he's like.'

'I thought I did – once upon a time' responded Ben with a barbed comment of his own, looking directly into the barmaid's gaze. 'Now I'm not so sure.'

'Well all that was a long time ago. You have your life and we have ours, so let's just leave it at that and let it go shall we?' This was Sue's final offering at temporary reconciliation. She knew she would have to keep any conversation with Ben brief because if Donny saw her talking to him he would inevitably kick off again. Meanwhile, Ben could feel Donny's eyes burning into the back of his head.

Returning with the drinks to the fold of his twin and father, he passed them over. 'Let's just go after this one shall we. Nothing ever changes in this place.'

His father felt obliged to defend his home. 'And that's a bad thing, is it ?'

Ben simply shrugged his shoulders and grasped the remainder of his pint.

III

After a Sunday session in the Black Bull, Graham Moyles could usually be found in his favourite armchair in the lounge with his head tilted to one side, his right arm dangling over the side and a broadsheet newspaper resting on his thighs. Only the faintest ripple of air from his vibrating lips and his closed eyelids gave away the fact that he was in a deep, beer-induced sleep. Ben was in Rich's room having a bit of downtime and enjoying some closeness with his twin, who was lying on his bed, arms behind his head. Ben was restless, walking around, picking things up and replacing them. Filtering through a couple of bookshelves, an old green-backed ledger manual caught his attention.

Ben opened the large pages of the analysis book and after recognising the print he started to laugh. 'Amazing, you've kept this all these years? I can't believe it!'

Rich appreciated the instant pleasure the find was giving his brother. 'Didn't think I'd throw it away did you?'

'Well I never thought you'd hang on to these memories that's for sure. We must have spent hours compiling this thing over the years. Look at this one – *The First Test Match between the Third Reich and a Winston Churchill XI* '

'Ah, what a game that was. I think Adolf Hitler had a duck, if memory serves me correctly – clean bowled by Clement Attley?'

Turning enthusiastically to the right page, Ben responded. 'Correct, Mr Sports Correspondent. How on earth did you remember that ?'

Rich revealed the secret of his recollection. 'Well if memory serves that was in the glorious summer of 1995 when the West Indies played England. We were thirteen and it was more or less the first time I became quite poorly with this useless ticker of mine. Rather than watch the Test Matches downstairs on the telly you spent most of the summer here in this room with me playing pencil cricket.'

'Who decided on the selection of the two teams ? It must have taken us a while to come up with these two – I mean Herman Goering wicket keeper and Anthony Eden opening bowler !'

Ben's laughter tickled his twin's funny bone and the contagion of hilarity spread quickly. Rich doubled up on the bed with a fit of the giggles, clutching the pillow as if it was a new-born baby and rocking backwards and forwards in uncontrollable glee. Rich made a plea to relent, 'Stop, stop or I'll wet myself. No more please!' It was only when he added, 'Look if we don't stop Dad will wake up and give us a row.'

Ben's regression came to a thundering halt. 'Give it a rest, Rich. We're both grown men. You're talking as if we were still kids.'

'Wish I was,' came the reflex response. 'At least before I became ill. I've almost forgotten what it was like to be just the four of us, fit and healthy and all together. They were happy days.'

Rich's comments brought a new level of solemnity to the proceedings and their rare episode of laughter quickly abated. 'Tell you what. Next time England play the West Indies out there in the Caribbean we should go. I'll take you and Dad and we can watch the cricket for real. You've always been keen on cricket. We can go and let our hair down for once.'

Rich interpreted this as a flight of fancy so took the initiative himself. 'No that's not good enough. You're always doing stuff for me. I'm the older brother. It should be me doing things for you. I'll take *you* to the West Indies and you can thank *me* for a change. All my life you've been looking after me and making sure I'm ok. Just for once I would like to do something for you that you could never do for me. Then I might feel as if we were equals.'

This cry of real anguish upset Ben who felt a need to justify himself. 'We are equals you idiot. I tell you what. I'll make a deal. Why don't we go *together* and plan it *together*. Listen…if I do stuff for you, it's because I want to …. because you're my brother and believe it or not I almost like you.'

This was too much for Rich who launched a pillow at his twin from the bed. ' Shut up you big girl!'

Ben thought that he had better respond in kind. 'Anyway who else is going to help me bowl out Joseph Goebbels on a non-turning wicket.' Rich made a noise that came from somewhere between laughter and tears. It was enough to surprise them both and restore a sense of balanced perspective in the room. Ben carefully placed the ledger back on the shelf and moved across to pick up a bedside portrait photograph of his mother. The picture had caught her perfectly, when she looked fit and well and had clearly been taken when she was in her prime.

Rich was the only one who could ask him the question without Ben feeling it was too painful to respond. 'You ever think about her, young 'un?'

'Only every day,' was the heartfelt response from his twin. 'Thing is, every time I think of her I also think about Dad and how hard it must have been for him. How old were we when she died, about fifteen?' Rich was listening intently to his brother's raw honesty, while sitting on the bed with his knees pulled under his chin. 'That would make him about forty then – that's still quite young to lose your partner in life. I can't remember him falling apart at the time, can you ?'

'I suppose he felt he had to keep going for our sakes. There was just that one time when he couldn't find his slippers – you remember?' Ben shook his head.

'He was looking all over the place, accusing us of deliberately misplacing them and losing his temper. It would be about six months after Mum died. He was shouting and carrying on and then he started throwing all the shoes from under the stairs all over the place.'

'Are you sure I was there ?' asked Ben, who felt guilty about being unable to recall the episode.

'Well, now that you mention it, you've got me doubting whether you were there or not.' Ben looked relieved. 'Thing was I'd never seen him lose control like that before. He went right off on one and stormed upstairs.'

'No, sorry bro' but I have no recollection of it at all.' said Ben.

'I went upstairs after him to try and calm him down. I remember feeling a bit frightened of how he might react. When I pushed open his bedroom door, there he was sitting on the edge of the bed, crying his eyes out.'

'What did you do?' It was the obvious question to ask.

'Well I was just going to walk in but then I saw he was holding something close to his cheek.'

Ben became positively animated. 'What was it?'

'It was one of Mum's slippers. He must have come across it while he was looking for his own. I guess the shock of finding something belonging to Mum must have caught him off-guard and released all his pent-up emotions. I didn't want to intrude on such a personal moment so I just withdrew quietly and came downstairs.

'I have absolutely no recollection of that, whatsoever,' claimed Ben with great relief.

'I remember now, you had been feeding the chickens and came inside just after I returned back downstairs. I think I just glossed over it. To be honest I didn't think it was my place to tell anyone, not even you.'

Ben gave an honest testimonial of his father's well-earned credentials. 'Well he hasn't done a bad job on us, when you think about it. I don't think he's ever showed any interest in anyone else. Do you?' Rich shook his head and lengthened his legs on the bed to a full stretch. 'I know Elsie is an old friend and thank God she does all the cleaning for us but she hardly constitutes a love distraction.'

Rich continued with the emotional generosity. 'He'll be sixty later this year. I suppose we should really do something special for him.'

Ben picked up on their earlier suggestion. 'Well I tell you what. Rather than just talk about it, let's see about going to the Caribbean somewhere and try and watch some cricket. He's always quite liked it as well. I can remember the four of us going to a match he played in once for Hubbleton against Mooreditch when we were little. What do you say ?'

Rich had an upsurge of limited energy. 'What I say is let's get out of here while he's asleep downstairs. How about a walk over the fields towards Slow Falls ?'

'Aye, c'mon old 'un. I'm ready if you are.'

The two brothers left the house and walked together into familiar countryside as they had done many times before.

IV

June that year had been particularly dry and the lack of rainfall had delayed the timing of haymaking on Moyles Farm, which normally began at the end of the month. While the sheep were on the upper pastures during the summer, the lower fields were shut off from grazing, allowing the grass to grow, in readiness for the production of the principal winter feed. July was already into the end of its first week and the weather forecast indicated rain towards the end of the month so it was time to begin to bring in the hay. Graham Moyles had asked Joe Setherton Junior to ensure his brother Eric would be available for some part-time work to ease the load but he was doing some casual labouring elsewhere for a few days. It meant that the presence of Ben on the farm was more important than usual.

This was not a problem for Ben who was an accomplished tractor driver, like his brother. Unfortunately for Rich, his father wanted to ensure that the time available for bringing in the hay was maximised and that meant working long hours. Graham considered this to be too onerous for his elder twin because of his heart condition so he was relegated to kitchen duties, ensuring that the others were fed and watered during short breaks from their labour. This did not please Rich who wanted to be seen to be doing his fair share, especially with his brother at home.

First thing Monday morning Graham was spreading hay on the outside feeder section of the cattle shed to satisfy the animals' endless appetites. The building had been transformed a year earlier into a more efficient operation. Previously the cattle had to be 'mucked out' at regular intervals. However, now all the animal excrement and slurry falling daily from their digestive system ran between the slats of wooden flooring in the stalls. Over time, an underground store of animal faeces and urine was produced as it flowed into a modern cesspit below the cattle. The slurry could then be accessed by man-holes along the side of the building and piped into a transportable tank, attached to a tractor. The 'brown gold' was then taken into the fields in winter and scattered over the land to help regenerate the soil. Gases such as hydrogen sulphide were at their peak when the cesspit was almost full shortly after New Year.

When Graham had finished admiring his ravenous cattle he moved to the nearby maintenance shed where Ben was already waiting. Father and son were soon side-by-side sitting in two tractors with the engines engaged. Ben was in the red Massey Ferguson MF 3600, while Graham was revving the engine of the older green John Deere model. The son was charged with 'tedding' the eastern pastures: this entailed turning the grass that had already been cut by his father to ensure that it could be dried in the sun. Graham was heading to those northern pastures that had not yet been mown. Meanwhile, Joe Setherton was already in the upper paddocks supervising the hired cutters who were clipping the sheep. Rich was restricted to light duties around the farmhouse. Other than making meals for the men this principally involved giving the daily feed supplements to the beef cattle and feeding the chickens.

Ben's working day was now a world apart from his job in Sergy. As soon as he manoeuvred the tractor through the paddock's gate with the 'tedder' trailing behind he realised what he had been missing. Driving the Massey Ferguson up and down the field a few times before moving onto the next was a freedom from the stress of having to prove himself every day. He was home, with his family and loving every minute. In the tractor-cab Ben had considered using his ipod and earphones so he could listen to music and provide a distraction from the boredom of manoeuvring the Massey. However, it was the mundane that was proving to be the attraction. The slow-moving tractor with the tedder thrasher behind was certainly noisy to anyone outside in the fields but inside the calmness of the soundproof cab the beauty of the view was undisturbed. Ben had time to absorb the scenery and drink in the greenness of the pastures and the fleeting sight of crows above, looking to scavenge anything that was available. The sun was bouncing off the glass tomb in which he was encased while he was in his own reality.

Stopping only to drink some tea from a thermos and eat his cheese and pickle sandwiches just after one o'clock, Ben suddenly realised that he had been working for half a day without talking to anyone. With one hand on the steering wheel and his other resting on his thigh, he was leaning forward in an attempt to stretch his back when saw the light on his mobile phone begin to flash . The notification text showed it was his father, no doubt keen for an update on how things were progressing. 'Hi Dad, how's it going with you? …yes, all good here … should return to the farm in about another hour … 'course I can return later… not tired at all.' These were going to be long days but Ben was loving every second.

At half-past six Ben pulled into the farmyard but rather than park the tractor in the maintenance shed he switched off the ignition when he was by the wall next to the farmhouse. Five minutes later his Dad arrived along with Joe, who had hitched a ride in the tractor's cabin. For Ben and his father this stop was nothing more than a meal break. Once they had eaten, both would be heading back out into the fields until dew started to form, which could affect the quality of the fodder. 'Coming in for something to eat, Joe?' was the least Graham could offer to the man who had been supervising the clipping of the sheep for most of the day. Joe was less concerned about food than he was about being asked to do some more work. He decided to make a quick exit, making up some half-baked excuse. 'No, I've got to get back to see to my old man so I'll be on my way thanks, boss. Same time tomorrow?'

There were only three days of intensive labour left before things could wind down a bit. 'Yes, thanks Joe. Any movement with Eric?'

Graham might have known what the answer was going to be because part-time work and part-time commitment just about summed up Eric Setherton. 'He should be finishing off in the next couple of days and then he can join us after that.' Rather than challenge Joe's response he just raised his right thumb and concluded with, 'Ok, mate. See you tomorrow.

Graham entered the kitchen where Ben was lathering his arms with soap, ready to eat some wholesome food. 'Something smells good,' claimed Graham as he stood behind his son, waiting for the soap and hot water to become available. 'Aye, our Rich has made a shepherd's pie. Smells nice doesn't it.'

A voice came from almost inside the oven, 'Yes that's me, not so much a farmer more a great cook.'

This self-pity was not going to be accepted by his father who responded with some justifiable irritation. 'Look Rich, we can't be in the fields and be expected to cook food as well and Elsie Thistlethwaite can't be here every day. What you are doing is just as much a contribution as what me and your brother are doing. Now for God's sake, stop moaning about it !' Rich backed off and made no further attempt to address his dissatisfaction. In almost complete silence apart from the scraping of plates, the shepherd's pie was wolfed down and with no time for the digestive system to fully complete its business, Ben and Graham were soon making their way out to the waiting tractors and heading back into the fields.

V

After four days of mowing, tedding and rowing, the hay was bailed and stored in the Dutch barn on the other side of the yard, opposite the farmhouse. The large circular bales had come to replace the smaller cubes of hay present during Ben's youth. This new development on Moyles Farm was a consequence of the owner's investment programme over the previous few years, which had also included the developments in the cattle shed. The baler may have cost thousands of pounds but it was a godsend at the end of July and had made the process of making hay much easier than in the past. Once the rains came and the weather turned more inclement, silage production would replace hay-making. At that time there was less pressure on hill farmers to work late because making silage was less dependent on dry weather.

Graham had instructed Ben to take some time off, intending to assign him only light duties for the remainder of his stay at home ; after all, he was supposed to be on holiday. This suited everyone now the immediate rush to make hay was complete. Meanwhile, Richard was glad to be charged with overseeing the weaning of the lambs that were being brought down from the upper pastures. It was more of a man's job than making sure everyone was fed properly. There were only three days left before life on Moyles Farm would return to normal and Ben would go back to France. The time had gone quickly.

Ben took the 'Green Goddess' into Hubbleton that morning intending to fill it up with diesel at the local garage and to enjoy being around his home village with little to do. Although they kept a supply of diesel at the farm, it was not the best quality fuel and his Dad was particular when it came to looking after the engine under the bonnet of the Land Rover. There were only two petrol stations in the Village, positioned at opposite ends of Hubbleton. Graham had a monthly account with the Shelco Garage and the owner, Mr Jenkins knew the Moyles family well.

Ben appreciated the amount of space that Shelco Garage commanded making it easy to fill-up and leave without fuss. It was easy to park and even had a mini-mart extended onto the back. He also enjoyed the Shelco orange signs, though he would never admit to such a childish fascination. Ben soon completed his task and after satisfying the Land Rover's appetite he passed some time talking to Harry Jenkins about his daughter Sarah who now lived 'down south.' Ben was more fascinated by Mr Jenkins' new uniform with its bright yellow logo on the chest pocket than hearing about how 'sexless Sarah' was doing. Eventually he broke free from their chat and after jumping into the Green Goddess he was ready to pull out onto the B352. Ben felt the power at his command as he drove along, although speed was not on the agenda today. Rather than pull away quickly with impressive horse-power under the bonnet, Ben checked his mirrors and gently eased his way towards the centre of Hubbleton. He wanted to take his time and saturate his memory with the images of the village so he could reminisce when he was back in France. Soon he would have to return to Sergy, a place he could only pretend to be his home, whereas Hubbleton was the genuine article.

The main street was busy with a mixture of locals and some visitors who had left their coaches in the main car park, just off the market place. The grey-brown darkness of the Northumberland stone-fronted buildings suggested a more dour environment than was actually the case. As Ben stopped at a zebra crossing to allow three people to cross the road by the bakery, he was taken by the brightness of the internal lighting contrasting with the shadowy stonework. Suddenly he sensed some movement to his left and noticed old Mrs Harris, a local character who was waving at the Green Goddess as if her life was in danger. She had clearly recognised the Land Rover without yet being able to identify the driver. An expression of disappointment crossed her face when she realised it was not Graham Moyles behind the wheel but someone much younger. She withdrew her hand to her mouth as if to say *'Oh dear, I don't recognise you'* but to save her embarrassment Ben returned her wave, although this simply caused her even more confusion.

Pulling away further down the main street and heading out of the far end of the village, Ben leant forward to get closer to the windscreen when he recognised a familiar figure walking down the street, on his side of the road. A woman was pushing a pram and holding the hand of a young boy who judging by her body language, Ben guessed must be her son. Sue Wallace was about to enter the local play-park, no doubt for some peace and quiet after a late-night shift at the Black Bull. Turning with her back to the road in order to open the metal entrance gate, Sue did not noticed the Land Rover pass by. However, the closer view confirmed Ben's initial instincts and he could see it *was* his former girlfriend. She was now devoid of her enticing public house uniform and almost unrecognisable in her motherly garb.

Rather than come to a sudden halt, Ben cruised past the family trio totally unseen before turning left. This took him alongside a residential street next to the park, where he brought the Defender to a halt. From that position he was able to observe Sue with her kids. They were approaching the area where the slides, swings and roundabouts were located, in a corner of the park. He wondered if he should get out to say hello or just carry-on about his way. Unusually indecisive, he sat inside the vehicle watching the family scene unfurl. The young boy ran off towards the nearest slide while Sue picked up the baby from the push chair to give her a cuddle. Ben felt guilty about intruding into their personal space but indulged his voyeurism a little longer as he sat totally focussed on what was happening. His mind wandered beyond the scene to a fantasy world where he considered what might have been.

Ben remembered how he and Sue had gone on their first date as teenagers, while they were still in comprehensive school together. They went to the cinema in Wooler, five miles away to watch *Titanic* and were almost not admitted because the place was packed with groups of young females all wanting to sigh over Leonardo di Caprio. That night was the first time they kissed properly. As he watched Sue play with her children he clicked his thumbnail against his teeth with frustrated anger. Suddenly feeling claustrophobic in the confines of the Land Rover he sprung out of the door and landed on the pavement with both feet.

The whole situation was ridiculous and he wanted to do something so he entered the park at the opposite entrance to the one used by Sue. Then he pretended to saunter over in her direction towards where she was sitting, but trying to appear oblivious to her presence. Ben had decided that if she saw him approach and then left the park, that would be all the indication of a total rejection he needed. If she remained on the park bench, his intention was to claim that he was just out for a quiet walk in his home village and their meeting was sheer coincidence. At least that part was almost true.

Neither eventuality occurred because Sue was so preoccupied with her children she did not see Ben approaching at all. Despite his cosmic attempts to make her turn around as he got closer, Ben suddenly found himself alongside Sue who was holding her daughter, Jessica. Her son Thomas had progressed to the swings by this stage and was completely oblivious to Ben's presence. For at least ten seconds Ben stood behind Sue in total silence, unsure of what to do next.

His response was feeble, 'Hello Sue, nice day. Fancy bumping into you here.'

The mother jolted slightly with the shock of seeing her former boyfriend. 'Oh, hello Ben.' She returned to adjusting her little girl's clothes and pondered how to react to the surprise encounter. 'You're still here then. I thought you must have gone back by now and resumed your new home in France.' The sentiment was said with feeling.

'*This* is my home, Sue. France is just somewhere I live at the moment. I don't think I could ever regard anywhere other than Hubbleton as home.' Ben was determined that if there was to be a spat, he was not going to make a retreat.

'That's not what you said when you came back from university, remember? You did not regard this place as your home then. If I recall accurately, you couldn't get out of here quickly enough.'

Ben was beginning to realise the depth of the pain that their one argument ten years ago had caused. Circling around from behind the bench he sat next to Sue and looked her straight in the eyes. 'That was a long time ago and we were both young back then. I was too immature to settle down in this place. I'd never been anywhere or done anything outside our farm. I wanted to see a bit of the world first. If I recall correctly you just wanted to settle in a nice little house in Hubbleton and start a family.' His eyes lowered onto the baby.

The rawness of their emotions was beginning to bubble to the surface. The movement generated by standing up in order to place her young daughter back into her push-chair was sufficient motion to bring Sue into battle mode. 'So how is it in that big beautiful world out there where you live now? Is it as good as you thought it was going to be? Have you made your millions yet or will that only happen when you inherit your father's farm here in little old Hubbleton ?'

Ben sat silently stunned for a few seconds and removed an imaginary thread from the leg of his jeans as he watched Sue kiss her daughter's forehead before putting her back into the push-chair and returning to the bench. He contemplated saying nothing further and leaving Sue to wallow in her own bitterness but before he could do anything, young Thomas had made his way over from the swings. The lad was standing in front Ben and staring at him as if he was from outer space. The boy was like a motionless mannequin, looking directly at this stranger without saying a word. His mother broke the silence.

'What do you want Thomas? Don't stare like that, it's rude.' The little boy did not react to his mother's reprimand. 'Thomas don't be naughty and pay attention. This is Ben, he is an old friend. He is Mr Moyles' son. You know… Graham who has the farm? Say hello to Mr Moyles, Thomas.'

After another long pause while the couple waited for Thomas to spring into action, he disappointed them by simply saying 'Hello,' without any warmth or emotion and in a way a nine-year-old boy could destroy any ego. Sue was becoming impatient and did not have time for this. 'That's better. Now what do you want ?'

After what would have been an unacceptable delay for an adult to respond, the little boy asked, 'Is it alright for me to go on the slide, Mummy ?'

Realising that she had taken out her bad mood on her only son, Sue inwardly recoiled and tempered her flustered state by showing some compassion. 'Yes, of course you can my darling. I'll watch you from here …..me and Jessica will come over in a moment.'

With that royal consent, Thomas half-turned to skip away but then remembered his manners. 'Bye, Mr Moyles. It was nice to meet you.' Having completed all the requirements of his social responsibilities, Thomas ran innocently towards the steps, excited at being able to mount the slide with impunity.

The interaction with Sue's son had helped bring the mood back onto an even keel. Rather than storm-off as his instincts had advised, Ben stayed to test his former girlfriend with a question of less bitterness that the one he had been asked. 'He seems like a nice boy – how about you, Sue? Is family life here in Hubbleton all you thought it was cracked up to be? Are you happy?'

Sue wished Ben had asked the question with more vitriol. It would have made her response easier. Her eyes misted over for a moment as she recalled those former times they had spent together. She wanted to tell him to clear-off because he had hurt her too much. She wanted to scream at him that she was desperately unhappy with a man she did not love and if she could turn back the clock, right here, right now, she would do it in an instant. Instead, she gave the only response she could give in the circumstances. 'I wouldn't change my kids for anything. If we had stayed together they would not have been born, so how can I ever regret us breaking up.'

With no place to go, Ben thought it was time to leave. Bumping into Sue had upset them both and their unspoken conversation was more deafeningly painful than their open dialogue. Ben was just about to stand to say a final farewell when Sue placed her hand on his forearm to prevent him getting up. She looked directly into his eyes and said, 'Bye Ben. I hope everything works out well for you. I hope you meet someone who deserves you.'

Ben returned Sue's gaze to see tears begin to well in her eyes. He moved towards her and they kissed each other in a way only lovers say goodbye, not caring if they were seen. It was a heartfelt gesture from them both and eloquently encapsulated the sentiment that neither had been able to say aloud. Pushing himself off the park bench, Ben stood upright and gave a poignant look towards the slide. After a few more seconds, he turned away, pressing his hand on Sue's shoulder with one final gesture of affection. Ben did not turn around as he headed towards the parked Land Rover. Once inside the car he turned the music on the radio to full volume and revved the engine before speeding off towards Moyles Farm. The full tank of diesel had come at quite a cost.

Pulling into the farmyard Ben could see the Massey Ferguson parked inside the machine compound and he was able to make out the distinctive shape of his father at the back end of the tractor. The scene suggested that all had not gone well with Graham's work in the lower pastures. Ben got out of the Land Rover and walked over to see what was going on. His Dad may have heard him come over but he chose to ignore all spectators and continue with what he was doing. There was some cursing going on which was fairly typical of the master of the farm when his work was interrupted. Ben tried to establish the nature of the problem but found it difficult because Graham's back was masking the rear of the tractor where the work was taking place. 'Alright Dad, it's only me. What's happening? Problem?'

Graham always tried to moderate his behaviour and particularly his language in front of his sons and although he could not see Ben, he could hear him well enough and became more civilised when he realised who it was. Speaking over his shoulder, Graham yielded. 'Oh, hello son. Yeah – a stone must have rolled down into the field from somewhere and when I went over it in the Massey, it caught in the power take-off shaft and ripped off the guard. I managed to pick it up and I'm trying to fit it back on but it seems to be damaged and won't fit properly. Bloody thing!' Graham was trying to position the thick plastic cover with one hand and bang it into position with the heel of his other. His son realised there was not much he could do other than offer moral support. There was insufficient room for the two men to work at the back of the tractor so Ben was left to stay close and offer feeble gestures of support. 'Do you want me to pass you a hammer or a spanner or something, Dad?' The proposal was met with silence.

A grunt of satisfaction suggested that the problem may have been resolved but this transpired to be only partly true. 'I seem to have got the guard back on after a fashion but I don't know how long it will last. Looks like I might have to get a new one. That'll be two hundred quid down the drain.'

Ben could see that his father was not keen on investing in something that was essential but just not top of his priority list and felt he needed to take him to task about the matter.

'Look Dad, you can't have a power take-off shaft spinning around and exposed to the open air. We need it to work the tractor attachments but we don't want anyone being dragged into it in the process. So buy a new guard before I come back here, for God's sake. Ben offered some further words of solace as they walked over to the farmhouse. 'If you need to get a new one so it's safe, then it's not money wasted is it? Make sure you order one and get it fitted properly.'

Ben's words appeared to fall onto stony ground. 'We'll see if that repair job works first son. I can't afford to throw money away just for a guard. That seems to be rigid enough for now. Leave it with me.' With that dismissive comment Graham got up and the pair made their way to the farmhouse.

It was coming towards the end of the day and it was time for something to eat. Ben was surprised to see Elsie Thistlethwaite in the kitchen. He knew she worked for his Dad but her presence had been scarce during his stay. Ben's visit had coincided with Elsie having to travel to Selby in North Yorkshire in order to help out with some domestic issues involving her own family. He had seen her only fleetingly while he was at home. Graham strolled over to the corner of the room near the stove and flumped into his favourite kitchen chair. It was an old brown leather seater, the only remaining part of a three-piece suit that Eva Moyles had bought new from Binns' Department Store in Newcastle during the 1970s. It was obvious to all the family why Graham had never thrown it out. Air escaped from a small hole in the old cushion when he sat down, making a deflating noise. Graham had become oblivious to the sound over the years and inquired of his hired help. 'What's for dinner tonight Elsie ? I'm starving.'

Elsie did not turn to look at him but busied herself stirring a large wooden spoon around the principal pot. 'Well I know it's not very seasonal but I've made a chicken stew with suet dumplings. There's enough to satisfy even your appetite Mr Moyles.'

While Graham showed vigorous approval, Ben scanned the downstairs area but there was no sign of his brother. Before he had a chance to ask Elsie his whereabouts she pre-empted his question. 'Richard has gone to his bedroom for a lie down. He told me to tell you not to disturb him. He's very tired and needs to sleep. He said he'll be down later to have something to eat.'

This concerned the two men and they looked at each other knowing what the other was thinking. Graham pointed to the ceiling with a raised thumb to indicate where he was going. Ben understood the message and then followed his father upstairs. Richard's health was sufficiently poor to allow no margin of error for any expression of discomfort, even if it was something as common as fatigue. Graham tapped lightly with the knuckle of his index finger on Richard's door and as there was no response he turned the handle knob and slowly pushed it open. He could see Richard was in a deep sleep on the bed but the nature of his breathing suggested that it was not a peaceful slumber. Graham walked over and sat on the edge of the bed, giving a deep sigh of anguish as he leant over his son's exhausted body. He swept Richard's fringe with his fingers before gently ensuring he was fully covered by the duvet. Ben stood next to his father with his arms folded and whispered, 'He doesn't look good Dad. What do you think we should do, should we send for the doctor?'

Graham repeated his thumb pointing trick and this time the two men left the bedroom and moved across the passage into Ben's room. 'I'm not going to send for Dr Elsworth tonight son. He's been like this before although it's something you never get used to. He wouldn't thank us for getting the doctor to see him. You know what he's like. He's a very proud lad, always fighting it off until it drags him down. You know he's on the list for a transplant, I suppose he's told you?'

Ben responded in a hushed tone. 'Yes, he told me he's been on the list for a while now but nothing has come along.'

'That's right. We thought we'd found a donor last winter but it proved not to be a match. I'd give both my arms to get him a new heart if I could. He always feels guilty about not pulling his weight on the farm but I never expect him to do anything heavy. In some ways I'd prefer it if he did nothing at all but just stayed in the farmhouse waiting by the phone for the transplant team to ring. At least that way I wouldn't spend every waking minute wondering if he's ok. The consultant has said it's only a matter of time before his heart gives up on him but Rich is having none of it. He's a stubborn bugger and no mistake.' Graham turned his head away and Ben was not sure if there was a tear in his eye or not.

He approached his father and patted him on the shoulder. 'Yeah, and I wonder where he gets that stubbornness from do you suppose? C'mon let's go downstairs and grab some food. If we're not going to send for the doctor then worrying about him is not going to do much good either.'

After dinner Graham returned to his comfy chair and entered a daydream world of his own. He only stopped twiddling his thumbs when Rich emerged from his bedroom about an hour later. With an exaggerated yawn and stretch as he entered the kitchen, the elder twin asked 'What's for dinner ? Something smells nice.' Ben and Graham looked at each other and stifled a laugh.

Graham took the initiative. ' You sit down and I'll serve it for you. It's Elsie's stew and it was lovely an'all. Want some bread with it ?' Richard unwittingly raised his thumb, something he had seen someone do somewhere before.

Rich took his stew into the lounge on a tray and while the three of them sat watching the television, Mrs Thistlethwaite poked her head around the door after seeing to the family's laundry. 'I've ironed your clothes and seen to the washing-up so I'm off now Graham. See you tomorrow boys.' The twins who were facing Elsie waved at her in silence, while Graham did not bother to turn around, simply raising a hand in acknowledgement. The scene of domesticity was complete when Richard laughed aloud as a character in the sitcom they were watching fell across the open counter in a wine bar. Twenty minutes later, the theme music of the programme signalled a change of action and Ben issued the challenge. 'Well I don't know about you two but I fancy a pint. Anyone coming down the Black Bull with me?'

Rich was the first one to respond, 'Nah, think I'll give it a miss tonight bro'. Tomorrow's your last night isn't it?' Ben took no notice of the question as he stood in front of the tv, deliberately blocking their view. 'I'll go with you then. I'm feeling a bit tired at the moment so I might have an early night.' The rapid fluctuation in Richard's energy levels was a symptom of his condition.

Graham decided to err on the side of caution, just in case a doctor was needed after all. 'Think I'll just stay here with Rich. Got another early start in the morning and I want to try out that guard on the power take-off shaft just to make sure it works and doesn't fall off.' Ben understood why Graham was declining his offer. His father supplied some compensation for his lack of company. 'The keys for the Land Rover are on the side there, son. Just take the Goddess rather than use your hire car. It's probably better for the roads around here, especially at this time of night. I won't be needing the car again, hopefully.'

With a throw-away farewell Ben made his way to his coat and said 'Ok if you're sure'. Five minutes later he was heading to Hubbleton for a change of scenery with thoughts of a Lockhead's pint.

Inside the pub, there were not many drinkers as it was a Thursday night. After ordering a pint of Best, Ben scanned the room and his heart sank. Although Sue Wallace was not working behind the bar as she did at week-ends, her husband Donny was in the corner by the dart board, deep in conversation with someone Ben did not recognise. There was no eye contact between the two former friends but Ben knew he would have been spotted sure enough. He considered doing an about turn and going down to the Red Lion for a change of scenery but decided against an act that would no doubt be construed as running away. Why should he be chased out of his favourite drinking hole when he had done nothing wrong?

Ben decided against any social interaction with the people in the bar. There were a few faces he recognised but after a couple of pints he thought he would simply go back to the farm. His previous enthusiasm for a drink in a friendly atmosphere now seemed to be wearing off. He gravitated to the end of the counter and used the wall as a back support and a shield, nodding occasionally to Joe Willbourghly, the landlord who often served on his own during the week. The lights of the one-arm bandit slot machine seemed to offer Ben a form of hypnotic escape as he stared at the bright lights while his mind wandered back to a time when he and Donald William Wallace were on better terms.

Although now reluctant and sworn enemies, Ben remembered the day as youngsters when he actually saved Donny's life. They were in their final year at junior school before leaving for the local comprehensive. Their class teacher Mr Kutz had organised a summer term trip from Hubbleton Primary to Marsden Rock on the North East coast. The plan was to stay the morning at the beach and the afternoon in White City near Whitley Bay, where they would be allowed to spend their pocket money on the fair-rides and amusement arcades. Four of the boys including Ben and Donny, went in the sea soon after arriving and waded out to the arch of the Rock, where there was a cave. Donny was wearing a top as well as his trunks, partly to keep warm but also to try and ensure his white, skeletal frame was not seen by the others. The strategy designed to avoid ridicule did not work because as they entered the water, one of the boys teased him. 'Come on Donny man, what you wearing that top for. Don't be such a sissy. Get it off!'

The others joined in. 'What you hiding under their Donny. Come on, show uz yer muscles, you big wimp.' Donny took no notice, prepared to allow his T-shirt to get sodden rather than expose his torso to even worse ridicule. It was bad enough that he could not swim.

Inside the domain of the Rock's hidden secrets, they were wrapped up in their own little world, able to shout at the tops of their voices and hear the echoes come bouncing back from the limestone walls. There was more teasing as well as laughing as the boys enjoyed their day out. They were having a great time unaware of what was going on around them but unknown to the group, the tide was coming in very quickly. The increasing height of the water level caught them by surprise and the sea filled the air pocket so quickly that it threatened their retreat. The brine was soon up to chest height and it was necessary to get out before the archway door was completely covered by the waves. Ben and two of the boys could swim so all they had to do was 'duck-dive' below the surface and re-emerge on the other side of the cave. However, Donny was a non-swimmer and that was a problem.

With the water up to his chin, Donny did not have the confidence to put his head under the water and push himself through the remaining gap. He panicked. The other two boys swam out of the cave and headed back to the shoreline, innocently unaware of any problem behind them. After one unsuccessful attempt, Donny became scared and re-surfaced *inside* the water-filling cave. The incoming tide was now above the level of the arch so there was no alternative but to dive below the water surface, something which a non-swimmer was bound to find difficult. Ben was treading water and trying to offer Donny words of encouragement but his friend was beyond listening and continued to thrash around desperately as his echoed calls for help were now totally confined.

Fortunately, Donny was wearing that T-shirt and when he finally disappeared below the surface Ben duck-dived after him and was able to grab the top. With all his might he yanked Donny under the water and through the narrow gap, onto the other side of the Rock. They suddenly found themselves in shallower water standing with their feet on a small sandbank. Donny was spluttering and spitting salt water and detritus along with his own sputum as he attempted to regain some composure as well as his breath. After a couple of minutes of crying, coughing and gasping the non-swimmer regained some self-control and began to wade back towards the shoreline just behind Ben. Once he had caught up, Donny put his hand on his saviour's shoulder and said, 'Don't say anything to the others Ben. I don't want them thinkin' that a'rm a wimp any more than they do already.'

Ben continued to push his legs through the resistant waves and turned towards his mate, responding, 'Ok Donny, don't worry, I won't say a thing.'

It was a dramatic moment in their childhood but from that moment, the relationship between the two boys began to wane. When they started comprehensive school after the summer break and were in different classes, they found new friendship groups and maintained a social distance. At the time, Ben was a little upset that his noble deed went unrecognised and unrewarded. He never told anyone about what happened that day but it was an episode in their lives that should have created a special bond between two childhood pals. In reality it was a constant reminder to Donny of a debt that could never be re-payed, making him the lesser man. Ben wondered if that was the reason he had jumped so keenly into a relationship with Sue, to prove to himself that he could get one over on the boy who wanted to leave Hubbleton.

The lights flashed on the one-arm bandit as one of the regulars gained a bonus for more beer. The noise of the winning coins dropping into the tray brought Ben out of his trance, although he could sense eyes glaring in his direction. Rather than return the gaze and look towards the dartboard, he thought he would pay a visit to the gents and then just finish his pint and go home. He did not need any aggravation, it had already been a difficult day. Standing adjacently to the door, Ben turned and exited into the passageway and then headed towards the pub toilets. After standing over the urinal and zipping himself up he turned and was suddenly thrown into a choke hold as his collar was thrust under his jaw. Donny had entered the toilet unnoticed and came to say more than hello.

'Next time you want to speak to my wife, I have some advice for you – Don't ! And stay away from my son. He told me that he had seen you in the park. Don't tell me, you just bumped into each other. No chance! She's *my* wife so just return to France or Switzerland or wherever else you have come from and don't come back!'

Before he had time to push Ben towards the wall, Donny was overcome by a stinging pain in his scrotum as his adversary brought his knee up to Donny's genitals with great accuracy. Donny fell backwards and brought a favoured hand to his crotch for some desperate relief. It did not matter, Ben followed it with a punch to Donny's jaw and this caused him to bounce off the wall before finishing in a heap, on his knees and gasping for breath. Ben was tempted to finish him off but decided against continuing the assault. That would only have prevented him from saying what had been on his mind for years. Standing over his vanquished foe, Ben pointed his index finger like a stork's beak. 'Don't go making yourself out as the victim here. You were the one who did the dirty on me! We were supposed to be friends for God's sake and friends don't do that to each other. She was *my* girlfriend and I trusted you. For the record, I'll talk to who I like and go where I want. This is my home as well as yours.'

Straightening his shoulders and brushing his dishevelled hair backwards with his fingers, Ben was just about finished. However, he turned for one final outburst. 'And one more thing – the day I saved you from drowning in the sea all those years ago was the biggest mistake of my life. I should have left you to choke in that cave. We would all have been better off!' Ben turned away and left Donny to absorb what had just happened. Slamming the door with distressed satisfaction he stormed down the corridor avoiding the entrance to the bar and left the Black Bull, uncertain whether he would ever return. No doubt the locals would spend the rest of their evening mulling over 'the fight in the bogs', or at least Donny's version of events, although Ben doubted he had the guts to even mention the incident.

Ben's drive back to the farm was less than a memory as he threw around in his head the incident with Donny. Fortunately, he did not pass any other traffic on his way back to the farm, which was just as well considering the Defender was hurtling along down the middle of the road. Pulling into the farmyard, Ben could see the light was switched on in the porch, while the rest of the house was in darkness. As Ben raised the latch to enter the kitchen he thought his home must be one of the last remaining houses left in the UK which could still be unlocked at ten o'clock at night. He saw a brandy bottle on the side of one of the cupboards, next to a used glass and recognised the label. Without bothering to wash the glass he poured himself a drink and downed it in two gulps but it made little difference to his clenched fists. Ben considered taking another drink but walked away in disgust as he thought about punching something within range. He decided against the idea and went upstairs to his bedroom in a state of fury. It was at least two hours before he was able to sleep.

VI

Saturday arrived, the last complete day of Ben's unusual holiday. There was a flight back to Geneva during the early hours of the following morning and there was a ticket with Dr Moyles' name on the stub. Ben was up early and in the kitchen just after his Dad, who had his usual pot of tea on the go. Graham was old school and making individual cups with a tea bag was considered inefficient and expensive. If it had not been so inconvenient to buy packets of the stuff in its natural state, he would have reverted to spoons and a strainer, like the good old days. He pointed to the tea pot without needing to say anything further to Ben. After cupping his mug with both hands and taking a treasured sip before sitting down at the kitchen table, Ben's thoughts turned to his brother.

'Rich up yet, Dad?' Although he could not discern exactly the words of his father's response, his body language and tone of voice suggested that Rich was still in bed so Ben followed it up with, 'Want me to go and wake him?'

This seemed to inject Graham with a little more civility. 'Yeah, ok. You go and get him up and I'll slap on some bacon and make a few butties.'

Ben placed his mug onto a coaster after taking another sip and went up the stairs to Rich's bedroom. He knocked firmly on the door but there was no response. Deciding not to give up, Ben gave one more loud rap and entered the room. He could see some movement from the bedclothes and was going to shout some obscenity about what his brother was up to but then he paused. Something about the way the sheets were gathered did not look normal. As he got closer to the bed Ben could see his brother was in distress, clutching his chest and appearing to be struggling for breath. He shouted through the floorboards to his father, who recognised the alarm in his son's voice. Graham immediately switched off the bacon and thundered upstairs.

By the time he got to the bedroom Ben had his hand on his brother's sweating forehead and was whispering something in his ear. Graham took one look at the scene and immediately dialled 999 on his mobile. As he spoke to the emergency services for an ambulance his eyes were transfixed on what was happening in front of him. It appeared as though Rich was having a heart attack and it was clear that they needed to act fast.

The medical team did not give Graham the reassurances he wanted about how quickly an ambulance could reach their isolated location. It was clear to the responder that more drastic action was needed. The level of anxiety in Graham's voice when asked about whether he considered his son's life to be in danger, was the clincher. An Air Ambulance was dispatched from Newcastle Airport with the intention of transporting the patient to the Queen Elizabeth Infirmary's Cardiology Department. Time was of the essence.

Graham pushed the mobile back into his pocket and approached the bed, where his son needed help. Easing past Ben he cradled his Rich as if holding an injured bird. While giving soft, authoritative words of reassurance he turned to address Ben. 'There's an Air Ambulance on its way and it should be here in the next ten minutes or so. They'll need somewhere to land so you go outside and direct them to the field beside the brook. It's flat enough for a landing and not too soft. You'll find a couple of flares in the storage box in the barn. Take them and set them off when you hear the helicopter coming. Quickly son, we haven't got a lot of time.'

Ben did not have to be told twice and after leaning over his brother to give some further words of comfort, he was off like a whippet towards the barn. He knew exactly which field his Dad meant and agreed that it was the best place to land a helicopter. His mind was in a turmoil of worry about his brother but he also needed to focus and give the best possible help to the incoming medics.

Pacing up and down in the field and scouring the horizon for any movement, time became physically painful. While he was waiting and partly to distract his thoughts, he examined a flare to ensure he knew how it should be activated because not one second could be wasted. As he was reading the small print on one of the labels, Ben thought he heard something. He squinted into the morning sun and prayed that it was not his imagination. Then he could see the yellow helicopter appear above the ridge. He ripped off the flare's cap and used it to scratch the black ignition button before holding it away from his body. The plume of bright coloured smoke exited the stick and was waved vigorously in order to maximise its power for pilot attraction. One of the crew inside the helicopter's pod was scanning the landscape and then pointed to the source of the smoke. The pilot headed straight towards the figure standing in the centre of a field, clear in his own mind that it was ok to land. After hovering for a few seconds to allow Ben to get out of the way, the air ambulance was skilfully lowered to the ground.

The first paramedic out of the helicopter was wrestling with his medical rucksack as he approached Ben and over the deafening sound of the deflating rotary blades shouted for instructions about where the patient was located. Ben pointed to the gate entrance and the male nurse ran towards the farmhouse, followed by another medic who was carrying more equipment. Rich's brother managed to overtake the pair and reached the door in first place. 'This way,' he garbled, gasping for breath. 'He's upstairs with my father.'

The medic ascended taking two steps at a time, calling indiscriminately for further instructions, 'Hello, it's the medical team. Anybody there?'

'Graham rushed to the door and waved them inside the bedroom with rotary arms of his own. 'He's in here! Quickly !'

The first medic was busying his hands looking for various aids while attempting to evoke a response from Richard. 'Hello young man, I'm a paramedic....my name is Norman... I'm here to help.... Can you hear me?' Turning to the two anxious faces he asked, 'What's his name.'

The two chorused as one, 'Richard!'

The medical team took over the situation with professional efficiency. Immediate relief was given via an oxygen mask, while Norman's colleague prepared an injection of adrenaline. A mobile cardiogram was taken giving a read-out of how the heart was performing. Almost instantly after the infusion of adrenaline there was a discernible improvement in Rich's physical demeanour. His breathing improved and his pallor began to be replaced by a more healthy pinkish hue. Sitting on the edge of the bed, Norman began to conduct an interrogation about Rich's medical history, while maintaining physical contact with his patient by holding his wrist to track the pulse rate. He listened intently as Graham outlined the nature of Rich's heart problems, the last time he was seen by a doctor and his presence on the transplant waiting list. Ben's eyes were on stalks as the reality of the seriousness of his brother's heart problems were detailed. Norman shot the occasional knowing look towards his colleague before eventually giving his opinion on what needed to happen. 'Ok, I think we will need to take him into Queen Elizabeth's where they can get a better picture of what is going on and provide the best diagnosis of what needs to happen next. We'll put him on a stretcher and take him there in the helicopter now. We can be there within a quarter of an hour.'

Graham pleaded with paternal anxiety, 'Can I go with him?'

The answer was a disappointment to Ben. 'We can only take one relative with us. We don't have room for anyone else I'm afraid.'

Ben took the initiative, aware that his father was obviously flustered and anxious. 'You go Dad and I'll follow on in the car. I'll see you at the hospital. It'll be alright.'

In the short time it took for Ben and his father to plan their own strategy, Norman and his mate had Rich on a stretcher and were about to make their way to the stairwell, before he ordered Graham to assist, 'Here, you take this and just hold it above your son's head.' It was a plastic bag full of a clear liquid that was being infused into Rich's system. Within an instant the patient and his father were inside the helicopter and as Ben's hair was ruffled in the downdraft, the people that mattered most were soon in the air and on their way to Queen Elizabeth's Cardiology Department in Newcastle.

Suddenly Ben found himself alone, bereft and uncertain about what to do next. In forlorn hope he scoured the horizon looking for one final sighting of the helicopter but even its distant whirling had evaporated into the ether. Allowing himself one indulgent sigh he then ran towards the farmyard to retrieve the hired SUV which he was soon driving back towards Newcastle. This was one race the Green Goddess would not win. On this occasion, travelling to Newcastle did not include any opportunities to indulge reminiscences about the landscape. Familiar features needed to be replaced by the anonymous views of a city landscape and the sooner the better.

Before he knew it, Ben was running out of the visitors' car park and into the main hospital entrance. After inquiring about the location of the department dealing with heart emergencies at the reception desk, he followed the volunteer's index finger down the long corridor towards Cardiology. In the treatment area he found his father sitting in a chair next to his sleeping brother. The frenetic behaviour associated with the word 'emergency' two hours earlier had been replaced by a level of calm. An oxygen mask covered Rich's mouth and nose and his breathing appeared to be easier than it had been back at the Farm. Graham jumped to his feet when he saw his younger son enter the treatment room. They quickly greeted each other with a sympathetic embrace before Ben asked the question. 'How's he doing, Dad?'

The response was more reassuring than Ben had anticipated. 'Yeah, he's a lot better, son. By a lucky twist the main heart consultant was on duty when we brought him in and he saw Rich straight away. He reckoned it wasn't a heart attack but was something associated with his dodgy valves. He gave him a shot of something that I didn't know the name of, and he seemed to stabilise after that. We've just returned from an MRI scan so hopefully that will show a bit more as well.'

Ben and his father sat beside Rich's bed for what seemed like an eternity. Their inner turmoil was trying to psyche the situation into a positive outcome. Neither of the two men were particularly religious but the power of their anxiety was the closest they got to prayer. Ben was beginning to get a bit concerned about the impact the day was having on his father, who looked worn out. He offered some sustenance. 'Would you like a cup of tea or coffee Dad, or something to eat? I can probably pick up a sandwich from somewhere. There's bound to be something around.' Before Graham had a chance to respond to Ben, Dr Chesney came into the treatment area holding several large transparencies.

'Hello again Mr Moyles, we have the results of your son's scan.' Turning to Ben he surmised who he was by his physical appearance although he was unaware they were twins. 'And you must be Rich's brother?' Confirmation came as he shook Ben's hand.

Graham wanted to cut to the chase. 'Er ...you were going to tell us about the results of the scan Doctor?'

'Ah, yes. I'm pleased to say it's better than we first thought. There is no further damage to your son's heart and he's probably had an *afib* episode.'

Ben raised the level of interrogation. '*Afib*? What's that ?'

The consultant saw the need to clarify. 'Sorry I didn't mean to slip into the jargon. An *afib* is an atrial fibrillation or irregular heartbeat. When it occurs it can seem like a heart attack, especially when the patient already has any form of heart disease, such as your brother has. It would explain why Richard struggled to get his breath. We were concerned that there may have been a blood clot causing the blockage but nothing has shown up on the scan. Just to be sure we've given him something that will thin his blood and remove the danger of any further clotting, if indeed that's what it was. The existing damage meant the heart muscle struggled to deal with the episode.

Ben asked his question desperately hoping for something positive. 'Is it serious?'

'Well yes, it can be but we want to make sure it doesn't develop *into* something serious. We've given him a couple of injections of a fairly powerful drug to stabilise his condition. When he's feeling better we will need to talk to him about things like lifestyle, diet and so on.'

Ben's second question was soon quashed. 'When can he come home?'

The consultant was more than prepared to err on the side of caution. 'I'm afraid not today. We will need to keep him here for a few days, to monitor his progress. We need to get the balance of any drugs we prescribe just right so they can do their work. A maximum of a week should see him return home as long as he promises to take it easy.'

Graham imposed his authority on the situation. 'You needn't worry about that doctor. I'll make damn sure he looks after himself. His days of working on the farm are over.'

'Well as you can see he is a lot better now than he was when you brought him in here. The sedative is doing its work so he will be asleep for a few hours yet. I suggest you both go home too and get some rest of your own. There's nothing you can do here now.

Graham looked at Ben sympathetically and encouraged him to do the right thing. 'Come on son, it's getting late and you have an early flight tomorrow.'

Ben tried to display some of the Moyles obstinacy but it was rebuked from a more experienced master. 'Ok but I'm not going anywhere until I know that Rich is on the road to recovery.'

'We'll talk about that in the car on the way back. Right now we both need some rest. We'll come back and see him in the morning. They'll ring us if there's any problem.

During their journey back to the farm Ben and his Dad stopped off in the village of Folkington to get some fish and chips. The homely attraction of the lights and the catchy name of 'The Chippy' were too appealing to ignore for their growing hunger. In addition neither of them felt like cooking a meal when they got home. While their fingers juggled with hot chips, sizzling fish batter was waltzed round the inside of their mouths by hyperactive tongues.

Graham resumed his paternal role as he sat with his meal warming-up his lap. 'You can't stay here son. You've got a job to go back to. What will your bosses say if you're late back from a holiday. You don't want to provide them with any excuses to sack you.'

'I know that Dad but how can I return to France when Rich is so ill. I couldn't live with myself if something happened to him and I wasn't around?'

Graham wracked his mind for a solution as he held the white foam tray above his head and lowered the remnants of the potato scrapings into his mouth. 'Come on we'll think of something. Tell you what, let's pop into the Bull for a pint on the way home and talk it through then. I'm going to have to face everybody's questions at some point and it would be better if you were there as well to fend off some of them. They will all have seen the helicopter heading towards the farm and put two-and-two together to make five. Better they know the truth about what's been happening.'

'Ok, Dad if that's what you want.' Ben needed a pint as much as his father.

As soon as they entered the bar of the Black Bull, Graham was surrounded by concerned locals quizzing him about the day's events. Although the place was busy on this particular Saturday night, people at the counter made space to allow Ben to get to the pumps and order a pint of Ordinary and a pint of Best Lockhead's beer. Sue Wallace was serving behind the bar, as she did most Saturday nights. She was pulling a pint for another customer and when she turned towards the till, Ben thought there was something different about her appearance. He leant forward to give his order and he noticed that her cheek seemed slightly red in colour, despite the heavy application of foundation make-up. Ben knew that he would be unable to engage in any lengthy conversation so when Sue placed the first full glass on the counter he moved closer and said discreetly, 'Did *he* do that to you?'

Sue was flustered and surprised at Ben's question. She thought the extra time that she had spent doing her make-up had done the trick but she was wrong. Sue tried to brush him off as she took his money and turned to pour the second pint. 'Did what?'

For a moment Ben wondered if it had happened before so he was not going to be deterred. 'Did Donny hit you because I was talking to you yesterday?'

Placing the pint of Best in front of him she took his money and replied, 'Just leave it Ben, I can handle Donny,' waving her hand dismissively as if swatting a fly. She returned from the till and placed the change from his order into his hand, leaning forward so their noses were almost touching. 'Don't do anything Ben, I'll be fine. Just don't make any more trouble.'

Ben's face flushed red with anger and he asked the question 'Is he in here now?' while scanning the faces in the bar.

'No he's not and he's not coming in tonight so just leave it alone, alright?'

Sue moved onto the next customer while Ben returned with the two full glasses to the group of friends surrounding his father. Graham could see that something was wrong but Ben was not going to disclose the reason for his fury. 'Everything alright Ben, you look flustered.'

'No I'm fine Dad, thanks. Just worried about Rich, that's all. Let's just smack these back and get back home. I've just about had enough of this place.

Ten minutes later the SUV was heading through Hubbleton towards the Red Lion when Ben spotted someone he recognised walking along the street. He screeched the car to a sudden stop which completely surprised his father. Without closing the door behind him Ben had got out of the car and ran across the road towards a startled figure. It was

Donny, no doubt on his way to drink in a different pub to the one where his wife was working in order to avoid any potential embarrassment. He was totally taken-aback by the sound of the brakes and the presence of a figure running straight at him. Ben did not give him any time to react and soon had him by the throat and pushed up against the nearest doorway.

There was no ambiguity in his message. 'Touch her again and I'll put you in hospital. I don't care if I'm in France or wherever I am, if I hear that she has so much as shadow on her face or anything else that looks like a bruise, I'll find out and come looking for you. Do I make myself clear?'

Donny's eyes were wide open with fear and he knew that Ben's threat was delivered with serious intent. He said nothing, only nodding his head in terror. At this point Graham pulled his son off his prey, having crossed the street once he realised what was going on. 'Leave him son, just get back in the car.' With those words of advice, Ben walked backwards across the road, still staring at the target of his anger. Graham had some final words of his own for Donny as he prodded him in the chest with his index finger. 'And if he doesn't do it, I will!'

Donny straightened his clothing and tidied his hair as his two assailants crossed the road to return to the SUV. The vehicle was then driven deliberately slowly past a stunned Donny, who was given an icy stare by its occupants before the car sped-off down the road and out of the village. The last ten minutes of the journey took place along the lanes to Moyes Farm. Ben broke the silence, to tell his father the plan he had cobbled together in his mind before they had arrived at the Black Bull. 'I'm going to try and swap my flight for a later one tomorrow, Dad. If Rich is better in the morning and shows signs good signs of improvement, then I'll return to France. I can take my stuff with me and when we visit and I can then go to the Airport from the Hospital. But if he's not much better I'm going to stay here and take my chances with work.'

Graham thought that was a reasonable compromise. 'Ok son, if that's what you want. As long as you know I'm not chasing you away?' His Dad had no cause to ask, the answer to his question was never in doubt.

VII

Sunday morning saw Ben wake early and rather than stew in bed he decided to pack his case, a much easier job than it had been two weeks earlier. Once he had finished he thought he would sneak downstairs and wait for his father to wake-up. Travelling back that day would not give Ben much time to settle leisurely into his flat before starting work, assuming he was actually going to be flying back later. He had just come off the phone to the airline and fortunately been able to arrange a later flight back to Geneva. However, that did not mean he would definitely return, it all depended on how Rich was doing.

When Ben entered the kitchen, movement from the chair gave him a start. 'Christ Dad, I didn't see you there, you almost gave me a heart attack. What are you doing up at this hour, even by your standards it's a bit early? The sun is hardly up yet.'

'Couldn't sleep for thinking about Rich. I know it's stupid and he's a grown man but I always think of you both as my two boys and if anything happened to either of you …'

Ben approached Graham and placed a hand on his shoulder to prevent him from breaking down. Anxiety was written all over his face. 'It's alright Dad you don't have to explain. I know.' After a moment of silence between them, Ben decided to take a practical approach. 'Fancy a cup of tea and some toast or bacon to start the day?'

It was more than Graham wanted. 'No, thanks son. I'll have a cup of tea but I'm not hungry. I don't think I could eat anything.'

As Ben busied himself with the kettle and the cups he asked his father whether he intended to ring the hospital to find out how Rich's night had gone. They jointly decided there was not much point as they were definitely going to visit the hospital anyway and even if they got through to the ward at such an early hour, they probably would not be told anything. Better to go and find out first-hand for themselves.

When they arrived at the Queen Elizabeth Infirmary it was only about seven-thirty in the morning, far too early for general visitors. The medical staff on the ward were buzzing around, no doubt ensuring every patient was washed, fed and medicated before the doctors' daily rounds. Staff at the ward desk demonstrated some frustration towards Ben and his Dad at having to deal with visitors given the early hour. However, they became more reasonable when Ben explained his circumstances regarding flying back to Switzerland and how as a twin he needed to be reassured about his brother's progress. Although the message about Rich's progress was garbled because staff were so busy it seemed to be generally good. The ward sister declared that '*It would be better if they spoke to his doctor.*' Ben and Graham understood that no one wanted to give an authoritative assessment of Rich's condition without a doctor's approval but first impressions seemed to be positive.

At first they were told they could not see the patient but Ben played on the fact that he had a plane to catch and eventually the sister relented. Her impatience was matched only by the demands of the job because she did not have time to argue. Graham and Ben were instructed to be quick and were given a maximum of five minutes so that Rich would not become too tired. The visiting pair were directed away from the examination cubicles where they had been the previous day and guided towards a separate area at the end of the ward. Rich was in Room Number 3, no doubt the first resting place for all suspected heart attack patients. Nervously tapping on the door before entering, Graham entered first and was physically relieved by what he saw. Rich was half-sitting up awake, supported by three pillows. Although his demeanour and tussled hair showed evidence of the trauma he had endured, he looked much better than either could have expected. When Rich recognised his father and brother his face broke into a pained smile and he beckoned them into the room with a flick motion of his hand. There was a tube running from his nose to a cylinder which Ben presumed contained oxygen to help control any discomfort. Graham sat on the edge of the bed and touchingly held his son's hand. Ben remained standing, almost confirming his intentions.

With arms folded Ben gave his assessment of events. 'You had us worried there for a moment, Rich. Thought you weren't going to get that chance you're always banging on about to pay me back.'

Rich smiled a response and opened and closed his mouth a couple of times to indicate intense dryness was causing some inconvenience. Instinctively Graham reached across to a plastic glass containing water on the bedside cabinet. Straightening the straw he held the cup for Rich who prevented his father from imitating his days of babyhood by taking the drink from him. Handing back the glass to his Dad, Rich retorted, 'Well I haven't given up on paying you back just yet but it might have to wait a week or two.'

Graham had enough of their prevarication and asked the key question. 'How are you feeling this morning, son? You're looking a lot better than you did last night. Did you sleep ok?'

Rich rewarded his father with the information he craved. 'Yeah, thanks Dad. I'm feeling a lot better now. I woke up once in the night but that was just because I needed to use a bottle. Otherwise I was flat out.' Then a flash of reality kicked in as Rich added, 'It's Sunday today, isn't it?' He was looking at his brother. 'Shouldn't you have gone back to Geneva already, young 'un?'

Ben responded. 'What and miss all this excitement. Not likely bro'. You've been the best entertainment I've had since I've been here.' Graham looked up from the edge of the bed and shot a look that could have turned Ben into stone. Rich picked up on the silent communication and twisted his face into an expression of mockery, which his father did not see. Rather than prolong any similar thread Ben decided to change the subject of their conversation. 'It's ok though, I've managed to switch my flight to a later one. In fact as soon as I've left you here, I'm off to the Airport with Dad.'

Ben threw a diversionary question at Graham. 'What about getting back from Newcastle, Dad? How are you going to manage to get back to the farm? I'd take you back but I've got to return the car to the rental company. They were expecting it yesterday so I don't suppose they're too pleased about things as it is.'

Graham had it all taped. 'Don't worry son, I'll give Joe Setherton a ring and he can come and pick me up.'

At that moment the conscientious nursing sister entered the room. 'Right gentlemen, that's your lot I'm afraid. Your five minutes are up. We need to sort out Richard's bed and give him a wash to freshen him up for the doctor's rounds. Can't have the consultant tell us off if our patient is not ready now can we?'

In a feeble attempt to defend himself Graham grovelled, 'Ok sister, thank you. It'll be alright if I come back later though?'

'Yes, I'm sure your son will be pleased to see you at the regular visiting time of seven 'til eight tonight.'

Graham put his hand on Rich's shoulder as a parting gesture. 'See you later, Rich. Take care.'

Richard sat-up in bed to allow his younger twin the opportunity to give a more demonstrative farewell. Ben took the initiative. 'Right then bro' – it's time for me to go back to France and do some proper work for a change. It's all very well spending my leisure time relaxing on the farm but there is some hard graft waiting back for me over the Channel.'

Rich knew his brother was more comfortable in the world of mickey-taking so he decided to wade in with some banter of his own. 'Well if that's what you call hard work I feel sorry for you. The winter time is when a farm sorts the men out from the boys. Not when you can sit in a tractor all day in the sun, admiring the views. That's just when we con the tourists into thinking they can be farmers!'

Graham gave a warning shot across his bow. 'I don't know whether you've noticed Richard Moyles but you have just experienced a physical assault on your heart. If you think I'm going to allow you to continue working on the farm in your former capacity you can think again.'

This was enough to silence Rich who was suddenly stunned by the reality of what his Dad was saying because he knew it was true. Ben leant forward and gave his twin an emotional hug before standing back. 'That's right Rich. You're going to have to listen to what the experts are telling you and take their advice. First things first. Get yourself well and when you get home I'll give you a ring to find out how you are doing.' Ben turned away to leave the room, pausing only for one last look at his brother as he reached the door. It was accompanied by a silent fist clench in the patient's direction and with a genuine smile of affection he said a silent goodbye.

The trip to Newcastle Airport did not take long especially on a Sunday and it was only about twenty minutes along the dual carriageway. Graham Moyles sat silently beside his son, while thinking of his other boy and wishing that the three of them were going home together. Ben could sense his Dad's sorrow and shared the sadness, occasionally pointing out some of the more noticeable cars with a level of indifference he could almost taste. While Ben pulled into the car-rental's vehicle compound, his father headed for the main Airport terminal, talking on his mobile to Joe Setherton to arrange a lift home. There was no problem, Joe knew he would get a handful of notes for his trouble and he could return them both to Hubbleton just as the Black Bull's Sunday lunchtime session was at its peak.

After reuniting in the terminal, Ben and Graham made their way to a ground-floor café to share some refreshments and wait for the next stage of their respective journeys. The eatery was the sort of bustling, anonymous place where people pay over the odds but complain only to each other. The queue was not particularly long but there was a delay at the front as someone ordered two mugs of hot chocolate with marshmallows that sent the spotty serving-youth into meltdown. Ben was conscious of his two cups of tea getting cold so he walked behind the chocoholic and paid for the drinks at the till before heading towards his father who was sitting at a table.

While Ben settled into his chair his Dad spoke with forgetful afterthought, 'Thanks son. What time is your flight again?'

Ben stirred a teaspoon around the inside of his cup and responded, 'Departure time is about four hours away but I've got to pass through check-in and then security and that takes about an hour so then I'll just sit and wait for my flight. I should be back in my place at about nine o'clock tonight as long as there are no delays. What about you ? You going to come back to see Rich during normal visiting time?'

'Yeah, Joe is going to ring me when he arrives in the car park and I've got some jobs to do on the farm before I come back into the City and see Rich. I'll text you afterwards just to let you know how he's doing.'

'Thanks Dad and keep me up to date with his progress over the next few weeks. I'm worried about him as I'm sure you are too. Let's hope they get his medication right quickly and he can settle down into a more relaxed way of life, without overdoing things.'

'I'm going to clamp right down on him and make sure he doesn't do anything heavy around the farm. Trouble is you know how stubborn he is. The thing about Rich is he is too competitive, always measuring himself against how *you* are doing. I don't know why that is but he's always been the same. It's as if he has to live up to being the older brother and look after you. When you have had to look after *him*, he takes it badly and seems to want to come back at you even stronger. That's when the trouble starts and he puts strain on his heart. I can't help feeling that unless we can get a heart transplant sorted out quickly he's only one attack away from disaster and we'll lose him.'

Ben's attempt to be reassuring was pre-empted by the sound of a mobile phone buzzing. It was Joe Setherton letting Graham know he had just pulled into the Airport's short-stay car park. The moment for father and son to say goodbye had come. Ben was surprised at how little time Joe had taken to get to the Airport but Graham explained that he had been doing a 'hobble' in Gosforth just down the road. As both men rose to their feet their scraping chairs fleetingly attracted the attention of a couple at the next table.

'So we'll see you when you get back, Ben lad. Look after yourself and don't let those *Frenchies* work you too hard. Remember, you've always got a home here whenever you want.'

While gripping his father's shaking hand, Ben also choked his emotion. 'And you look after yourself too, Dad. Try not to worry too much about Rich. I know it's bad at the moment but he's made of strong stuff. We Moyles boys don't go down easily.' Ben drew his father closer and they embraced each other as Graham kissed the side of his son's temple. Breaking from hold reluctantly, they patted each other's shoulders before Graham turned and made his way out of the café. Ben slumped back into the chair and stared into the cold brown puddle of tea waiting at the bottom of his cup. Searching for his large holdall under the chair with grovelling fingers he then got-up quickly and made his way to the check-in area.

Seven hours later Ben's 'plane was touching down at Geneva Airport. Standing by the luggage carousel he stood navigating his mobile phone while waiting for the waltz of the suitcases to begin. There was one message from his father who had just returned to Moyles Farm from his second visit to the hospital. The text confirmed that Rich was continuing to feel a lot better and the plan was to allow him home, probably on the Wednesday of the forthcoming week. Ben clasped the mobile and returned it to his pocket feeling a lot better. At that moment a warning siren preceded a whirling noise to indicate the passenger luggage carousel was about to start.

Taking little notice as the suitcases passed him by on their circular run, Ben's thoughts turned to work. He had not given much consideration to the experiment while on holiday. This had been partly intentional because he did not want any associated stress to spoil his enjoyment of being home. It had also been due to events that had occurred in Hubbleton, which had been extensive and consumed any time for conscious thought. Ben had helped out with hay and silage-making on the farm, spent leisure time with his brother and father and been involved in a spat with the husband of an ex-girlfriend as well as spending an extremely stressful day in Newcastle Infirmary. No wonder the idea of considering the consequences of an experiment was something he had shoved to the back of his mind. If he had spent time deliberating on what could happen, his ability to function would have been seriously impaired. A subconscious smile dawned in his eyes, reflecting the enjoyment he had experienced at home, where his priorities in life had been re-aligned.

It was close to ten o'clock when Ben finally arrived back at his apartment in Sergy. The lights were off in Gaston's place, which was not remarkable given his old friend's lifestyle. Turning the key to his own apartment, Ben was looking forward to finally having some peace. He switched on the lights and took the hold-all into the bedroom, almost throwing it into the corner of the room next to the wicker laundry basket. The next port of call was the kitchen where the fluorescent tube flickered before illuminating the room. He filled up the kettle and while it boiled, his eyes perused the familiar scene. Suddenly something caught his attention. There was something odd about the kitchen lay-out but he could not figure-out what it was. His head jerked back slightly as his instincts took control. Ben re-played in his mind the circumstances under which he had left the apartment. He re-called he had been in a bit of a rush because of being delayed by the dodgy floorboards and the security alert at the Airport and he remembered having to get a move on in order to be on time for his flight. The last thing he re-played in his mind was throwing his keys onto the kitchen work-space where they bounced off the micro-wave before finishing under the key rack. To make sure he recalled the events accurately he went back to the doorway and physically re-played the scene once more. Normally he would have ensured his work keys were neatly homed onto their peg but managing the effects of his tiredness made him rush. Leaving his keys looking untidy had been below his standards, even in his panic but he was now in a state of bewilderment. How come his work keys were now sitting prettily on their peg when *he* had not put them back there? There was only possible solution: while he had been enjoying a fortnight's break in his home village someone had been in his flat.

PART THREE

I

The hotel in the business park at Thoiry was only two kilometres outside Sergy and not the ideal location to spend a first night back in France. However, for Ben Moyles it represented a safe haven after discovering someone had invaded his privacy. That was the only conclusion he could reach after discovering that the keys inside his apartment had been moved during his stay in the UK. As far as he knew, no one else had access to his flat and there had been no sign of a break-in. Either someone close to him or someone with highly sophisticated knowledge and equipment could possibly have done the job. Waking in the sparse, cheap room of a basic hotel in Thoiry, Ben's mind re-played over and over the events which had led him to that conclusion and he still had the image in his head of how the keys had bounced off the microwave before settling onto the work space.

After coming to terms with the situation and while making a cup of coffee in his apartment he had tried to act as natural as possible in case someone was watching from any hidden cameras installed during his absence. His body movements felt unnatural as he self-consciously poured the water from the kettle while his mind went into overdrive. Ben's previous training in the UK before he had arrived in Sergy had prepared him for several possibilities and this was one of them. However, the reality of something actually happening did not prevent him from feeling sick and frightened. He had been tempted to head straight for the floorboards which housed his laptops and where his secrets were hidden but that would have been the most dangerous thing he could have done. Someone could have been watching and he would have fallen straight into their trap. Instead he had put down the cup and simply walked out of the apartment before sitting in his car for a few minutes to compose himself.

Ben's plan had been simple: look for a hotel and get some sleep before reporting for work in the morning and then telling someone he could trust about what had happened. The most logical person to inform was his line manager Jonas Brandli who would almost certainly send for Max Blosser, Head of Security. Ben had no interest in breakfast, it was the last thing on his mind. However, when morning arrived he paid his bill to the sleepy-eyed concierge in the lobby and walked past a couple of French white-van men who were also staying at the same cheap hotel. As he made his way to his car another thought struck him, perhaps his car had been bugged as well as the apartment. This was all getting too ridiculous for words, was he over-reacting, had he remembered everything accurately, had someone been in his apartment and copied his keys? He could only think that it was better to be safe than sorry.

Ben soon found himself in Jonas' office explaining his concerns like a schoolboy who had just found two of his teachers kissing in the stockroom. Jonas sat tapping his teeth with a pen, half-swivelling his chair and making sympathetic murmurings while Ben unravelled his tale. Brandli was not overly surprised and Ben thought he may have encountered this situation before with someone else. After giving his account the victim stood expectantly, hoping for some resolution to the matter. He almost stepped back as Jonas jumped out of his chair. 'Ok Ben, I'll get Max Blosser in here now. I don't want one of his minions investigating this. You're involved in too much important work to just gloss over this. I want it thoroughly investigated.'

Within a few minutes Ben was repeating his story to the owner of a black gringo moustache, wearing a Bosson International Security uniform and standing over him in Brandli's office. Max Blosser did not take his eyes off Ben while he was giving his account, no doubt deciding whether this man was a liar or a victim. He looked intently into Ben's eyes, not blinking while his mind turned over, all the time making an assessment of the situation. The whole scene was making Ben feel under scrutiny himself but he knew he had to go through with it. Blosser raised the fingers of one hand to his top lip, releasing his arm from its folded position to allow his moustache to be stroked with intimidating authority.

Then he broke into action. 'Ok Doctor Moyles, you're certain that you did not replace your keys onto their peg before you left but when you returned they were hanging on their regular spot ?' Ben shrugged his shoulders. 'In that case we need to do a sweep of your home and your car and check for any bugs. If we find anything then there will be no doubt now that someone has been in your flat. Does your home have security cameras fitted anywhere?'

'Good question', Ben thought to himself and then he remembered. 'Yeah – it does … just above the main entrance there is a camera and a security light so residents can see who is calling.' Ben hesitated before carrying on. 'Ah, but wait a minute ….they stopped working just before I left for the UK. I remember when I left, I took my suitcase to the boot of the car and it was very dark. I don't know whether they're still out of action or whether they've been fixed by now.'

'Right, we'll check that out. I'll need your home keys, and your car keys. Does anyone else have a set, a friend or neighbour or someone else?'

'Only my neighbour Antoine. If I need to let a workman in or if there's a delivery or something he would open the door for them. But I would always talk with him first and he's done that for me since I first arrived in Sergy. He would not have gone into my flat without having spoken with me first and I'm totally confident that Antoine would not have done anything untoward.' It felt like Ben was making a plea of innocence on his friend's behalf.

'Well, we'll have a word with him anyway, just to check whether he's seen anything or can help us with something he might have heard. In any event it is probably a good idea if we change the locks. Don't worry about paying for them, there is a contingency fund for things like this. Leave it with us and we'll get back to you. It'll probably take us the rest of the day.'

Suddenly Ben's mind visited panic and he started to sweat as a terrible thought clicked into place. What if they discover his laptop buried beneath the floorboards? Even worse, what if someone else had already discovered his hiding place and stolen his laptop ? How would he explain that to Bosson International ? He knew that would mean instant dismissal and probably a criminal prosecution. He needed to check before anyone else poked around his flat.

'Is it alright if I remove one or two personal items, just in case I need them for my work today?' While Ben looked anxiously at Blosser, hoping for a positive response, Brandli turned to give him a curious look. He thought he had better qualify his request. 'It's just that while I was away I made some notes and I knew I would probably need them when I started back to work. In my panic to leave my apartment last night I left them in the bedroom. Just don't want to leave them lying around, that's all.' Ben felt a sense of relief as he was aware that Brandli's gaze returned to the security uniform.

'Ok, that's fine. It's going to take me a few minutes to set this up. See you outside your home at ten o'clock. That's just under an hour's time.' Having been given a job of some importance, Max Blosser felt good about himself as he turned to leave the two scientists to their own devices before he would impose his presence on the investigation.

Just as he was about to exit, Ben gave one more feeble attempt at assistance. 'Don't you want to know where I live Mr Blosser ?'

Ben was blown out of the water with Max's final passing shot. 'I wouldn't be much of a security officer if I couldn't find that out now would I, Dr Moyles?'

Jonas Brandli's smile brought a semblance of perspective back to the proceedings as he watched the door close. 'I'm going to have to tell Professor Thompkins about this Ben, you know that, right?'

'I guess so, but I don't know how he can blame me for anything. It's not my fault if someone has targeted me. Just the opposite, it could mean they think my work is important. Certainly more than that big-headed so-and-so Thompkins does anyway.' Realising he had something significant to do, Ben concluded. 'Ok, I'll leave you to do that while I return to my apartment and sort out my place.' Trying to disguise his panic, Ben slinked out of the office before speedily heading for the car park. He had just under three-quarters-of-an-hour to get back and remove his laptops from under the floorboards to avoid a disaster.

Entering his flat twenty minutes later, Ben was beginning to feel that the speed of events had overtaken his sense of alarm. When he thought about the seriousness of what was going on he felt a flutter in his stomach that was not excitement. It was all very well chasing the intellectual thrill of scientific challenges, but it was something different altogether when an unseen, unknown enemy had begun to make you the centre of their attention. He pushed the door open wide and called into the empty arena. 'Anyone there ? The police are here with me so come out now if you're in there!' The absence of a response told Ben two things: the first was that it was safe to enter, the second was that he was nowhere near to being the brave individual he thought he was.

The absence of a response to Ben's naive question sprung him into action. Whether he was being watched by an unseen camera no longer mattered because he was in an impossible position: if he risked the company's security staff finding his hidden laptop he knew he would be instantly dismissed for breaking his contract ; if he was seen removing the source of his secrets then his personal safety would be in danger because whoever was watching would almost certainly seek him out. Ben reckoned the latter was the lesser of two potential likelihoods so he made his way cautiously to the corner of his bedroom and knelt down close to the familiar floorboards. There was no sign of any disturbance that he could determine so he lifted the wooden slats. He breathed a deep sigh of relief when he spotted that all the items were still there, the laptops, leads and flash-drives were just as he had left them. Quickly he began stuffing them into his rucksack relieved to get them out of sight again, although he was leaving to chance the possibility that he was being observed.

Ben wanted the opportunity to be the first one to speak with Antoine but a voice called out as Max Blosser knocked on his door expectantly. 'You in there Dr Moyles ?..... Hello?' Ben knew he had to respond and his call was the cue for Blosser and his team to enter.

'Did you get what you needed Doctor?' asked the security officer inconsequentially.

Ben was relieved that he did not seem to have a clue about what had just happened. However, there was still a problem: Ben could not go wandering around with such important secrets attached to his back, neither could he take them into work because he would never get them out again. The information on the laptops confirmed it was all his own work and that any success using the figures was due to *his* ideas. After some quick thinking he realised there was only one thing he could do. Returning to his vehicle Ben placed the rucksack under the spare wheel in the boot of his car and made sure that everything was thoroughly locked and out of sight. If he drove back to work and ensured his car was parked somewhere safe that should do the trick, even it was only a temporary solution.

Blosser's team of five men and one woman ignored Ben as they entered the flat and began to carry out their standard procedures when sweeping a room in search of surveillance bugs. Ben was invited to vacate the apartment and return to the laboratory where Max would find him later to inform him of the outcome of the search. This was fine by Ben who could not get out of the place quickly enough and soon he was on his way to exercise some subterfuge of his own.

The security team began waving their equipment over everything they considered a potential hot-spot. One of their crew was seated in front of a laptop screen hoping to see some evidence of interference or anything untoward. Starting in the kitchen it did not take long for something to register. The security man using a poker scanner saw its orange light change to red, flashing over a plug socket beside the kettle. Instantly he looked over his shoulder for confirmation which was dutifully supplied by the nodding laptop-man. A clicking finger to the others signalled that they were onto something and Ben's imagination had not been running falsely into overdrive. Having found another bug on the socket on the opposite wall they then completed their sweep of the kitchen and progressed to other rooms in the house. Eleven listening devices were discovered in total, located mainly in power sockets and light fittings. There were no cameras found anywhere, presumably because the snoopers considered it such a small environment that the devices would either be discovered by the occupant or their field of vision would have produced images that were not sufficiently useful.

As each bug was disabled one-by-one there was a reaction elsewhere as someone else's earphones were steadily losing signals. Removing the headset and clicking his fingers to a senior colleague this particular voice was strained with anxiety.

'What is it? Is he home from work already?' asked the *alpha-male* in the factory's darkened room.

'No, we're losing transmission. I can't hear anything at all. Here you try.'

Swapping positions, the more senior member of the team sat in front of the recording equipment trying to pick up any sounds coming through the earphones. He confirmed his colleague's findings by throwing the headset onto the table in anger. 'Go and get Zenib now. He's not going to be very happy about this.'

Five minutes later a suited man with a dark complexion entered the monitoring room. Some of those employed to scrutinise other screens were aware of his presence but considered it more appropriate not to turn around. When he was in the room, it usually spelled trouble for someone. 'Are you telling me that they have discovered *all* of the devices within twenty-four hours of Moyles returning to his flat? How the hell did that happen? Who installed the bugs?' The two other men looked at each other, nervous about giving any response. Zenib had a hard-man reputation. No one knew where he was from but they were aware that their highly paid jobs were dependent on his approval. However, in this factory no employee would receive a written final warning if their labour was considered sub-standard. Zenib preferred instant justice – his way.

'Come on, don't just sit there looking pretty, I asked you a question. Who installed the surveillance equipment in Moyle's apartment?' The name Lucas Gauthier was supplied and to the obvious relief of the reporting pair, Zenib seemed satisfied with their response. Lucas Gauthier ran an electrical installation business in Geneva, operating on a one-van, one-man labour basis. His workshop and low-key operation served as an effective cover for his more nefarious activities. Martin Amsler was the person who Zenib had instructed to sort out the installation of surveillance equipment in Ben's apartment. He was not happy that Amsler had used a two-bit felon like Lucas Gauthier to do the work. Clearly giving the job to Amsler had been a massive mistake and Zenib was not pleased with this cock-up. He knew that Lucas Gauthier had a police record and if there was any way the surveillance equipment found in Ben's flat could be traced back to him there would be even greater problems.

Within half-an-hour, Amsler was in the back of a car being questioned by Zenib. They were parked on an area of isolated wasteland on the outskirts of Geneva.

'I gave the job to you, Amsler. What were you playing at giving the installation work to that low-life Gauthier? Now we've got a can of worms to sort out.'

Amsler's shirt was soaked with sweat under his jacket. He knew he had made a bad error of judgement but perhaps if he said the right thing now, it could be sorted. After all, he was not the one who installed the stuff, Gauthier did that. Eventually he was motivated to speak. 'Sorry, Mr

Zenib but I wasn't to know that the bugs would be found in Moyles' apartment. Leave it with me Mr Zenib and I'll sort it out with Gauthier. What do you want me to do? Do you want me to get rid of him? I can do that. Just leave it with me to do the job and I'll put things right.'

Zenib paused for a few moments, in order to allow Amsler to sweat just a little bit more. 'Make sure you do. And this time don't make any mistakes. Now get out of my sight.'

Amsler turned to open the door to make his exit from the back of the car, only to find it was locked. 'I can't get out Mr Zenib, the door's locked.' There was more than a plea of desperation in the voice of the terrified employee. Zenib addressed the driver, a stocky Middle Eastern man with a square-shaped back, who had played an unspoken role up until that moment. Throughout the short meeting, the man in the driver's seat had not turned around.

'Mr Amsler can't get out,' stated Zenib, almost as if it was simply a matter of fact. 'Can you open the door for him?'

The driver turned around with a mocking smile and when Amsler could see what was in his hand he attempted to scream, although he did not have enough time to utter a sound. The fizzing noise supplied by the suppressor on the M9A3 hand-gun did its job. No one outside the car would have heard the shot, which propelled the bullet into the middle of Amsler's chest. As the two men watched the victim's eyes bulge, they were curious about how he would spend his remaining seconds. Amsler grabbed at the bullet's entry point and tried to say something. Whatever his last words could have been did not matter because they went with him to the afterlife as he coughed-up some blood with a gurgling, choking sound.

Some of the blood found its way onto the shoulder of Zenib's jacket. 'Now look what you've made him do you idiot. I've not had this suit very long and now you're going to have to burn it for me. Can't anybody do anything right?' Zenib shuffled across the back seat in order to get out of the side. He had two remaining orders. 'Make sure nobody finds his body and I mean nobody. Then sort out Mr Gauthier and make it look like an accident. I want him out of the picture before the police start poking around asking questions. Got it?'

The driver placed the gun under a newspaper on the front passenger seat and simply replied affirmatively in Arabic. With that parting comment

Zenib walked across to his black BMW parked on the other side of the waste ground, got into the driver's side and drove off as if he was on his way to another meeting. The first mopping-up job had been completed and he had no doubts in the ability of his minion to complete the second.

At the same time as Zenib was leaving the scene and making his way back to his surveillance location, Max Blosser was entering the Puissance complex to report to Dr Jonas Brandli and Dr Ben Moyles. The agenda included a report on what had been found in Ben's apartment. No one bothered to impede Max as he made his way through the company's security checks. If they could not trust the Head of Security, who could they trust? His startling moustache was as good as any swipe card and he was known to all staff. Jonas and Ben were waiting for Max in Brandli's office when he entered. As the most senior of the three employees, Brandli was sitting on his side of the desk prepared to face the other two. When they all took their seats, he opened the conversation.

'Well Mr Blosser, what did you discover in Dr Moyles' apartment .... anything?'

'You did the right thing reporting your concerns Dr Moyles. You were right that someone has been in your apartment.' Ben's blood ran cold as his eyes fixed onto the moustache of the Head of Security. 'We found a number of recording devices in the flat. Clearly somebody wanted to know everything about what Dr Moyles is up to. I will of course need to refer this matter to Professor Thompkins.'

'Of course,' was the only contribution Ben could think of before he moved onto the question he was desperate to ask. 'Was it all voice recording stuff in the flat. Any cameras at all?'

An ironic smile crossed Blosser's face as he toyed with thoughts of why Dr Moyles should ask that question. He wondered briefly if Ben had been up to some mischief after all. 'No cameras you'll be pleased to know, Dr Moyles. They probably either did not have time to put them in or they did not think it was worth it at this stage of the game.'

'I only wish it was a game Mr Blosser, but this is deadly serious,' responded Ben, still nodding at his acceptance of the security chief's assessment. Instead of punching the air with relief he allowed himself to rub his left thigh with the palm of his hand as he continued, 'What should I do now?'

'Well now the bugs have been discovered I don't suppose the culprits will try again. We're happy that we've removed everything that was there and we've changed the locks as well. The camera at the entrance has been secured and upgraded and will now be virtually impossible to sabotage from the outside, unlike the last one. We've spoken to your neighbour Monsieur Antoine Moreau and asked him if he noticed anything odd or unusual while you were away. He told us that someone did arrive to fix the camera but it was still not working after he left. He was unable to give us much of a description of the man but he did say that he had a van with him with some writing on the side. Unfortunately, he did not take much notice of what it said. He could be lying of course.' Blosser put pressure on Ben once again, regarding Antoine. 'Do you have any reason to doubt his account of things Dr Moyles, any reason at all?'

Ben sprung to the defence of his friend. 'None whatsoever. Antoine has had a spare set of keys to my flat since I've been in Sergy, when he helped me settle in. Why would he suddenly now help break into my apartment? It doesn't make any sense. The only thing I can think of is that someone with highly sophisticated skills has broken into my place because they believe they can find out something to do with my work. It has to have been motivated by someone with a working knowledge of Puissance.'

Brandli had been sitting silently while Ben and Max tried to clarify what had happened. 'Ok Max, I'll go and report to Professor Thompkins and no doubt he will want to speak to you as well. For the moment at least it seems that we have covered all the bases. All except one that is.' Ben shot a quizzical look at his line manager. 'What about Dr Moyles' personal safety. Anyone who has gone to these lengths in order to get closer to his work may try another way.'

Suddenly Ben became scared. 'What, you think someone may come after me, you mean?'

'Well it is a possibility Ben and we have to cover all options.'

Blosser offered some words of comfort. 'Personally I don't think that is the case. That's not how people like that operate. They're basically cowards who report to their paymasters. If they've not found anything then there's nothing to report, so they'll probably just back off. Anyway, the police will have to know about this and they will want to interview you Dr Moyles. If you feel anyway concerned for your safety I would certainly mention it to the *Gendarmerie*. I am sure they will step up their patrols of the area at the very least. They may even go as far as appointing a guard but I doubt it at this stage. If it wasn't for the work that Dr Moyles is involved with I doubt whether they would even consider the idea of protection.'

'Is that all for now then?' asked Ben somewhat relieved that things were seemingly under control. He felt a sense of satisfaction at having noticed the irregularity about his apartment keys. There was also a great deal of relief because if it had not been for those floorboards and that security alert at Geneva Airport on the day he was travelling, the infiltrators would have got away with their deed.

'Just one last thing, Doctor. You'll need these to get back into your flat tonight.' Max towered over Ben as he handed him some freshly-cut keys. 'And this…' Blosser then opened a long, narrow cardboard on Brandli's desk and took out a thick black rod. 'Use this from time to time when you're at home from now on, just in case. It's a bug detector that will pick up any type of modern surveillance equipment. All you do is pass it across an object or area of wall or something and if there is anything there, the light at the end will flash red. If that happens, leave the apartment immediately and get in touch with me or the police. I'm sure there'll be more questions to follow but that's it for now. I'll say good afternoon to you gentlemen.'

Before he left the two colleagues to sort out their own agenda, Blosser had one more question. 'There was just one other thing Dr Moyles.' Ben looked at him with some bemusement. 'When we were doing a sweep of your bedroom, we discovered a space under the floorboards.'

Ben was desperately trying to act surprised as he felt the pit of his stomach plummet. 'A space? What kind of space?'

'Well it looked like the sort of space somebody would use to store things, secretly I mean … er … a bit like a safe or some-such thing. Did you know it was there at all?

Ben continued to act bewildered. 'No… I didn't know it was there.'

'Ah well, never mind. It could be something that the previous occupant had used, perhaps to store his or her valuables. It doesn't matter in the scheme of things I'm sure. It's just that as it was empty I wondered if they had taken anything from your apartment that you might have been keeping in there.'

Ben thought he had better ram home the point. 'No sorry Max. I've never had cause to keep anything of value in my flat. You're probably right and it was something that the previous tenant had put in there.'

Fortunately Blosser seemed to be satisfied with Ben's response. Ben inwardly breathed a deep sigh of relief as the security chief left Brandli's office.

Jonas invited Ben to return to his seat and have a chat about what was going to happen next. 'I suggest you go home for the rest of the day Ben. You haven't really had a chance to sort out anything since your return and I'm sure you've got things to do. I'll have a word with Thompkins and arrange a meeting of the three of us. I'll ring you tonight and let you know what's happening. Meanwhile, you go home and settle in. It's been a very stressful time for you. Give some thought to what you are going to say to the police when they show up. Above all don't worry, you've done nothing wrong and it seems as though it's all now been nipped in the bud. It's possible that someone has got wind of the experiment and wants to know more about it. Incidentally, when have you arranged to check it out?'

'Towards the end of the next week is the time I was planning but perhaps I'll bring that forward now. It may be something that Thompkins might have a view about when we meet.'

Ben got out of the chair and prepared to leave but before he got to the door he turned and thanked Jonas for his understanding. Suddenly Ben's mind was full of a new agenda. He needed to phone his father to find out how his brother was progressing, he needed to think about what he was going to say to the police, and he needed to phone his bank to make an appointment for some urgent business.

II

Ben wondered whether his heavy sleep had been the product of a shortage of rest during that night in a seedy Thoiry hotel or the relief of hearing from his Dad that Rich would be out of hospital in the next few days. Perhaps it was simply because he was back in his own bed and able to relax, even though he still felt uneasy about his privacy having been violated during his absence. Either way it did not matter. He had enough time to go to the *supermarché*, stock-up with food for the coming week and have a hot breakfast at the in-store eatery. Jonas Brandli's phone call the previous evening informing him that Professor Thompkins wanted a meeting at eleven o'clock to discuss recent events gave him sufficient time to sort himself out and he was grateful for the extra slack.

Ben had been to the bank earlier to sort out his important business and was now in the *supermarché* which was busier than expected for an early Tuesday morning but at least the coffee was hot and the croissants fresh. In the corner table of the large in-house café Ben sat alone with his thoughts, trying to enjoy the sanctuary of an undetected breakfast. He had often thought that some of the so-called cheap places in this part of France were actually better than their snobby counterparts and this particular supermarket fell into that category. The aisles were well laid out and bright and there were always bargains to be had. As he toyed with these thoughts he almost laughed to himself that he was in danger of featuring in an advert for the place. Whatever was going on around him was at least helping him to find his feet again because it returned him to a normality.

Certainly the meeting with Thompkins was going to be important. How would his boss react to the possibility that he was being targeted because of his work? Thompkins would hopefully regard it as routine, after all Ben was totally unaware of how many other such incidents the Head of Puissance would have to deal with at any point in time. On the other hand, he could treat it as another blot on his record and terminate Ben's contract by citing some sort of technical breach of security. Thompkins had the authority to carry out such an act without being answerable to anyone.

Ben made his way back to his grocery-laden car, having earlier placed the full plastic bags in his boot before breakfast. On this occasion there was nothing secreted under the spare wheel. His laptops housing personal data of the utmost sensitivity were now in a safe place. Blosser's actions had given him some reassurance by failing to uncover any physical evidence of cameras installed in his apartment. He was protected, or so he thought. Perhaps more importantly, his work was now secure.

The short drive back to his apartment was routine but his mind was not really focussed on the roads. There was still the conundrum of Antoine and what to do next. Blosser had spoken to his neighbour and been given a believable story but was Antoine really telling the truth? How well did Ben really know Antoine Moreau? He was an affable old boy but apart from their drinking sessions together and their friendly banter, Ben knew little about his background. Surely an old man with mobility issues could not be spying on his so-called friend. If so, who was he reporting to? The more Ben kicked around the possibilities, the more he disbelieved all these unsavoury options.

Entering the apartment block with two full carrier bags in each hand, Ben was forced to push open the unlocked, heavy main-front door with his hip. Walking across the tiled floor to the stairs he sensed some activity in Antoine's flat. Rather than wait to see his door open as he had done many times before, he walked more quickly and ascended the stairs two steps at a time. This caused him some difficulty given the size of the load he was carrying. When he reached the top of the stairwell he could hear Antoine's door open, no doubt his neighbour was looking for a conversation. However, Ben was not ready to speak to him just yet. There was still enough doubt in Ben's mind to persuade him to wait and consider his next move. Arriving at his own front door he lowered two bags onto the floor and reached inside his coat for the shiny, newly cut keys. Ben still had to decide if he was going to leave the spare set with Antoine. Pushing open the door he suddenly questioned himself about whether it was safe to enter. The place did not feel like home any more.

In plenty of time for his meeting with Thompkins, Ben set-off in his car. There was something reassuring about travelling into work, a known routine that owned no threats. He had managed to escape Antoine's clutches when he left the apartment block, something that brought him some relief. The meeting with Professor Thompkins was going to be stressful but everything associated with his work at Puissance contained pressure not found in other places of work. This was simply an added idiosyncrasy, albeit with a bit more at stake than anything involved in a failed experiment. Since his return to Sergy Ben's frame of reference had taken a beating. As his daydreaming took its toll he almost failed to spot a cyclist approaching on the inside of his red Peugeot and he came close to pushing the rider off the road. He glanced in his rear view mirror to see an animated collection of lycra waving a fist from the saddle of a *Gitane* racer. There was no way he could offer any meaningful gesture of regret so the flash of his rear brake lights was futile. Suddenly even the journey to work had fallen into the same category as other recent bizarre events.

Making his way to Thompkins' office Ben was still kicking around in his mind all the things he still needed to do. Fortunately Jonas Brandli had already arrived and was waiting outside Thompkins' headquarters when Ben entered the danger zone. Trying to respond to the pretty receptionist's question and acknowledge the presence of his line manager, Ben then headed for the vacant chair next to Jonas, who was the first one to break the silence, though speaking in a hushed tone.

'Don't look so worried Ben, I keep telling you, you've done nothing wrong. I saw Blosser heading down the corridor as I was arriving. No doubt he's already been through yesterday's events with the Prof and given him the lowdown on his perspective of things. Since he seemed pretty satisfied the last time I saw him, this meeting should be nothing more than planning a way forward and tightening up on security in general.'

Ben felt a little bit more reassured by Brandli's comments but would have preferred Thompkins to have given the reassurance himself. The buzzer went on the receptionist's panel and she responded: 'Yes, sir. I'll send them in now.' Her follow-up instruction was ignored as Ben and Jonas made their way to the door of destiny without waiting.

Thompkins' handshake seemed genuine enough but Ben had been misled before by his boss. He detected no difference in length or sincerity between Jonas' greeting from the Professor and his own so that was the first hurdle cleared. Thompkins took the lead role, as ever. 'Please sit down gentlemen.' Once they had settled into the chairs in front of the leather-bound desk Ben and Jonas, were forced to look upward towards Thompkins who was revelling in his position of superiority. 'Now then Dr Moyles, I understand that you were involved in a bit of a circus yesterday. I've spoken this morning to Max Blosser who no doubt you are more familiar with today than you were two weeks ago. I've read his report and listened to what he had to say so I am satisfied that there has been no major transgression of our security protocols. In fact Dr Moyles I hear you are to be congratulated for the manner in which you spotted that your apartment had been broken into. I'm not so sure that I would have spotted the displacement of my keys after a fortnight's holiday. It was also good to hear that your training kicked in and your response to the situation was exemplary.' Ben was beginning to wonder if he had made an accurate assessment of this man's character. Perhaps he had a new best friend.

'Of course we need to decide where we go from here. Tell me Ben are you working on anything sensitive at the moment ?'

Jonas shot his colleague a look and knew they were both thinking the same thing: *'When did Thompkins ever call anyone by their first name ?'* Ben was more puzzled about his boss's apparent ignorance concerning the experiment that had been running while he had been on holiday. He decided to inquire about how much his new 'friend' had his finger on the pulse.

'I thought you knew about my experiment. Did Sebastian Thiroud not keep you up to speed on how my ideas were developing?'

This caught Thompkins off-guard. 'He may have done. I have not had time to read all the emails in my inbox. I am a very busy man after all. Nothing rings a bell about anything of any significance relating to your research. Perhaps I'll try and find his report later. Tell you what, when you have anything to report, get back to me and I'll get involved and I may share some of my knowledge with you. That should help.

However, first things first. I suggest you carry on with your work in Eta Lab and wait until you are contacted by the *Gendarmarie.'* Thompkins rose from his leather seat and offered his hand, clearly demonstrating his own agenda had been completed and the meeting was over. 'I think that concludes our business for the moment gentlemen, so I will say good-day to you.'

In the corridor outside the Professor's offices, Ben and Brandli took stock of the situation, the latter offering his assessment. 'Well, I suppose that could not have gone much better. I told you, you had nothing to worry about.'

Ben's eyes were surveying every light on the wall, while his thoughts were going all over the place in frustration. 'I suppose so. Thing is I'm not sure if I want to thank him or go in there and punch his lights out. Did you hear him ... *I may share some of my knowledge with you* ... The arrogance of the bloke. He's just full of it. Can you believe him!'

His line manager was more conciliatory. 'Just let it go. Something unpleasant has happened but at the end of the day there's no damage done. We're back where we were. Let's just go forward together.'

This was a bit too much for Ben. 'Jesus, Jonas – you got any more cliché's tucked away in that head of yours! I understand what you're saying but I was hoping that the arrogant sod would at least have known about what I was up to. Do you think Thiroud has even bothered to tell him about my experiment?'

'I've no idea, but you heard what he said. His report is probably sitting in his inbox and it hasn't had enough *pazzaz* to attract his intention. Mind you, I wouldn't put anything past that Thiroud either. He's far too greasy for my liking.'

With the minds of both men now becoming pre-occupied with other priorities, it was time to go their separate ways. A lot had happened in a short period of time and they needed to take stock. In particular, Ben had a lot of catching up to do and amongst other things, he needed to check his messages and assess what he was going to do next in relation to his experiment. There had been no reports of anything drastic having happened while he was away so that was encouraging. He thought he would call into the works' cafeteria and pick-up a sandwich. He did not feel very sociable and some 'me' time was called for.

III

Although there had been a few text exchanges with Veronique while he was away with his family, interaction between Ben and his girlfriend had been limited. When he switched on his mobile in Eta Lab he could see that there were four unanswered calls all attributed to her as the sender. He sat gazing at the screen of his iphone for a minute, considering whether to respond. The break had not been accompanied by pangs of longing and with everything else that had taken place, Veronique had slipped down Ben's order of priorities. For a moment he wondered whether this was the time to break-off their relationship. Then he remembered the sex and had second thoughts. Veronique was a bit of a wild-cat and that appealed to the more base instincts of the boy from the farm.

His daydream of desire was broken by the loud ringing of a phone on his desk. Ben pressed a number on the key-pad and responded to the call.

'Dr Moyles, there is a Captain Durand of the *Gendarmarie* on the line. Shall I put him through?'

After confirming that he would take the call, Ben listened while another new acquaintance introduced himself. 'Hello Dr Moyles. My name is Captain Jacques Durand and I am calling from the police station in Bourg-en-Bresse. We have received a call from your security officer, Max Blosser, who has informed us that your apartment has recently been broken into and that several surveillance devices have been recovered from your private rooms. We would like you to come to the Station here in Bourg-en-Bresse to make a statement and talk about the incident, monsieur. Would you like me to send a car or would you prefer to make your own arrangements?'

Having determined the location of the police station, Ben resigned himself to making his own way over and spending most of the afternoon in the company of the *Gendarmarie* . There was little point in starting any fresh work so he decided to give Veronique a call. It did not take her long to answer.

'Hello my darling Ben. How are you? I've been worried that I have not heard from you since your return. Is everything alright? Are you well? Did you miss me?'

Ben was taken aback by the rattle of her questions. 'Whoa there Veronique! One question at a time. Listen… I can't talk about everything right now but shall we meet up later and I'll tell you all that has been going on.'

'Certainly darling. Where shall we meet … your place or mine?'

Ben was forced to think quickly. Was it even possible that Veronique was also a suspect in what had happened. Was she culpable for the break-in? He had to be cautious. 'Let's meet at your place. Perhaps we can have dinner or something?'

'*Bien sur, mon chéri*. Rather than go out to eat, perhaps I can cook dinner for us. Then we can stay in and er…catch up… if you know what I mean.'

Ben's face illuminated with images of what was to come. 'Sounds perfect. See you later tonight. About eight?'

'I shall look forward to it. I can't wait to see you again, *à plus tard*.'

Just under two hours later Ben was walking across the car park at the headquarters of the *Gendarmarie* in Bourg-en-Bresse, west of Sergy. Although it was an inconvenience to have to drive so far in order to do nothing more than detail recent events and make a statement, Ben considered it preferable to being visited at his place of work by uniformed police in a marked car. Having to be questioned at Puissance Headquarters would have started the rumour mill and the task of being chosen as a target for discussion had already been achieved, even if it was unwanted. The journey was also exactly what he needed: a drive through a beautiful part of the northern Rhone Valley and the Regional National Park offered the kind of therapy that a boy from the Cheviot Hills would appreciate. The scenery was positively relaxing and the ride allowed Ben to wind down and put things in perspective.

At the front desk Ben introduced himself to an officer, who then proceeded to make a couple of calls before announcing that someone would be attending soon. Ben sat on a wooden bench in a waiting area that looked like it had just jumped out of a scene from a British police drama. Five minutes later a uniformed officer escorted him along a brightly lit corridor to an interview room where a detective was sitting behind a desk. Ben guessed correctly that it was Captain Durand who got up as they entered the room, offering his hand while simultaneously inviting Ben to sit on the other side of the bureau. Durand was medium height, neither slim nor overweight, clean shaven with wispy brown hair. The only distinguishing feature which made an impression on Ben was Durand's uneven eyebrows. They looked as if they had been stuck-on by his mother as an afterthought .

Using his well-worn monotone voice, the detective outlined the process involved. Ben proceeded to explain the events as they unfolded after returning from the UK, before scribing an account on some kind of official form which he dutifully signed. Captain Durand made very little comment about his interpretation of events, simply adding that the process was '*pour mémoire*'. It left Ben thinking that this particular policeman was not someone to be relied on in a crisis. Perhaps if the interview had taken place in Durand's office, Ben would have seen things differently and been more impressed by the *Médaille d'honneur de la Police nationale* and the *Médaille de la Gendarmerie nationale* hanging in a glass frame on the wall behind Durand's chair. These were the highest commendations that could be bestowed on an officer in either of the two French police forces and it was extremely rare for anyone to receive both medals. Captain Jacques Durand had accepted the honours with due humility while his colleagues held him in the highest regard. Both medals had been the product of the same terrorist incident in Paris when Durand's speedy interception of four armed extremists had saved the lives of a coachload of children and sightseers from a school in Lyons. After all the publicity, the humble policeman chose a quieter life in Bourg-en-Bresse near the Swiss border for the sake of his family and his sanity.

When the formalities had been concluded the two men shook hands, leaving Ben disappointed at the lack of eye contact from the indifferent detective. It was a low-key departure worthy of a lost dog report. When he reached his car, Ben shook his head in disbelief at what had just occurred. For a few moments he sat behind the wheel, zoned-out, staring at an attractive woman walking past on the other side of the street without paying her any heed. He could not believe that he had just reported an incident of potential subterfuge relating to world-changing research. The moment needed to be acknowledged somehow but in the absence of any other herald, Ben simply started the engine and proceeded to drive back to Sergy. The murky grey skies signalled a change in the seasons and served only to depress his mood still further, making the normally beautiful drive an equally dull affair.

It was almost five o'clock when Ben's dirty red Peugeot pulled into a residents' parking space outside his apartment block. He had time for a quick nap and a shower before heading off to see Veronique. However, when he reached the main entrance and proceeded to the lift on the ground floor, Antoine Moreau was standing in the open doorway of his apartment and his presence was unavoidable.

'Ello my friend. I trust you had an enjoyable trip to the UK. It seems as if things have been happening since you returned here, *n'est-ce pas*?'

'Indeed they have Antoine. I was going to call in to have a chat about it all.'

'Would now be a good time. I have some coffee made, perhaps with a little brandy?'

'I can't just now my friend but I will definitely talk with you tomorrow and perhaps we can clarify what has been happening.'

'As you wish, my *mon ami*.' With that half-hearted acceptance, Antoine turned into his apartment and closed his front door. Ben was not sure if his neighbour had been offended about what had happened with the security people or whether it was his own lukewarm response that may have caused some upset. However, this was the first time he had seen his neighbour in anything other than a friendly mood. There was no doubt about it, since he had returned to France there was a change in the air.

Ben pulled up outside Vernonique's residential block near the centre of Geneva and sat motionless in the car, in contemplation. This time he was not sure whether to continue as planned or return to see Antoine. It could mean the end of his relationship with Veronique if he rejected her at this stage. On the other hand things needed to be sorted out with Antoine, who he had known for a lot longer. He decided to clarify the situation with his neighbour and took out his mobile.

Veronique answered straight away and listened with some disappointment when Ben told her that something had come up at work and it needed to be sorted out. He promised he would make it up to her the following day and they would have dinner together at her favourite restaurant. Veronique wandered over to the window on the fourth floor of her apartment block and gazed at the view outside while she listened to Ben's apology. She noticed a police car with flashing blue lights speeding down the road just as a siren was sounding in the background on Ben's phone. Ten seconds after their conversation ended Veronique watched from her window as a red Peugeot with Ben at the wheel pulled out of her car park and turned left onto the main road. She walked over to the cooking hob and turned off the heat under a pan containing Bolognese sauce, staring at the bubbling liquid but thinking of something else. Veronique had a conundrum of her own which she needed to disentangle.

As Ben made his way out of Geneva he was suddenly overtaken by a flock of flashing blue lights. There was clearly a major incident of some sort judging by the number of police cars, ambulances and fire engines that were going past him at speed. About a mile away from Veronique's place he spotted a plume of rising black smoke with shooting flames and realised that he was heading straight towards its source. Whatever the emergency it must only have just happened. A motor cycle policeman was directing traffic at the head of a side-street, flailing his arms and ordering cars to keep moving while the drivers were trying to steal a peek at what was burning. An ambulance was attempting to pull out of the side-street so Ben's line of traffic was brought to a halt by the traffic cop in order to allow the paramedics a speedy exit. Ben could see a fire-engine dousing the flames of a white van parked outside what looked like a workshop, before its front windows had been blasted out. The back doors of the van had also been blown off. The remnants of one of the doors had been moved from its landing place on the road and placed along a wall. While the ambulance edged out of the narrow road before speeding away, Ben stared at the name of the workshop, or rather its owner. He could only just make out part of the name as the first letter had been lost somewhere in the atmosphere. The letters .. u.t.h.i.e.r' were discernible and Ben wondered for a moment if anyone had been hurt in the explosion. He was not to know at that stage that the emergency services were clearing up the mess after an explosion that had killed Lucas Gauthier

Ben's sheepish knock on Antoine's door had to be repeated before it was answered. As Antoine offered a half-smile, Ben presented his hand as a handshake gesture but on this occasion it was not for a greeting. It held a bottle of British brandy, a concoction from the West Country with a cider base. Ben had bought it at Newcastle Airport as a thank you present for his neighbour, who he thought might enjoy criticising the attempts of the UK to compete with the best French cognac.

'I have brought you a rare treat from my homeland my friend. I know you are going to enjoy this special drink. It is British brandy.'

Antoine looked at him without emotion and for a moment Ben thought he was going to close the door in his face. However, his face broke into a huge smile, followed by a familiar guffaw. 'British brandy you say. Well my friend, I do not think I can turn down such an opportunity. Come in, come in and I will get some glasses while you make yourself comfortable.'

As his neighbour turned into his apartment, Ben was pleased that Antoine was unable to see his expression of relief at being invited into his neighbour's flat. For a fleeting moment he wondered if the invitation was genuine or whether it was being seen as an opportunity to get information about what had been going on in Ben's place. Perhaps the drink would help reveal the truth.

Antoine poured the spirit into two large tulip-shaped glasses and then held one of them up to the light to explore the colour, before swilling it around to warm it slightly. 'Hmmmm .. it is a little light in colour compared to the real thing. Perhaps it will taste better than it looks.' He handed one glass to Ben before he took a swig from the other and stared at his opponent as the drink kicked in. Running his tongue around the inside of his mouth, Antoine finally gave his assessment. 'Not bad, not bad at all *mon ami*. I can taste the fruit. It is apples, *oui* ?' Ben continued smiling at his friend's effort to identify the flavour. 'It is a brave attempt and worthy of another glass at least, I think.' Ben felt a sense of relief that was palpable.

Ben intended to be as open as possible about the reason that Antoine had faced questions from Puissance Security, if only to warn him there could be further questioning from the *Gendarmarie*, though he doubted this would happen.

'You have probably guessed that something strange has been going on while I have been away?' Antoine sipped the brandy without emotion. Ben was not sure for a moment if the raised glass was an attempt to disguise a reaction. 'Well it seems as if someone has been in my apartment while I have been away.'

'*Croix*!' Antoine's shock seemed genuine to Ben. 'I don't believe it. Did they take anything?' inquired the old man with genuine concern.

'Nothing was stolen. However, something was added. Someone has attempted to bug my flat with listening devices.

'Why would they do that? You don't do anything in your flat … do you? I've never heard any noise coming from above, not even the moving of a table.'

Ben thought that was a strange example to quote but attributed Antoine's comments to his nervousness. Blosser will almost certainly have told him there were no signs of a break-in and Antoine was aware that others knew he had a set of keys. All logic pointed to Antoine being the most obvious suspect, and he was mindful of that fact.

'And you never heard anything ? Nothing strange at all … you did not notice anything different while I was in the UK?'

'Only the workmen who came to look at the camera but I told your man about that. There was no reason to suspect he was up to no good. He was wearing overalls with the name of a company on the back and he looked like an ordinary workman.'

'What was the name of the company?'

'The security man … he asked me that question and I couldn't remember. I have tried to think through the mist but I could not recall the name. I am sorry *mon ami*.'

'Don't worry about it. It's probably not important anyway. Has anyone else been to speak to you about what happened? The *Gendarmarie* for example.' Antoine looked surprised as if the thought had never crossed his mind. He shook his head in a claim of vigorous innocence, while Ben continued. 'They probably will at some point, though I don't expect anything will happen now. It seems as if someone has been attempting some industrial sabotage, trying to access information about what various scientists have been doing on the Puissance Project. It looks like I was lucky enough to have rumbled them. No doubt all senior personnel will be having their homes checked out as we speak. Somebody somewhere doesn't like what we're up to. No need for you to worry though so please do not concern yourself. Take another sip of British brandy and it will help you to forget.'

A couple of glasses later, Ben was saying goodbye to his friend before making his way back upstairs to his own apartment. His conscience began to trouble him about the way he had treated Veronique so he decided to give her a call. Although she was clearly disappointed about having to cancel dinner, she sounded more upbeat when Ben outlined his plans for the weekend. After all the strange events of the last few days, it was time to get things back on track.

IV

The shiny green automatic gates opened after the guard monitoring the cameras pressed the blue button, and the black BMW X6 pulled into the grounds of the magnificent mansion commanding a stunning view over Lake Geneva. The security presence was discreet although an increase in their number was only a phone call away. The limestone gravel that marked the spacious parking area sounded Zenib's arrival and as he alighted from his car he did not even feel the need to activate the fob over his shoulder to lock the doors, something that would only have offended the watchful staff. No one got in or out without their knowledge or approval.

An anonymous suit greeted Zenib before he got as far as the front door. 'Mr Connolly is on the upper terrace, sir. He's expecting you… I believe you know the way.' The subordinate moved to one side and waved an arm as a gesture of courtesy. Zenib said nothing as he entered the modern, glass lounge, where the natural light illuminated the classy, grey furniture and the original oil paintings on the walls. He ascended the open stairway and half-way up he could see the silver hair that made Connolly's appearance so distinctive. The multi-millionaire was dressed in white slacks, a dark blue sleeveless shirt and a pair of canvas shoes, looking like a throw-back to the early 1970s. He turned when he heard Zenib walking along the boards of the wooden terrace and pointed his glass towards the whisky sour that was on a circular glass-topped table. It did not matter if the drink was Zenib's favourite cocktail or not, he was going to accept it without comment.

This was not a social occasion as Zenib soon found out. 'So …this latest fiasco, can it damage us? You know the one I'm talking about, right?' Connolly was not looking at his employee but standing against the rail-guard looking out on the beautiful lake, without absorbing the view. The scene was preferable to the risk of further irritation by looking at the face of someone who had brought trouble to his door. A wispy breeze brought some movement along his silver thatch. 'I don't want any of this mess coming back to my door. If it does, you know what I'll do and I guarantee you won't like it.' At this point Connolly did turn, and looked at his minion with an icy stare, waiting for a response of subjugation and reassurance.

'It's sorted Mr Connolly. There's no way anybody can make a connection, if you know what I mean.' Zenib thought he would not be totally explicit, preferring to opt for a level of ambiguity that might be relied on later. There was a possibility that the conversation was being recorded and he did not want to be hung by his own words further down the line.

'So we still have a way in? I don't want there to be a major discovery coming out of Puissance and we are left standing with our pants around our ankles. We need to know what they are up to. The discovery of that surveillance equipment was made on your watch. It'll only be a question of time now before they scan the homes of the other principal players and no doubt they will then be on full alert. I don't want another repeat of that error of judgement, or I will have to make a decision on what to do next...if you get my drift.' While Zenib absorbed the implication, Connolly entered the glass fronted lounge and poured himself another drink from a decanter positioned on a table, just inside the door. For a few moments Zenib was standing on the terrace on his own, feeling more than a little vulnerable. Taking a sip from the crystal tumbler, Connolly returned and looked at his prey, waiting for a response.

'We still have people on the ground, close to the main players. If they find something we will soon know about it and we will know what to do. There's ...' His attempt to explain his plan was cut short.

'Don't tell me any of the details. The less I know the better. You are paid handsomely to do your job...so *do* your job. I've got a meeting next week in the Gulf and I know the Arab princes are going to be asking me if they should be concerned or not. I intend to tell them that everything is in hand because everything had better be in hand. We are both paid a lot of money to protect their interests ; they don't like their comforts being compromised. They tend to get more than a little tetchy with people who let them down and I like my head on my shoulders exactly where it is – I would prefer that it stays there. So let's put this latest ignominy behind us and move on. Keep me in the picture, I don't want to hear any bad news, I don't like unpleasant surprises.' After a final swig from the crystal, Connolly brought their meeting to a close, 'You know your way out.' With that clear message, Zenib replaced his glass to its original spot and made his exit with a sense of relief. Connolly returned to gaze at the lake and picked up a pair of binoculars to try and observe a pair of courting Great Crested Grebes that had been holding his interest before the inconvenience of Zenib's arrival.

Adam Danyel Connolly, known as 'AC' to his friends, was a self-made millionaire who had earned his wealth in the oil business after many years of hard work and ruthless wheeling and dealing. Known as a 'Mr Fixit' in the industry he had encountered most situations on the oilfields, sorting out everything from illegal strike action to erecting rigs in a war zone. Many years working in the Middle East had enabled him to become more than competent in Arabic, although he was born in Texas where he had cut his teeth on the oilfields at the age of sixteen. AC was a hardened individual, ruthless and not frightened to take risks, he did not accommodate failure easily.

Connolly's unique background also earned him the confidence of many oil executives all over the world, Arab and American alike. It placed him in an unusual position of trust with moguls from the Western and Middle Eastern oil-producing countries. As a speaker of Arabic he was an executive committee member of a Middle Eastern organisation established to protect the interests of countries lying within the Arab Gulf, known as the Arab Oil Producing Countries or AOPC. This meant he had influence when ensuring that oil prices were fixed at a rate that would guarantee the continued opulence and excessive lifestyles of the land-owning Princes.

Connolly also liaised with the American oil industry and acted as a bridge between two worlds that were instinctively wary of each other. However these cultures shared a common enemy: the twenty-first century had seen concern about fossil fuels polluting the world and adding to forces affecting climate change. There was a clamour for sources of 'clean' energy and the highest powers in worldwide oil production were even more concerned that one day there would be a discovery of a renewable energy source that would relegate oil from the premier league of power. As a result, Connolly had been given a mandate to work under the radar and ensure that competition from other sources would be quashed. The most likely current threat seemed to be coming from a group of scientists working near the French-Swiss border. Connolly was charged with the task of ensuring the Puissance Project failed – no matter what the price.

The cold, sincere warning from Connolly was still fresh in Zenib's mind as he made his way from the magnificent house by the shores of Lake Geneva, back to his own humble one-room flat near the site of the 'factory' on the border with France. He knew how to rectify recent mistakes and fortunately the two principal protagonists involved in that hiccup were no longer around to tell tales so he was satisfied that he had cleared up his own mess. It certainly seemed enough to get Connolly off his back, for the moment.

The next evening, Ben was sitting in *René's Restaurant* at eight o'clock waiting for Veronique, having already ordered a bottle of red wine. There was a flutter of anticipation in his body and he was feeling happy about making the correct decision the previous evening: it was necessary to sort out things with Antoine before indulging himself with Veronique. Ben's eyes started to wander around the restaurant while he was waiting and just as he raised a glass to his lips, his attention was caught by a solitary customer in the corner of the room who was finishing his meal. The man was reading a copy of *Le Soir*, a popular Swiss evening newspaper and the front page headlines were clearly visible: *"Deux hommes tués à Genève"*. Ben was curious about the drama and wondered whether the two men who were killed were victims of the explosion when he was caught up in the traffic, returning from Veronique's place. As the businessman took a final drink from his coffee cup and stood ready to leave, he plopped the newspaper on the table before walking out. Clearly, *Le Soir* had supplied all the news he required that day.

However, Ben's curiosity got the better of him and he swiftly shuffled across to retrieve the newspaper before it was removed by a waiter. Feeling uncomfortable about the deed he fanned the journal open so his face was hidden behind the front page, which he began to read. One of the men declared dead was the owner of the workshop that Ben had seen that day, someone by the name of Lucas Gauthier. His death was being viewed as 'suspicious' by the Swiss Police, who were investigating the cause of the explosion.

The body of the other man had not yet been identified, mainly because it comprised a male torso that had been recovered from Lake Geneva, where it had been dumped inside a black plastic bag. The head was missing along with the hands and feet. There was a gunshot wound in the centre of the chest, which police at this stage were regarding as the cause of death. It was clearly a case of murder and the investigating chief had pledged that he would uncover the people responsible for such a heinous crime. There did not seem to be any link between the two deaths, according to the journalist reporting on the stories.

Ben suddenly realised that he was on his second glass of wine and there was still no sign of Veronique. A glance at his watch showed that it was now almost quarter-to-nine. Ben's furrowed brow was followed by wide eyes when the waiter approached. He presumed he was going to be asked if he was ready to order yet and was prepared to plea for more time. Ben was just about to explain that his guest was late when the waiter spoke first, stating that he had a message. A Mademoiselle Veronique had contacted the restaurant to explain that a problem had arisen at work and that she would be unable to make their rendezvous. Perhaps they could make arrangements for another time, when they could meet at Monsieur's favourite restaurant. The wording was virtually the same as Ben had used the previous evening when he had cancelled their dinner date and it suggested that Veronique had been irritated by *his* cancellation. Perhaps Ben had taken too much for granted after all.

There was nothing else he could do but order a meal for one and re-appraise his strategy. Care was needed if he was to salvage their relationship and if that was indeed what he wanted. He wanted time to think straight, not only about his relationship with Veronique but also about everything that had happened since his return to Sergy. A part of him regretted ever having left for the UK although the memory of his family brought his thoughts back to normality. After eating a delicious one-course meal and leaving half a bottle of red wine on the table, Ben paid the bill before handing a used copy of *Le Soir* to the waiter on his way out, declaring, 'Someone seems to have left their newspaper behind.' On his walk to the car, Ben felt that he had misjudged Veronique.

V

It was unusual to receive a phone call on the landline but Ben knew his Dad only ever used his mobile for essential calls or when a 'proper phone' was not available. Although it was first thing on a Monday morning, Graham Moyles was calling to give Ben an update on Richard's progress and to find out how his younger son was settling back into life in France. Graham had already been out and about for more than an hour, seeing to the cattle and carrying out the routine of early morning chores. The time difference been France and the UK was not an inconvenience to such an early riser ; he did not even consider Ben's routine.

'So, he's doing well then Dad? That's a relief. How is he facing up to the prospect of a future not working on the farm and doing only light duties from now on?'

'Well that's going to take a long period of readjustment and I haven't really forced the point home yet. But I will, you can rest assured of that. The consultant has told us that he needs a transplant if he is to make any inroads into getting his life back but you know what that is like. We've already been waiting a while for an organ donor and had nothing but disappointment. Rich is still fast asleep at the moment and I know that he intends to give you a call this evening. I'm just telling you how the land lies so you don't say anything untoward when you *do* get the chance to talk to him. Anyway how are you doing son? Everything alright there in France? You settled back into the swing of things?'

Ben was certainly not going to disclose the concern about having had his apartment bugged while he was away. That would only have given his Dad even more stress, something he could do without. 'Na, same old boring routine I'm afraid. Nothing much has happened in the last two weeks. Next stop Christmas, I suppose.'

As soon as the handset was lowered onto its resting place, Ben's anticipation lurched to the day ahead. Although he did not discuss his own genuine concern about his twin brother out of consideration for his father, something else was more pressing. On this particular day, even his apprehension about the break-in had slipped down his personal agenda. This Monday morning marked the beginning of the third week since his return when a big reveal was about to take place and it was well overdue. Ben had told his Dad about the importance of his work in France and shared a little bit about his concern regarding job security. What he had never fully explained was how critical his own research could prove to be if his ideas were correct. There was a chance, admittedly only a smidgeon of a possibility, that the experiment he had initiated prior to visiting home could shed some significant light on the research that was taking place within Puissance. It was not essential to the renewal of his contract but given everything that had taken place earlier in the year, success of some kind could only serve him well.

Ben sat in his kitchen staring at the pattern on the splash-back tiles above the kettle and sipping his coffee to prevent it from going cold. He was still only half-dressed as the phone call from his Dad had momentarily diverted his thoughts and affected his routine. Returning to the bedroom to hunt for his trousers, he knew he had to do some reparation work to his relationship with Veronique. Her absence from their dinner date was almost as if she knew he had absconded from her apartment's car park, but he could not comprehend how that was possible. Whatever was going on with his girlfriend would also have to take a back seat for the moment. The knot of his blue tie was secured in a half-hearted manner and slipping on his jacket before re-visiting his *espresso*, he felt a distraction of butterflies at the thought of what he could be facing. The sensation was reminiscent of the time he went into university to collect his final degree results. Taking a last glance around the kitchen Ben paid special attention to the former locations of the surveillance devices, in an act of futile self-reassurance.

The worst part of going into work that morning was having to face that supercilious sycophant, Sebastian Thiroud. How he had ever become so close to such a prestigious physicist as Ian Thompkins was a mystery that would never be solved. Thiroud's intellectual capacity certainly outweighed his scientific knowledge and perhaps he had simply outwitted his competitors. However, the Puissance Project counted among its employees some of the most brilliant scientific minds in the world. It was unfathomable that someone could not have jumped over this particular little man. Perhaps he had some hold over Thompkins that no one else knew about ; it may have been something personal. Thompkins was not married and it was possible that something lurked in the shadows of his past. Although his boss had many unpleasant character traits, Thompkins emanated a certain degree of power and had a strong ego. Thiroud may well have been attracted to him for that reason. Ben even wondered if it had been Thiroud who had bought the large ring always flaunted on Thompkins' index finger.

The final set of traffic lights before entering the compound at Puissance was sufficient to break Ben's daydream and he snapped out of his fantasy. Now was the time for professionalism to take over and he realised he should no longer think about Sebastian Thiroud or anyone else for that matter. After completing the security checks that were part of his everyday routine, Ben made his way to Eta Lab and tried to engage his brain with positive thoughts. He forced himself to think that even if his experiment proved totally unsuccessful and he was subject to Thiroud's vile condescension he had to maintain some self-respect. *Dr Ben Moyles was a distinguished physicist who could easily move to another research position.* That was the mantra he recited with every step taken along the corridor to Eta Lab.

Ben settled himself down by preparing his research papers and he started analysing some of the data that had been transmitted back to Eta Lab's computers from the reactor. He was switching his attention between computer screens displaying images of figures and graphs so did not notice Thiroud approach. It was the sound of his voice that made him jump. 'So are you ready to see if your theory has any merit , Doctor Moyles ?' Ben did not bother to acknowledge his superior with anything other than a brusque shrug of the shoulders. Thiroud was enjoying the power of his position. 'Well I'm sorry to disappoint you but it's going to have to wait until this afternoon. Professor Thompkins has informed me that he wishes to attend the conclusion of the event, personally. Quite an honour for you I would have thought. Still I only wish I shared his optimism.'

This was too much for Ben to take and he felt it was about time for some retaliation. 'Have you got some sort of problem with me Thiroud ? If you have then spit it out because I'd like to hear it.'

This took his nemesis by surprise 'I don't know what you mean ?' he said, defensively.

'Well I'll tell you what I mean. Every time I have attempted to suggest anything other than what you or Professor Thompkins wants to hear, you engage your smug-meter and make comments like the ones you have just made here, now. And quite frankly, I'm sick of hearing them and I've a good mind to …'

Before Ben had a chance to finish his threat, the two scientists were joined by Jonas Brandli, who had spotted Thiroud entering the Lab. Although he could not hear the whispered venom of their conversation as he approached, Brandli was sufficiently astute to recognise hostile body language when he saw it and thought his presence at their so-called discussion could only be beneficial: his analysis was absolutely correct. Jonas was able to deflate the situation immediately. 'Ah, hello there Sebastian. I assume you were looking for me ? You will know of course that you need my official permission to enter Eta Lab before approaching any of my staff and I'm sorry if you could not find me … fortunately I am here now. I see you have already started to deliberate matters with Ben, here.' Turning to face Dr Moyles, he continued. 'No doubt Sebastian will have told you that Professor Thompkins himself would like to monitor the progress of your latest experiment. This is quite an honour, I'm sure you'll agree.' Ben had been glaring at Thiroud while the Head of the Lab had been speaking and it was only after a discreet knee-nudge from Brandli that he turned to focus his attention on the present.

'Er … yes Dr Brandli. Quite an honour indeed. I was just saying the same thing to Dr Thiroud here.'

The unspoken truth was best left exactly where it was, something that all three men recognised. There was no point in dampening any gunpowder at this stage.

As the morning progressed it became obvious that whatever the experiment's secrets were, they would have to remain a mystery for another couple of days. Thompkins' priorities elsewhere meant he was committed to more important pressing engagements and did not have time to tutor one of his minions. Once Ben received the official information that their meeting was postponed he had some extra time on his hands so he decided to contact Veronique and try and repair some damage following her cancellation of their dinner.

In order to avoid causing Veronique any professional embarrassment while she was working, Ben waited until the anticipated time of her lunch break before getting in touch. He listened to her mobile ringing with some trepidation, wondering if she would even accept the call when his name appeared on her screen. He need not have worried. 'Hello darling, how are you?' Without waiting for a response she continued, 'I am so sorry I could not make our date the other night. A last minute hitch to an important contract had to be sorted out and I just could not get away. I hope you got my message?'

She seemed genuinely concerned and her excuse was expressed with sincerity. Ben decided to give her the benefit of any doubt, fully knowing that his own behaviour had been more reprehensible. Veronique had seemingly made a choice between her professional and personal responsibilities, while he had dumped her in favour of an old neighbour. 'Yes, I got your message thanks. What a pity you could not make it. Never mind, what about tonight instead?'

'Oh, sorry *mon chéri* I'm tied up tonight with work but could do Wednesday if that's alright for you.'

Ben was not sure if Veronique had suddenly decided to play hard-to-get or whether she was genuinely unavailable. He felt a rush of emotion at the thought. 'Yes, Wednesday is fine for me. Shall I try and get the same restaurant?'

'That would be excellent. Text me the arrangements and I will be there. Bye.'

Before Ben had a chance to say anything, his mobile showed a red icon indicating their conversation had ended. Any doubts he had about whether Veronique had been involved in the intrusion into his apartment were scotched in that instance and he was glad that he would be able to pick up on their relationship -with all its benefits.

Ben had only one more catch-up call to make; it was to Camille who had probably forgotten the scheduling of his return from the UK and as a result had not bothered to try and make contact. For such an intelligent woman Camille was not very good at the trivia of detail unless it was important to what she was doing and then she had a mind like a steel trap. If the occasion contained an aspect that was somehow nebulous she tended to be carefree, almost to the point of incompetence. Gaston's birthday party had been a case in point: Camille had hired a catering firm to do the heavy work because she was totally disinterested in becoming involved in that aspect of the celebration. Even the birthday cake had been purchased from a local patisserie. However, she had organised the seating plan with the precision of a field-marshal and the layout of the placements was guaranteed to ensure there was the right balance of characters and egos sitting either together or apart. As a result, the evening had worked impeccably. Camille's strategy had functioned without a glitch and her friend Ben had even gained a new partner as a by-product of her arrangements.

Unlike the call to Veronique, it took Ben two attempts to get hold of Camille. 'Hello Ben, how are you? How did your trip to the UK go? How is your family?' The barrage of questions was typical of Camille, why bother to ask about one thing when an assault can reveal so much more. 'I noticed that I had a missed call on my phone and I was just about to give you a ring. I've only now come in from the garden as I've been seeing to my rhododendron, now the temperature has started to dip.' Judging by the scraping noise of a chair-leg Ben assumed she was making herself comfortable. 'Right tell me all, I'm listening. No better still, tell me nothing. Come over this evening and have dinner with me and Gaston. You can tell me then. I'll ask Veronique if she can come. I'll make something nice. Yes, come.. please say you'll come.'

Ben was beginning to wonder if he had any part to play in this one-sided conversation. 'Yes, my little whirlwind, I'll be delighted to come for dinner but there is no need to ask Veronique. I've already asked her if she would like to go out for dinner with me tonight but she said she can't make it. But I would love to come and I've a lot to tell you about since I saw you last.'

'Wonderful, wonderful. About eight ?'

'Yes, that would be perfect. See you later.' Ben pressed the icon to terminate the call and almost sighed as he did so. He was not sure if he had just been verbally assaulted or whether he had received a kind and considerate invitation from a friend to go to dinner. He decided it was the latter.

For the remainder of the afternoon Ben dealt with work trivia, all the while contemplating the results of his experiment. The data readouts sent to the Lab from the monitoring equipment inside the safety cell were encouraging but he had been down this corridor several times before. In the past when he thought the team had make a breakthrough they were always let down because the data could be misleadingly inaccurate. He did not expect a 'eureka moment' but he hoped there would be something positive to report and show the work carried out in Eta Lab was making a significant contribution to Puissance. At least he had a pleasant diversion planned for later that evening.

Ben also decided to phone his father just before setting off for the Dubois household that evening. There had been no point in trying to contact him during the afternoon as Graham would almost certainly not be in the farmhouse and mobile reception in that part of the North East was variable. Usually at this time of year Graham was at the local *tup* sales, trying to buy fresh stock in order to improve the quality of the sheep on the farm. As a consequence he could be anywhere, depending on where the particular market was being held. In addition, his Dad did not like to be distracted when he was going about his working day. Although he would not say anything to Ben about such an invasion, his son knew the situation well enough.

While Ben had begun to sort out his immediate priorities, Zenib was drinking his espresso outside a four-star restaurant on the shore of Lake Geneva. The view was a long way from the red mountains of the dry, rocky Middle Eastern desert that he regarded as home. He was alone with his thoughts as he watched the chic, elegant people going about their business. Lunchtime was approaching and the restaurant was starting to become busy. A waiter asked if he required any further service, which was coded language for *'You can't sit here all day unless you order something.'* The misty breath of the servant came too close to Zenib, who leant forward to indicate his irritation. 'I'll take another coffee.' The command was said with such curt authority that any further rebuke was unnecessary. While Zenib sat alone, staring at the beauty of the Lake, his gaze masked the whirring thoughts that were trying to address his latest problem.

Connolly's threat of possible punishment was lingering in his mind and although he could muster threats of his own, Zenib recognised he needed to gain favour with his boss.

All the information that had been gathered from secret sources indicated that Puissance staff were becoming more optimistic about the progress of their research. Connolly was not happy about the news and when that happened there was usually a ripple effect that threatened to drown his minions. However, Zenib was not going to be overcome by any of the subsequent waves. Thompkins did not present a problem, he already had that situation covered. The issue was with those independent researchers whose secrets were yet to be revealed. Three of them were giving concern at the moment. Dr Ben Moyles was one of them. The other two were in Alpha Lab, working more closely with their boss. Zenib's source was able to feed-back and give any necessary assurances without arousing suspicion. However, the monitoring of the scientists' behaviour from the sophisticated surveillance equipment in the 'factory' could not cover every situation. Perhaps it was the time to get closer to Dr Moyles and step up the work that was already in place.

The waiter returned with an espresso on a silver tray, preferring to focus on the cup and saucer with their golden trimmings rather than catch the gaze of the customer's cold eyes that were scrutinising his every movement. As quickly as he could move his hands without spilling anything, the items were laid to rest on the glass topped circular table and he returned to sanctuary inside the restaurant where the customers were less threatening. Suddenly the idea of a tip did not seem important. Zenib turned to peruse the view once more, instantly forgetting about the grovelling servant.

The caffeine kick stirred Zenib's cerebrum into action as he sat pondering the various possibilities. The noise created by a father and son organising their boat in the nearby marina was a momentary distraction before his thoughts returned to his options. Nothing drastic was needed yet, though things could change. The first priority was to establish the facts. The recent unsuccessful attempts to install the surveillance equipment had put Puissance's security on alert. Any attempt to repeat the process could bring horrendous consequences so a more subtle approach was needed. Zenib considered the people on the ground he could use and a glimmer of a smile crossed his face as he stood and drained his coffee cup. Placing some Euro notes under the clip of the saucer before shrugging his coat onto his shoulders, he knew exactly what to do. Zenib wandered along the shoreline path to contemplate his plan.

VI

Ben arrived at Camille and Gaston's house just before eight o'clock. The temperamental doorbell announced his presence and Camille ushered him into the kitchen after an extravagant *faire la bise*. 'I am just watching the sauce *mon chéri* . Gaston has not returned from work yet but he shouldn't be long. I hope you don't mind waiting with me while I keep an eye on the cooking.'

'Not at all. Perhaps I might learn something,' he laughed.

'I doubt it. Would you like a glass of wine while you sit with me?'

Camille had not noticed the bottle of red that Ben had left just inside the kitchen door. 'I've brought my own. Would you like some of mine?' This time it was Camille's turn to laugh as she stroked her hand down his chest as a sign of familiarity. While Ben poured, she stirred the shiny silver saucepans that were bubbling on the hob. 'It must be busy at work at the moment if Gaston is late. Veronique said she had something on tonight as well, otherwise you might have had an extra guest for dinner.' Camille offered a courteous smile in response, while Ben decided to take advantage of the lull in proceedings. 'Mind if I use your loo, Camille?'

'Of course my dear. You don't have to ask.'

While the hostess busied herself in the kitchen, Ben answered a call of nature. He knew it would have been alright to use the upstairs bathroom but also recognised that protocol directed him to the downstairs cloakroom. After completing his task and washing his hands, Ben heard the sound of cars pulling up to the lane beside the house. Thinking that it could not be Gaston because he would have driven straight onto the main driveway, Ben peered through the gap in the semi-open window, which overlooked the side of their home. He saw that it *was* Gaston and he was talking to Sebastian Thiroud. Both men were leaning against their cars, but were too far away for Ben to hear what they were saying. The familiarity of their body language heightened his curiosity, especially when Gaston appeared to pass Thiroud something from his wallet. Then he remembered they were in the same golf club and wondered if it was anything to do with that connection. Not wishing to prolong his stay in the toilet, he swiftly returned to the kitchen. Within seconds of entering the room he had wiped the incident from his mind.

Ben began to update Camille with his news about Rich, his stay on the farm and what had happened on his return regarding the break-in. Just as he was getting to the gist of the story about the surveillance equipment they both heard the front door open, followed by a '*Yoo-hoo*' from the master of the house. Entering the kitchen in response to Camille's answering call, he headed straight for Ben offering his hand and a few words of welcome. Camille teased her husband with, 'And what about your wife ? Do you not have any words of welcome for her?'

Gaston moved past Ben and gave Camille a compensatory embrace followed by a kiss on the lips. 'How could I ever forget about you, my beautiful wife.' While Ben was about to pour his newly arrived host a glass of red, Gaston held up his hand with an accompanying, '*Non, merci*. I need to get changed first and then I will have a well-deserved glass of whisky. Sorry I am late but it has been a busy day at work, as usual. Please carry on. I won't be a minute.'

The time gap allowed Ben to fill-in Camille with his account of how he discovered the 'bugs' in his apartment and his trip to Bourg-en-Bresse along with having to give a statement to Captain Jacques Durand of the *Gendarmarie*. She sat on a kitchen stool, glass of wine in one hand with the other supporting her chin while her elbow rested on a work-top. At some dark point when he was considering all possibilities, Ben had wondered if Camille had been involved in some way in the recent subterfuge. After all, she had generous access to his apartment. She could easily have made a mould of his key for someone else to copy or left a window open without him knowing. Part of him scrutinised her reaction to his tale but she listened with genuine interest and demonstrated natural curiosity about what Ben had endured. There could be no other conclusion than Camille had nothing to do with his recent problems.

At that moment Gaston re-appeared in the kitchen doorway, his wet thinning hair combed straight back after a quick shower. His suit had been returned to its resting place in the walk-in wardrobe and he was now wearing his favourite slacks and checked shirt. He clasped his hands together as if he was rinsing them clean. 'Right, that's me sorted. Shall we leave the little lady to finish the meal while we retreat to the lounge?'

Camille shot him a contemptuous look. 'Just as well we have a witness Gaston Dubois otherwise they would be finding another body in Lake Geneva.'

Ben picked up on the reference. 'Yes, I read in *Le Soir* the other day that a mutilated body was found in the Lake. Quite gruesome apparently.'

'You're not kidding. There has to be more to it than a simple murder. His head, hands and feet had been chopped off. Whoever killed him did not want him identified, that's for sure.'

'So they don't know who it was?'

'No, and I don't think they ever will. Come on, let's go and try that whisky I was on about.'

While Gaston and Ben retired to a more relaxing environment, Camille was left to complete the finishing touches to the meal. Despite her protestations, she was relieved the two men were out of her hair so she could get on with the job.

'It's a good whisky, *non*?' inquired Gaston as he handed Ben a generously-filled crystal glass.

'Very nice,' responded Ben, who would have complimented the drink even if it had been unpalatable. 'Where did you get it from? It's certainly not French … or Swiss.'

Gaston smiled politely. 'A client of mine has just returned from a holiday in the Scottish Highlands and he brought it back for me. This is a *Glencadam* whisky, which you can only get in Scotland apparently.' Gaston held-up the tumbler to the light before taking another sip. 'Very nice… very nice indeed.'

Ben felt a bit guilty at not having brought his friend a gift back from his holiday, though he did qualify his self-reprimand by considering the expensive wine he had brought along for the dinner. He decided to try and change the subject. 'So you're working late tonight, Gaston. Are things particularly busy at the moment?'

His friend went along with the small talk. 'Well, I certainly don't have time to go to the gym, like Veronique if that's what you mean. No wonder she has such a nice figure judging by the amount of exercise she does.

Ben did not respond to the comment, he was too busy thinking about its ramifications. If Veronique was going to the gym, why did she tell him that she could not go out for dinner because of work. Something did not feel right. Ben was beginning to wonder if he had taken Veronique too much for granted and she was now just playing him for her own ends. As he was about to interrogate Gaston about his girlfriend's behaviour, Camille came into the lounge and told the pair to move into the dining room because the meal was ready. As he carried his whisky out of the lounge, Ben felt disconcerted about how he was being seemingly treated by Veronique. Selfishly he did not consider his own actions on the night *he* pulled out of their dinner arrangements.

It was a lovely, relaxing evening with friends enjoying being together and catching up on recent events. Ben repeated some of the tales to Gaston that he had previously relayed to Camille, while she returned the finished plates to the dishwasher during a lull between courses. Ben inquired about their weekend visits to their ski-lodge in Interlaken and for a moment he felt envious of Camille and Gaston, not simply for the closeness of their relationship but also because of their material wealth. They seemed to have it all: well-paid jobs to accommodate their wealthy lifestyle in a chic part of Europe, with two lovely homes, one near the France-Swiss border. Ben could not even afford to hire a cabin in Interlaken and having been to the town once and witnessed its opulence, he wondered how the couple managed to accrue such wealth. Before his thoughts became more envious, he recognised that he should be grateful for being able to include them as friends.

It was approaching ten o'clock in the evening and Ben was forced to refuse another whisky. 'No, I had better not, Gaston. I'm pretty close to the limit now and I don't want to risk losing my licence at this stage of my career. It's probably better if I go home and get an early night. Tomorrow is a very important day for me. Professor Thompkins will be attending my unveiling of the experiment and I've got no idea how it will pan out. There's a good chance I won't have a job if things go badly.'

Gaston made an attempt to dissuade his guest about returning home. 'Are you sure. You can always stay in one of our guest rooms if you like.'

'No thank you my friend. It is time for me to go. Thank you for a wonderful evening. It was just what I needed to take my mind off things – and thanks to you my beautiful friend for a gorgeous meal. It was fantastic.'

Camille responded in kind. 'You're more than welcome. It's been great to see you again and catch-up with everything that has been going on in your life in the last few weeks. There's certainly been a lot to talk about.'

Ben stood and straightened himself ready to leave. He was escorted to his car by Camille and Gaston who were linked to each other in the sort of embrace only a closely married can deploy without looking silly. As Ben got into the car and lowered his window to offer his final words of gratitude and farewell, Camille called out with one final wave. 'Good luck tomorrow, I hope it goes well.'

Although Ben could not hear everything she said because of the noise of the car engine as he pulled away, he recognised it was a message of goodwill and waved affectionately as he left the driveway to make his way back to Sergy.

Soon he was entering his apartment block and although it was quite late, Antoine's door opened and it was clear from his state of anxiety that he wanted to talk. 'Ah, there you are Ben I have been waiting for you, *mon ami*. I received a visit earlier this evening from an officer of the *Gendarmarie* who wanted to ask me some questions about your break-in.'

Although Ben had been looking forward to an early-ish night he could tell that Antoine was stressed by what had happened to him and sensed the old man needed some reassurance. 'Shall I come in my friend and you can tell me all about it?'

It was clear as Antoine beckoned Ben through the open doorway that the old man was shaken. Ben declined the invitation to engage in more alcohol preferring simply a glass of cold water. He needed a clear head in readiness for tomorrow while for Antoine the brandy was working on a medicinal level. The pair made their way into the small lounge and sat facing each other. Ben thought that he had better lead the conversation. 'So, who was it who came to talk to you my friend. Was it Captain Durand?'

'No it was a sergeant, who was not pleased to have to come all this way to ask me questions that I could not answer. I cannot remember his name.'

'What time did he come? It must have been quite late. I did not leave my apartment until about half-past seven.'

'*Oui*, he came at about eight o'clock. I think that is why he was not in a good mood.'

'That is very poor, to come at that hour, knowing your circumstances. I will ring them to complain tomorrow.'

Antoine did not want to risk causing any further acrimony. '*Non*, please do not do that. I do not think they will bother with me again.'

'Even so, Antoine. That is not good enough. What did he ask of you anyway?'

'He just asked me what I had seen when you were away and could I recognise the man who had come to repair the broken CCTV camera. I told him I could not because I had no reason to study his face at the time. He was just a worker with a white van and a ladder. He asked me if there was anything else unusual that happened that I could think of. But I could not think of anything because of the way he was looking at me as if I had done something wrong.'

Ben attempted to console his neighbour who was an innocent bystander in the whole process. 'Do not worry about anything my friend. It is all over now.'

Antoine took another sip of his brandy and this seemed to stir a thought. His eyes were looking down at his feet while his mind was elsewhere, then he shared his deliberation, almost as a peace offering. 'The only other thing odd that happened while you were away was the visit from my sister's boy, Gérard. He came to see me on his way to a holiday in Switzerland.'

This stirred some concern. 'Why was that unusual, my friend?'

'Well I had not seen Gérard since he was a little boy. He is my sister, Madelaine's son. She lives just outside Paris but I have not spoken with her for several years. You would have thought that she could have let me know that Gérard was coming to visit. I did not recognise him: he has changed so much.'

Ben's mind was now in overdrive. 'So how do you know it really was Gérard?'

Antoine did not share Ben's concern and he was recounting the episode almost simply as a matter of fact. 'Well he said he was Gérard and he knew all about Madelaine and could tell me all about her. Who else could he be and know all that?'

Ben did not have the heart to tell Antoine that 'Gérard' could have embellished the basic facts with bluster if he was a confidence trickster. Anyone who had the nerve to break into someone's apartment and try to install surveillance equipment would not be phased by conning an old man. Ben felt he needed to push things further. 'So how long did he stay …this Gérard?'

'That's just the thing. He stayed for only one night and the next morning he just went without saying goodbye. We had drunk almost half a bottle of his brandy that evening and I must have been asleep because I did not hear him leave. He did not even say where he was going or anything. In many ways he was just like his ungrateful mother.'

Ben did not say what he was thinking. *'That was not your nephew, you old fool. It was somebody pretending to be him in order to try and get access to my flat. And it worked!'* Instead he was forced into diplomacy. 'That's families for you I suppose, Antoine.'

Lying in bed an hour later, Ben pondered whether to inform the *Gendarmarie* about Antoine's recollection of events but decided there was no point. Nothing could be gained by questioning his neighbour again. Even if he could give an accurate description of his 'nephew', it would achieve very little. The damage, such as it was, had already been done. Now the security had been tightened and no doubt the perpetrators would either try and gain someone else's secrets or give up altogether. Generating further investigation was futile so better to leave it well alone.

VII

Ben had entered the time of five o'clock on his mobile phone for an early alarm call on Wednesday morning. Today was going to be a big occasion and he did not know how it was going to affect his future. Slipping into his jogging kit and exiting the apartment block as quietly as possible, he was soon on familiar territory. It was lonely pounding the deserted streets at that time. The sun was yet to show its face and apart from the occasional car, the roads were quiet. The air condensing around each passing outtake of breath was testimony to the falling temperature at this time of year. Ben loved jogging in the bright sunny mornings and sharing daybreak with the chirping birds and inquisitive wildlife. However, these autumn months brought a different challenge. The absence of adequate light until around seven o'clock in the morning meant it could be hazardous running through the country lanes, even when wearing a high visibility vest. As a result, he preferred to jog through the streets of Sergy where the streetlights offered some floodlit safety. If the roads had been busy or if it had been daylight then perhaps it would have been more embarrassing to be seen running in vest and shorts along the pavement. Only a few songbirds clearing their throats in anticipation of sunrise were able to offer any croak of criticism.

Ben had neglected his training regime while in the UK and his body was feeling the strain. Some unusual dramatic events had taken over his priorities since returning to Sergy. He was replaying those events in his mind as a distraction to the discomfort in his cramping stomach, while trying to step up the pace. It seemed that the identity of the perpetrators of the break-in would inevitably go undetected. He contemplated what he should do in order to improve his own security and considered a number of options. At the top of his list was trying to find out who had betrayed him. Whoever had gained access to his apartment had used someone close to him either with or without their consent.

The indications seemed to suggest that somebody purporting to be Antoine's nephew had conned the old man into gaining access possibly by using the spare keys or gaining some useful knowledge of Ben's apartment. On the other hand, it could just as easily not have been the case that the betrayer was someone known and trusted by Ben. After all, not everyone knew that Antoine had a set of keys to Ben's flat, it would have to be a person who had a close knowledge of Ben's habits. Similarly, someone had clearly gone to a lot of trouble to find out a great deal of background information about Antoine and used that knowledge effectively. Such acts would require substantial effort and sophisticated ability. Perhaps the most sinister aspect of the whole affair was that the plan had been successful. If it had not been for Ben's personal vigilance, a great deal of confidential personal and professional information could have fallen into the wrong hands. As Ben jogged around the corner of Rue Concorde he almost collided with a man stepping out of his car. It caught them both by surprise.

'Désolé à ce sujet, monsieur,' the man said by way of an apology. Ben waved his hand in acceptance before continuing his run.

After a hot shower followed by a strong espresso and a slice of toast Ben felt the euphoria of active endorphins electrify his mind and body. He was ready for work and strode defiantly to his parked car, ready for the journey. The drive that he had taken repeatedly since moving to Sergy was nothing more than a distraction on this particular morning as he glanced at the rustic glow developing behind the distant Alps. This was the final week in September and sunrise was beginning to occur slightly later each day. Dawn was showing signs of beginning to lose its annual battle with the darkness, although at this time of year it was usually a draw.

At seven-thirty Ben was entering Eta Lab just as the sun's rays were beginning to turn a brighter yellow and he walked past Jonas Brandli's office, pleased that his line manager had not yet arrived for work. He lifted the papers from his desk and gave them a quick scrutiny. Placing a folder under his arm, Ben decided to make his way to the Radioactive Zone and prepare himself before the arrival of his bosses. Say what you like about Thompkins, and Ben often did, his level of professional punctuality was usually spot on. After a change of clothing and the usual safety checks, Ben entered the restricted area and decided to wait until the others arrived before going any further. He glanced over to the safety cell where a blue light above the door indicated that his experiment was still active. The next stage would be determined by his decision, he could either de-activate the set-up in the safety cell before the appearance of the others or wait until they arrived. The latter was the preferred option because he wanted to enjoy unwrapping his pet scheme in front of an audience.

At the appointed hour Professor Ian Thompkins accompanied by his ever-present assistant Dr Sebastian Thiroud entered the Radioactive Zone where they were met by Ben and Dr Jonas Brandli. There was no point in shaking hands, apart from the fact they already knew each other well they were all wearing gloves. Thompkins was the first to speak. 'Right, Dr Moyles, this is the moment you have been waiting for. We are in your hands and it is our role to simply observe, Dr Thiroud and I will take no part in the process of de-activation. We do not wish to risk contaminating the process, so it's over to you.'

Ben thanked his boss and the small group walked over to the door of the safety cell. After inspecting the dials on the wall adjacent to the door, Ben checked some basic data on his iPad. He then punched a set of numbers into a digital keyboard under the largest dial. This released the pressure inside the safety cell allowing the seal to be broken so the door could open. All eyes were now focussed on the entrance to the cell which was automatically lit as the heavy door slowly peeled back. It gradually revealed the mini-reactor encased in its synthetic cocoon, seemingly unscathed. If the experiment had been successful, the scientists would have expected to see a green glow radiating from inside the external casing as nuclear fusion continued to generate energy. Ben looked hopefully for signs of success but could not detect anything as he directed the reactor's trolley into the less confined inspection area. He was aware of expectant eyes attempting to peer over his shoulder, conscious that not everyone in the group was praying for success as much as he was.

The moment came to remove the outer shell and reveal the extent of the nuclear fusion. If the experiment was unsuccessful there would be no light on any of the monitoring boards. The green indicators that had been activated when the experiment was initiated would be off. However, everyone would have a clue about the result before the cocoon was removed because rays of escaping light would herald the outcome.

There was nothing to be seen and Ben could feel his heart sink at the inevitability to come. He felt Thompkins and Thiroud look at each other and almost expected them to laugh aloud.

However, when all the casing was removed a surprise improved Ben's mood considerably. Although the green lights were not glowing, they were not totally extinguished either. There were signs that the fusion process was still taking place, albeit not at the same rate as Ben had hoped. The experiment appeared to have been partially successful and more importantly it indicated a way forward for future research.

Thompkins almost pushed Ben out of the way as he stepped forward to get a better look. Without asking, he took Ben's iPad away from him to take a look at the data on the screen. He need not have bothered, it told him nothing except the code for opening the door to the safety cell. The most significant results would be included in the data that the reactor had been sending back to Eta Lab, where the most important analysis would be directed in the immediate future. Crouching down, Thompkins' gaze moved to the consoles beside the reactor and he examined the strategic chaos of wiring and the connectors. For a moment Ben wondered if he was going to slap the reactor with his fingers because it was reminiscent of a comic scene without a punchline. Thiroud stepped forward, attempting to offer grovelling support to his idol but he was equally stunned.

Jonas Brandli was the first to speak and he turned to face Ben, whose dumbfounded expression was yet to burst into a smile. 'Well my friend, it looks as if your experiment has produced success. Congratulations, Dr Moyles – do you realise what this means ? This discovery could be colossal.' Turning to address the others, he continued. 'We may well be witnesses to the most outstanding finding in modern history and be staring into the entrance of something monumental.' He offered his hand in a gesture of congratulations but his shake was significantly more vigorous than the one returned by a bemused Ben.

Thiroud was determined to rain on the parade. 'Hang on a minute, Dr Brandli. This proves nothing. Yes, it offers hope but it is hardly startling. We have come close to generating similar results in Alpha Lab using similar techniques. Clearly, a lot more testing needs to take place before we can make any firm claim of success.'

For once, Professor Ian Thompkins showed his credentials as a Nobel Prize Winner. 'No, Sebastian – Jonas is correct. This is a remarkable discovery and everyone associated with the Puissance Project needs to recognise the success that we have produced today. Congratulations on your work Dr Moyles, you have earned yourself a great deal of credit. What we must do now, as you say Dr Brandli, is conduct more tests over the coming months in order to improve these results before we can go public. This will be exciting work and you must play an important role with us, Ben.'

All this conversation went over Ben's head, he was still in a state of stunned euphoria, amazed at what had been achieved. Initially, he had been concerned that if the experiment failed he could lose his job and he never really contemplated that energy could still be produced by the mini-reactor after a month in the safety cell. The best he had hoped for was some encouraging data from the analysis of his prototype. A whirlwind of exciting possibilities was now racing through his imagination. The next few months were going to be very exhilarating.

Professor Thompkins waded in with some gravitas. 'If this secret becomes known, we may as well have targets on our back, gentlemen. Whereas *we* may be excited by the possibility of finding a new major source of energy, there are parts of the world who would now regard our work as a threat to their wealth and stability, if our theories are authentic. We must be very careful how we proceed. The first thing to do is to move this work into Alpha Lab where I can monitor its progress. We must also carefully check our security, professionally and personally. We already know that someone is taking an interest in our work. If they get wind of this development they may become more desperate. This is certainly an exciting development – it could also prove to be a very dangerous one.

VIII

Thompkins and Thiroud retreated to Alpha Lab to lick their wounds but for Ben and Brandli the taste on their tongues was sweeter and their mood was buoyant. Jonas could not restrain his excitement, 'Well, well ... who would have thought it. The major breakthrough in the field of energy has been achieved by a farmer's son from the Cheviot Hills of England!'

'Ok, Jonas I think I get the gist of what you are saying, but in the words of that well known sycophant Dr Sebastian Thiroud, *'This proves nothing'*. We still have a long way to go but at least we have a starting point. The trials over the coming months will be critical and I suspect that Thompkins will want to go into total lockdown while we investigate how to improve on the efficiency of the fusion process.'

Recognising that the experiment had not been without flaws, Brandli picked up on the point. 'What do you think went wrong with the experiment. It seems odd that some energy was still being generated after almost a month but what I wonder what restricted the power production?'

Ben had been thinking about the same problem while he was still in the Radioactive Area. That was the reason he had been unable to share in the unrestrained joy of his line manager. 'I'm not sure what it could have been but if I was to hazard a guess I think it must be related to the metallic hydrogen. The fact that prior to its deployment we had only failure but when we used it this time, we had some limited success. I suspect that the hydrogen was not pure enough. That would account for the fact that it still worked but with each cycle of the fusion there was a slight loss in energy transfer because of those impurities. Next time we will make sure the metallic hydrogen is every bit as pure as the original element and behaves in exactly the same way.'

'Well my friend, that is for another time. Today we must celebrate your success.' Brandli walked over to a filing cabinet in the corner of the room and slid open the middle drawer. Pushing back a concertina of suspension files he lifted out a bottle of single malt and removed two plastic cups from an adjacent water cooler. Ben looked at him quizzically, before his colleague explained himself. 'For medicinal purposes you understand.'

'Hmm didn't know you could get that on prescription.'

They laughed as Jonas poured and offered a plastic cup of whisky to Ben whose smiling eyes finally conceded he was happy.

'It's a pity you can't tell your family about your success. Not yet anyway,' said Jonas.

'They would never believe it,' Ben responded.

'Well whatever happens from here on in, it has been a fantastic morning.' Raising his cup in a deliberately flamboyant manner, he offered a toast to his principal researcher. 'Here's to you and your continued success, Dr Moyles. It could not have happened to a nicer scientist. Cheers.'

Ben could do nothing other than join in. 'Thank you Jonas, I really appreciate it. Don't forget the role you have played in it either. Without your guidance and support I would not have succeeded at all.'

Brandli's good mood continued. 'I think that you deserve to take the rest of the day off. No doubt Professor Thompkins will have some questions for you over the coming days, once he has had a chance to cast his eyes over the data. If he comes looking for you this afternoon I will cover for you. Go and celebrate or relax, whichever you prefer. You've earned it.'

Ben knocked back the remaining mouthful of whisky and enjoyed the kick it gave to his system. Shaking Jonas' hand as he stood, he appreciated the words of congratulations that he had received from a physicist he genuinely respected. Like a man who had just won the Euro Lottery, Ben was unsure what to do or where to go next. He decided to do what he normally did when there was a disconnect between his emotions and his body, he went home and then for a long run. Although his body had already experienced one shot of adrenaline, the afternoon light meant this time he could jog along the country lanes, always his favourite distraction, and he knew this would be a special run. Despite feeling fatigued due to his early start, stressful morning and the five kilometres already under his trainers, this run involved only indulgent joy.

Meanwhile, Thompkins and Thiroud spent their afternoon in Alpha Lab combing through the data printouts on the computers produced by the reactor in the safety cell. Their mood was sombre as the indicators seemed to suggest that Moyles had been right to pursue the density option rather than Thompkins' preferred strategy of focussing on laser heat generation. The Professor was trying to put a positive spin on the results, whereas if it had been his personal success he would have been euphoric.

'It looks as if the capital investment in the Puissance Project will be justified and that should release a lot of pressure for us. I know it's not the result that I had wanted because I was convinced that Alpha Lab was close to a solution. Although the results of this experiment are not yet definitive, we both know that over the coming weeks it can be refined.'

Thiroud realised a more cunning way forward. 'Yes, but do not forget that your name and Puissance are inextricably linked. When this becomes known to the world, it is the name Professor Ian Thompkins, Nobel Prize Winner that everyone will associate with this success, not some upstart. Don't forget that you also control everything that is associated with Puissance. No one can go to the media or make claims without your approval. The intricacies of the confidentiality clause in every researcher's contract fall within your remit. The wording is very specific in that regard. The publication of any research emanating from this international trial can only have your name on it, no matter who achieves the actual breakthrough. When we have refined Dr Moyles' reactor he will not be able to do anything with the findings no matter how upset he might get about it. Only *you* will be able to write any research papers or give lectures on the subject. When the media frenzy begins you will be at the vanguard, dear sir. Of that I am absolutely sure.'

A half-smile crossed Thompkins' face as he realised the implications of what his assistant was saying. It was he who held the power and there was nothing that Ben Moyles could do about it without breaking his contract. If he broke the terms of his original agreement it would mean one employee having to face up to the power of the world's greatest scientist at Puissance and risk being made bankrupt. It would be very easy to defame such a lowly individual as a researcher who was making claims above his station. Ian Thompkins was just the man to steamroller anyone who got in his way to fame.

After combing his wet hair and changing into some clean clothes, Ben was ready for an enjoyable evening. It had been a good day and was about to get even better with dinner at his favourite restaurant. Ben subconsciously and repeatedly tapped the steering wheel as he drove towards the Swiss border and the St Genis crossing, while the CD-player boomed out some of his favourite music. Once he was through the frontier check-point it was only another half-an-hour to the Italian restaurant. For Veronique, the journey was shorter and involved less hassle as her apartment was only just outside Geneva city centre.

Ben knew it was going to be difficult containing his success but understood the reasons for secrecy. However, he allowed himself to quietly luxuriate with the inner glow of achievement which he had been striving for ever since moving to France. There was no need to tell Veronique anything about his work, she already knew that he was involved in something confidential. Just as the familiar waiter was bringing a bottle of champagne and ice-bucket to Ben's table, Veronique entered with perfect timing. Ben's welcoming *faire la bise* developed into a kiss of passion.

'Wow, so that is what I've been missing,' said Veronique as the waiter averted his eyes before escorting her top-coat to the cloakroom. 'Champagne ! Are we celebrating something?' she inquired.

'Yes, we are – being together once again after a painful time apart.'

'Painful, *mon cheri*,?'

'Yes, of course. I have missed you.' Veronique was just about to add something when Ben put his finger to her lips. 'Before you say anything further, I just want to apologise for the other night when I had to cancel our dinner at your apartment.' She went to speak again but once more she was silenced by her escort. 'Ah.. no.. I suspect I upset you and if I did then I am truly sorry. …Pax?'

'Pax, you darling man.' This time it was Veronique's turn to offer a sensual kiss.

The waiter returned to de-cork the champagne and just as he was about to pour, Ben waved him away. It did not take a great deal of insight for the worker to realise that his presence was not required and he should return to the table only when passions had cooled a little. The attendant's disgruntled walk back to his station suggested that he did not like feeling superfluous to requirements. Ben poured the rapidly escaping champagne into Veronique's flute glass before filling his own. Once the bubbles had subsided he topped up the amount to a more generous portion, before raising his glass and offering *'A ta santé'*. Veronique chinked their flutes together and playfully accepted his toast. Eventually the waiter returned and after their three courses disappeared along with the rest of the champagne, they were ready to leave. Suitably buoyant and relaxed, the courting pair stepped out into the fresh, still air and began to walk back to Ben's car. The conversation soon turned to another aspect of their relationship.

'My place?' inquired Veronique, hoping for an affirmative response.

'Why not?' There had been a time when he had questioned Veronique's credentials but it had been such a great day that he could not resist going one step further. Within the hour Ben and Veronique were engaged in fervid sex and he realised what he had been missing for the last month. She had captured his passion, though not yet his heart.

The next morning Ben knew that his day in work would be raised to the next level and it did not take him long to find out what that entailed. As soon as he registered at reception, the security guard informed him that he should go straight to Alpha Lab and report to Professor Thompkins no less. New situations were picking up faster that Ben was dropping them and the whole aura around him suggested this was his time. Finally, he was beginning to realise that good things were happening. On arrival at his boss's reception suite his personal assistant Christelle flicked a switch on her ear-set and after a brief interaction she invited Ben to proceed through to Thompkins' office.

Ben was surprised to find two other guests already ensconced with the Head of Puissance and he recognised one of the faces. Captain Durand half-turned as Ben entered the room and he assumed the detective had driven over from Police Headquarters at Bourg-en-Bresse. In fact he had travelled directly from his home in Nantua, a small French town at the base of a limestone escarpment, located about halfway between Sergy and Bourg-en-Bresse. Ben did not recognise the other man, a more polished individual who was wearing an expensive suit with equally exclusive shoes that were next to his bright red attaché case. The two men remained seated while Thompkins rose from behind his desk to make the introductions.

'Ah, Ben good morning.' Glancing down at his two other guests he continued, 'This is *Ministres* Armand who oversees the *General Directorate for Internal Security* and Captain Durand who I believe you already know.' The two men rose from their seats and shook Ben's hand, the senior official making a more determined, crisp effort than his counterpart. Thompkins had everyone's attention. 'I have asked *Ministres* Armand and Captain Durand to come along this morning to conduct a major overhaul of security within the Puissance Complex. As you know Ben …'

He was absolutely astounded, *'Wow, he's actually calling me Ben in front of other senior professionals. Somebody slap me!'*

' … there was an attempt at a major security breach at your apartment and as we have since discovered, also at the homes of two other key researchers.' This was news to Ben, he had not been the only one to have had his home violated. 'We would almost certainly not have discovered the extent of this intrusion without the due diligence of Dr Moyles.'

'More compliments !'

'Although we have not had cause to question if this duplicity has gone still further, we cannot take any further risk. This is particularly the case following our recent historic discovery at Puissance. I have explained this at length to key members within the French Government, who are aware of our situation at the highest level possible.'

Ben could not help interrupting. 'You mean the *Président* is aware of our work?'

'Yes, Dr Moyles – that is exactly what I mean. The importance of what we are doing and the ramifications of our discovery have implications for the whole of the civilized world. We cannot take any chances, so we must make significant changes.' Ben was wondering what Thompkins was going to come out with next. All the time he was talking, the Minister was exploring text on his mobile while Durand's gaze did not leave the Professor's face.

'There is going to be a major overhaul of our security systems at every level. This will ensure beyond any doubt that our secret work will remain just that. It is vital at this early stage of our discovery that our enemies do not sabotage our development. The *Président* himself has plans to raise this issue in the New Year at the UN Economic and Social Council when the eyes of the world will be on us. These are glorious times gentlemen and we must be prepared.' Ben could not help but try to detect whether Thompkins' chest actually puffed out as he spoke with such pomposity. For the first time he also became suspicious about his boss's use of the word *'our'*. He had so far failed to acknowledge to anyone outside the Radioactive Zone that the discovery was the work of one of his researchers, namely one Dr Benjamin Moyles.

Ben wanted some answers to some of the questions fizzing around in his head. 'When will this overhaul begin Professor?'

'It will start later today. Captain Durand and his team will begin scanning key areas of Puissance immediately. He will manage the vetting procedure and liaise with our own security team then report back to myself and *Ministres* Armand.

'What about our own personal security? How do we ensure that we are not at risk ourselves?'

'Well for the next two months we will be under police protection. We will be moved to safe houses for our own safety and for the next two months our movements will be restricted. We will review the position after that.'

Ben was becoming concerned. 'But you can't expect us to hide for that length of time, surely?'

'I absolutely understand what you are saying Ben, but this discovery is huge. Certain agencies would not hesitate to resort to any means, violent or otherwise, to nip this discovery in the bud. At the moment only a few individuals are aware of the situation. Hence the need to maintain secrecy. Once our trials are concluded and the results are refined under my supervision, we can publish the discovery to the scientific world and the general public. At that point others will be aware of what it means and it will no longer be a secret. We can then relax our personal security and begin to live normal lives again or at least as normal as they are going to be following our discovery. These are only going to be temporary arrangements, for a month or two at most, if all goes well.'

Ben still needed some reassurances. 'As you know, my own apartment was the subject of a security breach in the last few weeks. How safe is my place going to be?'

Thompkins was luxuriating in his role as leader, enjoying every aspect of being in control. 'I've already thought of that Dr Moyles. You will be moved somewhere safer, where it will be easier to police. Only a few people will be aware of your new location. I will do the same, as will Dr Sebastian Thiroud and Dr Jonas Brandli.'

Ben was becoming irritated. 'Supposing I don't want to go? Perhaps I don't like the idea of becoming a prisoner all of a sudden. What then?'

For the first time, *Ministres* Armand interjected and imposed his seniority and political gravitas onto the discussion. 'You have no choice Dr Moyles. These directives come from the *Présidents'* Office itself. We cannot take risks, either with what's at stake personally for you and the other members of the Puissance Project or what we are risking in the international community. If this work was to fall into the wrong hands the results could be catastrophic. I repeat what Professor Thompkins has just said. These are only temporary measures.'

'But what happens if I want to phone someone or go out to meet a friend. Is this not permissible?'

The Minister once again had a solution that allowed no wriggle room. 'We have already thought of that. You will receive a new mobile with a collection of SIM cards. After each call you will destroy the used card and replace it with a new one. You must never make two calls with the same card. That way it cannot be traced. Similarly if you notify Captain Durand here that you wish to leave the safe house, you must inform him beforehand where you are going and appropriate security will be provided. I recognise these measures may seem draconian but they are better than the alternative, as I'm sure you agree.'

Ben did not have an answer and he sensed that it was a case of the bigger the discovery, the greater the risk so he decided to go along with the arrangements.

Within the hour Ben had returned to his apartment, accompanied by an entourage of police intent on helping him move some personal possessions. The high profile police presence attracted some local attention and certainly did not evade Antoine's notice. The old man stood at his open doorway trying to attract anyone's attention in an attempt to elicit information about what was going on. A uniformed policeman walked past and the old man took his opportunity, 'Who is in charge 'ere … can someone please tell me what is happening.' His appeal was brushed aside and on hearing Antoine's voice as he descended the stairs Ben was able to put him out of his misery.

'Hello Antoine, how are you ?' His neighbour did not have to say anything in response as Ben could recognise from his body language the signs of stress. 'Do not worry old friend, they are simply helping me to move.'

'What! You are leaving ? ...why, where are you going?'

'I am moving somewhere safer for now, but I shall return before Christmas if all goes well.'

'Is this to do with that break-in you had recently? Was my nephew involved in this ? If he was I will ...'

Antoine did not have a chance to finish his sentence. Ben curtailed their conversation with further words of reassurance. 'No, it is nothing like that. It is simply something to do with work. Before you know it I shall be back in my apartment and sharing some more of your lovely Napoleon brandy. Make sure you do not drink it all my friend.' Offering his hand he simply added '*Au bientot*.'

Ben then turned away as his friend leant against the frame of the open doorway still perplexed at proceedings. Before he had a chance to ask any further questions, his young, clever friend disappeared in a car cavalcade. The sound of the engines made Antoine realise that he had no contact details for Ben and he shuffled across the passageway to try and catch his neighbour before he left but he was too late. The frenetic activity generated by the move had caused Antoine to forget to ask for a forwarding address. In the time taken to open a bottle, his friend had gone.

Ben was sitting in the back seat of the middle car of three police vehicles, the last one containing his personal effects. Thompkins had assured him that he would be escorted to work in the short-term and would not need to drive anywhere. It was all related to the extra measures which were going to be applied over the next couple of months. There was going to be a major difference to his lifestyle and his personal security was going to be much tighter, at least in the short term. Ben was not sure whether to be excited or unnerved by what was taking place. The mixture of emotions was too heady a cocktail to drink easily.

The cars were driven through a large, open metal gate that was the entrance to a country lane. The armed officer positioned at the entrance of what appeared to be some sort of private mansion saluted as the vehicles passed at speed. When they were out of sight the minor official closed the entrance once more and continued to act as intimidating as his salary would allow. Ben had never become used to seeing armed policemen. In the Cheviot Hills communities rarely saw any member of the local constabulary and when they did there was more likelihood of a smile than a bullet. The scrunching noise of the cars pulling up on the gravel drive outside a magnificent looking chateau could be heard by anyone within a stone throwing distance and it was clear that they had arrived at their destination. During the journey Ben had tried to work out where they were going. It had only taken about thirty minutes but they had headed south, away from the Swiss border. The chateau was isolated between the villages of Mordex and Choudans at the foot of the Jura Mountains and just outside the line of villages that sprinkled the base of the escarpment. Although access was good, the place was very isolated and as it was surrounded by woodland it was ideal for the task.

Ben entered the wooden hallway, his shoes tapping on the hard surface, offering a half-echo by way of comfort. There was little indication of anyone else living in the place and Captain Durand was already waiting inside the large reception room, which had several landscape oil paintings on the most prominent walls. There were three mounted, stuffed heads in one corner of the chamber and at some point in the past a keen huntsman must have resided in this large manor house. The macabre setting was not Ben's idea of a game's room and the glazed eyes of the two wild boar and a majestically horned stag did little to add to the warmth of the place. Durand invited Ben to sit on an immaculately upholstered chair and gave his charge the low-down on the living arrangements. It was a task that the policeman felt was below his pay-scale and it did not sit comfortably on the shoulders of a man who had encountered significantly greater dangers.

Half the mansion was already sealed-off with locked doors and the furniture inside the rooms covered by dust sheets. Ben's accommodation was on the middle floor, where there was a well-maintained, modern kitchen with all the gadgets he needed. His warm bedroom was just off a corridor adjacent to living quarters where there was a television and a desk if he needed to work. Security was based on the lower sections and the outside grounds were patrolled by a specialist, armed team which contained uniformed and plain clothes officials. To a lad from the sticks it all seemed somewhat over-the-top but he recognised that this was a new arena he had just entered and life needed to change accordingly. Captain Durand explained that although this particular chateau was not known to him, to the government officials it was very familiar. The place had been used in the past to house vulnerable informers and foreign defectors and its location was known only to a few, on a need-to-know basis.

As the two men sat opposite each other, one talking the other listening intently, Durand began to explain the way the plan would work. His monotonous voice was reminiscent of their meeting in Bourg-en-Bresse and Ben sensed he was beginning to lose concentration as the Inspector droned on about the tedium of the domestic arrangements. Eventually everything was explained and Durand pointed towards a policeman who was standing in the open doorway before adding, 'Officer Savoie will help you to bring in your possessions from the van and you will have time to settle in. Tomorrow a car will take you into work where I presume you and Professor Thompkins will be able to continue with whatever it is you are doing. There is no need to worry about anything. You will hardly notice us here at all. Do you have any questions?'

'Yes I do, actually. What happens if I want to go out or socialise with friends. What happens then. I don't intend to be a prisoner in this place for the rest of my life.'

'It will not be for the rest of your life, monsieur. As I understand it, our brief is to supply security for a few key personnel for up to two months. You are one of those personnel. If you wish to see friends they can be brought here to you. If you wish to go out anywhere – to a restaurant, the home of a friend .. that sort of thing.. you must inform me personally at least twenty-four hours in advance. I will consider your request and inform you if it can be approved. I must remind you however, Dr Moyles that my instructions come from the very highest level in our Government. While I am not privy to the details of your work, I am aware that it is of the greatest level of importance to everyone here in France. For that reason alone, I and my officers will take no risks with your safety – at least for the next two months. After that, who knows….?' The Gaelic shrug was typically French, even from a small man almost disappearing into a large chair. There was nothing else Ben could do but accept his temporary fate. At least his working days would continue as usual. The more he thought about it, the more excitement began to replace anxiety. Ben smiled consciously at Officer Savoie and the two men headed towards the van outside.

Across the border in Switzerland, Zenib was focussing on the monitor screens from the safety of his 'factory' location. Something unusual had been brought to his attention by one of his overpaid minions. The VDUs showed that a group of about five men and two women were moving along the various corridors of the Puissance labs and they were carrying equipment which looked familiar. The troupe seemed to have a common purpose and the speed of their actions suggested that they were experienced in whatever it was they were doing. It did not take long for the thought to register, they were scanning the rooms looking for breaches in security. Zenib began watching their work with cold concern. Mayhem seemed to ensue when the cluster entered the conference room where Ben had upset Professor Thompkins a few weeks earlier.

A fudged face filled the entire monitor screen and stared without awareness directly into Zenib's eyes. As the look was returned with anonymous anger one of the light switches became a source of interest to the interested observer. A second distorted image waved a probe over that part of the conference room and then suddenly the VDU went blank. Zenib's anger began to vulcanise when slowly and efficiently each display unit turned into a picture of oblivion as the security team discovered one-by-one the items of his sordid little secret. Eventually and quickly every picture on the wall monitors disappeared as Zenib's surveillance of Puissance secrets was discovered. Suddenly Zenib roared with anger, simultaneously sweeping everything off the desk in a grotesque outburst of frustrated rage. Others in the room looked at each other in startled fear. One of the men in the firing line jumped out of his seat, his actions generated by a sense of self-preservation. The workers looked at the seeming destruction of a soul as Zenib continued to lose any semblance of control. 'Get out !...get out! … all of you get out.' He looked directly at their terrified expressions. 'I told you what to do… now do it… or I'll shoot every single one of you.' Seeing Zenib's hand move inside to his holster they did not need to be asked again. Jackets were swept off the backs of chairs and the group jostled for the speediest route out of the factory. This was not a time to hang around, a thought that was reinforced by the banging, swearing and smashing of equipment that could be heard by the terrified workers as they headed for their cars and the safety beyond.

Zenib's arms were stretched and rigid as he gripped the edge of a table covered in sprinkles of shattered glass. He knew he would need a plan of action and retribution to submit to Connolly, if for no other reason than his own self-preservation. All the signs seemed to suggest that Puissance had made some sort of breakthrough. He would need to consult with his informant on the inside before meeting anyone else. What Zenib did know was the whole project had been upgraded. Whatever actions were needed from that moment would require a fresh level of ruthlessness. The anger that Zenib was feeling could only be sated by an act of indulgent violence.

IX

The quartet of scientists headed from Thompkins' office towards Alpha Lab with a sense of purpose. The Professor had Thiroud grovelling at his heels, while Ben and Jonas Brandli followed, excited at the prospect of beginning something new. They shared a sense of history, on the verge of discovering a new epoch of scientific energy comparable to the development of steam power by James Watt almost three centuries earlier. Whereas to the layman and schoolboy Watt's image of watching a lifting kettle lid explained his discovery of steam power, scientists knew it was really because he introduced a separate condenser to an existing engine. Similarly, the Puissance project was doing more than extracting sustainable energy from sea water. The controlled nuclear fusion involved using complex variations of heat and pressure to distribute neutrons of hydrogen and transfer the energy source without losing any power. Dr Ben Moyles had made the step possible by introducing sophisticated techniques involving metallic hydrogen and powerful magnetic forces. The four men were now about to embark on processes that would refine his methods. The outcome could change the world's balance of political and economic influence for the foreseeable future.

One half of Alpha Lab had been cordoned off to everyone except the top team. If extra labour or insight was needed, trusted personnel were to be introduced gradually on a need-to-know basis. This was top secret work and it would begin by following the thread of success arising from Ben's experiment. The small group was gathered around several monitors, some of which were connected to an interactive whiteboard. Ben began to navigate his way around his constellation of data while the others watched as the numbers, graphs and virtual reality animations unfolded Ben's intellect. They sat silently hypnotised by the demonstration of frolicking data, sometimes glancing at the mini-reactor positioned to Ben's left.

Occasionally he strode over to point to various parts of the apparatus to explain how his theory was tested in the real world. Thompkins pitched in with one or two questions for clarity, usually followed by a variation on the same theme by Thiroud, overly keen to demonstrate support for his master.

'I think the problem lies with the metallic hydrogen conductor,' Ben claimed in the summary of his exposition. 'There was no doubt that the energy being generated within the reactor was still active but equally it was becoming less powerful over time. This is clearly shown by the data – here.' He used a laser pen to point towards the whiteboard at downward trending line graphs, decreasing bar heights and smaller slices on various pie charts. 'Granted, producing any sustainable energy to the point where it has lasted virtually a month represents a huge shift forward. There is no doubt that the progress was also due to pursuing the theme of extra pressure rather than trying to concentrate on lasers and heat.' Ben glanced towards Thompkins and for a moment thought he saw him physically flinch, although he acknowledged to himself that it might have been his wishful imagination playing tricks. However, there was no doubting Thiroud's icy stare.

Ben continued, 'I think if we can remove the miniscule impurities in the metallic hydrogen we can increase the sustainability of our power source. With the brains we have in this room right now, I believe we can improve these ideas to the point where the energy can be produced continuously using clean sources.' Ben looked at the silent trio, waiting for a reaction. He had been on his feet, leading the way for two hours, occasionally taking sips of water but giving his all in an attempt to impress his superiors. Thompkins tapped his fingers on the table's surface to indicate his appreciation of a job well done. Jonas Brandli was more generous offering un-constrained applause, while Thiroud feigned a cough as an excuse to do something else with his hands.

Thompkins was the first to speak, using his authority as the lead scientist within Puissance. 'Congratulations, Ben this has been sterling work, really first-class. As I see it, we now need to address the problems with hydrogen purity and see how we can increase levels of pressure and also generate more heat using lasers.' Ben could only think to himself at that stage, *'For God's sake, give it up man. You have just seen how a successful experiment has avoided using lasers. Just accept you are wrong.'*

The rest of the working day was spent pouring over the data, figure by figure, occasionally returning to the mini-reactor and teasing out various possibilities before deciding the best way forward. Ben estimated that it would take at least another two weeks before they would be at the stage of re-running the experiment with improvements. He knew it would be intense and exhausting work but the prize was too great to let anything get in the way.

At 7.00 p.m. it was time to call it a day and the Professor drew matters to a conclusion. 'Right gentlemen – it is time to go home. We have made a start, an encouraging beginning I believe. We shall return tomorrow and the next day, and the next, until we are all in agreement that we are ready to go once more. Then we shall engage the reactor and with my added expertise I have no doubt that we shall this time achieve real success. I say goodnight to you all and look forward to beginning work again in the morning. Shall we say, meet in my office at 8.00 a.m. prompt for another exchange, yes?' There was no attempt by anyone to challenge Thompkins' direction as it made sense. So with handshakes all round, the four men separated, each one heading to his new destination, known only to the Professor and the security authorities.

Ben's driver was waiting for him just outside the main entrance. This was the second professional courtesy within Puissance indicative of his newly acquired status. Becoming familiar with the inside of Thomkin's office and working with a small team of the top scientists within Alpha Lab had given Ben his first taste of professional exclusivity and he liked the feeling. The driver saluted and introduced himself as Claude, who Ben learned later was a bodyguard trained by French elite forces. Claude emanated the sort of physical, silent assurance that was ideal for the situation and Ben knew that he certainly would not like to mix it with his new friend. If his bulging biceps bursting from within the expensive suit did not convince anyone to stay away, then the extra tailoring that was needed to accommodate his Glock 17 would do the trick.

Claude took a different route to return to the chateau, something else that was to become a familiar routine. For security reasons it was important to vary their itinerary each day. The special forces knew more than Ben about the dangers involved when the stakes were high and were taking no chances. What Ben did not see was another car following him and Claude each day. This contained two more agents shadowing behind, on the off-chance that they were needed if their charge, codename *Giroflée* (Wallflower) was in danger. All four scientists were subjected to the same security protocols in their different locations. Only Jonas Brandli had a family to consider and they were provided with safety measures all of their own.

The expressionless face of Jacques Durand was also something destined to become familiar within the confines of the chateau. When Ben arrived back at his new home, the Captain was watching from the other side of the gravel driveway scanning the scene, looking for any threatening signs of danger. To Durand this particular bout of duty was a serious but onerous task which could only disrupt his final year of service before he could forget about everything and return to becoming a normal human being once more. He caught Ben's gaze as he alighted from the car and stood arms folded, looking discreetly authoritative.

The kitchen was well stocked and Ben set about making himself something to eat. As he busied himself with the microwave and saucepan, his mind wandered towards his family. It was about time he gave them another call to check-up on Rich's progress. The last time he had spoken with his father, things seemed ok, his brother was making slow but steady progress and was becoming more used to doing fewer onerous tasks on the farm. Joe Setherton Junior did not mind that too much as he had begun to experience more time and extra responsibility on Moyles Farm. Ben recognised there was a greater onus on him to make more calls home, now that he was technically uncontactable.

Ben's new living quarters were comfortable and functional, although he suspected after a few days of confinement he would start to go a little stir crazy. A saving grace was to become the early morning runs with two of the security men in attendance. They also liked to keep themselves fit and their competitive edge added an extra dimension to Ben's normally leisurely runs. Like the journeys to work, each day the routine was changed – just in case. The working days were similarly 'groundhog' in nature with constant tweaking of statistics and examination of data, all under the expert supervision of the almighty Professor Thompkins. Ben felt guilty about the truncation of contact with Camille and Gaston but he suspected they may have picked up some awareness of the situation by virtue of their familiarity with Sebastian Thiroud. He had no reason to think this was the case but wishful thinking was beginning to be another friend.

Of course there was also Veronique. After a couple of weeks of phone calls but without any physical contact with his partner, Ben was becoming more uncomfortable, in all sorts of ways. The security arrangements seemed to be working: progress was being made at work, there were no signs of any attempts to find out where he had moved to, and he was still able to make contact with the outside world. Ben was not used to being confined in this manner and it was inevitable that he would attempt to break the cycle. The arrangements may have been convenient for Puissance but there were becoming a frustration to Ben. However, events took a turn for the worse when Jacques Durand suddenly appeared at the entrance to Alpha Lab and asked to speak with Dr Moyles. The quartet of scientists had not yet left Thompkins' office and their early morning briefing was still under way.

Ben looked surprised when the receptionist rang through and he was informed of the policeman's presence. The receptionist tried to look busy while eavesdropping on their conversation but the Inspector was too experienced to be deceived by such a primitive ploy and he escorted Ben away from the area to a more discreet location. Ben's surprise turned to stunned attention as everything about the policeman's behaviour suggested something serious had happened. His first thoughts turned towards the health of his brother. Durand was his usual platonic self as he disclosed to Ben that his neighbour, namely one Monsieur Antoine Moreau had been found first thing that morning lying in the doorway of his flat. He had apparently dragged himself towards the entrance after having been severely assaulted, presumably in the early hours. Durand wanted to know if Ben could think of anyone who had a grievance against the old man.

Ben's response was predictable. 'Where is he? I want to see him!'

'I'm sorry monsieur, but I cannot allow that. He is in hospital and the last I heard he was unconscious so there is no point in you even being there.'

However, nothing was going to get in Ben's way. 'I don't care if you cannot *allow* it, I'm going and there's nothing you can do to stop me. I don't know how you treat your friends here in this part of France but where I come from when the time comes to show that you care, you do it. So either take me to see my old friend or get out of my way.' As Ben attempted to step forward, the policeman moved to the side and stood in his way. There was an uncomfortable few seconds of silence between them before Durand relented and stood aside. 'Ok, monsieur but at least allow me to accompany you to the hospital.' The Inspector's analysis of the situation convinced him there was very little danger involved in allowing Ben to visit Antoine Moreau. He also thought the old man may even tell Ben something that he was either unable or unwilling to disclose to the police.

Within half an hour Ben and Durand accompanied by a second car containing two armed detectives arrived at *Local Hospital Du Pays De Gex* and were soon at Antoine's hospital bedside. The old man had a badly split lip and swollen right eye and at least two broken ribs. He had taken a severe beating and was under sedation when Ben arrived, a saline drip attached to a vein in his right hand.

'Who would do something like this?' pleaded Ben, who was upset at the sight of his friend. 'He's an old man who wouldn't hurt anyone. What possible motive could anyone have for attacking someone as vulnerable as him?'

Durand moved his hand up to his chin as he unfolded his arms to give his assessment of the situation. 'Well, there are several motives we can rule out straight away. Clearly, it was not theft or a crime of passion. In my view whoever attacked your friend was trying to gain information. I am assuming you did not give him your new address or tell him where you had moved to?'

Ben did not like the veiled insult about his level of discretion. 'Of course not. When I last saw him I did not even *know* where I was moving to. Even now I am not sure of the actual address.' At that moment Antoine began to stir and was clearly in distress so Ben bent down close, took his hand and began whispering words of comfort in the old man's ear. 'It's alright my friend. We shall find who did this and they shall be punished. You are safe now.'

Antoine attempted to speak but his words were lost amongst the painful mumblings of his injuries. Ben gave it another try. 'What is it Antoine, what are you trying to say?'

In the faintest of whispers and with Ben's face only inches away, the old man whispered, 'I did not tell them, *mon ami*. I did not tell them anything or give them her address.

'Whose address Antoine? Who were they looking for?' The question accompanied Antoine into the sanctuary of sleep, as the old man's hand squeezed Ben's finger and he returned to silence.

Ben and Durand looked at each other as they stood beside the hospital bed, both pondering possible reasons for the assault. It did not take long for Ben to offer his analysis and his voice trembled as he tried to mask his state of panic. 'Good God, Antoine must have been talking about Veronique!'

Durand's detective brain engaged, 'What does he know about her – does he know her address?'

'No, I don't think so, although he does know she works in a bank somewhere in Geneva.'

Durand's response did not exactly allay Ben's fears. 'In that case, it would not take them long to find her given the resources they seem to have at their disposal. They clearly want to know your new location and have realised their anonymity may have been compromised with the discovery of the surveillance equipment. We must find her before they do monsieur. Quickly, we must go to Geneva. I will contact the Swiss authorities and seek their co-operation in locating her present whereabouts.'

There was a frantic dash from the hospital to Geneva, twenty kilometres away. The journey was shortened considerably by the flashing blue lights and honking French police sirens persuading the traffic to pull over to the side of the road. Following Ben's instructions they found the Schtern Bank quickly, arriving shortly after the cantonal police cars. The local police had been alerted by the Swiss Federal Office. Gaston Dubois was waiting at the doorway of his office, alerted by the sirens and the apparent chaos in reception. Ben was the first to speak. 'Where is Veronique, Gaston? She should be here shouldn't she?'

Gaston was his usual, calm and aloof self, not easily moved out of his comfort zone. 'Hello Ben. Is everything alright? Are the police with *you*?'

Ben was way past offering social niceties to his friend. 'Never mind me, Gaston. Where is Veronique?'

Dubois responded as if it was not his concern. 'She's not at work today. One of her friends phoned earlier and said she was sick. Damned inconvenient actually. I was …'

Ben was still in determined mode. 'Friend. What friend? What is the name of this *friend*?' Gaston looked towards Veronique's agency replacement for support but received nothing other than a blank expression. Ben turned to Durand who was happy to be guided by his charge. 'We need to go to her apartment straight away and make sure she's alright. C'mon we need to go now!'

The navy blue entourage left the bank almost as quickly as it had arrived, this time heading out of the centre of Geneva towards Veronique's apartment. Once again the attention-seeking cars were defaulted into their emergency honks and fastest wings. It was about ten minutes before they arrived at Veronique's place. Anyone still lingering around any potential crime scene would have heard the commotion and scarpered accordingly. The door to the flat was open and had been forced. Durand ushered Ben behind him as he removed his holster and silently directed his first assistant forward to inspect inside the flat, with uniformed officers in close attendance. Spinning into the kitchen the professional's reflexes indicated no persons present, though there had clearly been some sort of disruption. They crept further down the hallway, hand-guns at the ready before Durand called out. 'This is the police! If there is anyone in here, declare yourself now.' Everyone stood still, some praying for a response but there was no immediate answer. 'We have the flat surrounded and you have no chance of escape so come out with your hands above your head.' Still nothing.

Then Ben heard a low level groan coming from Veronique's bedroom. Without any consideration for his own personal safety or a semblance of awareness for professional protocol he pushed past the cautious line of police and darted into the room. Alarmed and embarrassed by his fearless actions he was closely and swiftly followed by two armed officers. Veronique was lying on the floor, hair bedraggled, blouse torn open and holding a bloody nose. She seemed completely disorientated but at least she was conscious. Ben quickly went over to her and tried to offer words of comfort, as he had done with Antoine. He was sitting on the floor holding his partner in his arms, trying to console a distraught Veronique, whose whole body was shaking.

'Who did this to you, my darling ?' Without waiting for a response he continued, 'Don't worry, you are safe now.'

Captain Durand offered some further words of reassurance. 'An ambulance is on its way, mademoiselle. It will be here immediately. Can you give a description of who assaulted you?'

This was a step too far for Ben. 'Not now, Durand. Can you not see that she is too upset to answer your questions? We must see to her injuries before we can try to get to the bottom of this.'

However, Veronique was more co-operative than Ben had anticipated. She mustered some strength and looked directly into Ben's eyes. 'They were asking me where you lived, where you had moved to … but I could not tell them and they did not believe me. I think they believed me … eventually.'

At that moment the paramedics arrived and saw to Veronique's immediate needs before she was lifted onto a stretcher and whisked off to Geneva's University Hospital. Ben wanted to go with her but was prevented by Jacques Durand who maintained that it might play into the hands of her assailants if his attendance was exposed. 'We have established a routine to protect your safety, monsieur and it works. Whoever is trying to get to you is becoming desperate. We must go back and then we can talk about ways that you can see Mademoiselle Perrin but on our terms. Right now we have to get you out of here without anyone seeing us. Rest assured that your girlfriend is ok and has not been seriously injured. I suspect if they had wanted to inflict serious harm on her, they would have done.'

This made sense to Ben: Veronique was safe and she was going to be protected by an armed guard in hospital. There was no reason to suspect that the perpetrators would return, at least not in the immediate future. The way events were unravelling, things could change pretty quickly. Whoever was trying to get to Ben would then have to assume a different tack. Durand called through his radio for three police cars to be made available and to meet him and Ben in the residents' underground car park.

'They will let us know when they think it is safe to make our way out and head back to the manor house. I do not think it is a good idea to return to the Puissance complex today. We can assume a different routine tomorrow. Professor Thompkins and the other scientists will just have to do without you today, Dr Moyles.'

The policeman's summary was accepted with silence and the two men were left alone in the bedroom of Veronique's flat, pondering events and trying to make sense of it all. Ben allowed his thoughts to ramble. 'I don't understand what is going on. First Antoine, now Veronique and for what? Why this need for violence and why are they trying to get at me? I am not the only scientist working on the Puissance project but they seem to be focussing all their efforts in attempting to get to me.'

Durand had spent more time thinking about that question than Ben had given him credit for. 'There can only be one reason *monsieur*. Whoever is doing this must know that the scientists here in Sergy are on the verge of a discovery and that it is the product of *your* work, *your* knowledge. Therefore, it must be someone who knows you, someone close to you. They must have someone on the inside who is working for them. So, we need to work back from the day of your discovery and consider the people who are aware that you have made this breakthrough, whatever it is. Whoever did this today – they are not the people we want. The CCTV may show us something but I doubt it.

We must also step up our current level of security. I understand from Professor Thompkins that you are at the stage of running the next phase. I want you to think of the actions of those around you and consider whether anyone close to you has started acting out of character. Give serious thought to anyone or anything that you think is suspicious.'

At that moment a message came through on the Captain's earpiece reporting that the police were ready in the basement car park so the heavily protected duo made their getaway and headed out of Geneva and back to the safety of the chateau.

X

The chauffeured limousine with darkened windows pulled up at the end of a dirt track overlooking Lake Geneva. Zenib had been waiting for its arrival and as soon as the engine was switched off he made his way out of the small copse and headed for the car. Adam Connolly was sitting in the rear passenger seat with the indifference that can only accompany a colossal level of arrogance because he did not even look up from his laptop.

'So my friend, what can you tell me? You owe me some good news so I hope you have some.'

Zenib felt confident but only because things had progressed and he had something positive to report. 'Yes, Mr Connolly. We know what has been going on inside the Puissance Research Centre and I am pretty sure we know how to stop it. That young scientist I was telling you about …' Connolly looked straight at Zenib and raised his eyebrows as an aid to recollection, before nodding in affirmation. Zenib continued, 'His name is Moyles, Dr Ben Moyles. Well it seems they think he has made some sort of breakthrough.'

'Breakthrough?' The question was more of an accusation than an inquiry.

'Yes, while he was away during the summer he had left an experiment running and when he returned it seems as if it was successful. They are currently trying to refine the project though there is no evidence they have yet succeeded.'

Connolly looked out of the window, absorbing the information he was being given. 'Well it's up to you to make sure they don't succeed. That's what I pay you for.'

'There are four main scientists working on it now. The only trouble is that since their discovery they have been placed in secret locations. We are trying to find out where their new living quarters are but the French security services have become involved and have tightened everything so no one's talking. We are focussing on Moyles and trying to get to him. I think we are pretty close. At least we know enough not to waste our efforts on anyone else. He appears to be leading a team and my sources tell me they are about to initiate another test. If it works they will go public.'

'What sources are we talking about here?' Connolly showed very few outwards signs of stress, though given the high pitch stakes involved it had to be more of an act than a genuine state of mind. 'AC' did not want to report any threatening developments arising from the research at Puissance to the Head of Security Committee on the Arab Oil Producing Countries. The people they were all serving did not take kindly to failure, though no one knew the identity of Connolly's real paymasters. The power of the people backing him was to be feared.

'We have someone on the inside who is giving us the information we need. As long as this pathway remains open, we are in control. We should know where they are hiding this Moyles character in the very near future. My plan is working.'

'Good ... very good my dear Zenib. Keep me informed and make sure you succeed. We all have a lot to gain but also a lot to lose. And I don't like losing.' This was the time to leave no doubt about what he meant as he looked menacingly into the depth of Zenib's eyes. 'If you understand what I am saying?'

Zenib showed no signs of disagreeing and as Connolly returned his gaze to his laptop, he simultaneously flicked his left wrist. Zenib took this as his signal to leave.

There was a possibility that the experiment would finally be initiated but the decision belonged to Professor Thompkins. The next stage had even been given a code name to mark its authority. It carried the name *Aion* after the Hellenistic deity for unbounded time, another reflection of the lead scientist's pomposity. Ben was clicking his heels in the chateau's driveway, shuffling around bits of gravel with the toe of his shoe while waiting for Durand to show his face. Eventually the policeman appeared and before he had a chance to volunteer anything Ben was at him. 'How is Veronique? I hope you have called the hospital this morning and made arrangements for her safety.'

Although miffed at the insinuation about his professional competence, Durand retained his calm persona. '*Oui,* monsieur. Everything has been arranged, she was discharged from hospital early this morning and is now recovering from her ordeal in a safe house, or rather a safe apartment. A female officer is with her at this very moment. However, I do not expect her assailants to return. Whatever they did or did not find out has clearly been assuaged. I would expect that Mademoiselle Perrin will be able to return to her own apartment within the next couple of days.

'Have you been able to identify anything from the CCTV?' asked Ben with a certain amount of anxiety.

'Only that it appears that there were two men. Both were wearing face masks and knew their way around the cameras. The masks were very professional, the sort of thing that pranksters on modern television programmes use. It seems to be the case that whoever is behind all this subterfuge does not the lack resources nor access to the most potent of strategies.'

Ben stretched his lips in agreement with the Captain's assessment. It was time to set off for Puissance and he made no further inquiries. He entered his car via the rear passenger door being held open by Claude. The journey took about fifteen minutes longer than normal, presumably because the vehicle was being driven back along itself for some distance in an attempt to appear to change its route. Given what had happened the previous day, it was understandable. It was not long before the four main scientists were consulting once more in Thompkins' office and as usual the Professor was leading the discussion.

'I am happy about the way my plans for *Aion* have progressed recently. If things go well today we should be in a position to initiate my next stage of the experiment. I would like us to meet at the end of today to discuss my proposal at length, rather than meet here tomorrow morning. Shall we say, 6.00 pm gentlemen?' The proposal was met with agreement.

Ben was never surprised at the number of times Thompkins used the word '*my*' whenever he spoke. As a more junior researcher he did not have the professional clout to correct his boss about whose theory and ideas had led to *Aion*. It seemed like the Professor was trying to take all the credit and Dr Moyles was not about to let that happen without a fight.

By the end of the day, Ben was happy that his calculations had seemingly been able to correct the fault he had identified from his first experiment. The level of impurities within the metallic hydrogen had now been reduced to zero or at least within a decimal place that had no relevance, meaning the transfer of energy from the fusion process would be exponentially more efficient. In essence, whatever energy was produced within the reactor would be transferred to the target without any deterioration. The only thing to do now was to run the test.

That evening the atmosphere surrounding the four scientists in Thompkins' office was producing energy levels of its own. The men from the Puissance Project had been working on Project *Aion* for almost a fortnight under the most stressful circumstances and now everything was ready. The Professor had somehow produced four glasses of dry sherry to toast their success. It was so typical of Thompkins' arrogance, believing in his personal success without anything to substantiate his claims other than his own self-confidence.

'Gentlemen, it feels that we are on the verge of history. I wanted to have one final meeting before we launch my experiment tomorrow. We are all confident that the changes we have made together will be successful –yes?' There were beaming smiles as they raised their drinks and chinked their glasses as murmurings of congratulations overlapped. 'To the future gentlemen. This will make us all famous and produce a new world order within energy production. Good luck !'

Sebastian Thiroud had one more grovel up his sleeve. After taking a sip of sherry he added, 'I'd just like to say Professor that we could not have reached this stage so early without your leadership and unquestionable expertise. Any success is down to you.' Without pausing for a challenge Thiroud raised his glass and championed, 'To Professor Thompkins, gentlemen!' Ben could only offer a mumbled half-hearted supporting toast. He was becoming increasingly anxious about his own efforts being side-lined.

As the car transferring Ben to his secret location entered the driveway the automatic floodlights exposed the area alerting everyone to his arrival. The duty officers waved their electronic devices over the car before Ben alighted. Looking for breaches in security was the paranoia of their work. Fortunately Ben did not have to succumb to this indignity: like all personnel he was simply obliged to walk under a surveillance archway at the entrance to the chateau, before he could ascend to his apartment. He looked around for Durand only to discover that he was unusually absent. Ben had wanted to ask him once again about Veronique's progress but he was hungry so this particular task would have to wait.

Entering the kitchen to transfer a ready-meal from the small freezer to the microwave, Ben noticed a note on the work-surface. It was from Captain Durand and simply read: 'Mademoiselle Perrin will be released from hospital tomorrow and will be in her own flat in the evening.' The policeman's signature was at the bottom of the note. The news gave Ben an extra spring in his step and as he went about his meal-making task he distracted himself with thoughts of visiting her in her own environment. After setting-up the *Aion* Project with the others, Ben anticipated an enjoyable furlough in a couple of days' time. Fantasies about his former exploits with Veronique caused a rush of passion that he was keen to release. He had already alerted his bodyguards of his intentions to visit his girlfriend and nothing was going to stop him from catching up on some personal physical relaxation.

There was a feeling of anticipated excitement the next morning as Ben made his way to the car. If *Aion* was successful, news about their discovery would spread like a bushfire not just within the scientific community but across the world. The work of the Puissance Project would be the focus of the international media and instant fame was guaranteed for all those closely associated with the work. Some would undoubtedly receive instant worldwide recognition and were inevitably bound for the annals of scientific immortality. Ben knew and expected that he would receive the lion's share of the limelight. After all, he was the one who disagreed with the principles espoused by the Professor at Puissance and had the nerve to follow his own beliefs. Those ideas were the ones to have finally made the breakthrough. Ben could not wait to walk into the Radioactive Zone and assemble the reactor's components.

After making their way through Alpha Lab and into the preparation area all the team were ready. Inside the Radioactive Zone there was a further group of about sixteen experienced scientists. This assembly comprised a mixture of male and female nuclear physicists and organometallic chemists at the top of their respective fields of expertise. All had been assigned specific tasks within *Aion* relevant to their area of specialism. None knew at this stage the precise final objective of their work but knowing the prestigious nature of the lead members of the Puissance team involved, each of them sensed they were working on something special. With very few words at the beginning of their assembly the large group dispersed into their specialist areas. Thompkins had assessed that it would take about twelve hours before most of the group could be dismissed. Once they had finished, the main components would be assembled by six men: Thompkins, Thiroud, Brandli and Ben along with Dr Heinz Kranck a specialist in deuterium once shortlisted for the Nobel Prize and Dr Dominic Flinthouse whose early work in magnetic confinement fusion had led to the formation of the Puissance Project, twenty years earlier. Most of the day would be involved in setting up the reactor, a larger version of the one Ben had set in motion over the summer. They would eat 'on the move' when they were hungry but such was the pace of their adrenaline release, no one really wanted food.

Everything went to plan and just before eleven o'clock in the evening Thompkins was prowling around the assembled reactor that was the culmination of generations of work. 'OK, gentlemen, I think that's it. In just over two weeks we will see if our position on the esteemed peak of the world's greatest scientists has reached the summit. All we need to do now is to activate the fusion process and transport the reactor into the largest safety chamber then we can all go home, or at least what constitutes our home at the moment.' It took three of them to move the reactor across to the cell, using a remote controlled tramway system. Once inside the chamber, Thompkins acted out of character and gave the final instruction to activate the fusion process.

'I think it only proper that the activation process is initiated by Dr Moyles. After all it is largely as a consequence of his commitment and self-belief that we have got this far with our work.' Stepping back from the equipment, he added 'Over to you Dr Moyles.'

Somewhat surprised at the turn of events Ben activated the sequence of commands on the reactor's console. Once completed he looked at each of his colleagues before declaring, 'That's it, gentlemen. I feel I should make some sort of announcement equivalent to 'three small steps for man' but right now I can't think of anything other than to say thank you for your work today. Let us all pray for success when we reflect on today's events.'

There was no time for anything other than sleep when Ben returned to the manor house. *Aion* was under way but it was still to be determined if the world would change as a result.

XI

Ben woke at about half-eight, a lie-in by his standards. Ten minutes after putting on his running garb, he was one of three joggers heading along a narrow path in the woods. Although leading the way without knowing where he was going, Ben was outpacing the two security men. He knew their shoulder holsters and constant scanning motion would inevitably affect their normal running speed so he expected to 'win'. After forty-five minutes of sweating they were running up the chateau's driveway in a final sprint. Ben finished first, bent double and gasping after pressing the stopwatch and discreetly examining the time. Recording the running interval was a futile exercise as each daily run differed in length so the timing meant nothing. However old habits die hard.

Durand was at the main entrance, smoking a cigarette and trying to merge into the background while leaning against one of the mock Grecian pillars that attempted to give the place some character. As Ben approached, the policeman offered his usual acknowledgement, only this time his charge did not walk straight past but made a demand and there was to be no compromise. 'After breakfast tomorrow I want to be taken to see Antoine Moreau before I go to work. Then, I intend to visit Mademoiselle Veronique Perrin in the evening. Please see to the arrangements.' Without waiting for a response Ben brushed past and ran up the stairs to his apartment. The success of the previous days' work had revitalised his confidence.

The following morning after another enjoyable run and a quick breakfast, Ben took one of the disposable SIM cards from the group leader of his security team, intending to phone home. If the news about his brother was not encouraging he would try to compensate with a positive to report to his Dad about his *own* progress at work. He slipped the card into the back of the mobile after discarding the old one into the authorised container. The disposal method was a condition of the deal whenever he wanted to make a telephone call from the chateau.

Graham Moyles answered the call almost immediately. Ben was lucky to have contacted his father so quickly, expecting that he would have to try more than once. He soon realised it coincided with his father having a cup of tea during his morning break. Graham liked to use the same red, tartan-covered thermos that he had cherished since his wife died. There was nothing more relaxing than finding a sheltered spot on the farm, drinking hot tea and looking out at the raw beauty of the Cheviot Hills. It was a time above all others that the Master of Moyles Farm relished, admiring his domain, where he was king of all he surveyed. It was fortunate for Ben that the elevation enabled a signal to reach Graham's mobile and it was doubly remarkable that his Dad even had the phone with him at all.

To Ben's further surprise, his father was up-beat. Although there was little change in Rich's condition, there was a possibility that everything was about to change. A young woman had been involved in a traffic accident and suffered catastrophic head injuries. She was currently on a life-support system in Newcastle General Hospital. Early indications from blood analysis and other tests suggested she was a good match for Ben's brother. The girl was not expected to live and the Moyles family had been informed to prepare for action at a minutes notice. That was one of the reasons why Graham had been so responsive to Ben's call. There was a possibility that Rich could have a new heart before Christmas if things went to plan.

Unlike his father, Ben felt guilty about the upsurge of positivity he was feeling. While they perceived the young woman's situation as fortunate, somewhere in the region a father and mother were grieving at the imminent loss of their daughter. When their mobiles became silent, Graham Moyles took in the morning air with a strong sense of hope. Given Rich's circumstances Ben decided not to tell his father about the ongoing experiment and what it could mean, nor did he refer to the stressful situation he was currently experiencing while in protective custody. He knew it would be better to exercise his mind with other thoughts

Antoine had been released from hospital and was allowed to return to his own flat. Two, low-level officers were assigned to patrol outside the apartment block, Captain Durand's gesture at increasing Antoine's level of security. In reality no one thought that Antoine was in any further danger. He had provided the assailants with some information which they had followed to Veronique's place. The thugs would be aware that Antoine knew very little after his so-called 'nephew' had paid a visit. However, the attack had affected him badly.

Ben did not spare any expense and bought the best French brandy he could find; he felt that Antoine deserved a treat. The uniformed officers had been told to expect Ben and since his face matched the image on their cell phones they allowed him to enter the building. One of them knocked and opened the door and as soon as he entered the hallway, Ben called out to his friend. 'Where are you, *mon ami*? I expect the nurses are recovering from your attempts to seduce them all. Speak up so I know where to find you.' There was no response which gave Ben cause for concern. The normally boisterous play-acting was missing. Ben turned into the small lounge and his heart sank.

Antoine was sitting in his favourite chair staring at the floor, with his walking stick by his side. The bruising on his face had erupted into blackness following the beating and his left eye was still closed. A large bandage covered the five stitches on the side of his temple. Everything about him screamed fragile old man and his body language showed that he was broken. As Ben entered, Antoine did not move his transfixed gaze and he continued to stare at a stain on his small rug beside the gas fire. Ben tried to be up-beat: 'Look what I have for you my friend. The best brandy in France and it's better than any medicine prescribed by a doctor, *n'est pas*? I will get two glasses and you can tell me how you are feeling.'

Ben knew the place well enough to find the glasses and pour the brandy. It was to prove more medicinal than intended and when offered the drink Antoine remained motionless. Ben had to wrap the old man's fingers around the glass but there was still only a limp grip. The drink simply fell lifelessly into Antoine's hand with the tumbler collapsing onto his thigh. The young neighbour lifted his friend's hand to his mouth and he eventually took a sip, before Ben moved back slightly to taste from his own glass. Any attempt to toast the situation, no matter how light-heartedly would have been misjudged and futile.

He knelt down and returned to Antoine's level in the chair, speaking gently to his companion. 'It is alright my friend. They will not return –

not today, or the next day or the day after that. They will never come back, believe me. I am sorry that you have been harmed in this way and I blame myself . It was *me* they were trying to find. They harmed you to get at me, I hope you know that.'

Antoine finally moved his eyes to look at Ben and eventually said just one word ….. 'Gérard.'

Ben did not quite hear the mumbled words. 'What did you say, my friend? I did not hear you.'

The word was repeated and Ben withdrew slightly, trying to think on his knees. Eventually words of consolation sprang forward. 'That was not your sister's son who came to visit you in the summer. It was someone trying to convince you that he was your nephew, Antoine. The person who did this to you, they were not related to you if that is what you are thinking. That was not Gérard who came back. He was an imposter, you understand ? *Un imposteur, n'est pas.*'

Antoine repeated what he had just heard. '*Un imposteur*?'

'Yes, your sister's son Gérard is working in a university in America. It could not possibly have been him. They must have known that you had not seen Gérard for some time and tried to trick you. They were trying to get into my flat.' Ben realised it was not the time to disclose they had been successful and it was all the old man's fault. 'The police have checked it out. That man was definitely not your nephew. Do not concern yourself about any upset within your family, your sister does not know about any of this.'

At last there was a flicker in Antoine's eyes as he realised the implications of what he had just been told. Ben surmised that it was not just the attack itself which had decimated his neighbour, it was the thought that someone from within his own family could have been party to the assault. Once Antoine had been reassured about the truth, his mind was able to find a haven of acceptance. It would take a while, but Ben knew Antoine was going to be ok. There was only one thing left to do: Ben said goodbye to his drinking companion, silently boiling with anger at what his own behaviour had caused this innocent old man to endure. 'I will return to visit you soon, my friend… *A plus tard*.' Antoine lifted his arm before it flopped back into its place of rest, mumbling an inaudible '*Adieu*.'

Ben found it difficult that afternoon to complete any work. The visit to Antoine had upset him greatly and his mind was full of irrational thoughts. Somehow considerations about neutrons, nuclear fusion and SI units seemed irrelevant. There were more than enough scientists pouring over the data being transmitted from inside the safety cell for Ben's absence not to be noticed. A feeding frenzy was taking place in Alpha Lab and no one was concerned whether he was there or not, least of all Ian Thompkins. It was with some relief that he returned to the sanctuary of the chateau, where the usual faces were on parade, ready to greet him with their bug-scanners and surveillance probes. At least tonight was going to be different and he would finally be able to visit Veronique in her own apartment. Durand did not want him to go but that was not going to stop him. Ben was desperate for some real relaxation and hoped he was going to find some in the comfort and seclusion of her place in Geneva. He was not worried, he would be accompanied by security men and there were no signs that he was the target of any further interest from unseen and unidentified enemies.

With the familiar protocols out of the way, Ben found himself being transported swiftly through the routine border checks and into Switzerland, where there was a sense of snow in the air. It would soon be December and although Geneva received less snowfall than some other places in Switzerland, courtesy of the moderating effects of the Lake, the white stuff was never that far away. Swiss efficiency in all its services inevitably meant that road closures and other disruptive effects were less significant than those experienced in the Cheviot Hills back in the UK. However if snow fell at home, Ben had never minded the postcard scenery that often characterised his beloved hills. Somehow being blanketed in snow and inaccessible to the rest of the world brought everyone together in their farmland communities. That is certainly how Ben's memory recalled those cold days growing up on Moyles Farm. As he looked upward from within the car, recollections of precious times with his mother began to trickle through the falling flakes of his mind. Fortunately that particular anguish was brought to a halt as the car pulled up outside Veronique's apartment block. Swiftly the mood changed. Ben was required to stay in the car for a few moments while the area was scanned by the eyes of security men. Two of them approached Veronique's front door before sending back the message that all was well.

Veronique was expecting Ben's arrival, Captain Durand's efficiency had seen to that. When she opened the door Ben was angry and embarrassed at the way she looked. As with Antoine, the results of her recent assault created colourful bruising around her eyes, although the swelling to her lip showed signs of abating. He went to kiss her but Veronique flinched during their embrace, a consequence of being punched in her ribs during the attack. Ben withdrew with the shock. 'Sorry, I didn't mean to hurt you. Was I squeezing too hard?'

She offered a smile of reassurance. 'No, it's ok. I'm just still a bit sore, that's all'.

He took out his anger on a policeman standing close behind him, in the doorway. 'That'll be all for now thank you, unless you would like to come inside and watch.' The disdainful look from the dutiful officer had been well practised with other members of the public over a long period of time. Nevertheless, he was obliged to take the insult as the door closed in his face.

The physical aspect of their reunion did not take long to materialise and after only the briefest of introductory chats, Ben and Veronique found themselves in bed. Although it was early evening, it was dark and cold outside and the warm bed offered reinforced comfort, which they both relished. They were naked under the sheets as their post-coital tryst developed into an analysis of recent events.

'Those thugs kept asking me where you were. I couldn't tell them anything because I didn't know but they wouldn't listen.'

'How many of them were there?' inquired Ben, almost in a Durand-like tone.

'I'm not sure but I think three. They just didn't believe me when I told them I didn't know where you had moved to.'

'Well at least they won't be coming back. And if it's any consolation you weren't the only one to be beaten up and interrogated. They did the same thing to my neighbour, Antoine.'

'What that loveable old man who lives downstairs?'

Without answering, Ben leaned over and kissed Veronique once more. He thought that initiating another round of lovemaking would be preferable to telling her that the only reason her assailants knew where she lived was because Antoine must have told them about her. She did not need to know and at that moment Ben could think of only one thing. It had been too long since he had last seen Veronique and he had missed her more than he had realised.

'Why don't you stay the night – unless you want to go back to your new place, wherever that is.' said Veronique, supporting her head with her elbow leaning on a pillow. The heavily scented fragrance emanating from her body was proving irresistible. Ben decided that he could not think of a rational reason not to stay. Rather than return to the manor house that evening he would sleep at her place and go back in the morning before leaving for work. If the security people did not like it then too bad. So far he had done everything they had asked and he was not in the mood to be side-lined when there was no evidence that he was in immediate danger.

Ben slid to the side of the bed and reached for his discarded boxer shorts which were lying on the floor. Being a fundamentally shy boy from the North of England, he stood with his back to Veronique and raised the underpants to cover himself so she could not see his embarrassment. In this semi-naked state he made his way out of the bedroom and opened the front door where his bodyguard was standing. Handing the poor man a flyer from the local take-away he ordered, 'Get us two pepperoni pizzas, please can you. Neither of us are in the mood to start cooking and we've both worked up a bit of an appetite.' Ben was beginning to enjoy his position of apparent superiority and for some reason had taken a dislike to this particular bodyguard. Perhaps it was his surly outlook. 'Just ring the bell when it's ready, thank you.' While the security man tried to maintain some composure, Ben jogged back to Veronique and launched himself onto the bed from about a metre away with an exuberant leap. She curled into a ball under the sheets and let out a scream of anticipation.

'We are naughty,' she maintained. 'Didn't he say anything about having to send for a pizza? It's hardly in his job description.'

'Well what could he say? I've got them over a barrel at the moment. I know it won't last forever so I'm going to make the most of it while it does. I don't think it's too much to ask. We are *hungry* after all. At least I am.' With that, Ben leapt on top of his paramour and began tickling her and messing about in a light hearted outburst of sheer tomfoolery. The jocularity ceased when Veronique was forced to call out in pain as the horseplay became too boisterous.

'So tell me about this new place of yours.' Ben shot her an awkward look before she continued. 'It's alright, I don't want to know where it is, only what it's like. Is it a nice place?' she asked as she smacked his lips with a kiss.

Ben thought it such an innocent question that he could think of no reason in the circumstances not to respond. So he told her about his apartment, how modern it was but also stressed some of the safety protocols that now dominated his routine, before declaring. 'Anyway, enough about that, I want to hear about more of what you have been doing while I have been out of circulation.' He then launched another amorous attack.

While Veronique shrieked and fidgeted in total complicity, the helmeted motor-bike delivery boy arrived with two large flat boxes containing identical twelve-inch pizzas, the insides of which were examined by the reluctant duty policeman, who rang the bell.

'Crikey, that was quick,' said Veronique as if making a performance management assessment of the delivery boy.

Ben explained the apparent high level of efficiency. 'I'd rung from the car on my way over. I reckoned we would be hungry round about this time.'

Veronique's stunned expression of exasperation torpedoed her into an attack. 'Do you mean to tell me …..that you… you knew were going to …' Veronique's fun loving accusation remained incomplete as she mockingly feigned a clenched fist in Ben's direction. Meanwhile he opened one of the two boxes now lying on top of the duvet and took a huge bite of pizza that over-filled his mouth with pepperoni. As he sat there wearing a wide, slurping smile, Veronique threw her head back onto the pillow in exasperation. There was only one thing left that she could do, she joined him in devouring the in-bed meal.

XII

Although Durand did not like the latest demand being made by his charge, there was little he could do. Ben's late phone call had given his protector no opportunity to make alternative arrangements so the security team had to improvise. Ben wanted to stay the night with Veronique and had no appetite to get out of bed and be whisked back to the chateau late at night. Given his experiences during the last three months he was not going to budge and his intransigence meant the security team would have to stay within reach of Veronique's flat during a very cold night. For those responsible for Ben's immediate safety, the change in arrangements meant remaining awake or at best taking turns to grab to sleep for a few hours in a car. They were not going to be happy but Ben did not care and for a few moments he wondered if his success was making him more arrogant.

After walking up and down the dark, deserted streets to keep awake and clicking their heels to keep warm, the five members of Captain Durand's security assignment were becoming more than a little impatient as the hours ticked over. They considered six o'clock in the morning was long enough to wait for a spoilt British scientist, no matter what he had discovered. One or two cars went past and the steam rising from passing engines indicated not just the early hour but also the still coldness of the Alpine air. One or two people were beginning to make their way to work and the sound of the not-too-distant engines from the first *mouettes* crossing Lake Geneva indicated the City was beginning to wake-up. The herald of the daily hustle was also being signalled by the chinking of the first TPG trams as more people left their homes to go about their business. Hopefully Dr Benjamin Moyles would soon consider it appropriate to leave his paramour so the guards could get some decent sleep.

The sentry sitting on an improvised passageway chair on the other side of the door to Veronique's flat was the first to notice that Ben was now on his way. The researcher was halfway out of the door and offering a final farewell to Veronique, alerting the sentinel's attention. Ben offered a gesture of acknowledgement which was not reciprocated by the muscle mountain fed up of waiting. The two men made their way out of the apartment block together and at the end of the lift's short journey, the ping of the doors opening was the herald of good news the security men wanted to hear. Two other officers were waiting in the foyer and stern expressions of disapproval were directed at Ben, not that he cared. The principal driver was propping his head against the car's headrest, dozing in an effort to get some rest when the team were preparing to leave. Once the streets had been scanned and safety levels approved, Ben received the signal to exit the building and head towards his vehicle parked at the bottom of the road, about fifty metres away.

Ben's walk was brisk and his mind elsewhere as he headed towards the car. In the sleepiness caused by the last twelve hours of their surveillance activities, no one noticed an early morning jogger running around the corner of a side-street at that precise moment. He ran straight into the group, knocking Ben to the ground and catching everyone by surprise. The runner helped Ben back to his feet, offering profuse apologies to all concerned when the two security officers belatedly moved into professional overdrive. The runner was suddenly lifted and rammed against the adjacent wall.

The policeman's initial interrogation of 'What do you think you are doing, you f.....?' was curtailed by Ben's interjection. 'It's alright officer, I'm fine. We're all fine. Nobody is hurt here. You can put him down now'. The release of the runner's chest hair allowed him to take a deep intake of breath. The icy growl of the gorilla with sausage fingers now loosening his grip had been enough to convey the appropriate message. The second security officer was more restrained as he addressed the frightened jogger with greater professional compassion. 'Right sir, you can go now thank you. Just be on your way.' The high-viz vest disappeared quickly into the darkness as all the men got into their cars and made towards the French border.

On arrival at the chateau it was still dark, although the automatic floodlights lit up the way as the cavalcade swept into the drive. The shadow in the covered entrance belonged to Captain Durand and he was not in the greatest of moods. In fact he was seething with anger at the way Ben had changed the arrangements the previous evening. As Ben alighted from the car, Durand stepped forward, out of the shadows. Ben felt a sinking feeling in his stomach reminiscent of when his father castigated him for tormenting his brother.

'I need to speak with you, *docteur – immédiatement.*'

'About last night I presume,' came Ben's reply. He attempted to side-step the senior officer who was not about to be ignored. Although smaller by a few inches, Jacques Durand was going to say what he had been stewing over all night and no one was going to stop him. His tone was quietly menacing.

'We had an agreement, monsieur. If you were to venture outside this compound the arrangements would be vetted and approval given beforehand. There was to be no variation from this protocol.' Ben went to speak, but Durand's raised index finger ordered him to remain silent. 'I and my officers are acting on behalf of the French Government in order to protect the interests of my country and our allies. I have already reported my concerns regarding your behaviour, which I consider to be reckless in the extreme. Not only did you put yourself in unnecessary danger, you abused the rights of people trying to protect you. Did it not occur to you, monsieur *'scientifique'* that my officers also had homes to go to, and wives and children who were expecting them home last night. Why did they not arrive ? It was simply to satisfy your lust for some mademoiselle. I am not having it monsieur, *non* I am not having it at all. My senior colleagues agree with me that if you vary from our arrangements at any time from this moment, your security will be repealed. If your bosses at Puissance wish to protect you after that, they can employ their own private security firm. Do I make myself clear, Dr Moyles?'

Once more Ben attempted to side-step his protector and once more he was prevented. On this occasion one of the security team who had been up all night protecting Ben's interests also stepped forward. The abused bodyguard relished the prospect of putting his hands on this Englishman who was showing disrespect to his renowned boss. This time Ben had no alternative.

'Oui je comprends monsieur, je suis désolé.'

As Durand rubbed out the end of his cigarette into the driveway with the sole of his shoe, he allowed Ben to carry on and enter the house. The police captain's facial expression as the Englishman walked past was one of total disdain. As Ben completed the usual protocols and walked under the electronic scanner's arch on his way to his apartment, a red light suddenly illuminated the entrance area, followed by a security bleeping noise. The security officer on duty at this point gave an unambiguous order.

'Stand completely still, monsieur. Do not take another step.'

Durand also heard the noise and was soon standing closely behind his stationary charge. The duty officer took a small poker probe and moved it around Ben's upper torso but there was no further sound. Then it was moved down his left leg – still nothing. When the right side was monitored however, the repeated clicks from the probe indicated the presence of a foreign object. It appeared to be coming from the small stamp pouch just above Ben's larger right-side trouser pocket. Once positioned directly over this area the click became one continuous sound.

Ben went to lower his arms in order to reach inside but was immediately prevented by Durand. 'Ah-ah monsieur, allow me.' Carefully the policeman inserted two fingers into the smaller pocket while he gazed directly at a stunned Ben. Slowly the object was lifted out of the pocket into a visible position for all to see. It was a small, round piece of silver about the size of a Euro coin and was instantly recognisable to Captain Durand as a common tracking device, the sort often attached to key rings. The device was common enough to be widely available, making the purchaser virtually untraceable. However, it was also sufficiently effective to anyone who knew their stuff.

'*Merde*!' exclaimed the policemen. Those around him all looked at their startled superior officer. 'It is a tracking device. Someone has been very determined to find out where you are living monsieur. Your location has been compromised. We must move you immediately.'

Ben was dumbfounded. 'What! But… I don't understand. How did that get there?'

'That is a question for another time. You are now in danger. While you have been stationary here now at this location whoever has been monitoring the device will know that you must have arrived at your destination. If they are as sophisticated as I suspect they are, they will be coming here –

and soon! There is no time to waste. You must leave everything here and come with me.' Durand signalled for his second-in-command to attend instantly, giving the instruction to contact everyone within the operation to receive the coded message, '*The water is out of the lake*'. This was the phrase designed beforehand to indicate that Ben's location had been discovered and escape protocols would be engaged. There was another safe house previously prepared for just such an eventuality. The task now was to transfer Ben before any assassins arrived at the chateau.

XIII

While Durand hustled his team together, giving instructions and directing security men to different strategic positions, Ben was left with a couple of bodyguards in the safety of the chateau's stairwell. There was no mistaking the nature of the butterflies in his stomach. They were not feelings of excitement on this occasion, he was beginning to sense real fear. Ben lowered himself onto the third step and not for the first time began to think about who was after him. Who was so determined to suppress a discovery that still had not yet been confirmed? The methods that had so far been deployed were highly sophisticated and required a lot of planning, they needed extensive resources and a network of people dedicated to their task. This was no 'fly-by-night' organisation but something operating on a scale comparable to the Puissance Project itself. What country or corporation was so committed to destroying the prospect of a clean, sustainable source of energy? The obvious answer was that whoever was behind all of this had to be connected in some way to oil. Either it was an international oil organisation intent on suppressing all competition or the agents of another state, perhaps a country in the Middle East whose status was totally dependent on its oil industry.

Ben was still thinking about potential suspects when his bodyguards started to react to messages coming through their ear-sets. It was time to move. The quickest way to extricate Ben from danger was by helicopter but the sun was still asleep and there was snow in the air. The next best option was to use a convoy of cars and given the need for speed, it was Durand's chosen course of action. Ben was swiftly ushered into the back of a large, black four-wheel-drive unmarked police car. It was the middle one of three and the cavalcade speedily revved out of the driveway towards the network of country lanes. Durand was in the passenger seat in the same car as Ben, walkie-talkie at the ready.

There was no doubt that the cars were driving too quickly for Ben's liking, especially at this time of year and on such poor roads. The main question under consideration was whether they were acting in time or had the tracking device done its job? The answer soon came when rounding one bend, the lead car drove into a fallen tree blocking the road. Fortunately, the two vehicles behind had the opportunity to veer off down a slope onto a minor track.

Ben's car was now the lead vehicle hurtling down narrow country lanes. The experienced driver was totally focussed on the task in hand, with little time to be concerned about strategy. Durand was demanding further back-up down the hand-set but was not totally confident there would be time for others to come to their aid so he would have to rely on his years of experience.

The two cars went around another sharp bend, when Durand suddenly shouted, 'Look out!' He pointed to an overhang where there were two armed men seemingly waiting for their arrival. One was kneeling down but had something on his shoulder that looked like a missile launcher. It was being swivelled around by the other man behind who was clearly targeting the cars. Suddenly there was a flash from the back of the launcher tube. As the cars went around the bend, a missile shot behind Ben's vehicle, hitting a tree which instantly burst into flames. The panic of the situation must have affected the vision of the second driver who swerved off the track and overturned down an embankment.

The final car contained the person the assailants were after. Ben was hanging onto the driver's headrest from the rear seat, gripping it with all his might and swivelling around at every turn. He had witnessed two cars being taken out containing people who were intended to be his protection. His concerns were not about the occupants of those cars, but his own safety. Suddenly terrible thoughts began to come to the fore. What would happen if he was captured? What would happen if the car crashed? The permutations stopped there as Durand turned to give a stark message.

'They are directing us where they want us to go. We must get out of the car and make our way by foot. Reinforcements are aware of our situation and will be here imminently. Ben could only wonder if '*imminently*' was quickly enough.

First light was beginning to appear over the surrounding mountain and Ben prayed it was not also going to be his final sunrise. Durand ordered the driver to stop the car around the next bend. All three men got out of the vehicle and pushed it off the road, down into an steep gulley. As the bodyguard pulled out his gun from his shoulder holster, Ben turned to ask, 'What's your name, my friend.'

The driver responded with a puzzled expression, 'Claude?'

Ben felt foolish having already asked the driver his name days earlier. The man shot another perplexed look and simply shrugged for no other reason than he could not think of anything more appropriate.

Meanwhile, Durand's eyes scanned the countryside through the shadowy daybreak as he looked for inspiration. Then he spotted something. 'There! We need to head down there. That clearing in that patch of woodland. If I can signal for them to pick us up there, we should be ok.'

Ben was not sure where he was referring to or how they were going to be picked up but he recognised this was not the time to ask questions about detail. Constantly looking over their shoulders like nervous sparrows, the trio left the roadway and made their way down the incline towards Durand's clearing.

Three quarters of the way down the slope they heard a car pull up on the road above them; it stopped opposite their abandoned car. It had not taken the assailants long to find the point where it was supposed to have been hidden. Durand knew at that moment that a tracking device must also have been attached to the car. He hoped that none of them had a similar device hidden on their person.

Their position was masked by a small copse of trees and they could hear voices shouting in anger coming from the road higher up. They appeared to be speaking Arabic and the pitch of their voices was unambiguously aggressive and determined. One of the men started to shine a strong beam randomly down the slope using a large torch, trying to illuminate his prey. Meanwhile, three other men were frantically arguing with each other about what to do next.

The beam came within centimetres of the group. Ben threw himself to the ground when he sensed it was too close for comfort. Durand resorted to silent pointing as there was a danger the still air would carry their voices further than was safe. He was indicating a large rock and suggesting that they take cover behind it, suspecting he knew what the next tactic of the would-be assassins was going to be. Crawling on all fours like stalking lions they covered the few metres together and arrived behind the rock just in time. Above them, the Arab men had rigged up a Mk.48 machine gun. A nod from their leader was the signal to his minion to release a hail of bullets down the hillside. It was a similar tactic to the torch trick, hoping that if they fired enough bullets some would hit their target. Fortunately for the fleeing trio, the shelter of the large rock provided protection. Several bullets ricocheted off the limestone roof above where they were hiding. The noise was deafening as shells rebounded off the rock towards adjacent trees, forcing all three to cover their ears. Claude went to peer around the bluff, hoping to fire off a few rounds of his own. However, he was prevented from shooting by his wily boss who knew that any light from a firing gun could easily give away their position.

Once the machine gunning had stopped Durand whispered simply, 'Now, come on quick!' indicating that they should break into a run and head for the wood around their clearing. In the minute it took for the killers to re-load they had made good their escape from immediate danger. The group was now out of sight and the protection of the trees was enough to convince any shooter there was no point in firing into that area.

In the improving light, Durand heard it first. 'Did you hear that?'

Ben responded with a further whisper, 'Hear what?'

'Shh ..... that. Can you hear it?'

Claude was the first to spot what Durand was referring to. 'There.. look – up there.' The noise was emanating from a blue and white Dauphin police helicopter appearing over the top of the adjacent mountain. Durand recognised the sound immediately and he knew the on-board cameras had almost certainly been adjusted to 'heat mode' to make it easier to spot people on the ground. He started to wave and encouraged the other two to follow his lead. The experienced officer knew that if any more people on the ground were being spotted from the helicopter, only friendly forces would be the ones waving. The trio all ran towards the clearing as the descending chopper got closer. They made their way through the trees to the edge of the dell and lying low, they waited for the helicopter to land.

Within a couple of minutes the Dauphin had landed, its rotary blades chirping while it remained stationary. The next course of action was clear. Durand shouted at Ben, 'Run, my friend. As fast as you can!'

While the helicopter's door was being slid open Ben sprinted as quickly as his jogging legs would allow. He was soon followed by Durand while Claude brought up the rear, gun in hand. The noise of the helicopter covered the shouting Arab voices that were now echoing through the adjacent woodland. The first awareness Ben had of any convergence with the enemy was the stinging sound of a bullet fizzing over his shoulder. The helicopter's presence had made it clear to everyone what the escaping group were attempting to do. The men from the Middle East now made for the clearing as quickly as they could. One of their bullets hit Claude in the shoulder and he fell to his knees. Uttering an angry expletive he turned and had the satisfaction of finally being able to fire back at the men who had been chasing him for the last hour. He hit the lead man in the leg causing him to squeal loudly before he was overtaken by an uncaring accomplice. Another Claude bullet hit the second man, removing part of his ear before he fell to the ground in shock. Following further waving from Ben and Durand who were now inside the helicopter and standing at the doorway, Claude ran to the position of safety and launched himself from about a metre away, the adrenaline removing any temporary pain from his bleeding shoulder. He was hauled inside the helicopter with the help of Ben and Durand who were grateful that Claude was wearing a belt with a large buckle.

Seconds later the door was closed and the Dauphin took-off heading away from the peanut-shooting guns of their chasers. The downdraught from the helicopter rippled the grasses while the two injured assailants were assisted by their partners in crime. The noise of the Dauphin disappearing from the clearing was soon lost into the air as quickly as it had arrived. The ordeal of the three men was over – for the moment.

It had been the second occasion in the last four months that Ben had signalled a helicopter to land. The first time he was concerned for the health of his brother. On this occasion it was the his own safety that was at stake. As he slumped back into the seat and looked at Durand applying a first aid dressing to Claude's bleeding shoulder, Ben closed his eyes and tried to think only pleasant thoughts. After all, Christmas was only just around the corner.

XIV

The second safety house made no compromise on security. This building had oppressive protection as the basis of its deterrent, rather than secrecy. The red brick structure was at the centre of a four-hundred metre, open gravel surround. The perimeter comprised an electric fence with manned turrets at its four corners. It was used only as a last resort, usually for political miscreants and high profile criminals. It was officially called *L'Agence Nationale de la Sécurité* but within government circles it was also known as *Le Bouton Carré* since it stood out like a square button. Most people had heard of '*Le Bouton*' and knew it would take an army of tanks to get through the security protocols. There were even two barriers before the main reception gate, each one covered by its own security camera. Staffing within the complex was of the highest level and manned only by elite Government troops.

In making their escape, the Dauphin had flown directly from the chaos of the woodland clearing and landed on a large blue letter 'H' marked out on the southern part of the exercise yard of '*Le Bouton*'. There were one or two bullet impact marks on the outside of the helicopter but given the distance the aircraft was from the handguns and the calibre size of the bullets, the occupants had never been in any real danger. Ben felt a huge sense of relief on touchdown, an emotion shared by his protector, Captain Durand. The helicopter doors were opened to reveal a medical team ready to take any injured individuals directly to the on-site infirmary. The two men stood back to let others help Claude to the waiting stretcher where he was instantly treated by enthusiastic paramedics. Before his two companions had a chance to say anything to him, Claude was quickly whisked away.

Ben and Captain Durand were greeted by the *Commandant de Police*, who had been alerted about developments while in an official morning meeting in Geneva. The *Commandant* was shaking hands while giving a simultaneous summary to his two new guests.

'Right gentlemen, I have arranged firstly to have you checked out by our medical staff. After something to eat and a freshen-up I suggest we meet in my quarters to discuss what you have just been through. I find it always best to review the situation on a full stomach as soon as possible after the event. That way your recollections are still fresh. I will send someone to bring you to me at the appropriate time. Meanwhile, Lieutenant Faure here will show you where to go.

Just for your information, there is no need to worry about your Puissance colleagues, they have all been moved, as a precaution. I am told that no one has experienced anything remotely comparable to your recent escapade. We need to explore the how and why of what has just happened as well as the *what* we are going to do about it. Meanwhile, we shall take our steps one at a time.' With the exposition completed, the *Commandant* offered a salute, which was half-heartedly returned by Captain Durand.

Ben was bemused by the speed and nature of events. The tranquillity of his experiment running within the confines of a secluded safety cell seemed a world away from the consequences it was creating. Neither of the two escapees had the energy or desire to look at each other. They simply followed Lieutenant Faure as far as the primitive living quarters where they entered two adjacent but identical cells. Each room contained a bed, a shower and a toilet but apart from a clean blue jump-suit and flip-flop slippers on top of the sheets, not much else. They were instructed to put all their clothes into a plastic bag that was handed to them as they entered their respective cells. As a naked Ben entered the shower he felt the soothing running water over his body positively therapeutic. In the warm wetness he pushed back his hair and wiped the water away from his eyes before pinching his nose. Then he turned his back on the running water, allowing it to cascade over his shoulders and into the warmth of his lower back, all the time thinking and trying to analyse recent events. Ben and Durand hardly spoke to each other, even as they were being accompanied by officers to the dining area, where they ate an unedifying meal. Ben dropped his cutlery onto the plate and the sound echoed across the large, empty refectory. Durand looked at him and was just about to say something when Lieutenant Faure returned with the orders, '*Le*

Commandant is ready for you now gentlemen. Please follow me.' The scraping chairs indicated their compliant reluctance and soon the two men were sitting in the guarded office of the most senior officer in the region.

The *Commandant de Police* finally revealed his identity, courtesy of the highly polished plaque on his strangely small desk. He was Philipe Brignac a legend in eastern France, where he had earned his reputation following several high profile cases which the national media had lapped up. Being favoured by newspapers in this part of the country allowed his name and his image to become as popular as any other French dignitary. Brignac was astute enough to recognise the other policeman facing him. He had known of Durand's desire to get to the retirement finishing line after the burn-out he had endured dealing with the terrorist incidents in Paris. Settling into a quiet police backwater in this part of France would be a natural choice for anyone seeking simply to melt away. Brignac's gentle approach was symptomatic of his respect for Jacques Durand.

The 'man on the ground' gave his detailed report of the previous hours and his boss listened intently to how the tracker device had been found in Ben's clothing, how their attempt to escape had initially been foiled with a planned response by some unknown assailants, and how Claude was shot before they could affect their escape. When he had finished his account Brignac sat in silence for a few long seconds before he sprang out of his chair and wandered over to the window to gaze at the scene outside without looking at the view.

With his back to the two men, he began to speak, arms folded. 'So what you have described Captain Durand could only have been the outcome of three possible causes. Either Dr Moyles here knew of the device in his clothes and was hoping to get away with revealing his location for purposes yet to be identified...' Ben became extremely prickly at the very suggestion and had to be prevented from getting out of his chair by Durand who grabbed his arm and looked directly into his face, before purposefully shaking his head.

Brignac began to turn around to speak directly to the two men. 'Or secondly someone else put it there and if so, who? Thirdly, it may have been a distraction: these unknown assailants already knew the location and the purpose of that device was to throw us of the scent.'

Ben interrupted Brignac in an attempt to introduce some humanity into the *Commandant's* cold analysis. 'What about the men in the two other cars? How are they?'

Brignac felt a waft of embarrassment as he realised he should have begun his account with a summary of how Durand's colleagues had fared. After all they had been forced off the road in very violent circumstances. It was a miracle that the shoulder-fired projectile had only just missed one of the cars, although it virtually obliterated a nearby tree. 'Ah yes, I am told they survived their experience. Two of the them have nasty injuries but they will be ok apparently . The others suffered a mixture of cuts, broken bones and minor injuries. Our experts are examining the missile now to get an idea of where it came from. Early indications are that is similar to those used in the Middle Eastern war zones.'

Brignac returned to his analysis of how the tracking device had ended up in Ben's jeans. 'So who had the opportunity of putting it in your pocket without your knowledge Dr Moyles?' He did not give Ben a chance to respond before continuing with his own analysis. 'Clearly when you were with Mademoiselle Perrin she had the opportunity to slip the device into your pocket so we must regard her with suspicion.'

Ben attempted to spring to her defence, 'Yes but ….'

Brignac was too determined a character to have his thoughts side-lined. 'You cannot deny she had a chance on that occasion Dr Moyles so I must keep an open mind. We do not know if she had any ulterior motive for finding out where you were living. There is no concrete evidence to cast any doubts on this woman but what do we really know about Mademoiselle Veronique Perrin?'

At that moment a light was switched on in Ben's head. 'Hang on a minute,' he said excitedly. 'When we left her apartment block someone ran into us. I remember he came out of nowhere and knocked me off my feet. Supposing in the ensuing melee he managed to slip the device into my pocket. There was a lot of confusion at the time and he must have had the opportunity. I know he looked scared when the bodyguards jumped on him but supposing it was an act and that was his intention all along.'

Durand seemed more supportive than Ben had anticipated. 'Mmm… it's a possibility I suppose.'

Brignac followed the lead. 'Ok there may be some CCTV coverage of that incident. We should check it out to see if there is any evidence to support this theory. It seems a strange thing to have happened in the circumstances. I want you to take a few hours to gather yourself together before we do anything further. Meanwhile I will do some digging on Mademoiselle Perrin to see if she *is* all she seems.'

Ben was no further forward. 'What about me, what am I supposed to do?' he asked.

Brignac proposed a way forward. 'You must stay here for the rest of the day at the very least *docteur*. We shall make the appropriate arrangements and you can be escorted to work at Sergy tomorrow or until your work has concluded. Meanwhile you must not attempt to make contact with anyone outside *L'Agence Nationale de la Sécurité* . I need to contact my Government colleagues to find out exactly what we should do – not just with you Dr Moyles but also the others on your team at the Puissance Project. This decision must be taken at the supreme level from within our Government and I must have a directive from someone higher up before we can act decisively.'

With very little to add at this point, their meeting was adjourned and Ben was the first to leave, returning to his cell through an elaborate system of sealed corridors, accompanied by a uniformed officer. Once inside his room, he gave some instructions to his guide about the retrieval of his clothes and other personal effects from the chateau. It had been quite a day and a continuation of an ugly nightmare that had entered his life. For a good hour he lay on his bed looking at the pattern on the ceiling and trying to think of a way forward that he could control. He reached one principal conclusion and that was to ensure the experiment was a success. Once the genie was out of the lamp there would be no going back and no point in anyone pursuing Dr Benjamin Moyles. The enemy's focus would then shift onto a different spotlight.

XV

The following morning the atmosphere in Thompkins office was palpable. Even the taste inside Ben's mouth was strangely tangy, almost nauseous. One person was missing and until he arrived, no one wanted to say anything. An odd cocktail of misfits was sitting in silence and for once, Ian Thompkins had nothing to say. At the back of everyone's mind was the contemplation of their new reality. Fame was welcomed, but threats and violence were something else altogether. Everyone knew what had happened to Ben the previous day but nobody wanted to unpick the detail, they each had their own worries. Since the clampdown on security, Ben was not the only one to have been moved to a safe house as they all had scurried to safety.

Captain Durand entered the office, accompanied by his trusty sergeant who made no attempt to sit with the others, preferring the safety of guard duty by the door. Jacques Durand no longer presented a dishevelled, uninterested persona. This man was focussed, on task and he meant business. He was the police officer who had gained recognition through *Médaille d'honneur de la Police nationale* and the *Médaille de la Gendarmerie nationale* and had finally broken free from the cocoon of the mundane duties he directed from the police station at Bourg-en-Bresse. The scientists in the room were not the only people to have been affected by the attempt to assassinate Dr Ben Moyles. They had also attempted to deprive his children of their father.

Durand opened the proceedings. 'I don't intend to unpick yesterday's events with the people in this room. Not just yet anyway. We still do not have all of the facts and are awaiting on several tests and reports before we can say with any clarity what happened and even more importantly, who was responsible. Suffice to say that you must be careful, though I doubt whether I need to press the point.

I understand from Professor Thompkins that within the next two days the results of your ongoing experiment will be concluded. At that point we hope and expect that the threat level will be decreased. When this unknown menace has been identified and the nature of the work of Puissance becomes public, we expect you will be able to return to something resembling your normal lives. But not just yet, not until we have found out who is leaking key information out of this complex to the detriment of you all.

It is almost Christmas and we hope that details about the experiment will be in the public domain before the New Year. Until then, the present security arrangements will continue. Any questions?' The stunned silence was not unexpected. 'In that case I will leave you in the hands of Professor Thompkins who will conduct the rest of your meeting. Meanwhile, I need to get on with my duties.'

There was a collective intake of breath as the door was closed and the two policemen vacated the room. As chief scientist Thompkins took the lead. 'Well gentlemen, you heard what the man said. He has his job to do and we have ours. The sooner we uncover whether our expectations are proven correct, the better. I suggest we agree that tomorrow we should enter the safety cell and establish if our theories work. Perhaps after that we can experience some degree of normality. Today we must make our own preparations to ensure we are ready. I know it's not going to be easy but we must try and treat these days at Puissance as ordinary working days. Try not to be concerned, I have every confidence in the authorities who are protecting us.' The group dispersed with only Thiroud staying behind to seek solace with his hero. The others went off to their respective locations within Alpha Lab to resume their duties.

Ben was not concerned about making preparations because he did not share Thompkins' confidence regarding their safety. It was all very well for the others to talk platitudes, they were not the ones who were being targeted. For whatever reason, unknown assailants had singled out Ben for special treatment. The puzzle that was being played out in his mind was simple – how did they know the experiment was applying *his* theories and not those of Professor Thompkins? The security breach had to be coming from someone close to Ben, someone he knew. He played around in his head with several possibilities but nothing seemed to make sense. It had to be somebody who was aware his experiment over the summer had been successful, but that information was limited to a select group who he counted as friends or trusted colleagues. Clearly he was wrong, that seemed clear now.

Meanwhile, there were others he also needed to protect. In the confines of Alpha Lab he had access to some of the most powerful computer hardware in the world at his finger-tips so he reconciled to use these resources while he had the chance. Ben's first-class honours degree in Computer Science meant he knew how to hack into just about any system given sufficient resources. He reasoned that if he was in danger, then so was his family and he was not prepared to accept that situation. Ben went into his office, locked the door and set about his mission.

Five hours later, Graham Moyles, Richard Jacob Moyles and Benjamin Jacob Moyles no longer existed on any computer data base anywhere in the world where Ben had been able to find their names. This included electoral roles, national insurance and tax system accounts, dental practices as well as banks and creditors and airline passenger lists. In fact, everywhere that Ben could think of within the time period. Their 'missing lists' also included any miscellaneous sub-branches of any website where it was feasible they may have previously featured. Ben inflicted a rogue virus 'worm' onto every worldwide computer system he could access; nothing was left uncontaminated. Anyone who tried to get at Ben Moyles by tracking down his family on a computer system would be left frustrated.

There was one exception to Ben's exploits, a single access point that was still needed, where discovery of their location could be traced if the desire was sufficiently clever or determined. The internal network firewalls on Queen Elizabeth Infirmary's Cardiology Department system were still enabled, allowing the family to be contacted if a suitable donor was ever found for a heart transplant for his brother. Ben considered anonymity from all other internet presence might present some temporary collateral damage but inclusion on the transplant register was a must. There was no point in protecting Rich from a potential assassin if he was only then to die because he could not be located in time to receive a new heart. If everything went to plan Ben reckoned that he would be able to revert to the status quo without some of the list hosts ever being aware they had been hacked.

The day had gone without being noticed, a consequence of another full agenda. Satisfied for the moment that at least his family were tucked away snugly in some Internet black hole on the Dark Web, Ben felt that he was now beginning to fight back. It was good to think that some of the control he had previously felt was ebbing away was now returning.

Three cavalcades of two identical cars, each protected by two armed vehicles sped out of the Puissance compound, but only one column contained a research scientist. The other two sets of vehicles were decoys designed to throw from the scent any saboteur who was still determined enough to have a go. All three convoys were additionally protected by an overhead helicopter equipped with heat sensitive cameras as well as a heavily armed number of highly-trained, specialist personnel. Even a draught was going to have difficulty accessing Ben's car. However, it was still not a nice feeling for a young man who only had noble intentions. Throughout his chase for success Ben had been motivated by trying to find a source of energy that would help all mankind but it appeared that his dream was not something that everyone shared.

There were only two weeks remaining before the Christmas holiday period. Usually a skeleton staff of enthusiasts and loners manned the essential components at Puissance during Yuletide. It remained to be seen if this was still going to be the case. Other routine procedures were taking place inside the corridors and laboratories. This included the maintenance staff replacing fire extinguishers very early in the morning before most of the workers arrived for their daily duties. Completing the task at such an hour meant that disruption to everyone's usual routine was minimised. It was customary to upgrade the extinguishers in December as a gesture to the Health and Safety Handbook. Ben used to think that it must have something to do with a one year guarantee expiring before the beginning of a new calendar year, not that he spent much time contemplating such mundanity. He had to walk past a group of three service men in green jumpsuits who were exchanging unused fire extinguishers for brand-new ones. The bright red casings would no doubt be replaced in an unused state at the same time *next* year. Ben smiled to himself as he walked past the workers, who did not need the large yellow lettering 'Maintenance' on their backs to advertise their function. One of the men responded to his passing with a gentle '*Bonjour*' and an accompanying half-wave.

Ben continued walking along the corridor before arriving at the double glass doors that marked the entrance to Alpha Lab. Without looking back he swiped his security card and entered a code. An almost inaudible click, signified the access point was now unlocked. There was the taste of anticipation in his mouth as he knew the others would soon be arriving to discover whether the recent threats to his life had been an unnecessary act of terror or whether his scientific calculations would mark his time in history.

There was almost another half-an-hour before Thompkins *et al* were due to arrive but Ben was not going to be late today, not on this occasion. Thompkins may have been the senior scientist but the team were implementing *Ben's* ideas. He was not going to follow them into the arena like some trivial theatrical extra, his intention was to stamp his authority on the situation. This was a time for silent contemplation and although there were no external windows in Alpha Lab to reveal a glimpse of the world outside, there was a sky-light which Ben had used before when inspiration was needed. It pointed south-east towards Lake Geneva and the view highlighted the beautiful snow-covered peaks of the Swiss Alps. Of all the restricted views visible from inside the Puissance complex it was the one that reminded Ben most closely of his home in the Cheviot Hills. He sat in moments of total silence wondering what his father would be doing. It was the time of year when Graham Moyles usually attended the lambing sales or perhaps he was seeing to one of the cattle that was calving. Whatever he was up to, Ben wished he could talk to his Dad about the excited anticipation racing through his body.

In a world of his own for a few minutes, Ben was enjoying his fantasy when he almost jumped out of his skin as Jonas Brandli burst into the room. His line manager clearly preferred to express his emotions through buoyancy rather than contemplation. 'Morning Ben' said Jonas as he approached with his hand extended, signalling a change of behaviour on this special occasion. 'How are you feeling today? All my instincts tell me this is going to be a good morning. I've been here since six o'clock examining and re-examining the data coming from the safety cell and it all looks perfect to me. If we find that the energy source has extinguished I shall be amazed. Come on my friend, put a smile on that gloomy face of yours. We are about to make history.'

Ben decided that Jonas was right, especially given the recent escapades that could so easily have prevented him from seeing daylight, never mind a successful outcome to his experiment. A reluctant smile confirmed that Brandli's optimism could be shared. Just to make sure, Jonas grabbed Ben's shoulders affectionately and gripped them firmly, almost to the point of discomfort. 'Yes, that's better,' he continued. 'Don't look so worried, everything is going to be fine. You need something to settle your nerves ... fancy a coffee?'

Before Ben had a chance to respond, Thompkins' entourage entered the room. '*There* you are Dr Moyles. Good morning to you. I hope you are ready to discover the outcome of my experiment.' Without waiting for a response, mainly because he was not even looking at Ben directly, the Professor continued. 'This could also be a good day for you too, my young fellow.' Resisting the temptation of telling his boss where to go, Ben remained silent. There were two new faces in Thompkin's group on this special occasion but no one attempted to make introductions. Ben assumed from their demeanour they were not scientists, their faces more indicative of awesome ignorance than inquisitive excitement. Rather, he supposed they were representatives of the French Government and were present in order to report back to their political masters. However, they did exude some silent authority and were being treated respectfully. At this point Thompkins was on a roll, 'Right gentlemen ..and ladies'.... He turned to two distinguished female physicists at the back of the group. 'If you are ready, please accompany me to the key area where we should now prepare ourselves for the discovery of a lifetime. 'It is now eight-zero-five so I suggest that we make our way to the Radioactive Zone and re-assemble outside the safety cell at eight-forty-five. Agreed?' There was no point in responding to the question, everyone understood the situation.

At the appointed time, ten male scientists accompanied by two female colleagues were booted and suited in appropriate protection garb, finally gathered for the great reveal. Thompkins made his way to a large computer console that contained the master keyboards controlling the whole sequence of events. He entered some data before turning to look at a monitor positioned on the wall above their heads. It showed inside the safety cell where the target of their affection was positioned. Thompkins then manoeuvred a joy stick which moved the webcam and he looked up once more to scan the internal scene. Like a crowd of tennis spectators, the heads of the others moved in synchronicity with their lead player. From the back of the group it may have seemed comical but this tie-break was of the utmost importance.

Once satisfied that nothing untoward had taken place inside the safety cell, the maestro entered a different set of notes causing a massive noise to echo across their space. The loud thump was the result of the door-opening process being activated. The jolt of surprise was followed by nervous laughter among the gathering as they looked towards the cell entrance. The housing containing the reactor slowly began to move along the narrow tramway rails out of the cell, under Thompkins' stewardship. The Professor was finding it difficult to contain his excitement as he guided the mechanism remotely from the console. All eyes were focussed on the moving object but there was nothing to indicate what was going on and the reactor still held its secrets.

The skilled hands of assigned workmen beavered at the outer casing, removing the relevant clasps and bolts. Suddenly, like magician's assistants they stood back in unison as if waiting for a round of applause revealing the synthetic cocoon wrapped around the reactor. Thompkins stepped forward and prepared to remove the final overcoat. With typical pomposity he tried to ape the words of Neil Armstrong on the Apollo 11 moon landing. 'This may be the stallion of Puissance jumping over the wall for mankind.' Its clumsy meter showed just how out of touch Thompkins was from the real world and in that moment Ben could not have felt greater contempt.

Even before the Nobel Prize Winner had unwrapped the outer layer, Ben had spotted a green glow emanating from under the lower portion of the synthetic material. He was aware that this could only have happened if light was still being generated by the reactor. As Thompkins peeled back the final portion there was massive cheering, hand clapping and hooting from a group of normally conservative scientists, who recognised that light was still being produced. The readings on the adjacent panel were superfluous, the bright green bulbs showed the only results that mattered. Their attempt to correct the problems associated with metallic hydrogen impurities had done the trick. The experiment was a success.

Immediately, the group surrounded the Professor and the reactor. As Ben looked on, the noise of congratulations continued and even the four technicians were clapping without knowing why. Those waiting their turn to shake Thompkins' hand occupied their time examining the reactor in close detail, while others slapped him on the back before issuing the mandatory '*Well done*' and '*Congratulations*' in true sycophantic melody. This was the good news everyone had predicted. Ben's preference for caution could now be displaced because this was true success by anyone's standards. A new source of clean, sustainable energy had been found and this could change the balance of the world's supply of power. It would probably take at least another five years of refinement to make the principles economically viable but the death knell had been sounded for fossil fuels. The world was now on the brink of a changing political order.

Thompkins addressed the group in an attempt to bring harmony to the joyous chaos. 'Thank you everyone for your kind words and your presence here today at this magnificent discovery. I could not have done it without the hard work and skills of my brilliant team. I would implore you to refrain from discussing with anyone what you have seen here today and remind you that your contract explicitly prevents you from going public with this knowledge. Sufficient to say at this point that I shall be making a statement to the media within the next twenty-four hours. My able assistant Dr Sebastian Thiroud has already prepared the ground in this regard and I shall make my announcement to the world's media at ten-thirty tomorrow morning. As for now, I invite you to return to my office where glasses of Moët and Chandon will be supplied in copious quantities.'

During the course of those five life-changing minutes Ben had made no attempt to communicate with Thompkins. He had watched the events unfold almost as if he was simply another member of the invited entourage. Not once had Thompkins made reference to Ben by name or even acknowledged the source of the new direction the work at Puissance had taken. He felt betrayed and was concerned the situation would become even worse after tomorrow's press conference. Ben heard the noises made towards Thompkins but the sounds of truth had not progressed beyond his shield of disbelief. There was no point in sharing the joy in Thompkins' office because his boss had moved into a higher gear and left the rest of the team in his egotistical wake. While others left for the changing facilities of the Radiation Zone, Ben and Jonas Brandli stayed behind to inspect more closely the data that the experiment was still providing. It was also the opportunity to take stock.

'Congratulations Dr Benjamin Moyles. How are you feeling? I told you I felt very positive about how things would go today. And it's all down to your work, my friend. Only good things can happen to you after this. You must be elated.'

Ben could not pick up on this cue. He was confused and concerned about what was going to happen next. 'I'm obviously pleased that all that hard work has paid off. Trouble is I think my theories are about to be hijacked. That smug so-and-so Thompkins has his eyes on the prize and it's not going to be easy to convince the scientific community that the concept of focussing on pressure rather than heat during the fusion process was down to me. Before I had that success over the summer few people were interested in listening to me and now they all think the idea came from the *great-I-am* himself.'

'So what are you going to do about it. I'll back you up if he proves to be difficult. I don't like him any more than you do. Your ideas were the product of working in Eta Lab after all. You would not have been so-called promoted to Alpha Lab without having earned your spurs with us first. So don't worry about me on that score.... I'll support you.'

'Thanks Jonas, that means a lot. Come on, let's get out of this gear.'

The two men trooped off slowly to the cleansing area just outside the Radioactive Zone. As they were getting changed together, Brandli pursued his curiosity. 'So what are you going to do, Ben?'

During the periods of contemplation Ben had been anticipating how things would unfold if the experiment was successful. He had already prepared a professional paper which was good enough to release to the scientific community. If Thompkins was not going to give him the credit he felt he deserved, the only solution was to declare his ideas unilaterally. With each layer of clothing added Ben was becoming more stubbornly aggressive. 'I intend to see him first thing in the morning, before the press conference. I will show him my paper and tell him I intend to submit it to the *International Scientific Association Journal* for consideration at their symposium in January. They have the professional kudos and integrity to give a serious and well-balanced assessment of my claims. I have the times and dates to support the progression of my views, leading to the summer experiment and now the further application of those concepts which have produced today's outcome.'

'He won't like that. He doesn't enjoy being threatened. Remember his reaction the last time you challenged him?'

'Yes, indeed I do. I was proved right then as well and I'm in no mood to be fobbed off or bullied by the likes of him, Nobel Prize Winner or not.'

The two men were now fully dressed and facing each other in the changing room as Brandli reached inside his jacket to produce a comb. While brushing back his hair he asked Ben, 'You going along to Thompkins' office for some bubbly?' He already suspected what Ben's answer was going to be.

'I don't think so Jonas. The stuff would stick in my throat right now. I don't care if Thompkins thinks I am deliberately raining on his parade, though come to think of it, I'd be surprised if he even notices I'm missing. No, I'm going to ask them to take me back to *Le Bouton* for some peace and quiet and to think things through. How about you ? Are you going?'

'I'm not going in there if you're not. After all if you are undermined then so is the whole of Eta Lab and I'm not having that. No, I think I'll go home as well.' Leaving Ben sitting alone on one of the changing rooms bench seats Brandli brought their discussion to a conclusion. 'See you tomorrow?'

'You certainly will Jonas. And thanks once again.' With a flick-wave salute Jonas left the room and made his way back to his own home arrangements. Ben found himself alone with his thoughts. He knew tomorrow was going to be a difficult day but he was up for the challenge.

XVI

When Ben stepped out of his bullet-proof car he sensed a permanent change in his life was going to be inevitable. The only good thing about travelling to work with an escort seemed to be the clearance procedure on entry to Puissance. The circumstances surrounding recent events proved that he was beyond reproach as far as any subterfuge was concerned so the usual onerous security inspections that he had endured over the previous five years were no longer required. He walked past the scanning arch and basket checks and headed for the corridors leading to the various labs. One woman placing her personal effects onto the conveyor belt nudged her friend with her elbow and pointed at Ben as he walked quickly past their curious gaze. He wondered for a moment if the reason for their interest was due to word leaking out already about yesterday's success. One reason for holding the press conference later that morning was almost certainly because it was going to be impossible to keep a lid on the situation. In many ways Ben was glad that the world would know about the discovery, at least then he would begin to get his life back and experience a normal existence.

Entering Alpha Lab he headed for his promoted spot where his small office was located. There were a few other workers busying themselves around his area and his paranoia extended to concern about the way they were looking in his direction. He had about half-an-hour to act before news about the meeting with the media would become widespread and Thompkins would become unreachable due to the ensuing euphoric confusion. Ben unlocked the top drawer of his desk and removed a pink folder containing a bound depth of about four centimetres of A4 notes. The heading on the front cover read: *Maintaining the process of nuclear fusion through sustained pressures using metallic hydrogen as a conductor of clean energy transfer.* Underneath the title was the key phrase, *'by Dr Benjamin Moyles.'*

The contents of the folder represented Ben's work and theories developed during his years working in France. It was fundamentally a war manifesto, laying bare his intention to claim success for the major breakthrough created by the recent experiment. If Thompkins had shown any magnanimity throughout the process, Ben would have been more than willing to share any glory. However, the leader of Puissance had made it abundantly clear that he intended to claim the glory for himself and that was fundamentally unfair. They had crossed swords over the direction of the research and Ben had endured the stress of potentially being removed from Puissance altogether. If that was not enough, serious threats had been made to his life because someone on the inside recognised that the breakthrough was down to a scientist by the name of Dr Ben Moyles. Whoever was responsible for trying to kill him was yet to be revealed and there was no guarantee that he would be completely safe, even after the press conference.

Ben stared at the folder and smoothed his fingers over the glossy cover as if it was a treasured family album full of happy memories. He flipped through the pages as a final farewell before suddenly rising from his chair to begin a purposeful walk towards the office of Professor Ian Thompkins. Within five minutes he had successfully negotiated Christelle and entered the inner chamber where he was greeted by a smiling boss, who was unaware of what was about to happen.

'Ah.. there you are Ben. Come on in my dear boy and take a seat. We missed you at the celebratory drinks yesterday. I hope you didn't stay away because you thought you weren't invited. I would have been more than pleased to have seen you celebrating my success.'

This was almost too much for Ben who was wondering what part of Thompkins pompous assumptions he should take issue with first. Choosing to keep his powder dry he carefully and precisely placed the pink folder on the green leather mat directly under Thompkins' gaze and then stood back and parted his hands and arms. The reveal gesture was completed by pointing his palms toward the ceiling. Thompkins shot him a quizzical look.

'What's this, dear boy? It looks impressive but I don't have time to look at it now I'm afraid. I'm just about to leave to give a major press conference that will be headline news all over the world. Can it wait for another time?'

Ben's powder was getting warm. 'No Professor Thompkins, I'm afraid it can't wait. In this file is the evidence to show how and why *my* experiment worked to produce sustainable energy from the process of nuclear fusion. It is evidence produced from years of *my* work, while here at Puissance. It shows categorically that the route taken previously within the project focussing on heat to attempt to sustain fusion was misguided and documents some of the difficulties I have faced trying to develop my own ideas on the fusion process. Ideas I might add that have now been shown to work and are at the centre of where we are right now. I intend to submit this document to the symposium of the *International Scientific Association Journal* following your press conference. A press conference by the way that I feel I should also have been invited to attend. In a gesture of professional good-will I present this document to you now so that you can lend your support to show that the fundamental breakthrough came from within Eta Lab as a result of *my* work and *my* research. If you fail to do so, I will have no alternative but to resign and declare my theories unilaterally.'

Thompkins rose from his chair and for a moment Ben thought he was going to reach out and agree with an amicable handshake but he was wrong. Instead the Professor pressed a button on his desk console and spoke to his personal assistant, while Ben looked on in suspended animation. 'Is Dr Thiroud with you at the moment, Christelle ?' After a few seconds pause he continued, 'Could you please send him in now ... *je vous remercie*.' Thompkins then looked directly at Ben without a flicker of emotion as Sebastian Thiroud meekly knocked before entering the room. 'Ah, Sebastian, please come on in. I have just been having an interesting discussion with Dr Moyles here about my successful experiment. Could you please remind Dr Moyles of the conversation we had with him a little while ago regarding the conditions of his contract. He seems to be of the opinion that the results of my experiment belong to him and he should be the one holding this morning's press conference.'

The obsequious assistant relished the opportunity to put Ben to the sword and his facial expression demonstrated that he understood the gist of what must have just taken place. 'Yes, indeed Professor Thompkins.' He spoke the words without looking at his master as if he was about to embark on a previously rehearsed scene, only this time it was for real.

'You may remember Dr Moyles that following the limited success of your experiment over the summer you were asked to sign a contract agreeing not to disclose the results of this experiment to anyone. This was in addition to your general contract of employment here at the Puissance Project, which covers the same sort of conditions but in more general terms.' Reaching inside his attaché case he produced copies of the contracts which he waved under Ben's nose. 'I have copies for you here Dr Moyles, if you would like to see them. I'm sure you will find these papers in order and they will undoubtedly support what I have just told you.' Ben pushed the documents away from his face and his expression demonstrated raw, silent anger. Thiroud continued, 'This was of course before Professor Thompkins deployed *his* incredible skills to refine the process, the success of which we all witnessed yesterday.'

Thiroud was enjoying every prick of discomfort his hissing diatribe was inflicting on the young researcher. 'If you try to claim any credit for either the principles underlying the experiment or the method deployed by using Puissance resources here in Sergy, I can guarantee that not only will no other major scientific project ever employ you again but I will personally ensure that the best lawyers the French Government can provide will take you for every penny you have. Do I make myself clear, Dr Moyles?'

Ben stared intensely through to the back of Thiroud's eye sockets, seething within his soul while considering his options. The first thing to decide was whether or not to head-butt the odious little toad standing before him. That is how similar scores would have been settled inside the Black Bull in Hubbleton, although he had come a long way from such a culture. In that single life-changing moment, Ben's naïve political savvy was exposed for his enemies to see and enjoy. He may have predicted that Thompkins' ego was big enough to ensure he took the lion's share of any credit but he had grossly underestimated how calculating and proactive Thompkins and Thiroud had been to ensure it happened. Ben stood alone, feeling physically sick as if his integrity had been gutted like a fish. The duo must have been plotting behind his back while seemingly being supportive throughout the development of the experiment. His life was suddenly being sucked back into non-existence but fortunately his intellect came to the fore.

Ben said nothing because there was nothing he could say. Instead, he looked down at the pink folder resting on Thompkins' desk and reached to pick it up. Thompkins moved forward as if to prevent him from doing so but Ben looked at him with an expression that bordered on demonic. As a result, the Professor withdrew. 'This is my work, written on my paper, which I bought myself. If you think it belongs to you, think again because if you try and prevent me from removing this document from this office I shall forget my position as a well-respected scientist and express my feelings in a manner you will not like.' There was no need to say anything else. However, Ben did attempt to follow the threat with, 'I shall see you in court, gentlemen.' Nobody in the room considered that would become a reality.

Ben grasped the document tightly in his right hand in an attempt to divert his compulsion to transform it into a fist. He walked out of the office in a temper that he had never previously experienced, leaving Thiroud and his boss looking at each other, before they both broke into a knowing smile of contented smugness. The senior scientist broke the silence, 'Right Sebastian my friend, it is time for us to face the world and claim our reward. We should make our way over to the ante-room where we can meet the others and decide exactly how we are going to declare our findings to the world.'

The modern, glass-surround Lecture Theatre was at the opposite end of the complex to where all the labs involved in vital research were located. Generally, the Theatre and its adjacent buildings were not considered to contain sensitive information and security was more relaxed, though not today. On this particular morning it was full of the world's media, with the front row looking like a firing squad of cameras. The lights from the expensive iphones were being tested by seated journalists before the main protagonists arrived. One or two others were adjusting their settings for audio-record, to ensure that every word would be covered and reported accurately for the international media. The vehicle compound was overflowing and some of the Puissance employees' cars had to be left outside the fenced area such was the demand for space. Experienced engineers in headphones were not concerned about any inconvenience to the natives. They had seen it all before and were not in the least intimidated by the irritation of any local complainers. Giant satellite dishes attached to white vans with television company logos were testimony to the level of interest being shown to this historic event. The press conference was already running late, although no one in the room had expected it to proceed on time.

There was a buzz of expectation within the lecture theatre, it was the sort of murmuring that happened very rarely in the modern media world. The reporting jackals sensed blood and they were not about to be disappointed. A group of about eight key players walked slowly down to the front, where they sat behind their name-plaques. A xylophone of microphones had been set-up by tv companies trying to out-do their rivals with gaudy covers designed to reveal the name of the television company they represented. Brightly covered three-lettered acronyms were pointing towards the central voice of whoever was going to lead the session. That person soon became known as the room settled to something resembling silence. It could only be one person.

'Good morning ladies and gentlemen. Thank you for coming to this press conference this morning on what is a very special occasion. I would go so far as to claim this is a historic day, one that will forever be stamped on our minds as we share something momentous together.' Leaning forward to adjust the largest microphone, Thompkins also hoped the cameras would home in on his better side, as he swept back his hair in characteristic style, before continuing. 'I wish to announce that scientists working under my leadership are now able to claim that I have discovered the Holy Grail of sustainable energy. Under strict laboratory conditions my team have been able to demonstrate that the process of nuclear fusion can be controlled to generate power over a sustainable period of time, using only clean sources as the basis of the process. In short ladies and gentlemen, I have shown how it is possible to produce enough electricity to sustain the power needs of any modern household without the need of any fossil fuels. The days of oil, natural gas and coal are now numbered.'

At this point shouting and finger pointing reached fever pitch as journalists sitting near the front stood to try and interrupt by asking questions in order to be the first ones to get him to reveal the secret. Thompkins' voice became lost in the cacophony of noise that erupted in front of him. He held up his hands in a gesture of surrender in a feeble attempt to return to calm. Eventually, as even the most obstinate of reporters became aware it was necessary to revert to civilised audibility, the Professor was allowed to continue.

'I shall answer any questions to the best of my ability in a few minutes. However, I would like to congratulate others who have helped to make this discovery possible, in particular my trusted colleagues sitting to my right here, Dr Sebastian Thiroud and Dr Jonas Brandli.' Cameras flashed to a blinding light as fresh photographs focussed on the assistant stars, causing Thiroud to shelter his eyes by raising his hand to his face. 'Tomorrow I shall give a lecture to all my fellow Puissance scientists to explain how I have achieved this remarkable feat before releasing a paper detailing aspects of my research to all my fellow scientists throughout the world and indeed to the public at large.'

Watching from the back of the room was the silent dejected figure of Dr Ben Moyles, standing with his arms folded, watching his nemesis luxuriate in falsely-earned adulation while he leaned against the wall, trying to push it down with his shoulder. Every word coming from Thompkins' mouth was like a dagger through Ben's hopes. He kept trying to tell himself that his day would yet come, but it was little consolation in the fervour of the present forum. He thought how typical it was that the lead scientist of such a prestigious project as Puissance would prefer to make the announcement to the world's media first, before disclosing the results to his colleagues and peers. It seemed that with every stride he took, Thompkins' ego simply grew bigger.

As more chaotic shouting followed each sentence, Ben decided to leave and without any ceremony he slinked out of the door and made his way to the main entrance. After a few words of explanation to his driver, he made his way back to *Le Bouton*, where he knew exactly what he was going to do.

XVII

Monitors at Geneva Airport were displaying images of the morning's press conference at every Departure Lounge and there were similar broadcasts on all large screens in the public esplanades in the city centre. Politicians, scientific experts and anyone with an opinion were being interviewed to give their views on the future now that a new, clean source of energy had been discovered. The 'Greens' in every country in the civilised world were ecstatic at the prospect of having their whole *raison d'être* being ratified. Although the international oil companies were saying very little, they were clearly the organisations with the most to lose. Middle Eastern countries under immediate pressure announced they would be holding an emergency meeting in Batar to consider the worldwide implications for oil prices.

At the centre of everything was the image of a smiling Professor Ian Thompkins being lauded by his Puissance colleagues. News clips showed him raising his hands like a gladiatorial champion in recognition of the acclaim being hailed in his direction. It was being predicted that within five years the first homes in France would be trialling mini-fusion reactors in order to satisfy their energy needs. People inside the Airport Terminal were suitably buoyant having heard about nothing else from the news media all day. Good news is a rare commodity and people were relishing the positivity. Newspaper front pages were similarly euphoric. 'Puissance', a word previously known only to science experts, was suddenly in everyone's lexicon. The whole circus was too much for Ben. He did not want to be around to be viewed as one of the anonymous physicists. Having to listen to his boss make false claims about how his theories had come to fruition while Ben's ideas were to be expunged from their rightful place in history was beyond the pale. There was only one thing he could do in the circumstances and that was to return home to the bosom of his family.

Ben was able to take his own car from the compound in *Le Bouton* without needing the approval of the top brass. There was a phrase that he could not remove from his mind and summed up his predicament: 'from hero to zero'. He repeated it constantly to himself as a silent masochistic mantra, preferable to the reality he was experiencing. There was no escape from his pain and indignity. Only his physical removal from the epicentre of agony offered any prospect of relief. Given the time of year he was lucky to get a flight from Geneva to Newcastle and there was only an expensive, business class ticket available. However, the high cost was the least of his worries and not worth a second thought. He reconciled not to phone his Dad and tell him that he was coming home, simply to announce it as a Christmas surprise when he arrived at the farm. Meanwhile he welcomed the solace offered by the anonymity of the Departure Lounge.

The evening flight meant he would not arrive in Newcastle Airport until late, though the time difference helped a little. He would have to take a risk hiring a car, it would probably incur further expense but that was not a consideration, he just wanted to be back home at Moyles Farm. While waiting for the flight to be announced Ben sat in Departures with a whisky companion, staring at the floor in case he caught site of yet another tormenting television screen. If he had to look up he preferred to ogle the display board, trying to spot if his flight was delayed, already knowing that a prolonged wait was almost an inevitability on this dark day. Conditions at Geneva Airport were not ideal for air travel but in a country used to dealing with snow and ice, their efficiency meant any delay was minimised. However it was a different story elsewhere; the report on his iphone suggested that the weather at Newcastle might offer more of a challenge. Snow was predicted for the North East region in the UK. In the Cheviot Hills that particular inconvenience was always possible, it was just a question of how severe the problem was going to be.

Unfortunately, the journey home went quickly and Ben soon found himself waiting at the car hire desk behind two other people. He could see through the panoramic windows that snow was beginning to fall, just as predicted. It was forming a cover and that meant trouble for drivers. The late hour also produced a different assistant at the car hire desk to the one normally seen by Ben. After twenty minutes in the queue peering over the shoulder of the man in front and trying to indicate clear impatience in an attempt to speed up the process, Ben was eventually greeted with, 'Good evening sir, sorry we had to keep you waiting, how can I help you?'

There was no point in continuing with the strategy of impatience so despite his true feelings, Ben was polite. This ploy worked and he was able to hire the only four-wheeled drive still available without prior booking. Yet again it was expensive but he was past caring.

The main roads around the Airport were being kept clear by the constant traffic transforming the falling snow into slush and then water. Although it was late and unwelcoming it was also a busy time of the year. Some people were visiting relatives, others were engaged in late-night shopping and the various activities demanded by Yuletide. It was a different story on the country roads. The snow was getting heavier and drifts were beginning to form in adjacent fields. Ben had to engage double-speed for the windscreen wipers to ensure the view was safe for him to continue. At one point he stopped the car to sweep away gathering snow from the bonnet as even the engine's warmth was finding it difficult to stave off the accumulation of whiteness. The traction system on the four-wheel SUV enabled a safer journey than provided by some other vehicles but extra care was still needed nevertheless. Four miles from home two abandoned cars had been left at what used to be a lay-bye. There was no sign of the drivers which pleased Ben, the last thing he wanted to do was offer any charity to a stranger in distress.

When he reached his home lane, Ben could see that someone at Moyles Farm had anticipated events and made an attempt to clear the gathering snow in the driveway, presumably as a last act before retiring inside for the night. One good thing about living on a farm was that heavy machinery was ready and available to attack any of nature's threats. On this occasion it looked as if it was an honourable draw, at least for the time being. As Ben pulled up into the farmyard the front door of the farmhouse opened. The bright light from behind the figure made it difficult to spot the person's face but the size of the silhouette was a give-away. Graham Moyles must have been wondering who was crazy enough to visit him on such a God-awful night, which was getting worse with each falling snowflake. It did not take long for the two protagonists to recognise each other. Ben stomped along the path to remove any lingering snow on his shoes before entering the porch to be greeted by his stocking-wearing father.

'Well this is a nice surprise. I wasn't expecting you, especially on a night like this,' said Graham in a manner that was genuine, even for Christmas.

Relishing the bear hug for reasons his father would never understand, Ben muffled into his Dad's embracing shoulder. 'Thought I would come home for Christmas if that's ok with you?'

'It's more than ok, son. I'm really pleased to see you home again. Rich will be just as delighted. I know that for a fact.'

'Where is he? Is he inside?' Ben asked, although there was also a spur at the back of his mind that his brother may have been in hospital. He knew his Dad did not tell him everything in order to avoid any upset, something Ben had also learned to do in return.

'No he's gone to bed… you know, tired and all that.'

Ben and his Dad continued their conversation as they made their way to the warmth and red glow emanating from inside the kitchen. Graham held up the kettle to check the water level before switching it on, still listening to his son's voice. 'Any developments with the transplant Dad ?'

His Dad allowed himself the luxury of sharing part of his load. 'Na … that young lass I was telling you about died, poor thing and her heart was not a good match as things turned out. So everything remains the same with the transplant- still waiting for a donor.' The end of Graham's sentence was almost lost in the noise of clinking cups and a boiling kettle as he continued to make them both a strong cup of tea, before going to the cabinet and pouring an accompanying glass of whisky.

Just as they sat down to enjoy a catch-up there was a loud click and the lights went off. It was then accompanied by a whirring sound, symptomatic of their boiler winding down. 'Blast!' cursed Graham through the darkness, 'Wouldn't you just know it. At this time of year as well.'

Power cuts were something that Ben had experienced many times before on the Farm, especially in the days of his youth. 'Looks like we could be having an old-fashioned Christmas this year. Must be all this winter weather.'

'We haven't had a power cut for a few years. The weight of the snow on the overhead power lines must have brought down the cables. I'll give the electric company a ring in a minute, once we've finished our drink. The glow from the oven fire will have to do for the moment.'

'No problem, Dad. It'll be just like the old days when Mam was alive. Remember that Christmas when Rich got a bike and was angry as hell because the snow stopped him from riding it.' Graham shrugged a smile at the thought of happier times. Glancing out of the window, he continued, 'Look at it coming down now!'

For a few minutes the two men sat in silent comfort, enjoying not only each other's company but also the softly falling flakes reflecting the light from the window onto the snow, creating a scene from Victorian times.

Eventually Graham rose from his chair and after pouring a whisky refill for them both, he reported the power cut to the electricity people on his mobile phone. Holding up the iphone like a trophy as he re-engaged his backside into its regular moulding he declared, 'Damn clever these phones. What is it you call them ? ...*eye*-phones or something. In olden days I would have had to scramble through Yellow Pages in the dark to get that number. Now I just typed their name into the space on the *engine-thingy* and it came up.'

For the first time that day, Ben afforded himself a genuine laugh with a joke at his own expense. 'Yeah...wonderful thing technology. If only computers could make sure we never got any more power cuts. It's about time somebody came up with a better energy system.' It was all he could do not to break into hysterical laughter. His Dad was a little taken back by the intensity of his son's response to his own joke, but supported the sentiment nevertheless.

'How long was the power off for last time, then Dad?' For a fleeting moment Ben wished he was going to say '*For about six months*,' because after what had just happened in France, he was ready to quit everything and ask his father for his old job back. Working on the farm was suddenly more attractive than it was yesterday.

'Just a few days, son. It depends what happens further down the valley. If the lines are down and the towns and villages are cut off as well they will see to them first before they get to us farmers in the hills. It's just as well we are prepared. I'll go and get a couple of paraffin lamps from inside that cupboard in the porch in a minute. We've got plenty of logs, wicks and oil for the lamps and there's more than enough to eat. It was only yesterday that I went down to the hypermarket in Steddon and got a load of food in, ready for Christmas. With you and Rich in the house as well, I've got everything we need. There's hay and feed for the animals so it can snow as much as it wants and we'll still be alright.'

After the warmth of their whisky, they took a lamp each and went towards their separate bedrooms, turning up the wicks to generate more light. Their shadows cast a dancing display as they ascended the stairs before wishing each other a good night. The snow was still falling heavily and there was the first appearance of cold breath as they spoke their final words for the evening. Then they retired to the cocoon created by the thick duvets in their respective beds. Ben snuggled down, feeling safe from the outside world which he now had good cause to hate. No one could touch him while he was cut off in the safety of Moyles' farmhouse and for the first time in ages, he slept like a pupa moth.

The following morning there was still no electricity, something that was evident to Ben when his breath appeared before his eyes as he was still lying under the bed covers. With chattering teeth and skipping toes he made his way to the bathroom like a tap-dancing polar bear. At the same time as he arrived at the door it opened and his startled brother took a step back in shock, shrieking simultaneously and causing Ben to give a mocking laugh. 'Sorry bro, I didn't mean to startle you. Are you alright, I wouldn't want to give you another heart attack.'

'Not funny little boy. If I had gone into shock it would have served you right.' For a moment they stood looking at each other, not sure where to take their mock battle, until Richard broke into a smile and after dropping his towel, decided to give his brother a hug before asking 'When did you get here anyway. Did you hitch a ride on Santa's sleigh or something?'

'Yeah, I can forgive you for coming up with that theory. Have you seen it outside, it's going to take us ages just to dig our way out of this one.

'I don't think we need bother. Dad saw the forecast yesterday and went out into the fields with straw for the sheep. All the others he has brought down here, at least as best as he could. The cattle are in the sheds as well. All we need now is a manger and we're set for Christmas.'

Ben flicked the towel from the floor with his foot and his brother dutifully caught it nonchalantly. Rich was half-way out of the bathroom doorway as Ben spoke to him and said, 'See you downstairs in a minute. You can make me a cup of tea ready, if you want. Two sugars. Just ask Dad for the recipe if you're not sure how to make it!' Rich's middle finger salute told his brother all he needed to know.

Scrubbing his wet hair with a towel as he entered the kitchen, Ben exclaimed with pleasure. 'Phoah ... it's nice and warm in here. It's blooming freezing upstairs.'

His Dad was crouched on his knees poking the oven fire to try and generate an even bigger blaze as he turned to speak to Ben. 'Morning son. Yeah it's bitter out there. I've just come in from feeding the chickens and seeing to the livestock and you don't want to go out there in a hurry. I've even put a basket and blanket by the back door there for Archie. It's too cold for him in the barn, even inside his kennel.'

'Well it is Christmas Dad – goodwill to all men and dogs, and all that!' offered Ben.

'Not yet it isn't bro. It's not even Christmas Eve until tomorrow.'

Ben's face re-appeared from under his towel head-cover. 'Thanks for correcting me.'

Rich continued the family banter. 'Always my pleasure to put you right little brother. I'm never too busy to do that.'

Their father intervened. 'Give it a rest you two will you. I'm trying to make us some breakfast here, at least the best I can in the circumstances. I suppose even you two bright sparks have figured out that the electricity is still off. We've got no phone connection either and my mobile batteries are flat. I forgot to switch it off last night. How about yours, are your phones working?'

Ben was the first to defend himself. 'Sorry Dad, mine's flat as well. I didn't get the chance to charge it, what with coming here from the airport and everything.'

Rich attempted to save the day. 'I put mine on charge last night before I went to bed. It should be in the lounge. Hang on, I'll go and get it for you now.'

While Rich was out of the room, Graham recovered from his haunches and replaced the poker into its stand before dusting down his hands on the thighs of his thick moleskin trousers. Busying himself by unpicking a pack of bacon and sausages, he turned to his younger son. 'I'll get this done and then maybe me and you can sit down and have a proper chat and then you can tell me why you are really here.' Ben threw up his arms in front of his defeatist expression as he finished towelling his hair. 'What … you didn't really think I was going to fall for that surprise nonsense did you? I can see it in your face. Something's wrong and I want to know what it is. Don't worry, we can wait until Rich is out of the action. He normally has a kip in the middle of the afternoon so we can do it then. Let's get breakfast out of the way first.'

Rich re-appeared at the kitchen doorway just as his brother and father were in the middle of their pregnant pause. 'What ? … talking about me while I was out of the room were you? Come on then, tell me what he's been saying about me.' Rich's eyes moved in the direction of his father.

Ben treated the question with due contempt. 'How's that paranoia coming along these days Rich? It seems you're cultivating it quite nicely, bro.'

'Oh, haaa-haaa. It's only started to get worse when you arrived, anyway.'

Graham took control once more, grabbing the mobile out of his son's hand. 'Look… just give me that phone and go and cut some bread. Ben – you stoke the fire and put those sausages and bacon slices into the frying pan on the oven hob and keep an eye on them while I try and get hold of the electricity company to find out how long the power cut is going to last.'

The battery icon on Rich's phone showed an energy reading of only five percent and Graham assumed that the power cut must have curtailed the charging process. He was not too happy about it, 'Damn! there's hardly any life left in this phone either.' He looked accusingly at Rich who felt it necessary to defend himself. 'Sorry Dad, I put it on charge last night, honest.'

Graham's first attempt to get through was met with an engaged tone. He switched it off to wander over to the oven hob to make sure Ben had not burned their breakfast. 'It's ok, Dad – I'm on it.'

After finally getting through via four dialling option choices, Graham was forced to listen to Vivaldi before he was informed he was sixth in the queue. He busied himself by helping his son with the food preparation while constantly holding the phone to his ear to make sure that he did not miss his turn. After ten minutes, just as he was cracking an egg one-handed into the frying pan he could hear an ingratiating voice. 'You're through to the Emergency Service at the Northern Electricity Board – sorry to have kept you. How may I help?'

Recognising the need to cut to the chase, given the amount of battery life left on Rich's phone, Graham garbled his question. 'Can you tell me how long the current power cut is likely to last please.'

'Certainly sir, can you give me your post code and I will check that for you.'

'Yes, it's NE72 6BD.' After the announcement of the six in the postcode the phone went dead, the silence only broken by a frustrated caller. 'Hello, hello ..damn and blast!'

'Ben was the first to try and console his father when he saw Graham raise his eyes to the ceiling. 'Never mind, Dad. Come and get your breakfast. We'll just see what happens. It's not a problem, just relax and enjoy not being in the fields today.'

The first job of the day was to assess the situation. Around the farmhouse and towards the various outer buildings it was necessary to clear a path to create some access. Members of the trio each took a heavy duty snow shovel and waded through deep drifts to the maintenance shed. From there, they started to create a path towards the respective outer buildings. A trail was made from the farmhouse to each area where they would need to visit daily, especially to where the animals were housed. It was hard work but in the context of a snowy Christmas it was immense fun and after a couple of hours they were finished so headed back to the comfort of the farmhouse.

The two brothers sat beside the fire in their kitchen, chatting and waiting for their Dad to return from his mission to feed some of the livestock after clearing his own pathway to the barn. Before Graham returned they both started to glow in the warmth of dry clothes and the recovery from some physical labour. Ben knew from the scratching sound of Archie's paws on the back door that their father was on his way. The sound was unheard by Rich whose eyes were beginning to close in the hypnotic peace of the occasion. Ben slinked out of the room unnoticed and returned with a thick blanket which he placed over his now-sleeping brother. At that moment he could hear his Dad approaching the front of the farmhouse so Ben went to the porch and like a conscientious car park attendant pointed for Graham to go around to the back of the house.

By the time he had made his way to the farmhouse's rear entrance, the master of the farm was met by a dutiful Ben holding a freshly made cup of tea and a finger of whisky. Archie was trying to jump at Graham's knees and gain some attention, but the sternness of the rebuke saw him instantly return to his basket. Graham raised his eyebrows and Ben responded by pointing in the direction of the kitchen, 'He's asleep. I think the hard work and the cold have knocked him out, especially once we had got changed into some warm clothes and he got a hot drink inside him. I think it best not to wake him.'

Graham simply raised a thumb in acknowledgement before instructing his son, in a similarly hushed voice, 'Thanks son, that's great.' Refusing to accept the drinks there and then he continued, 'Just take the drinks into the lounge, son. It should be warm in there,'coz I lit the paraffin heater just before we left. I'll see you in there now, once I've taken off my boots and got Archie settled.'

Ben did not see his father go into the kitchen to check on his other son, now fast asleep in a resting pose under a protective blanket.

Entering the lounge where his replacement cuppa was waiting next to a glass containing his snifter, Graham asked and received an update on how their snow-shifting session had gone. Ben reassured him that they had made good progress and though it may turn out to be only temporary respite if the snowfalls continued, paths to the buildings around the farmhouse were clear.

With all distractions now removed, Graham took control of the situation and decided it was the time for a proper catch-up. 'So, young man, are you going to tell me why you are really here. You can cut out the rubbish about wanting to see us at Christmas, etcetera etcetera.... I want to know what has happened because you have never been able to hide anything from me. You're like your brother in that regard. So let's have it.'

Ben knew there was no point in trying to mislead his Dad any longer and given the way he was feeling he did not want to do that either. He felt he needed the comfort of a sympathetic ear and there was nobody in the world able to offer that kind of consolation more than his loving father. Ben placed his cup on the small table beside his chair and moved forward in his seat. 'You're right Dad, something has happened and I don't know what to do about it so I'd really like your advice.' Ben proceeded to recount the tale of what had taken place immediately before his arrival at the farm, deliberately omitting to refer to the occasion when his life was in peril. He knew that no father would want to listen to an account of someone trying to kill his son. Ben restricted his version to include only those facts relating to the duplicitous behaviour of his superiors and their apparently successful attempt to usurp him from his rightful claim for the scientific achievement he had accomplished.

Graham listened intently, taking occasional alternative sips of tea and whisky before declaring, 'So what are you going to do about it?' His tone was reminiscent of an occasion when Ben had reported to his father that another boy had been picking on him at school. Although the actions needed then were different to this more serious situation, the intent was the same; whatever you do, do not simply lie down and accept it but muster all the determination you can, and if you are right then the truth will out.

Ben asked a question, regressing to a childhood scene. 'What do you think I should do, Dad?' before receiving a blunt answer.

'It's no good telling you what *I* would do. I want to hear what *you* are going to do. So tell me what you intend because you must have been thinking of *some* solution.'

'I think I should go to the press and hire a good lawyer to go on the offensive on my behalf. I've got proof that the ideas on nuclear fusion were mine because the data on my research pre-dates what has just happened. I can prove that the principles used in the experiment were based on my original ideas. There's no doubt they will deploy a heavyweight team of corporate lawyers to go on the offensive. They're probably already briefed and ready to go but if I can get the media on my side and then public opinion, I might have a chance at some success.'

'Ok, son. It sounds like a plan. Once we have got Christmas out of the way, that's what you should do. I'll back you all the way. If you need money for a good lawyer don't worry, I'll help you out. What's right is right and there's no way some snotty Aussie scientist is going to get the better of any son of mine.'

At that moment a yawning Richard Moyles entered the room stretching and rubbing his eyes, to bring their discussions to a conclusion.

'Ah there you are you two. I must have dozed off. Why didn't you wake me? Have I been asleep long?'

Graham dished out another portion of paternal love. 'Not at all son, just had forty winks that's all? Come on sons of mine, I think it's time for something to eat and I'm not going to make it on my own.

For the next six days and nights the Farm was cut-off from electricity and the outside world as the amount of further overnight snow surprised them each morning. It was the heaviest snowfall since the record blizzard of 1947. Christmas Day came and went without a programme being watched on the usually overworked television. The absence of electricity meant that phone chargers were redundant but the abundance of paraffin provided plenty of light in the kitchen, where the open fire and old stove embarrassed their modern competitors. The dark evenings were spent playing cards and board games. On one evening the boys decided on a game of pencil cricket, which saw Rich's Walt Disney XI beat a team of Hollywood Stars thanks to a half-century by Donald Duck. The family trio were enjoying each other's company as well as the alcohol. The bright, sunny, crisp days were spent seeing to the livestock and clearing the snow. For the twins it was like old times; Ben and Rich relished being together as they both regressed to a childhood that was timeless. Graham tried to use the tractor to help ease the transport problems caused by the snow and one morning with Ben's help they attached a snow-plough shield to the front-loader. Most of the snow was pushed to one side to the joy of the cheering twins and although it was good enough to clear their driveway, there was no point going any further because the main roads were still blocked without any sign of a reprieve.

Eventually the snow thawed and on the seventh morning there was a loud click as the lights throughout most of the house came on, the heating system re-engaged and Archie jumped to his feet, concerned at the strange turn in events. Graham was pleased that a temporary reprieve seemed probable and their unusual routine could be replaced by something more constructive. Apart from an overhead helicopter hovering over the farm after three days, the men were cut-off from the outside world over most of the festive season. It had not taken much waving for the crew to be convinced that all was well before the aircraft continued scanning the region looking for anyone in more desperate need. At least now things could change.

It was New Year's Eve and after experiencing some withdrawal symptoms Rich switched on the television in the lounge, in an attempt to catch-up with the news and hear about what had been happening in the world beyond Moyles Farm. Hearing the sound of another voice, Ben and his father wandered into the room to join him. None of them was prepared for what happened next.

PART FOUR

I

This was a big moment for Professor Ian Thompkins, one that he hoped would be the first of many when he could luxuriate in his recent hard-earned success. The day before he had informed the world's media of his major breakthrough in discovering a method of producing sustainable clean energy and his monumental findings were greeted with inevitable euphoria. However, their questions regarding his methods were not really challenging, such was the style of modern media investigative reporting. They were less concerned with the how, only with the consequences which were going to be globally massive. Thompkins saw their response as worthy only of contempt. This forum was going to be different because it contained the world's top scientists and they were bound to exercise his intellect. The group comprised his colleagues at Puissance, who in their own way had helped him to achieve his success. Today was the occasion for lecturing them on his methods and their interest would be massive, their awe phenomenal. That was the scenario being played out in Thompkins' mind as he preened himself in front of the wall mirror in his office, preparing to face his admirers.

There was still about an hour to go before all his colleagues would learn his secrets, conundrums that would become synonymous with the name Professor Ian Thompkins. Another Nobel Prize was not even a consideration, it was an inevitability along with an honorary knighthood. He rehearsed it over in his mind, *Sir Ian Thompkins* the scientist of the century, ranking alongside the greats whose names adorned any superior television quiz programme. A name that would feature in every schools' national curriculum to herald a change in history and world power. Like a wasp in a jam-jar the thought bounced around in his head and just for a fleeting moment he wished the lid could allow the pressure of joy to escape.

The intercom from his personal assistant buzzed through. 'Dr Thiroud has arrived Professor, shall I send him through?'

'Yes please, Christelle.'

The beaming sycophant was soon at his master's side. 'You look very smart, Professor, fitting of the occasion if I may say so.'

'You may indeed, my dear Sebastian. This is a special day. This is my day. I presume the arrangements are all in place?'

'Indeed they are, sir. I've just come from the Lecture Theatre and everything is arranged. In fact a few of our colleagues have started to arrive already. No doubt they wish to grab a good seat in order to witness history being created. It is something that they will be able to tell their grandchildren about in years to come, while they are enjoying the comfortable warmth that your brilliant mind has created for them.'

'Good, good. I want to go over my lecture with you, dear chap. There are a few places where I would value your opinion.' A smiling Professor turned to his friend and continued, 'I thought I would begin by going over some of the developments and challenges I have faced over the years, here at Puissance and then pick up specifically on how I have managed to overcome those difficulties to manage a breakthrough.'

For the remainder of their time in Thompkins' office the finishing touches to his important speech were made with some tweaking, courtesy of Thiroud's input. There was hardly any mention of the research work carried out by Dr Benjamin Moyles. The only reference to a change in direction of the investigation emphasised Professor Thompkins' stewardship.

The Leader of Puissance allowed himself one final tie-straightening manoeuvre in front of the over-worked mirror before declaring 'Right Sebastian. I am ready.'

The two men walked past Christelle and began to stride down the maze of corridors towards the far annex that housed the prestigious Lecture Theatre. The Professor could already feel that it was a suitable venue to accommodate such an important seminar. As the two men entered the room there was a burst of instantaneous applause in acknowledgement of their arrival. Sebastian Thiroud diplomatically stood to the side to join in the echo of clapping, allowing his boss to wallow in the adulation being offered by his peers.

Thompkins stood at the raised lectern beaming in feigned humility before gesturing with lowered hands for everyone to sit, but inwardly thinking he would like them to continue for a few moments more. After a couple of minutes the standing ovation abated and Thompkins picked up the interactive white board's remote control, ready to scroll through the many slides to show how his experiment had unfolded. For some reason Sebastian Thiroud slipped out of the Lecture Theatre after walking past one of the security guards who was manning a door at the rear. Looking down at his mobile phone, he seemed to be reading a text and gave the impression he was leaving to sort out a problem.

However, Thiroud carried on walking out of the building, avoiding the world's press journalists who were being kept well away from the Lecture Theatre. Instead, they had been forced to gather by the barrier at the main entrance, about half-a-mile away. They were all waiting to pounce on the scientists once the lecture had finished and failed to notice the insignificant little figure in a woollen hat ghosting past them on his way towards the car compound. There was a white SUV with blackened windows parked in a lay-bye nearby, its engine was running as Thiroud slipped into the vacant back seat. Reaching inside his jacket pocket he produced his mobile phone and pressed a speed dial number. When the call was instantly received he left a message.

'The lecture has started. …I trust that is my part of the bargain completed and we are now even?' There was no response from the recipient, the message was received and understood.

Meanwhile the driver headed for Geneva, to take Dr Thiroud to his chosen destination.

II

Those sitting at the end of the rows, along the side of the Lecture Theatre and closest to the fire extinguishers were engulfed in flames within seconds. Several innocents were more or less vaporised immediately as the devastating explosion blasted the Lecture Theatre to the cosmos. The annihilation was triggered from a remote device controlled by Zenib in the pseudo headquarters of the phoney factory. Almost sixteen kilometres away from Puissance, the activation process was more or less undetectable but the power of its effects was catastrophic. All Zenib had been waiting for was to hear the telephone call from Dr Sebastian Thiroud that the lecture with all attending scientists had started.

Thiroud had been on the payroll of Zenib's organisation since the early stages of Puissance. Whereas Thompkins had been involved in the Project for scientific prestige, his minion was more interested in the money, an impulse born of desperation. Initially, Thiroud's gambling addiction was cultivated in Casino Suisse in Hotel des Alpes on the shores of Lake Geneva. The promise of a three-night stay in opulent five-star luxury as a guest of a mega-rich oil broker he had befriended at the roulette table one night, had been all the enticement needed to gain control over the weak little man. It was Thiroud's vulnerability to gambling that Zenib had seized upon. Before Thiroud could do anything about it, the senior Puissance scientist had been caught in a net of deceit created by his own weakness for baccarat and more dangerously, stud poker. It had been easy to entice him into the bed of a beautiful prostitute, manipulate a run of 'bad luck' and then threaten to call-in the subsequent debt of over a hundred thousand Swiss Francs by the time the free hospitality had expired. While he was winning lots of money with a beautiful woman on his arm, the insignificant Thiroud felt like the king of the world. Once the losing streak had started it was impossible to stop. Ben's nemesis wanted to continue chasing the dream even when his failing luck inevitably started to turn sour.

Zenib's phone call to Thiroud's office while he was at work in Puissance two years earlier had made the scientist shiver with fear. It meant his debt collectors could get at him where it hurts and if his superiors were to learn of his gambling problem his reputation and standing within the world's scientific community would collapse. It had been easy to keep Zenib up to speed with developments at Puissance and as Thiroud viewed it at the time, hardly a big deal in his eyes. It was not as if the possibility of a breakthrough was much of a reality, the Puissance projects were going nowhere. All Thiroud had to do was keep the Arab in the loop and grease the workings somewhat. That had meant approving the paperwork granting the maintenance contract to a company operating from a factory in Geneva. At the time, it meant only a little inconvenience and a smidgeon of guilt for Sebastian Thiroud. However, it enabled the surreptitious installation of surveillance cameras to proceed and gave the company control to observe what was happening within the Puissance Project on a day-to-day basis.

Unknown to everyone, the regular overhaul of fire safety equipment in most of the key buildings just before Christmas had let unknown agents install powerful explosives within the extinguisher capsules placed on the walls of the major laboratories within Puissance. On this particular day in the festive period, their heavy duty installation in the Lecture Theatre had allowed the instant annihilation of all the world's leading energy physicists at the press of a button. The huge fireball lit up the sky like an atomic bomb and the explosion could be heard across the still air into Switzerland.

From the back of the white SUV Thiroud turned around to see the orange glow rise above the level of the Alpine peaks. The explosion took him by surprise, he thought his phone call was the signal for some potential disruption to Thompkins' lecture. It had never crossed his selfish mind that Zenib would act in such a devastating manner. Thiroud had grossly underestimated the savagery of the person pulling his strings. In the instance between the stirrup and the ground he hoped that the apocalypse was not the result of his actions but that the timing of his phone call and the explosion was nothing more than a bizarre coincidence. It was false optimism because in that split second of horrible reality, he understood what he had done. Suddenly, Dr Sebastian Thiroud felt very frightened and very vulnerable and he wanted the car to cross into Switzerland as quickly as possible. Casting a glance at the chauffeur in the driver's mirror, Thiroud could only see a steely pair of eyes staring back at him and his blood ran cold.

Everything had changed when Thiroud reported to his paymaster that a potential breakthrough in the energy market had been made possible by a researcher called Dr Ben Moyles. Suddenly the stakes became much higher and the threat to the oil industry more manifest. Once the surveillance equipment had been discovered in Moyles' apartment and other various locations within Eta Lab, the options became significantly reduced. Zenib was aware that his own paymasters would not be pleased with the way things were going and drastic action was needed to put things right. Time was also working against the suppression of the news and there was no opportunity to finesse an outcome. If Thompkins had not gone to the media first, fewer people would have lost their lives. The speedy solution had to be wholesale and indiscriminate though no one expected such a level of carnage.

Zenib stood on the flat roof of the factory in the industrial estate, his binoculars trained westward towards Sergy. Once he heard Thiroud's voice over the phone he had flicked the switch which activated the explosives hidden in the fire extinguishers, using a radio signal from within the disguised factory. After a couple of seconds he was raising the field glasses towards the clouds and the rising fireball in the distance. He did not need an expert to tell him that his scheme had worked, no one close could have survived such an explosion. Lowering the glasses to his waist he afforded himself a wry smile. He knew that as long as the principal protagonists involved in the research at Puissance had been wiped out along with their secrets, his work would be appreciated by those who had hired him. Anything less would have seen him incur Connolly's wrath.

Zenib took out his mobile from his rear trouser pocket and pressed the relevant number. There was no two-way conversation, he simply said 'It's done,' before curtailing the call and picking up the detonating console. Then he made his way below where two men were waiting for his instructions. 'That's us finished gentlemen. Remove everything of value you can and what you can't take away make sure is completely destroyed. I think you know what I mean.' Their actions confirmed they were aware of what to do. Half-an-hour later, as Zenib was handing his coat to a waiter in his favourite Geneva coffee shop, the deserted factory complex was ablaze, the consequence of what would be reported as an electrical fault. As far as Zenib was concerned, he had cleaned up his own mess. Once the fire in the factory was allowed to take its course, there would be nothing to link him with anything related to the catastrophe. Connolly was bound to be pleased, and for Zenib it was a case of job done.

Connolly was as good as his word. The following morning Zenib logged on to his online Swiss bank account and after entering the relevant code he could see a deposit had been made, amounting to half-a-million Swiss Francs. He was going to have plenty of time to enjoy life before contemplating his next move.

However, for Sebastian Thiroud the future was less promising. The dawning reality for Thompkins's side-kick was an awareness that he had now outlasted his usefulness and could be considered a liability. Zenib had squeezed every last morsel of information that he had been able to provide. Compared to the size of the sums of money at stake in this whole conspiracy, his gambling debts were insignificant. Compounding everything was Thiroud's awareness that he was involved in sabotage up to his neck and more importantly, he knew too much. Even a fool would realise that his shelf-life was passed its sell-by date and there were few places to hide. As soon as he crossed the border into Switzerland, Thiroud reconciled to try and disappear.

The response by the official rescue services to the explosion and the ensuing fire was pandemonium. Within seconds Puissance's own security fire service was attempting to douse the flames but it was immediately obvious that the scale of the disaster required more support. The noise had carried several kilometres over the airwaves and emergency calls were flooding into call centres. *Service d'Aide Médicale Urgente* (SAMU) and *Service Mobile d'Urgence et Reanimation* (SMUR) were quickly on the scene with their mobile intensive care units, aided by the Swiss Militia Fire Brigades (*Miliz-Feuerwehr*) which had thundered across the border to assist. Yellow safety hats and thickly clothed uniforms were running in every direction, uncertain on how to proceed, only sure that they needed to be seen doing something. The roof above the Lecture Theatre had collapsed and from the top of a ladder extension an unmanned hose was gushing a thick jet of water into the centre of the devastation. Flashing blue lights were everywhere and those people who had survived or were suffering shock were being comforted by the ambulance staff and blanketed in aluminium-coloured sheets, either on the roads away from danger or on stretchers preparing to take them to hospital. No one seemed to be in charge and journalists and cameramen were running to any scene that offered an appealing shot for their newsreels.

Television programmes across Europe were interrupted while strips of coloured text moved along the bottom of screens giving news updates, even as the presenters were attempting to give their own version of events. A cascade of dishevelled reporters on the scene were attempting to rationalise some order onto the chaos that viewers could see in the background. Directors from their mobile units were shouting instructions down ear-pieces being pressed against the sides of heads. Tightly-skirted dollies were trying to give a report only because they were in the right place at the wrong time and were operating clearly out of their depth. After the commercial breaks the scheduled programmes were curtailed and replaced by ones showing a panel of 'experts' sitting around a coffee table, attempting to give their own interpretation of events, all speaking out of ignorance and supposition:

'I always said it was too dangerous to have such research near a populated area.'

'This is clearly a terrible accident.'

'The most obvious explanation is a terrorist attack by agencies yet to claim responsibility.'

'I'm not sure what has gone wrong but we must send our sympathies to the families of those concerned.'

'It seems strange that this explosion has occurred when it did, given the enormity of the announcements being made at the current time.'

Watching from a coffee bar in the centre of Geneva a smug smile crossed the face of Zenib as he watched the product of his work with detached satisfaction.

Meanwhile, Captain Jacques Durand was being blue-lighted in a police car as a blasting siren was persuading most drivers to pull over to the side of the road. He was being rushed from the police station at Bourg-en-Bresse to the source of the fireball in Sergy. No one had anticipated any problems when the lecture was planned so Durand had left the Puissance complex early before Thompkins had started to give his address. The routine security had been delegated to a junior police officer and Max Blosser. Durand had been about to enter the roads around Bourg-en-Bresse when he heard the explosion and turned to see the same fireball that Thiroud had witnessed rising in the sky. Durand did not need to ask any questions about what had happened, he only knew he had to turn around and return to Puissance. The local uniformed police were attempting to do their best to liaise with the fire chiefs and medical staff but once Captain Durand arrived, he assumed control.

For several hours the fires burned and smoke from the simmering embers were still too hot to be approached. Reports were suggesting that the number of deaths was eighteen, so far. At least that was the tally of bodies calculated by journalists counting blanket-covered stretchers being solemnly marched to a procession of ambulances during the course of the day's events. Viewers were being warned that the death total could rise once the rescue services were able to access the inside of the Lecture Theatre. This area appeared to be the epicentre of the disaster and it was feared that Nobel prize winning physicist Professor Ian Thompkins was one of the casualties. At one o'clock in the morning the smoothly skinned news presenter announced that the fire chief had told one of the network's senior reporters that the operation stages had now moved on from rescue procedures to recovery protocols: anybody not yet accounted for was to be presumed dead.

The morning news reports on most Christmas Eve mornings usually contained light-hearted, trivial tales about such things as a family pet dressed as Santa Claus or a long-lost relative suddenly being found to everyone's open expression of joy. Not this morning. The smoulders being observed rising from over the reporter's shoulder were testament to a very solemn occasion, totally lacking in festive cheer.

'I have spoken to the Fire Chief this morning and he has confirmed that only now are his brave and very tired staff being able to pick through the embers after what is being described as a colossal explosion here yesterday. In addition to many dead bodies being recovered from the debris, we still await news about the welfare of the lead scientist here at the home of the Puissance Project, that is Nobel Prize Winning

Professor Ian Thompkins. The Australian physicist remains unaccounted for along with several of his senior colleagues. The Professor was due to give a major lecture here this morning, when he was expected to explain to his peers how he had been able to produce a sustainable source of clean energy, a major breakthrough in power production. That clearly did not happen.

Early reports from the scene are yet to determine the source of the explosion and questions are already being asked as to whether the huge nature of the explosion was in some way linked to Professor Thompkins' research.

Only a couple of days ago I was reporting about the world-breaking research that promised so much for the future. It appears now as if is that future has been plunged into uncertainty.

This is Claude Fiscalle reporting from Puissance Headquarters, here at Sergy for IFF News.

It was the same on every channel throughout Western Europe. It seemed as if the promise of a brighter future had been removed in an instant and that optimism was being replaced by sombre reports of death. The most popular theory being touted about the cause of the explosion was that it had been a tragic accident somehow related to the recent nuclear research taking place within Puissance.

On Christmas Day, the official services were finally able to reach the source of the explosion. The scene was one of devastation and ghoulish cameras were being kept well away. Sheets reminiscent of a large marquis tent had been erected around the critical area in an attempt to create some respect for those who had perished. Not even those long-serving officers who had seen it all before were prepared for what they were about to encounter. Charcoal skeletons in poses reminiscent of ancient Pompeii were everywhere, the crusts of human beings now transformed into forensic objects of study. The intense heat had reduced the size and weight of the human remains which were missing eye sockets and other physical characteristics of human decency. Some bodies had been blasted to fragments and it would take months of intense DNA and dental investigation work before their names would be known and their remains released to the family.

Captain Durand perused the scene from the edge of the disaster arms folded, seething with frustration and anger. Standing next to him was *Commandant* Lucques Belmont the most senior fire officer attending the scene and few words passed between them as they looked on with solemn faces. Durand was the first to speak.

'I think we are not going to find out much today *Commandant*.'

The incident commander agreed. 'Yes, you can see that my *pompiers* are shattered. Duty demands that we send these brave firefighters home to be with their families and salvage what remains of their Christmas Day.'

'And us also, monsieur. I think we will all hug our children a little tighter today after what we have seen.'

'Agreed. Let us return tomorrow and then we can at least begin our investigation in earnest.'

III

The day after Christmas was one of reflection for Captain Jacques Durand. He had arrived at his daughter's house in Poncin near Bourg-en-Bresse late on Christmas Day after his wife Cecille had abandoned hope of ever seeing him enjoy a smidgeon of the family's festivities. The couple's grandchildren had already opened their presents and the main sting of the occasion had been soothed when he finally arrived home. He had apologised to all concerned but after more than thirty years in police service his family had become immune to the situation and his pleas for forgiveness. However, on this occasion even they were taken aback by the timing and scale of this particular case. The last thing they wanted to do was add to his woes.

When he pulled up to the Puissance compound in Sergy the following day, he was waved through the cordon by a uniformed officer. The scramble of journalists trying to question anybody arriving at the complex was less energetic than the day before. Presumably, like everyone else at this time of year, their *Réveillon* had slowed them down just a little. There was no attempt to intercept the main investigating officer, who had already spent the first hour of this particular working day updating his superiors and government representatives about what was known at this stage. There was some concern regarding the way many of the fire extinguishers had reacted at the time of the explosion. The remnants of the capsules suggested that the heat had not caused their outer shells to burst open, rather it was something related to some unusual chemicals they contained. There was a strong possibility that they had contained explosives and the most likely candidate was *semtex*, which could be set-off by an electronic trigger. If each extinguisher was packed with the stuff, the combined effects of their detonation would be comparable to what had been experienced. Since the explosive was one favoured by many terrorist groups, it seemed to be the most likely cause.

Durand was walking up and down an aisle created by tables of evidence. On top of each stand was an unusual or suspicious object that could be pertinent to the investigation. A block of offices on the Puissance site had been transformed into temporary headquarters for the investigating team. At this stage of the process a provisional mortuary also included the charred remains of anyone who had been in the Lecture Theatre at the time of the explosion. The atmosphere in the hall was reminiscent of the reverent silence inside a large church and Durand's leather soles clopped along the wooden floorboards like those of an unwanted intruder. He stopped to pick up a twisted piece of metal from one of the tables and was examining it when Lucques Belmont approached him and spoke first by way of an introduction. 'Have you seen that, my friend?' he said, pointing along the tables toward three men covered in white uniforms, all wearing protective face-masks.

'What are they doing?' inquired Durand who was working his way towards that end of the room.

'They think they have found the remains of the Professor. They are doing what they can to take samples of what is left of him. If it is him, it should not take long for their identification to be conclusive.' Durand murmured a sound of groaning acceptance as if to say: *'Yes – and what next'*. The two men then ambled towards the black crisp that once contained one of the world's finest minds. The body was now nothing more than a crime exhibit.

Durand informed Belmont of developments. 'A press conference has been set up for two o'clock this afternoon. The Minister of Justice herself will be leading the media circus and I believe we are both expected to be there. No doubt somebody else is trying to give you this information as we speak.'

'What does she intend to say?'

'Well, I think the line that they aim to promote to the outside world is that the explosion was caused by an on-site fault in one of the reactors involved in the nuclear fusion process associated with the recent energy experiments.'

'And in reality?'

Durand was beginning to get a little tired of being questioned, but given the important nature of events and the seniority of the person he was with, he continued. 'Well, agents of *Direction Générale de la Sécurité*

Extérieure have already been alerted and their network of informers are being squeezed for information.'

'What does the DGSE intend to do once they have found out who it was?' asked the *Commandant*.

'I think that is a question we are better off not asking, my friend.'

The two men could see that the level of interest being taken over this particular corpse was significant. The remains of a detached arm were being adjusted into position inside the shoulder socket of a crisp body. One of the scientists spoke to the interested group. 'Yes this is the correct arm. As you can see, it is a perfect fit..'

One of the others offered a question. 'And what is that ...' he pointed to the hand, which caused the senior pathologist to peer more closely. ' It looks like a ring of some kind.'

'Indeed it is, though it seems strange to find it on the index finger.'

From what Captain Durand had already gathered during the course of his investigation, it provided all the proof he needed. They had found the body of Professor Ian Thompkins.

At the appointed hour, the line of four key individuals marched past the mass gathering of journalists and sat at the front of a crowded room, behind a bush of microphones. The Minister of Justice read a pre-prepared statement, adjusting her glasses at irregular intervals to stress her intellectual competence.

'I can confirm that at 11.32 local time on December 23rd a violent explosion occurred at the research headquarters of Puissance International located just outside Sergy. Substantial damage has occurred as a result of this explosion, the cause of which I am unable to confirm at the present time. As you can appreciate substantial and significant investigation is currently underway and it would be ill-advised of me to speculate.

I can confirm that eighteen bodies have so far been recovered from the scene but I must stress this cannot be presumed to be the final number of deaths, as the recovery process still continues. Regrettably, I can also confirm that one of the deceased is the distinguished physicist, Professor Ian Thompkins, whose family in Australia have already been informed.

That is all I can say at this stage and I will not be answering any questions here today. As you can appreciate investigations into the cause of the explosion are still ongoing and another press conference is scheduled for the same time tomorrow.

Thank you very much ladies and gentlemen.'

There was an eruption of journalists as they stood trying to hurl questions at the reluctant foursome as soon as the Minister finished speaking. Those in the front row rushed forward and tried to thrust their microphones into the faces of the stunned quartet. The flashing of cameras all firing at the same time produced a blinding light so fierce that the Minister and her colleagues had to protect their eyes, holding up their hands like surrendering captives emerging from a cave. The four officials did not attempt to escape using the same route by which they had entered, opting to make their getaway behind the screens which had provided a backdrop. A number of heavy duty uniformed policemen made it clear to the approaching throng that the event was over and nobody was going to answer any questions. The one tit-bit which the journalists had been fed and which they would no doubt use for their evening headline on the front page was straight forward, *'Professor Ian Thompkins Confirmed Dead.'*

Jacques Durand left the building and made his way back to the site of the Lecture Theatre to see if any more clues had been discovered among the debris. As he kicked his way through some of the external rubble, toying with a stone under his shoe, his mind tried to piece together what he already knew. At the time of one of the most important lectures ever given, explosives had been planted in the guise of fire extinguishers in one of the most highly guarded complexes in France and set off at precisely the correct time to cause maximum damage. This was also at the workplace of someone who had previously reported having had his apartment invaded by sophisticated surveillance equipment. Was it by chance that two dead bodies had also been recovered in the Geneva area about the same time as all this other stuff was going on ? One of the bodies was recovered from an explosion in a garage owned by someone with a dubious background, the other killing involved the discovery of a torso of a dismembered body of a male yet to be identified? There seemed to be too much of a coincidence that all this was happening in the same place, at the same time. Durand had never really believed in conspiracy theories but the more he thought about it the more he came to think that someone operating at the highest level in his country was trying to suppress something for their own gain and seemingly nothing was going to get in their way.

The worst of it was Durand had no real leads and did not know where to start. Inside the make-shift headquarters on the site at Puissance he called a meeting of his most senior police colleagues. They were all facing their respected boss, confused at what they should be doing and such was the pitch of their anxiety that everyone was standing. Durand rattled off a series of commands to several sub-groups, each assigned with a specific task to gather information relating to the key components of their investigation. They were to call-in favours from the criminal fraternity, interrogate all their usual informers and do whatever was needed to gather information which they could collate, ready for a brainstorming session the next day. Although they all were given a new sense of purpose, Durand was not sure if they would be any further forward in twenty-four hours' time. He only knew that the pressure to get results was soon going to be unbearable.

IV

Sebastian Thiroud was anxious. The size of the blast he had witnessed over his shoulder as he pulled away from the Puissance buildings confirmed that he had been played. He was not sure why he had been asked to phone that particular number once all the scientists were in the Lecture Theatre but had certainly not been prepared for what he saw as the car pulled away. As his driver made his way to the Swiss border the thought that grew in his mind was the realisation that he was part of the same research as those who were killed. The more he considered events, the more he realised that he had no protection from whatever was going on. The doubt did not take long to grow in his mind that he was now in danger himself. Questions would inevitably be asked by the authorities about why he had left the Lecture Theatre. It was an obvious question and one he could not answer and he became increasingly concerned with each passing metre that he had to act to preserve his own safety, all the time knowing he had been set-up.

Once the car had passed through border control into Switzerland and entered the jurisdiction of the *Romandy*, Thiroud was under the impression that he would be taken to the casino. The plan had been to enjoy an afternoon playing baccarat knowing his gambling debts had been settled by the phone call. However, that was before he felt the vulnerability of fear and he was having a major re-think. The little man sat hunched on the back seat staring out of the window at the passing buildings while pruning his finger nails, chewing on them anxiously and trying to think hard. Travelling along the lakeside road they came to a set of traffic lights which turned red at the junction with *Rue du Mont-Blanc.* Thiroud saw his chance, and lifted the door handle a split second before the driver intended to pull away. Ignoring the shout of 'Hey!' from behind the steering wheel Thiroud ran along the bus lane, under the red awnings of the Bristol

Hotel before the overweight chauffeur had a chance to unbuckle his seat belt. While cars behind beeped their horns in annoyance, the driver had no recourse but to slap his hands on the steering wheel in a gesture of frustration, knowing that Thiroud had escaped.

The senior scientist had intended to go to his apartment in Geneva's Old Town where the trendy cobbled streets offered convenient small bars and cafés, ideal for the night-life of a loner. He now found himself walking quickly through the shadowy streets created by the tall buildings near the railway station, a less salubrious part of the city. Thiroud needed to find sanctuary quickly because everything about his behaviour was telling passers-by that there was something wrong. Wandering along *Rue du Prieuré*, a street containing tobacconists, cheap restaurants and curry houses, he noticed a narrow vertical sign trying to indicate the India Hotel, but the letter 'a' of the first word was missing. This was not the time to consider other options so he reconciled to check into the 'Indi Hotel' and buy some time to re-group.

Descending a couple of steps into the darkness that contained the reception desk, there was no one present at check-in. An old television was positioned on a high shelf above a doorway behind the counter. The former scientist was horrified to see breaking news about a huge explosion at the Puissance complex near Sergy. Suddenly a small man of seemingly Indian ethnicity appeared and politely inquired if he could help. While trying to retain one ear on the tv commentary, the sweating customer inquired, 'Do you have any rooms available?'

The receptionist had presumed that he was going to be asked for directions and was a little surprised that someone so well dressed would want to stay at this particular hotel.

'Yes sir, we do. Is it just for yourself, sir?' Thiroud nodded while removing his wallet from the inside pocket of his jacket. He was disappointed at the amount of cash it contained.

'Credit card, ok?' He knew he would need some cash if this particular corner of downtown Geneva was going to be his sanctuary until things blew over.

The stress of the situation was proving to be too much for this flawed individual. The receptionist did not show him to his room in case anyone else wandered in from the street, preferring to stay at his station by the counter. Inside his particular chamber there was no television, only a bed, a washbasin and a wardrobe. The room's main advantage was its anonymity. It was hardly likely that anyone would think to look for him here. The hotel was also surrounded by similarly low-key cafes and bars where he could hide-out during the day without being noticed. If the early reports of the explosion were accurate, his absence from the Lecture Theatre might remain undetected and he might even be declared among the dead at Sergy. That would be a definite bonus, enabling him to start again somewhere new. After all, he had never sought publicity the way Thompkins' had courted the media so it would be relatively easy for him to 'disappear'. Absolutely exhausted by the stress of the situation, he flopped down onto the dark green duvet cover and found the temporary comfort of a deep sleep.

On the first night of his new life Thiroud risked having food in a nearby Turkish café. The cuisine was passable but the environment was dire and only a couple of other people were eating there. Thiroud was eyeing the non-eaters inside the place with suspicion especially as the evening newspaper was full of the Puissance story. Reading the account and examining the photographs he was unnerved to the point where he felt compelled to retreat back to his hollow. For the next three days he scavenged an existence and although it was Christmas, there was very little evidence of it in this part of Geneva. Without a change of clothes he was beginning to challenge aspects of his personal hygiene and with three days to go to the New Year, he knew he would have to take some calculated risks.

Thiroud understood that none of his friends or acquaintances would be looking for him, rather they were probably expecting his name to be mentioned in a press conference as one of the casualties in Sergy. As for the others, his knowledge about what they might be planning was threadbare no matter how hard he tried to reassure himself. His phone call was supposed to have been the final instalment of his gambling debt, an act designed to erase everything he owed, or so he thought.

His mind was racing in the loneliness of his isolation while he sat with his sad glass of cognac. At least he would not have to deal with the staff at Schtern Bank any more. It was bad enough having to grovel and embarrass himself about a loan and he still recalled how he could not even access an

ATM in Sergy. The arrogant machine flashed the words *'Fonds Insuffisants'* on the digital screen when he tried to withdraw some cash. He had to go and look for his friend from the golf club to try and help sort it out. Gaston Dubois was good enough to give him some cash to help tide him over when he called at his house. It had been a close shave because Thiroud remembered how he almost ran into the upstart researcher Moyles who was having dinner with Dubois and his wife Camille that evening. Fortunately he had spotted the pretentious nobody's car parked outside Gaston's house. The embarrassment he would have felt if one of his minions had discovered he was a gambler in heavy debt would have been unbearable.

Sipping the cognac in the dark corner of a scabby bar he reconciled to return to his own apartment in a couple of days and try to spot if anyone suspicious was hanging around. If he went when it was late, their presence might be more easily discernible. Suddenly his attention was drawn to a photograph of a face which filled the television screen above the bar. It belonged to someone he recognised: Dr Jonas Brandli had been declared dead at the Puissance site in Sergy. His body was initially identified by a charred family photograph in his wallet and his uniqueness was later confirmed thanks to DNA testing. The newsflash then switched to his home where his widow and two teenage children were being interviewed about what the loss meant to all of them. Their tearful demeanour told the viewers all they needed to know. Thiroud felt sick watching the screen, knowing he had been complicit in his colleague's death.

The little bell above the door tinkled as Thiroud left the café. In the street he pulled up his collar and tried to slink lower into his jacket. It was a cold night and his frosty breath persuaded him to keep moving, although the thought of returning to the hotel was not much of an incentive to walk quickly. Instead he marched to the end of the street just to see if there was life beyond his oasis of exile. On the corner leading into central Geneva a bright ATM light caught Thiroud's attention and being short on cash he decided to see if his credit was good or not. To his surprise he was able to withdraw eight-hundred Swiss Francs without any trouble. He presumed that the closure of the banks over the Christmas period must be working to his advantage.

In fact he did not realise the opposite was true. Although Shctern Bank was indeed closed for the holiday period, online information could still be accessed remotely and his transactions were traceable. Someone had decided to allow Thiroud free admission to his account in order to track him down. Payment for a room to the 'Indi' Hotel had been made using his credit card and that transaction had not yet been processed. However, the withdrawal of cash from the ATM could be identified immediately so the delusion of freedom that was making him feel more reassured was misguided. Thiroud did not know that a car was being directed to *Rue du Prieuré* where the ATM was located. From that moment of interaction with a deceitful machine he might just as well have had a target on his back.

Although Christmas may have only tickled the community around this seedy part of Geneva, New Year's Eve was a different story. From inside his room on the ground floor, Thiroud could hear the revelry outside as groups of people intent on having a good time were making their way to any place that served alcohol. The bars and poky eateries around the hotel were suddenly alive with activity and rather than become anonymous Thiroud decided to hide in plain sight. Most people were singing up to the sky rather than looking directly into faces and he thought by mingling with the masses he would be safe. On his way out of the hotel he noticed an overcoat under a seat at the vacant reception area. Without looking back he quickly swept it upward and within ten metres he was doing up the buttons in an attempt to keep out the cold. The coat swamped his puny demeanour and his self-respect was in danger of disappearing altogether.

He furtively looked around to see if anyone suspicious was looking in his direction but did not notice anything. Content that he was safe, he made his way to his 'favourite' bar to enjoy a coffee and cognac which had become a cheap night out. However, when he got to the door he was surprised to see a massive Turkish bouncer asking people if they had enough money for the entrance fee in order to gain access. There was no point in even trying to get in without paying so he decided to tag along with a group of party revellers who were on their way to the city centre. There was a loud bang and Thiroud's body twitched with fear, before he realised it was a firework exploding in the sky above the group. The others stopped to watch as the display of shooting stars, bursting colour and loud cracking hypnotised their drunken attention.

Thiroud did not see who it was who approached from behind or what weapon he used. He only felt the intense debilitating pain surge through his kidneys as the metal blade caused an upsurge of blood to cascade from his lips. He went to scream but no sound came out as his head went back with horrific realisation at what had just happened: he had been stabbed. Thiroud fell forward onto the shoulders of someone who was standing in front of him while his assailant mingled backward into the crowd. For a second, the support provided by the innocent by-stander allowed him to remain almost upright. The supporter was not pleased with someone invading his space and responded angrily. 'Here watch what you're doing. You almost knocked me over there.' Thiroud continued to fall and as the reveller moved sideways his body hit the road with a terrific thud. Most people were unaware of the severity of his injury, thinking he was simply another drunken reveller. It was only when one of the young girls spotted a seepage of blood emerge from beneath his stolen overcoat that the fireworks took second place and she screamed alarmingly. By that time the perpetrator had escaped into the ether, no doubt keen to claim his reward from the criminal fraternity that had offered a tantalising bounty. Suddenly Thiroud's body entered into death throes with a final dance of death. The twitching corpse made a grotesque site, destroying any potential enjoyment for those in the immediate vicinity.

It was not until the following morning, just after Durand had given his colleagues their daily briefing regarding the Puissance investigation, that the detective received a phone call from a colleague in the *Einsatzgruppe TIGRIS* based in Geneva. The federal task force had become involved when the identity of a stabbing victim in the area down by the railway station had been confirmed. Dr Sebastian Thiroud a chief research scientist, presumed to be among the carnage in the Puissance complex at Sergy, had been found in a pool of blood in a seedy area of Geneva six days after the event. Jacques Durand listened in stunned silence as the detail of the incident was relayed. Twenty-four hours earlier he was gloom-ridden at the total absence of any leads. Suddenly things had changed and there was now a thread that he could follow. Hopefully the trail would lead to the source behind this massive conspiracy.

V

'Wow! Have you seen this bro'. That's your part of the world, isn't it?' cried Rich, pleased at being in control of a situation.

Ben circled around the lounge to get a better view of the television before he sat on his knees right in front of the screen seemingly hypnotised by pictures of foreign buildings. Rich was just about to call out and complain about his brother's selfish behaviour when Ben held up his hand in a one-armed surrender. It was followed by a gesture with more authority and some finger pointing. 'Shhhh.. I need to hear this. That's where I work… right there. What the hell is going on?'

The story now a few days old was being re-hashed as the third item on the BBC News programme, after other clips featuring the country's disruption due to snow and the Queen's plans for New Year at Balmoral. However, the seriousness of the situation in France was in no doubt. Bodies were still being recovered from the debris and a number of key personnel were not yet accounted for. The television announcer re-iterated the news that the leader of research at Puissance, the renowned physicist Professor Ian Thompkins, was dead and his body had been identified and recovered. A brief snippet was shown of the UK Prime Minister sending her condolences to the families of everyone involved , before the newsreader moved on to the next item.

For a few seconds there was stunned silence in the Moyles lounge. Rich was the one who asked the question. 'Are you telling me that you should have been at that lecture, bro?'

At first Ben could only nod his head, before he offered a shocked response. 'That's exactly what I am telling you. That *'renowned physicist'* who they are talking about is the arrogant git who stole my theory and was about to tell the world about how *his* discovery works. I was supposed to be there to listen to him pontificate about how wonderful he is, or rather *was*.'

The enormity of what Ben was saying was beginning to sink into the awareness of the others in the room. His Dad pitched in with a dawning question of his own. 'Did you tell anyone that you were coming home and were not going to be at that lecture?'

Ben could only shake his head in affirmation, 'Uhh-uhh.'

Graham continued, 'So everyone out there thinks you could be one of the dead?' Ben's head-shake turned into a silent nod. 'They could be looking for your body right now? I think you had better let somebody know that you're safe, don't you? Do you want me to get the phone for you, son?'

Whereas his father and brother were naturally concerned about Ben's close shave with death, his mental agenda was following its own path. The one thought dominating his next move was that perhaps this second close call with death was not yet over. If Ben was to call the emergency services in France and declare that he was safe and well and there was nothing to worry about, that would alert others less sympathetic to his well-being. Worse still, if he was to announce to the press that his ideas had been stolen by the Professor and he was nicely tucked away in the family farm in the Cheviot Hills he was basically placing an advert in the window saying '*Assassins this way, please.*'

Ben needed to clarify a few points of his own and asked his brother about what was in the news programme's content before he arrived in the lounge. 'Did they say if they had identified the cause of the explosion yet, Rich?' His twin did not notice the concern in his brother's voice and casually confirmed that the nature of the explosion was still being investigated. 'What about other people? Have they found Sebastian Thiroud or Jonas Brandli? Are they safe?'

After the second question Richard could see his brother's face was covered in anxiety and recognised this was not the time to mess about. 'They didn't mention anyone else, only that the operation was now looking for bodies, not survivors. It could be they are safe but just had not yet announced it.' In an attempt to give his twin further assurance, Rich added genuinely, 'Thank God you came home, Ben. I shudder to think what could have happened to you.' As Ben rose from his kneeling position he tweaked his brother's knee in a gesture of affection before he headed out of the lounge. While his brother continued to watch the television, Ben beckoned his father from the doorway to accompany him into the kitchen.

He realised this was the time to tell his father the whole truth. There was no point in trying to play down the severity of the danger he had experienced and could still be facing. What they had just witnessed on television sent a shiver more penetrating than any snow storm. Ben was not sure how to proceed and he needed his father's advice now more than ever. The two men entered the kitchen with only one of them concerned about how to open their conversation.

'I've got something to tell you, Dad.' Graham looked wide-eyed at his son, not sure what he was going to say, before he continued. 'Things are worse than I actually told you.' The look on his father's face was not only one of concern but also genuine fear.

For the next half-an-hour Graham sat opposite his son engrossed in every nuance and pause while Ben unburdened himself of his tale of woe, omitting nothing. He spoke of the attempt to bug his place on his return to Sergy in the summer, how his neighbour Antoine had been duped in order to gain access to his apartment, how it became necessary to move to a safe house following the successful experiment when he was carrying a huge secret and how his location had been compromised by a tracking device before someone tried to actually kill him. He told him how a random jogger had knocked into him while he was leaving Veronique's flat and how his girlfriend had been beaten up in an attempt to try and find his whereabouts. It was melodrama on a colossal scale, except it was all true.

Once he had finished he took a deep breath, not knowing how his Dad was going to react. They looked at each other, bound by a common gaze before Graham gave his opinion. 'So this Captain Durand, who you say you reported everything to, what does he have to say about it all? Does he have any opinion as to who is behind all this?'

'Well, if he does, he's not telling me. All he has said is that whoever is the cause of everything must be well organised and well resourced. It could be a big global energy company, possibly someone from within the oil industry who has a lot to lose if my energy source takes off. It could even be some Middle Eastern state that has an economy based around its fossil fuels and has too much to lose.'

'No I don't mean it like that. The thing that strikes me about everything you have just told me and from what I already know, is that someone close to you can't be trusted. Someone is giving away your secrets for whatever reason. Who do you have in your life who is aware of what you are doing but you don't really know that well ? Do you have any ideas about who this could be?'

Ben just slowly rotated his head in an act of bemusement. It was a question he had asked himself quite a lot recently. 'There are other scientists within Puissance who know about the nature of my research but at the moment we don't even know if they are alive either. They could have been killed in the explosion so I don't think even they would go that far.'

Graham was more interested in his son's personal friends. 'What about that couple, you know… that banker and his wife. What's her name… er.. that Camille woman. How much does she know?'

'What, you mean Camille and her husband Gaston ? They know very little about what I *do* ? But then again, you could be right, I don't know. I guess in the great scheme of things I don't know them that well. I've been with them socially quite a few times but we've never really talked, you know… on that level.'

'So that just leaves that girlfriend of yours… that Veronique. How much do you know about her? How did you meet?'

Ben explained about how Camille had fixed him up with Veronique as a date at Gaston's fortieth birthday party and after he got drunk she took him home after he passed out. From there, the relationship grew and they had spent a lot of time together.

This seemed to arouse Graham's interest more than any other aspect of Ben's account. 'It's not like you to get drunk, especially at a party like that. Did you have a lot to drink, then?'

Ben blinked in surprise at the question and thought about what his Dad had said, before something swept across his dawning mind. 'No, I remember being surprised the next morning about having been drunk and my head was thumping like a steam-hammer. I was so drunk I was out of it in the car when she took me home.'

Suddenly a penetrating query from his Dad. 'If you were so drunk that you were unconscious in the car and it was the first time that you had met, how did she know where you lived? Who gave her the instructions on how to get to your place? Did she drive straight there?'

Ben leaned back in the chair and placed his interlocked hands behind his head while he pondered his recollection of events. 'I can remember we had come back from the gazebo and I stumbled up the step, which was the first indication that I was unsteady on my feet. Everyone laughed and just thought that I'd had too much wine. Camille suggested calling me a taxi but Veronique volunteered to take me home. I don't remember her asking anyone for directions and I was certainly too far gone to tell her. We didn't drive around looking for my house either. I *do* remember throwing up the next morning and feeling like death.'

'So somebody could have spiked your drink – or was it just the volume of drink you'd had, do you think?'

Something was emerging from Ben's evaluation of events. 'No, I do recollect thinking that it was unusual for me to be feeling that bad after what I had drunk. I couldn't even remember …' Ben decided not to continue.

His Dad picked up on his hesitation 'What …you couldn't remember what?' Ben considered it undiplomatic and unnecessary to explain to his own father that he was not even sure if the pair had consummated their relationship that night. Similarly, he did not want to go into too much detail about how keen Veronique was to have such intense sex so early into their relationship. It was not every girlfriend who would make love in the open air the day after meeting someone.

Graham got out of his chair and walked back into the lounge to see his other son, who was still engrossed in television catch-up while wallowing in the enjoyment of a room now getting warmer. Meanwhile Ben stared at the wall trying to unpick other aspects of his relationship with Veronique. For the first time since his world had been upside down, his father had alerted him to a possible interpretation on his relationship with Veronique that was different to his own. He now had some doubts about his girlfriend.

When Graham soon returned, Ben seized on him with another question. 'But she was beaten up by somebody who was trying to find out where I was. I saw the bruises for God's sake. Surely she wouldn't have gone along with that just to find me, no way!'

His Dad did not relent and still had an explanation. 'Who says? From what you've been telling me these are big stakes and she might well be central to the whole thing. Taking a couple of smacks in the face for something so massive, might be pain worth taking. If someone wanted to give me a punch to the face for a million quid, I'd say go on then – wouldn't you?'

The counter interrogation continued. 'But what about that runner who almost knocked me over. He could easily be the one to have planted that tracking device on me.'

'Who knows, maybe he was. Or perhaps it was nothing more than a coincidence or a diversionary tactic designed to make you *think* it was him. I'm just asking the question. That's all I'm saying.'

The pair jumped as Rich came in with a sudden loud announcement of his own. 'Your phone's charged up now Dad if you want to use it.' He became conscious that a discussion had taken place to which he was not privy. 'You too been talking about me again?' This time Ben had no witty retort about his brother's paranoia; he was too busy taking in the ramifications of what his father had asked about his so-called girlfriend from Lugano.

While his father phoned around some of the locals to find out how everyone was doing in the snow, Ben was doing some phoning of his own. He was trying to book a seat on the first available flight from Newcastle to Geneva. Rich found himself with no one to talk to so he retreated once more into the lounge where a popular sitcom repeat seemed preferable to feeding the animals yet again. It was hardly holding his attention when Ben filtered back into the lounge and slumped into the chair beside him. 'Who you been phoning Ben? Telling everybody that you're safe and well?'

'Nah… I've been trying to book a flight back to Switzerland but the earliest flight to Geneva is not until the day after New Year's Day. Until then I think all I can do is sit and watch how things unfold on the news.'

Rich's curiosity was beginning to grow. 'So you've not heard from that girlfriend of yours, what's her name Veronique, isn't it?'

'No, nothing…no texts or messages.' Ben then sounded as if he was doing more than answering his brother's question. 'It's almost as if she wasn't expecting me to be around anywhere.'

The boys were joined by their father who had a local update. 'Apparently a snowplough has cleared one track along the main road out there so I think I'll get the tractor out and make a fresh pathway to the farm entrance. Then we should be able to get into the village and see how the land lies. Not sure how the shops will be doing for stock. They might not have had any deliveries. They're normally a bit short at this time of year anyway so God knows what the situation is like now because of the snow. I wouldn't be surprised if there's not any bread and availability of some of the other stuff is probably restricted to stop folk hoarding food. At least it doesn't matter to us because we've still got plenty in our big chest freezer in the shed. It will not have defrosted, in fact it's probably colder in the shed than it is in the freezer.' Turning to Ben he continued. 'What about you son, make any progress?'

'I can get a return flight in a few days' time and I've decided not to tell anyone where I am. When I get back I'll report to Captain Durand who is bound to be involved in investigating the Puissance explosion. At least he's someone I can trust. When I land in Geneva I'll let him know I'm safe and we'll take things from there. I don't intend to say anything to Veronique or try and phone any of the others. I'll just wait till I get back and see how they react when they see me.'

The farmhouse was beginning to get back to a state of normality. There was more warmth inside because the boiler was now surging and the re-connected electricity meant the oil lamps could take a back seat for the moment. Graham moved them to the front porch so they could be easily accessed if there was another power cut. Rich volunteered to make some food while Ben and his Dad went out to the maintenance sheds to start up the tractors. Once in action, Ben followed his father, who had the main snow plough attachment. The low loader at the front of Ben's tractor was good enough to move small accumulations of snow missed by his father. Within the hour there was a pathway to the main road and Graham decided to take the Green Goddess into the village to make an assessment of the local situation. If the Black Bull was open he might even treat himself to a pint. However, Ben decided not to go into the village because the fewer people who knew he was on the farm, the better.

Graham returned a couple of hours later and the boys helped him unpack the limited supplies he had been able to get his hands on. Rich noticed the crate of Lockhead's bitter at the bottom of the groceries. 'Feeling a bit thirsty, eh Dad.'

Graham had the answer ready and waiting. 'Well we can't bring in the New Year without a drink and anyway we need to toast your brother's luck before he heads back to France or Switzerland or wherever the hell it is he's going.'

The dusting of grit along their pathway and the salting of the main road was the final punch of retaliation against the snow which had seemingly now passed over the whole of the UK; no further falls were forecast. At least the absence of any more weather disruption meant that Ben should make it to Newcastle Airport without too much trouble and the farm could revert to the sort of normality that was typical of a winter in the Cheviot Hills.

A couple of days later, after some minor family revelry on New Year's Eve, it was time for Ben to return to the Continent. With slightly more concerning advice from his father than usual, Ben made his way from Moyles' farm to the Airport. His father looked worried as Ben was waved off that morning but the whole affair needed to be sorted out, one way or the other. Too much had happened within a short space of time and Ben's life had been turned upside down since his return to Sergy in the summer. People had died, his own life had been threatened and a major scientific breakthrough was at the heart of it all. Ben wondered if it had been worth the grief as he sat back in his seat on the aeroplane; he could only conclude that he preferred his life before all the drama.

During the flight back to Geneva Ben smiled to himself at the image of his brother's two-finger salute behind his Dad's back when he had said goodbye. His stay on Moyles' Farm had been an island of normality in a sea of turmoil. As a family they had done very little out of the ordinary but it was perhaps that routine of simply sharing their home together that made Ben glow inside. Twenty minutes into the journey as he gazed out over the grey clouds, he reconciled to return as soon as this mess was sorted out. One way or another he was not going to go back to the frenetic chase for fame. He had seen enough of that and he wanted nothing more to do with the cut-throat pitch of the world he was about to re-enter. A flutter passed through his body as the thought of what he was about to challenge on his return lingered. There was some dangerous stuff still to be negotiated and he was uncertain of his own safety. Making plans for the future at this stage was highly optimistic.

While Ben was in the air, Captain Jacques Durand was in the pathology lab of the headquarters at the Centre for Police and Customs Cooperation (CCPD) in Geneva. The central investigation team had moved from its temporary base on the Puissance site in Sergy, to a more central location where proper investigative facilities were available. Cross border partnerships between the French and Swiss governments ensured close co-operation and in this particular investigation Durand's authority would not be compromised. Durand and his Swiss counterpart from *Fedpol*, Inspector Tim Favre were standing behind protective glass in a viewing gallery looking down at a covered body on a slab, which was waiting to be dissected by the Professor of Pathology at Geneva Medical University.

The only thing that Durand and Inspector Favre knew more than this medical expert was the name of the corpse. It was that of Dr Sebastian Thiroud a leading figure in the research project based at Sergy who somehow had avoided the massive explosion at the Puissance complex, only to be found in a Geneva side-street during the New Year's Eve celebrations a few days later. What the police wanted to hear was the most likely cause of death. If the autopsy pointed towards a suspect then great, but nobody was holding their breath on that one. The investigating officers were too long in the tooth to expect a second Christmas bonus.

The Professor lifted the sheet to expose the upper torso of the corpse, before sweeping it away like a magician whisking away a tablecloth. It was a flamboyant routine he enjoyed every time. The doctor started his monologue by directing his speech into one of the two miniature microphones dangling from the ceiling. For the first five minutes of his pronouncements there was little new information, confining his description to the obvious characteristics of the body, such as weight, the approximate age of the deceased, hair colour etcetera. When he began the autopsy in earnest he turned the body onto its side to reveal an incision about five centimetres long just below the left lung. Further unpleasant body cuts and organ-weighing moments later, the Professor declared that the weapon of destruction was a thin blade approximately thirty centimetres long with a serrated edge, possibly the sort of knife used by a trapper or slaughter-man in a *boucherie*. The edge had been thrust upward where it had caught part of the lung before passing into the heart. It must have been delivered with some force to have penetrated these vital organs from behind. The wound would have caused massive internal haemorrhaging and death was almost certainly instantaneous. After an hour of further slicing and pontification, the doctor looked up to the gallery and concluded, 'I would suggest gentlemen that whoever killed this man knew exactly what he was doing. It was no fluke, you are almost certainly looking for a professional.'

That was all the two detectives needed to know so while the Professor concluded the routine duties associated with his task, they left the autopsy arena and made their way back to the hub of the investigation, where a meeting was called. Standing in front of display boards covered in photographs relevant to the Sergy crime scene, Durand led the summary of the investigation.

'We now know that Thiroud was definitely murdered and we know how he was killed. Someone out there knows something so I want to you to approach every informant you have and put out feelers. Let everybody know that we do not intend to give up on this one. I want to know what Doctor Sebastian Thiroud was doing in Geneva when he should have been at Professor Thompkins' lecture and killed in the explosion like everybody else.

I want every aspect of the man's personal life examined. Who did he know? What was he up to outside his life at Puissance? I want his medical records examined, his bank account trawled and his inside leg measurement on my desk by the end of the day. Do I make myself clear?'

There was common agreement amongst his troops and they knew what to do. One or two officers returned to their desks but most headed for the exit doors, intent on doing their boss's bidding. A day of intense investigation would hopefully produce the leads they needed. Durand needed thinking time and he returned to his glass fronted temporary office to go over everything once again. Although he was convinced the bizarre series of events were somehow connected to a conspiracy, he had to tie together all the inter-related facts. Little did he know that his best witness was on his way to Geneva.

VI

While Ben watched the baggage carousel begin to move the suitcases around their circular identity parade, he was not too concerned about trying to spot his own luggage. His mind was still whirring with the one thought that had dominated his daydreams during the flight back to Geneva: Veronique. The questions his father had posed on the family farm were natural and came from an objective source he could trust. The main puzzle for Ben was deciding whether those uncertainties contained any merit. There was only one way to find out. Before he phoned Durand to tell him he was alive he needed to confront Veronique.

Ben could not share with his father aspects of his sexual relationship with Veronique. Father and son chats about the facts of life had caused moments of embarrassment for the twins when they were adolescents. Graham was a remarkably blunt farmer at the best of times and when he came to have 'that chat' with the boys, his explanation was more biological than emotional. As a result, all parties found such a topic for discussion was best avoided in the future, even into adulthood.

Ben re-called how he was surprised at Veronique's 'full-on' approach regarding their sexual exploits. She was hot stuff alright and he was more than pleasantly surprised at her feminine freedoms. That first session in the open air under a tree in Avouzon was particularly memorable but he recalled his thoughts during their post-coital afterglow. How did she find him so attractive after such a short time together? Yes, he was a decent bloke and not bad looking but she went straight for the pleasure dome without a second thought. What was she after? She was also a stunner who had seemingly fallen out of the sky and he did not do anything to court her, other than turn up to a party. Camille had fixed them up together; was she privy to all the other paraphernalia as well, along with Veronique? Ben was in danger of contracting some of his brother's paranoia. There was only one way to find out if Veronique was culpable: he had to surprise her and then make a judgement on her reaction. That would tell him all he needed to know.

Eventually his familiar suitcase made its way around and he swept it up onto a luggage trolley. It took another half-an-hour to proceed through passport control before he was standing outside the Arrivals section of Geneva Airport. There was less snow in the air than he was used to but it was bitterly cold nonetheless. The frosty breath of passengers outside the terminal going about their business was reminiscent of a steaming rugby scrum half-way through a match as it seemed to rise like a single cloud. The crisp cold climate of Geneva was something Ben enjoyed. There were allusions to the stillness of summer mornings, although temperature levels were an obvious difference. Looking around the concourse for any possible suggestion of trouble, Ben pondered his next step. His car was in the long-stay car park but was it a beacon for any would-be assailants? Then Ben thought any potential followers could also be scanning the car hire places at the Airport. He decided to opt for convenience and made his way to collect his own car before heading for downtown Geneva.

The last time he had seen Veronique she was back in her own apartment so that was the place he decided to aim for first. Hopefully she would be there, surprised but pleased to see him with open relief that he had not been killed. If things went well in less than an hour he could be sharing a bed and engaged in hot sex with someone he could now trust. It was lunchtime and he had also given some consideration to stopping off somewhere first for something to eat, an idea that was soon side-lined. The high level of activity in the restaurants and cafés that he passed on his way to Veronique's apartment made him re-think his decision. The drive took him through the centre of Geneva, on his way to the Villereuse side of the city and Veronique's apartment. The garden chairs positioned on the pavements seemed a little incongruous for the time of year, though most people had naturally sought the comforting warmth inside the restaurants.

Ben pulled into the carpark and looked upwards towards Veronique's apartment. The crude symmetry of the lego-style architecture contrasted with the sophisticated interior of the chic rooms in this part of Geneva. Veronique's place was on the fifth floor of this particular concrete block, overlooking a busy road but convenient as a central location. It was only twenty minutes from the Schtern Bank where she worked for Gaston. Ben contemplated how lucky she must have been to get such a place, given the circumstances under which she had started her employment. For a fleeting moment as he ascended in the lift, Ben wondered if Gaston's previous personal assistant had been 'encouraged' to leave her employment in order to make way for Veronique but then he gave himself a mental rebuke for engaging in an overactive imagination.

The gentle ping of the lift told Ben he had arrived on Floor 5 and when the screens glided open he walked the short distance along the corridor to Veronique's apartment where he noticed something was not quite right. As he got closer he could see a plastic bucket was holding the door ajar and he called out gently in order not to alarm anyone inside. Silently he made his way into the apartment unsure if it was occupied. Then suddenly he heard a shuffling noise coming from inside her bedroom. It sounded like someone was moving furniture around. He poked his head through the doorway to see a woman in a tabard polishing a bedside table. As the woman turned she screamed loudly and backed into the wall at the shock of seeing a man who she did not recognise suddenly appear in the bedroom.

Ben did his best to pacify her and held up his arms in surrender. 'It's ok… look I'm not going to harm you. I am a friend of the owner of this apartment, ok ?' He could see why she had not responded to his entry calls. The young, slim woman must have been listening to loud music, judging by the earphones now dangling by her side. She did not seem to respond to his attempts to placate her and her wide eyes suggested that she was still afraid. He tried a couple of other languages by way of a soothing introduction but it was not necessary as the girl was French. Her inability to communicate at that moment was a reflection of her fear rather than her nationality.

He accompanied her out of the bedroom and into the kitchen where he was pleased to witness her composure beginning to return as she sat on a high-stool by the breakfast bar. Ben poured her a glass of water in another attempt to calm her down further.

'I am sorry if I frightened you. I am here to see Mademoiselle Perrin. Do you know where she is?' While the woman continued to regain her composure Ben's eyes flitted around the room. The kitchen cabinet doors were open and other than basic crockery there did not seem to be anything inside.

The cleaner shook her head, while gulping the cold water as if it was lifesaving medicine. *'Elle n'est pas là. Elle est partie.'*

Ben could not contain his surprise, '*Croix*!' Without further challenge Ben went into the bedroom and looked inside the wardrobe and drawers, only to find they were empty. It was the same story throughout the apartment. Returning to the kitchen he asked the girl if she knew where Veronique had gone but she simply responded that she had been informed by her employment agency to clean the empty flat, though she did not understand why. Apparently a person from the apartment next door had informed her that the previous day there had been a lot of activity in Veronique's place. A team of industrial cleaners had already gone through the flat from top-to-toe with powerful sanitisation equipment. She said that her own presence that day was not really necessary and up to the point of Ben's scare she was enjoying having an easy shift. Ben thanked her and apologised once more. He felt he should make some sort of gesture of goodwill so reached inside his wallet and gave the girl a 50 franc note. She thanked him and her refreshed demeanour suggested that her day had just improved.

Ben left the apartment, stunned at what he had seen while he was trying to work out the myriad of possible explanations for events involving Veronique. He pressed the zero sign on the elevator panel and began to make his way to the ground floor. As the lift came to a halt he stood motionless for what seemed like an eternity. His sleep-like state was only broken when the doors suddenly re-opened by a resident who was surprised to see anyone inside. Ben did not look at his face but brushed past, uttering an obligatory *'Pardon, monsieur'* as he did so.

Returning to his vehicle in the car park, Ben looked up to the apartment once more. It seemed like a fog of truth was clearing as he settled into the driver's seat. Then he produced his mobile phone from his inside pocket intending to ring someone who could give him a better weather report. This was an important call and Ben needed to gather his thoughts and decide on what to say before making contact. After a few minutes of contemplation he made his move. The call was answered immediately.

'Hello, Captain Durand?' He had decided not to say anything at all if it was not someone he knew he could trust.

'*Oui, ça l'est. Qui est-ce?*'

There was almost an audible sigh of relief as Ben recognised the voice at the other end of the call. 'This is Dr Ben Moyles, Captain – I believe you may have been looking for me.... or at least my body.'

Ben was a little disappointed that the policeman did not appear shocked, no doubt years of professional cynicism had prepared him for anything. 'Where are you Dr Moyles? Yes...we have been looking for you.' When Ben explained that he was in Geneva and he was not far from the Centre for Police and Customs Cooperation, Durand's instructions were succinct and authoritative.

'Stay in your vehicle and I will have a police car with you within five minutes. Do not move. They will bring you to a safe location and I will be waiting to talk to you.'

As good as his word, Ben was quickly and discreetly ushered into Police Headquarters in *Rue de Berne* onto the second floor where Durand was in his office, waiting behind his desk. After an initial courtesy handshake, the detective set to work.

'So Dr Moyles. I guess my first two questions are self-evident. Where have you been and why weren't you at Professor Thompkins' lecture on the day of the explosion?'

Ben was also not in the mood to circumvent the truth any more than the detective. 'I have been with my family since the day of the explosion and only heard of events in the last few days. My family's farm has been cut off by winter snow with no electricity and I returned to Geneva as soon as I heard the news. You can check if you want, it should be easy enough to verify. I got back as quickly as I could and only landed here about three hours ago. The reason I did not go to the lecture is quite simple: I was very angry with Professor Thompkins. He had stolen my ideas and was trying to pass them off as his own.'

'How angry were you with Professor Thompkins, *docteur*? Enough to want to kill him?'

Ben pondered the question for a moment, puzzled at the new direction and becoming frustrated and annoyed. 'Hang on a minute. What is this? I thought that the explosion at Puissance was an accident, that is what they are saying on the news. If you are telling me here now that it was not an accident but was deliberate, that's new to me. Do you really think I'd be stupid enough to try and kill everybody who I had been working with over something like the theft of an idea? Apart from anything else, my friend Jonas Brandli was in that Lecture Theatre and as we speak I don't know yet if he is safe or not.'

'No Dr Moyles. I do not think you are implicated in the killings. Following your call half-an-hour ago I checked with Geneva Airport to see if you were on any flights recently and they substantiated what you have just told me. In addition we know how the explosion was detonated and not even you could have done that from ten thousand metres off the ground. No monsieur, we suspect someone else of that deed, but you understand why I had to ask the question?'

'Yes of course. So you believe it was a bomb that killed all those people?'

'*Oui, monsieur*, it was a planned, calculated act. Explosive devices were disguised as fire extinguishers and placed in each laboratory and other key areas on site at Puissance. We have checked the CCTV footage to try and identify any of the people installing the extinguishers but you will not be surprised to learn that the cameras were disabled at the time. We went to check on the location of the Maintenance Firm and it turned out to be a factory on the outskirts of Geneva. Unfortunately, the same factory was burning when we arrived. Our fire experts are preparing to go through the debris as soon as everything is under control and the building is safe to enter. You will not be surprised to hear either that none of the staff of the company concerned can be traced at the current time. We are also working on that *maintenant*.'

Ben had more pressing concerns. 'What about Jonas? Can you tell me what happened to him. Is he safe?'

Durand did not answer the question, opting simply to shake his head while looking at Ben and supporting his response with the words, '*Je suis désolé, monsieur*.'

Ben stared at the notes on Durand's desk, not wanting to raise his eyes which he sensed were beginning to fill with tears of pain and anger. 'Poor

Jonas. He supported me a great deal, particularly facing up to Professor Thompkins. He was a good friend… His poor family.'

Durand needed to press on with more questions. 'When you phoned me, Dr Moyles you had just been to visit Mademoiselle Veronique Perrin? What can you tell me about your relationship with her?'

Ben sensed a degree of inevitability in the question but considered it necessary to follow the journey. 'Nothing more than you know already. As you are aware she and I were in a relationship.'

Durand picked up on the tense, '*Were* in a relationship, *docteur*?'

'That's right Captain – but she seems to have vacated her apartment and I'm not sure where she has gone. I have not spoken to her since I left for the UK. I could not phone her from my farm because there was no electricity, the snow had brought down phone lines and reception was poor. I simply decided to wait until I got back here only to find out that she has gone.'

The detective reached into a drawer on his desk and pulled out a thin yellow file which he plopped down onto the desk in front of Ben. 'You might be interested in this file Dr Moyles. I'm afraid it's not very thick but it contains enough for us to hazard a guess about what has been going on.'

Ben looked down at the file and then again at the policeman, puzzled by what was on the desk. He carefully flipped opened the front cover of the A4 folder. A pink page of writing was headed: Veronique Perrin, also known at Angelina Fricetti, aka Maria Santaberno. Below the heading there were six passport-sized photographs all appearing to show Veronique in several guises, each one differing in choice of hairstyle and the shape of her eyebrows. Ben's question was asked in a state of genuine confusion. 'I don't understand. What is this?' The incredulous look on his face was about to be replaced by an expression of the penny dropping.

Durand enjoyed exercising his muscles of detection. '*This*, my friend is your girlfriend, or rather I should say this is the woman who purports to be your girlfriend. In reality she is a paid member of a criminal group with strong ties to Lugano. We think she is in the employ of Salvatore Castanelli a Mafia boss based in Naples. Unfortunately for you, she is a '*puttana*' who no doubt has been paid for her services. It just so happens that she is a very expensive, highly skilled and convincing *puttana*. She was never interested in you at all I'm afraid Dr Moyles, only what she could get out of you, or rather what information she could get out of you. She is very skilled at fooling men interested in her obvious attributes and who provide her with information in the most intimate of circumstances… if you know what I mean. Essentially, she was after information about those scientists who worked on the Puissance project. In this particular case, that was *you*.'

'You mean to tell me that she was never interested in me?' The truth was beginning to sink in, although Ben made one last desperate bid at dignity. 'But she was beaten up by people trying to find out where I was.'

'No, monsieur. She *said* she was attacked but I suspect it was really all staged. The man who ran into you when you left her apartment that night may have been nothing more than a distraction or could even have been a jogger out for a run and genuinely bumped into you by accident. Clearly Mademoiselle Perrin's puppet-masters thought she needed to be convincing. After all what are a few bruises and a cut lip worth? No doubt they were charged for the privilege of beating her. It was *that* allegation that led us to discover who she really is… or rather, was. There was a very short list of people who could have planted that tracking device on your person.'

'So where is she now?'

'Oh, I don't think we will ever see her again. She has probably returned to Italy or some distant corner of the world, probably to do the same sort of thing with some other poor sap. Certainly we shall try and find her but with the backing she has I doubt we shall ever know where she has gone to. It was definitely *her* who planted the tracking device on you. Whoever she was working for must have decided you were the principal player in the research project and the one who needed to be eliminated. Once the explosion occurred and they believed you were one of the casualties, she had no reason to stick around.'

Ben was in shock. He sat motionless while his mind went into overdrive. 'The dirty, lousy ….'

His potential foul-mouth rant was curtailed by Durand's next question. 'What can you tell me about Sebastian Thiroud, monsieur?'

'Thiroud ? … Well I can tell you that he is or was..?' Ben waited for confirmation one way or the other from Durand, who simply held up his hands as a gesture for his witness to continue. '…well anyway, as I was saying I can inform you that he is an obsequious little toe-rag, who would do everything and anything for his boss Thompkins. He was an able scientist but a completely obnoxious individual who was central to ensuring the Professor was able to cream off all the credit for himself. You know the sort of weasel… someone who reads the small print first and then makes sure it's followed to the letter. He made certain that I could not go public with my claims. I hate the man. Why? Has he been found or something?'

'Yes *docteur*, his body has been found alright but not where you may have thought. He was not in the Lecture Theatre at the time of the explosion. Like yourself he managed to avoid being killed…. at least for a little while.' Ben squirmed uncomfortably in his seat and wondered if he was still under suspicion for something. Surely recent history was enough to convince anyone that he was genuine. 'Dr Thiroud's body was found during the early hours of New Year's Day in a rundown part of the City. He had been stabbed.' A look of surprise spread across Ben's face and for a fleeting moment there was a trace of sympathy. 'He was clearly in hiding for some reason. We suspect from going through his bank details that he was in serious debt and our intelligence information tells us that he had a gambling addiction. It may well be the case that whoever he owed serious money to caught up with him – or his death may be connected to this conspiracy that seems to be around us. There were some interesting deposits made into Dr Thiroud's bank account and our friends here at *Fedpol* have senior officers examining some of those details right now.' Then Durand's mind appeared to go along a fresh track. 'Did Dr Thiroud know Veronique Perrin at all, Dr Moyles?'

Ben was surprised at the question and wondered why it had been asked. 'I'm not really sure. They may have met at the home of Camille and Gaston Dubois sometime but I'm not sure about that. I'd be guessing really. Camille knew Veronique reasonably well I think. She was the one who fixed up our first date together at Gaston's party. I don't think Veronique knew Thiroud socially, though he may have met her through some bank business related to Puissance. It's a possibility. Then there's a link between Gaston and Thiroud who were members of the same golf club, I suppose though I can't imagine that Veronique had ever met him *there*. Golf clubs were not exactly on Veronique's social hit-list though I'm beginning to reappraise my view on that particular lady.'

'Did Thiroud know Gaston Dubois *well* ? It seems strange that Dr Thiroud played golf. There is nothing in his background to suggest any interest in sport.'

'No, I don't think he played. I presumed he was just a social member. It would not surprise me if that's where he did most of his major sucking up. The number of prestigious personnel who were members of that elite club must have been too much to resist. Thiroud liked nothing more than to ingratiate himself with people in powerful positions. It probably made him feel important I suppose. It's almost as if he was a classic case of *little man syndrome*.'

Both men sat looking at each other, Durand trying almost psychically to evoke a further response. That moment of intense silence seemed to do the trick as something in Ben's mind came racing to the fore. 'Hang on a minute ... yes... there was something... I'd forgotten all about it. There was one occasion when I went to dinner at Camille's place, just after I'd got back from my summer break as I re-call. Yes, that's it, I remember now.... It was around the time we'd just found the surveillance stuff in my apartment and I had just arrived at Gaston's house. I was bursting to go to the loo and went there while Camille was cooking the dinner. The toilet window was open and I could hear voices outside. I looked out and could see Gaston and Thiroud talking together and I remember thinking to myself that they looked familiar with each other, at least that's how it looked to me at the time. I couldn't hear what they were saying but Gaston gave Thiroud something from his wallet. I just presumed it was something to do with their relationship at their golf club. I didn't make anything of it and when Gaston entered the house he never mentioned it either. I just forgot all about it.'

Durand seemed to be kicking around various leads in his mind with each new snippet of information. 'Mmm.. there seems to be a financial connection between Monsieur Dubois and Dr Thiroud. Clearly money is involved in some way and it is interesting that some of the people we are talking about have a banking connection.' The detective became aware that he was thinking out aloud and did not want to betray his considered theory of possibilities. 'Never mind about that for now. I think we need to investigate that issue further with our Swiss colleagues. There seemed to be a money trail with Thiroud also: he had gambling debts and knew both the head of Schtern Bank and his personal assistant, professionally and possibly socially. Early investigations had indicated the sums involved were substantial, certainly something that would have been known and managed by both Monsieur Dubois and Veronique Perrin. Dr Thiroud was vulnerable in a number of ways and that needs further investigation.

Durand was feeling more confident and decided to change track once more. 'So Dr Moyles, where does this leave you? At the moment your name is on the 'Missing Presumed Dead' list at Puissance. No one in Switzerland or France is aware that you have survived, other than one or two people you have spoken to since your flight landed. There is a possibility that if people yet to be identified become aware that you are alive, then you could be at risk. Equally, when the UK media become aware of your involvement in Puissance and your name is on the list of potential dead they may well follow up your story and contact your family, although that might take them a little longer.'

Durand was in default mode. 'You say that the data that led to the discovery of a sustainable energy source is the result of your work?' Ben indicated that the detective was correct. 'I presume you still have that data and its whereabouts are known to you. However, what do you intend to do with the information? The last person who tried to reveal that material was wiped out in the most dramatic of circumstances. We need to think this through.'

Ben listened attentively as Durand pronounced his theories before making a suggestion of his own: 'With your permission, I think it is best if I remain on the list of presumed Puissance dead and keep as low a profile as possible. That means returning to the UK and the sanctuary of my family's farm. That should give me a couple of weeks to prepare all the data and information for the world's media. Whoever is after this data will have to then change their strategy because it will be known and available to everyone. Perhaps then I will be safe.'

Durand's curiosity got the better of him. 'So do you intend to sell your ideas to the highest bidder? Within the hands of private companies this could make a fortune.'

Although he did not show his feelings, Ben was annoyed at the suggestion. 'No I do not intend to sell my theories. I believe this discovery should benefit everyone, not just corporate organisations or governments.

Believe it or not, I did not go into scientific research for the money. I became a research scientist because I wanted to help people, not just the rich countries but those who were seeking to develop with limited resources. Call me naïve if you like but it has never been about money. I want my name to become known for the right reasons and not because I have discovered something that will make me rich.' Durand pursed his lips in admiration.

'Ok monsieur. Leave it with me for a few moments. I will check the time of the next flight out of Geneva and we will discreetly escort you to the Airport and you can return to your family. With your permission I will alert the police authorities in the UK to your situation.'

'No, I do not want you to tell the British police. If you want me to sign some sort of waiver or whatever to specify that I don't hold you in anyway responsible if things go wrong then I will do so but I think the fewer people who know about this, the better.'

'If that is how you want it *docteur* then I completely understand.'

After about twenty minutes Captain Durand returned to his office where Ben was still seated while waiting for travel information. 'Unfortunately there is no other flight to Newcastle Airport today but there is one to London Heathrow in a couple of hours. From there you can catch a plane to Newcastle at 22.35 this evening or drive home, whichever you prefer. It means you will get home very late but that might not be such a bad thing. There will be fewer people going about their business.'

Within twenty-four hours Ben was catching the second of his two-way flights between the UK and Geneva. The information he had gleaned from the trip acted not only as a warning for his personal well-being but it also prescribed a strategy that would hopefully lead to his safety.

VII

Adam Connolly was waiting in his car which was parked in a discreet spot overlooking a small marina on Lac Léman. A tap on the window made him raise his head away from his iphone where he was checking emails. A beckoning index finger indicated that Zenib should enter and he slid into the adjacent passenger seat in the rear of the car. At the same time the driver got out and stood about five metres away, just out of earshot. Connolly handed a black leather attaché case to Zenib who clicked it open and took a peek inside.

'It's all there, you can count it if you like, just not here,' was Connolly's only curt instruction. 'It is the sizeable bonus we agreed.'

'I'm sure it is Mr Connolly. I think I can trust you.' The comment evoked an ironic smile on Connolly's face.

AC summarised his employee's work. 'A job well done my friend. My employers are going to be very pleased. There may even be another bonus. Yes, they are going to be delighted. It was a close call, even if I say so myself. What is the latest body count?'

'Eighteen confirmed dead was the last I heard but they may never find the remains of some of them.' With a sense of relief he continued, 'I guess that's the end of our business?'

'Almost – but not quite. Until all the names we want are included on that list there are some final checks I want you to do.'

'On who, Mr Connolly? I don't think anyone is left to identify.'

'Well at the moment, there are no indications that the remains of Moyles have actually been located or identified. Thompkins and his immediate associates are accounted for but my associates will want one hundred per cent confirmation. How you get it, I will leave up to you. We know that fool Thiroud will not bother us anymore and may even end up taking the wrap for the whole thing. The girl has gone back to Italy, though I think she will be moved-on until all the heat blows over.'

'What about the other one? Is that secure?'

'That's water-tight. Nobody's going to blab on that front so there's no need to worry there. Everything is as sweet as a nut thanks to all the money we have turned over to ensure silence.'

'Ok Mr Connolly, you'll hear from me as soon as I have anything.'

'Make it quick, that's all. The sooner my people can increase their oil prices, the sooner you'll get your bonus.'

Zenib got out of the car with the attaché case gripped tightly in his left hand, while his right reached inside his jacket to shadow hold his shoulder holster. Half a step away from the car he looked around, trying to spot anything suspicious, he trusted no one. After satisfying himself that it was safe to proceed he waved a thumb at the driver, who acknowledged the signal before returning behind the wheel. Connolly's car was already on the highway before Zenib had arrived at his own about fifty metres away. He was not sure what further checks he could carry out on Moyles to confirm everything was in order. There was no chance that he could have survived that blast. The only possible alternative was that he decided not to attend the lecture without telling anyone. It did not matter too much, everyone left a trail and if Moyles was still alive Zenib would soon sniff him out.

Meanwhile, Ben was boarding his flight and making a temporary escape to the Cheviot Hills. It was after midnight before he arrived back at Moyles Farm. There were still pockets of snow lying around the countryside, reflecting cars' headlights back onto the wet, shiny roads. Small mounds of ice lay under hedges and along the sides of ditches on the route home from Newcastle Airport. Ben was becoming something of a regular at the car hire desk. The four-wheeled drive SUV was now also more familiar to his touch and as soon as he set off from the rental compound he reached for the heater switch. As well as the snow, there were also occasional patches of ice along the lanes at that time of night but the scrunching noise under the tyres indicated that the gritting lorries had been out preparing the roads for the consequences of plummeting temperatures. Ben spotted the orange light of one yellow truck blinking on the roof while it was scattering its load. For a moment he was concerned that the spray of grit splattering on the bonnet of the rental might cause some damage, a thought that soon passed when his mind addressed more serious matters.

Ben was unsure how much to tell his brother and father about the situation but by the time he arrived at their driveway he had decided on a policy of complete honesty. In theory it was not just his own safety that he was placing in jeopardy by returning home, the rest of his family were at risk if his whereabouts became known. The absence of any lighting in the farmhouse caused Ben to close the SUV's door quietly as he crept into the house and up the stairs without making a sound. Once inside he placed his suitcase on the bed and sought the toilet down the corridor. He suddenly jumped when he saw a large silhouetted figure standing in his doorway.

'Dad! You scared the living daylights out of me!'

'Sorry son but I heard you come in.' Ben wondered how that was possible. 'Everything alright?'

'Everything's fine, Dad. Go back to bed, I'm sorry I woke you. We'll talk about everything in the morning.'

It was ten o'clock before his father returned to the farmhouse from his early morning shift in the fields. Ben was in the process of updating his brother on some of the bare details about his return, omitting the more sensitive issues. He made them all a cup of tea while his Dad warmed himself by the stove. Finally, when they were all seated and comfortable Ben declared, 'I need to talk to you both….' Just before his brother pitched in with some attempted wit, he was cut short by his twin, who added. '… seriously.'

'Ok son, we're listening.'

While the animals were feeding in their respective barns and the chickens clucked around the yard Ben began his tale. He told his father and brother about Veronique, the break-in to his flat, Antoine's assault, the experiment, the need to live in a safe house and the assault on his life. He left out nothing and although most of it was already known to his father, for Rich it was all a complete shock. Ben informed them of the real reason he had returned to the UK: people had been killed and someone was after him too. He had been betrayed by Veronique and Sebastian Thiroud and possibly others. Captain Durand of the French police was working with members of the French and Swiss Governments to find out the source of the conspiracy and identify who was at the heart of the whole affair.

'One of the things I intend to do while I am home is to prepare in writing everything that Professor Thompkins was going to tell his team of scientists but had been prevented from doing so by the explosion that killed them all. Someone has a vested interest in preventing this information from reaching the world's scientific community. I intend to ensure that this discovery is made available to every country in the world. What they decide to do with it is up to them but I intend to share this knowledge.'

'But it's going to make you rich and famous, right little bro?' asked Rich with all the enthusiasm of an excited child.

'Yes Rich, it could make me rich and famous but it's not about that. This discovery will change the world. It is equivalent to the discovery of the atom, or penicillin or the silicon chip. It is that important and that's not just me saying it.'

His father, as ever saw straight through to the heart of the issue. 'But my first priority is to make sure you're safe and at the moment from what you've just told us, I'm not sure you are.'

Ben's honesty continued. 'As far as I'm aware, no one knows I'm here and I think it's best for all of us if it stays that way. I don't intend to go into the village and if either of you two go there, it's probably best if you don't mention me at all. There's no need for anyone else to know where I am. It's only a matter of time before a journalist or someone sniffs out an interest and it all leaks out. But by then I hope to have got the data out into the scientific community. After that, I'll be safe and we can get on with our lives.'

Rich sought some reassurance. 'What if they try and trace where we all live?'

Ben had an answer. 'Before I came here at Christmas I removed all our names from as many computerised public lists as I could find ; things like electoral rolls, telephone directories and so one. With just about everything I could think of I was able to hack into various records and take off our names. The only thing I didn't touch was our highly personal stuff, like medical. It won't stop us from being traced eventually but it will buy us time, certainly enough for me to do what I have to.'

The seriousness of the situation had still not got through to his brother. 'Wow, respect! You were able to do all that? Jeez, have I got a seriously clever brother or what!'

Graham did not say anything but left the room and went outside with a sense of purpose. Ben and Rich shot each other a puzzled look until Rich screwed his face and turned his arms upward as if to question what was happening. Ben raised himself out of his chair intending to follow his father but failed to stand fully upright before his Dad returned carrying a shotgun, which was unloaded and broken. Ben looked worried as his father spoke with some authority.

'I want you to keep this somewhere handy. Maybe in the boot of the SUV or even your bedroom. There's a box of shells for you but don't load it until you have to. Pointing to a lever which was central to loading the gun, Graham continued. 'Always point the barrels upward when you break the gun. That way any shells left in the barrel will fall out and there won't be any accidents. To load the shells, simply do the opposite.' Looking then directly at his elder twin, Graham instructed, 'The same for you as well Rich.'

His son felt as if he had to defend himself. 'I know how to use my shotgun, Dad.'

'I'm just saying. Make sure you know where it is at all times. I hope we don't have to use these things but if we do, I don't want us to have to look for them. Now Ben, give me your car keys and I'll put this one in your boot right now.'

Ben reached inside his jeans and presented the keys to his Dad. While Graham had his back to his sons, Rich mimed a firing action, aiming directly at his father. Ben shook his head in disgust as a rebuke to his immature brother. Although the episode was treated light-heartedly, the seriousness of the situation was not lost on any of them.

VIII

Zenib cruised into the industrial estate and left his car in the communal parking area, before stepping into the modern, glass-fronted building. He looked like a typical small-business manager, with suit and brief case. It was his side-kick who looked incongruous, a little man with rimless spectacles who although with youth on his side, looked positively unhealthy. Anyone looking at him would assume he was in need of a fix and they would be right. Zenib had control over his puppet not only by exerting his physical presence but by being able to dominate his body's craving for drugs.

The small silver plaque at the entrance was inscribed 'Orion Inc.' a cover for the activity actually going on inside. Zenib had moved his centre of operations from Geneva to Lausanne, a city further along Lac Léman but still in the French-speaking part of Switzerland. Geneva had attracted more than its share of attention and it was the place where the bodies were buried – literally. If anyone was following genuine leads from the explosion, they would never find him here, they would never find him anywhere. The operation that had occupied the last year of his life was almost complete.

The only thing left to do by way of reassurance to his bosses was to confirm that Ben Moyles was dead. Confident of success already achieved, Zenib did not really expect to find anything but he was being paid to look so why not? The office in Lausanne was ideal for the job: it was part of a computer complex with good access to a powerful mini-hub and when he finished the job, the bogus company would simply disappear. His companion was a computer whizz with weaknesses almost as big as his ability with a keyboard. Zenib did not possess the hacking skills himself but this 'wimp' could get the job done.

There was a complication arising from breaking into public databases at this time of year. Most everyday data was kept alive for a month or so, depending on the agency concerned. However, virtually all services deleted their active data at the beginning of a new calendar year, when they would also make storage back-ups. This meant anything relevant to Moyles' possible movements immediately around the time of the explosion could present difficulty. If Moyles had been anywhere or done anything in the new calendar, the 'wimp' would find him. Zenib flicked open his attaché case to reveal several packets of white powder wrapped in small clear plastic bags. The *Wimp's* eyes lit-up when he saw the packets and Zenib teased him with an incentive from close distance. Bending over him nose-to-nose he spat out the words like a hissing cobra.

'If you find what I'm looking for you can have all these my friend and lose yourself wherever you want, either in this world or that other one you find so fascinating. Fail me and you will regret it, do I make myself clear?' The *Wimp* adjusted his glasses and nodded enthusiastically, though he would have said yes to anything this monster asked of him in that moment. 'Now – do your work.'

Zenib moved over to a corner of the room where he sat on a large swivel chair, almost lost in its sumptuous leather. He started to pick at his nails with a small file while staring at the frightened little man who was punching the keyboard for all he was worth. Occasionally Zenib looked out of the window to stare at any passing young ladies. Sensing that all was not progressing satisfactorily his man-management skills persuaded him that further inducement was needed, especially as he could see how much perspiration was soaking through the shirt of his accomplice.

'Here take this.' Zenib threw one of the small packets of cocaine into the chest of the addict. 'Perhaps that will stop you sweating.'

After three hours of boredom, the computer expert suddenly sprang to life. 'Is this what you're looking for?' Zenib wearily got out of the chair and moved over to the computer monitor where he viewed the screen without really knowing what he was looking at. 'There … see? These are passenger lists for *Helvetalp Airlines*. They show the names of people who have booked in the last two weeks on flights between Geneva and London. You can see there, look … two days ago Dr Benjamin Moyles on Flight LHO5843 from Geneva to Heathrow.' After focussing on the text, Zenib's fist came down on the table with a mighty thud, causing his companion to lurch backwards in his seat. He thought it best to try and offer further service. 'Do you want me to see if he was on any flights out of London?' The throbbing vein on the side of Zenib's temple which was pulsating in rage gave him the answer he needed, especially when it was accompanied by a penetrating stare. 'Ok, Mr Zenib, sir. I'll keep looking.'

Zenib knew that if Moyles was alive and had flown back to London, he could be anywhere by now. A thought for his own self-preservation crossed his mind as he stepped outside to make the phone call to Connolly. He knew 'AC' would not be pleased at the news. 'Mr Connolly, I'm afraid our friend is on a holiday we did not know about.' Following an expletive rant on the other end of the phone call which did not serve as a favourable testimony to Zenib's capabilities, he continued. 'Yes sir, I know what to do.'

Connolly gave some final words of caution. 'Don't ring me again unless you have the news I want to hear. Do I make myself clear?' As the call went dead Zenib looked at the phone and tilted it towards his inside jacket pocket before grinding his teeth and returning to his source of information.

Meanwhile in a luxury chalet seventy kilometres away in the ski resort of Flaine in the French Alps, 'AC' Connolly walked out of his lounge and onto the veranda overlooking the magnificent snow-covered mountains. He took a sip of his best malt whisky from a crystal glass tumbler and considered his options. If Moyles could not be silenced it might be necessary to advise his superiors on alternative forms of investment. It was becoming necessary to distance himself from this mess. Too many mistakes were being made and this was the Arab's last chance to put things right.

As Zenib returned to the office, he was greeted by a nervous smile on the face of the *Wimp* which suggested further progress had been made while he was out of the room. 'I've found him on another flight on the same day as he left Geneva.' This tempered Zenib's anger to some degree. 'He was on an internal flight from Heathrow to Newcastle. There you can see, it's Flight No HONW3...'

'I don't need to see it. Is that the last flight where his name is shown?' The bedraggled clothes responded affirmatively and Zenib gave him another threatening stare. 'In that case your work here is done.' Zenib clicked open his attaché case and removed the remaining sachets of cocaine before dropping them in front of bulging eyes. 'There – take these with you and go. Knock yourself out.' The other man considered asking his temporary boss how he was expected to get back to his place but took the wise decision that it was a question better left unasked. He scooped up his pay cheques and headed out as fast as he could, disappearing into a sordid underworld where he was more comfortable.

Zenib was left to consider his options and decided he had no alternative but to go to Newcastle Airport and try and pick up the scent of Moyles' trail. His home address had so far been untraceable because somebody had removed his name from every list that had been tried. However, someone must know where he was and Newcastle was the place to start.

While back on the farm, Ben varied his work between reproducing data from the final experiment and completing some light duties to help out his Dad. He knew that the trail he had attempted to cover in order to sustain his anonymity would not last forever but still calculated that he had enough time to do what needed to be done. However, he had overlooked the possibility that while he had removed some computer references, his most recent journey on an aeroplane had not escaped detection. Given the stress he was under and the many important decisions he was having to make, it was an understandable error. Ben was suddenly at risk but he did not know just how much of a threat he was facing.

IX

Ben was working in the maintenance shed with his father, who was reversing the John Deere tractor into a parking space before switching off the engine. Graham had gathered a large bale of hay into the front loader ready to take around to the sheep-shed the following day. Ben was grinding grain, using power from the activated engine of the larger Massey Ferguson and ensuring there was some ready feed for the cattle. There were a few polythene sheets constantly blowing back into the shed caused by the strong wind eddying outside the entrance. The slippery plastic covers were the remnants of some empty bags of fertilizer although to Archie they were simply interesting canine toys. Ben cursed as they became entangled in his stride, his frustration worsened by the dog's constant barking. As he picked up the bags, Ben had a few words of chastisement for his Dad, who was now getting out of his tractor. 'I see you still haven't bought a new cover for the power-take off drive. It's just about hanging off. I told you to do it the last time I was home – having an unprotected shaft is dangerous. You need to do something about it before it goes altogether. Just as well we don't have any young kids on the farm otherwise you could find yourself in serious trouble with the health and safety people. Those polythene sheets almost got tangled up in it a minute ago, never mind Archie running around.'

Graham felt it necessary to defend himself. 'I've been too busy to bother about stuff like that. Don't worry about it. It's alright if you know what you're doing and the only people working on *this* farm do know what they're doing. At least they better had otherwise they've got no place being here.' Ben shot him a scornful look as his father relented, the old man taking his temper out on poor Archie. 'Aye, alright I'll do something about it. Get over there Archie. Stay!' The collie meekly retreated into the corner of the maintenance shed, not daring to move and unsure on what he had done wrong.

'Promise? You better had otherwise or I'll get one myself.' Graham turned his back on his son and made his way to the farmhouse. He was hungry and Rich was preparing the evening meal. 'I'm just going to check on our Rich, *he's* bound to be moaning on at me as well because he's cooking the food again.'

Graham had not really wanted to tell Mrs Thistlethwaite to stay away from the farm for the next few weeks but she was known for being a gossip and if she had seen Ben staying at the house, the news would have spread all around the village by the end of the day. The old man had made-up some story about Rich having to avoid contact with everyone else because the drugs he was taking could make him vulnerable to infection. Mrs Thistlethwaite's irritation was only placated when Graham assured her that she would still be paid for her trouble.

The missing member of the Moyles' clan suddenly appeared at the entrance to the maintenance shed. 'Dad, the hospital is on the phone. They've got some news, can you come quick and talk to them.' Hearing the tone of concern in his son's voice, Graham increased his pace while Ben jumped into the Massey to switch off the ignition and deactivate the grain grinder before following his Dad into the farmhouse. As the two boys brought up the rear Rich tried to give one of the polythene sheets to his brother but it blew over Ben's head. 'Never let it be said that I don't give you anything,' said Rich, immature as usual.

Ben was not amused and he folded the plastic sack and tucked it under his arm while continuing towards the farmhouse at quite a pace.

There was no time to remove muddy footwear as Graham picked up the receiver on the small table where the house-phone rested. It was positioned just off the porch so the workers would not tramp mess all the way through the house. Ben and Rich both watched their agitated father listen to the news that was cascading into his ear. His eyes were dancing around the carpet but he was not looking at its pattern. The brothers were desperately trying to interpret the information he was receiving by reading his body language. After getting nowhere for minutes, it was only when they heard him say, 'So you want us there straight away?' that they were able to piece together the importance of the call.

Eventually Graham replaced the receiver and turned to address both his sons. 'Right, listen carefully you two. Apparently there was an accident earlier today on the A697 near Wooler. A motor cycle rider was knocked off his bike and seriously hurt. He's not expected to make it through the next twenty-four hours. He's currently on a life-support machine but that is only while they contact his parents and inform them of the seriousness of his condition. It sounds like they are going to give them the option of switching off his life-support.

Apparently the young fella was carrying a donor card in his wallet when he collided with the lorry. The consultant seems to think that his heart could be a match for yours, Rich so they want us to go to the hospital where they can check everything out. Apparently a surgeon in London has been contacted and he's flying up here now so it's a serious probability that doesn't sound like another false alarm to me. Now, we've got no time to lose boys so get your skates on. Rich – you get that bag of yours that's been packed and ready to go since ever I can remember. I'll go and pack some stuff to get me through the next few days in case I need it. Ben – I want you to drive us there.' Looking at each of his two sons in turn, Graham concluded. 'Fingers crossed boys, this could be what we have been waiting for.'

In a state of disorganised excitement the three men did what they had to do. In the car on the way to the hospital the conversation was purposeful and direct. This was not the time for family banter and when one of them spoke, the other two listened intently. Ben made the first constructive offer for some practical changes. 'While you're at the hospital don't worry about the farm, Dad. I'll see to that. I'll pop into the village on my way back and track down Joe and Eric Setherton and offer them some work. They won't turn down the possibility of earning some money so that should be enough to keep things ticking over for a while.'

Some concern crossed his Dad's mind. 'What about people knowing you're back home though son. Once news gets out things could change pretty quickly.'

'Don't worry about that now. That's not the most important thing at this moment in time. We need to see to our Rich first.' Turning around to look at this brother in the back seat, Ben continued. 'How you doing back there, bro. You ready to get a new heart for a new year?'

Rich simply held up his thumb as a response. The one thing that had not happened was any expression of concern for Rich's reaction to the important news. Ben and his Dad had taken it for granted that Rich would be as enthusiastic as they were at the possibility of getting some normality back into his life. Rich was more concerned about whether he would survive the operating table.

Pulling into the hospital's car park there was a sense of realisation within the family trio. They recognised this was a significant moment for all of them. Whereas Ben would simply have dropped them off for a normal appointment and pulled away without bothering to park, on this occasion he got out of the car and stood to face his brother. 'I'll come in with you' he said, without a great deal of conviction.

Rich was more resolute. 'No need, bro. You've got things to sort out and I don't want to see your ugly mug around me when I'm trying to concentrate on more serious matters.'

Ben knew what Rich was really saying and saw through the coded dialogue. 'In that case I'll say goodbye now.' The two boys hugged tightly and Ben whispered into his brother's ear after wishing him good luck, 'I love you, man.'

Rich feigned a punch in his brother's direction. 'Get off me you big girl. If I'd wanted a sister I would have asked Dad for one, not you.' The mistiness in his eyes was something Rich could not disguise and both knew the real truth of their feelings towards each other. Graham looked at his younger son and screwed a grin into his lips. With one hand resting on the roof of the car and his foot in the well of the open door, Ben watched his father and brother walk all the way out of the car park until they reached the main entrance and became lost in a crowd of people.

From the car park Ben tried calling Joe Setherton and his brother Eric in case they had not switched off their phones but was not surprised when there was no answer. At that time of the day their mobiles were probably on silent mode, the men not wanting to be contacted no matter what the emergency. It was understandable: working out in the open air at that time of year was not easy. They would not have wanted to risk being dragged out into the cold at that hour of the day. However, Ben also knew that they were probably in the Black Bull so that was his next stop.

There were not many people in the pub that night, just enough to make it interesting. Ben felt eyes burning into him as he walked through the door. Sue Wallace was working behind the bar and in the corner playing dominoes were Joe and Eric, accompanied by none other than Donny Wallace. Ben smiled in Sue's direction before wandering over to the gambling threesome. The Setherton boys were facing Ben, while Donny's back did not turn as he approached. However, Donny knew what was going on because he had spotted Ben's reflection when he entered the bar. Ben opened the conversation in a friendly manner. 'Evening boys.' He received a reciprocal response from only two of them, Donny preferring to remain silent. 'Just to let you know that our Rich has been taken into hospital and my Dad's gone to be with him. Looks like he could be in for quite a while so that's going to take Dad out of action as well. Gonna need some help and wondered if you boys were interested?'

Joe took the lead in the negotiations. 'How much and for how long?' In this part of the world, farm labourers preferred to talk without frills.

'Time-and-a half for both of you. Not sure how long yet but it's going to be at least a month by my reckoning if the operation goes ahead. Failing that a guaranteed two-week's work. What d'ye say? Interested?'

'What's he gone in for Ben?' asked Joe.

'Well if it all works out it could be the big one – a heart transplant. They think they might have found a donor.'

Joe looked towards his brother whose face stared back with exactly the same frozen expression as when Ben entered the bar. 'Yeah, that sounds good to me, Ben. Can you manage for tomorrow on your own though? We've still got some work to finish off first for Tommy Horton up in his farm in the Till Valley. After that we're all yours.'

'No problem,' responded Ben. 'See you the day after tomorrow.' Three of the four men were nodding in agreement. Donny remained slouched over the table, with a handful of dominoes still waiting to be played. Just before he turned to go, Ben concluded. 'Evening, Donny.' The best offering he received in response was nothing more than a reluctant grunt. Donny failed to turn or acknowledge Ben in any way beyond an incoherent mumble.

Ben turned and within the three strides to the bar he considered whether to have a pint or not. The absence of a convivial atmosphere persuaded him to keep walking. Although from behind the bar Sue did not move a muscle, her eyes followed Ben all the way out of the pub. She lifted the counter-flap and walked over to her husband where she picked-up three empty pint glasses with the fingers of one hand. With the other she poked Donny in the back. 'What did you do that for? He was only trying to be friendly. Isn't it about time you two patched it up. You were friends once.' Donny ignored the advice and placed his 'double-four' domino at the end of the small line that had started their game. Sue had not finished her nagging. 'If you ask me, you're the one who needs a new heart.' The scathing comment from his wife made Donny think deeply about the message although he showed no sign of having taken any notice. As he looked up from the table he mouthed a silent obscenity at the Setherton boys, who were unsuccessfully stifling a snigger, laughing like two adolescent schoolboys.

As Ben got in the car ready to make his way home, there was a notification on his mobile and he opened the text, which was from his father. 'No news yet. Will speak tomorrow. Goodnight son.' Tomorrow was going to be a big day.

X

The two men did not appear to be travelling together, occupying different seats on the same flight to Heathrow. They could easily have been mistaken for professionals going about their routine business. The plan was that from the Airport at London they would be met by their contact who would supply them with transport and weapons. Very few words had been exchanged with Connolly, Zenib had assured him there would be no further slip-ups in his delivery of this particular assignment. He was doing the job gratis, in recognition that it was part of the original assignment. The five hour journey in the white SUV was straightforward, driving north of London on the M1, then straight onto the A1(M) at Leeds all the way to Newcastle. The pair exchanged driving only once as they covered the four-hundred and fifty kilometre distance in good time.

As they pulled into the short-stay car park at the Airport, Zenib issued the instructions. 'You get a parking ticket, I don't want us to come all this way and then attract attention because we didn't pay to park the car. You got British pounds, yes?' The man in the driver's seat nodded. 'Ok I'll go into the terminal and ask the questions, you follow me and stay ten metres behind me, *capeesh*?'

Zenib left the car and strode over towards the sign indicating Arrivals above the revolving doors of the Terminal building. One of the car rental desks had a small queue but the other two were deserted except for their respective attendants. The employees were sitting behind a desk counter that was too high for their chairs. Zenib approached purposefully and produced a photograph from the side-pocket of his jacket. Looking down on the startled worker he opened the conversation politely. 'Hello sir, I wonder if you could help me please. I am looking for this man, have you seen him?' He showed the attendant a grainy photograph which had been removed from Ben's file in Human Resources at Puissance. The man simply shook his head and returned to the roster that had occupied his attention before the arrival of this curious individual. Zenib received the same answer at the next counter and moved on to the final car rental hire office just as a satisfied customer was leaving. Again, he asked the question but this time received a different answer.

'Yes, I know him. Dr …er.. Mole or something like that, I think. I remember he was here just a few days ago. Nice chap as I recall. We've supplied him with a car a few times over the last couple of years or so.'

Zenib began his stalking. 'Can I see his booking form, please. I need to find him urgently.'

'No sorry sir, I can't do that. If you want me to try and relay a message to him, I'll do what I can.'

Zenib raised his act by one gear. 'Sorry, I don't think you are hearing me properly. I *need* to get hold of him straight away. If you check his booking form, the information on there will help me find out where he is.'

'Sorry sir, that's against company policy. I can't divulge a customer's personal details, unless you are a policeman with the necessary documentation.'

Zenib had not come this far to be obstructed by a jobs-worth but only had a couple of seconds to choose a strategy; he decided to hold back from threats at this stage. He reached into his wallet and produced a wad of English currency, totalling somewhere in the region of five-hundred pounds. 'Well my friend, if you were to leave his documentation accidentally on the desk, while you left for five minutes and counted just how much there is here, I'm sure we will both be satisfied.' They looked at each other for a couple of more seconds until the hire representative relieved Zenib's slender hold of the cash before punching a few details into the computer. The monitor was turned towards Zenib so he could read the information comfortably. 'Right, sir. I just need to go to the toilet for a moment and will return in about five minutes time. I trust that is not too inconvenient for you?' The slightly raised voice was to ensure that others on the next desk could hear what he was saying. Although the cash seemed like a lot of money the car hire worker was not going to lose his job over it and wanted a guarantee that company policy was being seen to be done. He left via the *portakabin's* slender door at the back of the serving area, leaving his new benefactor to lean over the counter and view the screen. The monitor text displayed details such as the name of the person hiring the car, its make or model number and appropriate mileage and several other facts not of interest. However, at the bottom of the online form Zenib found what he was looking for: *"Contact Address – Moyles Farm, Hubbleton, Northumberland."*

Returning to the car, Zenib handed his accomplice the note. 'Enter this address into the *satnav* and see what it tells us.' After a few seconds the man turned to his boss who was now in the rear passenger seat over his left shoulder. 'It shows the place, Hubbleton but there is no reading for Moyles Farm.' A sly smile crossed Zenib's face. 'Tonight we will find somewhere to stay before we go and look for Moyles. Tomorrow we will find the village and then ask someone about the location of the farm. One of the locals will know. Once we have had a good look around the area we will pay our doctor friend and his family a surprise visit.' Feeling in control for the first time in a while, he pointed forward with his index finger and the driver started the car.

After a night in a motel near the airport, the two men made the final leg of their journey. It was around two o'clock in the afternoon when their car entered the village of Hubbleton and the light had not yet begun to fade. The driver laughed as they passed the entrance sign showing, 'Welcome to Hubbleton. Please drive carefully.' Zenib also afforded himself a grin of appreciation. Their eyes scanned the streets half-hoping that they would get lucky and spot their target out in the open. However, before they knew it they had driven through the village and found themselves heading towards open countryside.

The driver spoke first. 'Christ, was that it? What a dump this place is. Could it really have spawned someone who is supposed to be an important scientist. Unbelievable!'

Zenib gave his orders. 'Just turn around somewhere and drive through again. If we simply go around this wilderness looking in hope for the farm, we'll never spot it. Find a garage and we'll ask in there.'

The orange lights of the Shelco Garage attracted their attention and they drove onto the large forecourt. There appeared to be a mini-mart inside so Zenib indicated that he would go and buy something as an excuse to ask some questions. Placing a tight woollen beany hat over his hair and a set of heavily rimmed glasses as further disguise, he tucked his lapels closer to his body. Swiftly he walked across the open tarmac, glancing up at the outer wall above the main entrance to see if he could spot any CCTV cameras. The blinking red light indicated there was a working system in operation.

Entering the mini-mart Zenib could see only a couple and an old lady inside, perusing the aisles for any food offers and attractive deals. He picked up a bottle of wine from the off-licence shelves and made his way to the check-out. As he turned a corner he almost knocked over the attractive redhead and got a scornful look from her husband before he apologised profusely. 'I'm so sorry, are you alright? I didn't see you there. That was so clumsy of me.'

Her husband spoke with some intimidation. 'Yeah, you should watch where you're going.'

The redhead attempted to gloss over the situation. 'It's alright, Donny. I wasn't looking either.' Turning to her accidental assailant she added, 'Really I'm fine. Don't worry about it.'

The three of them progressed together towards the check-out where Mr Jenkins' employee was supervising a new girl on the till. Handing her the bottle of wine Zenib asked the question that was the whole reason he was there in the first place. 'I don't know if you can help me but I'm looking for Moyles Farm. I know it's around here somewhere but it doesn't show up on my satnav. I'm trying to find my friend Ben Moyles. I don't know if you know him?'

Ever keen to help, Mr Jenkins waded in. 'Ah yes, I know Ben and his Dad. Not sure if he's at the farm though. He's probably still in France, where he works. He's there most of the time and only comes home now and again when he gets the chance. Are you a friend of his then?'

'Yes, I know Ben from way-back. I was in the area so I thought I would drop in and see him.'

Donny and Sue Wallace could hear this conversation taking place in front of them but were surprised by a couple of things and shot each other a puzzled look as they stood in the queue with their loaf of bread and bottle of milk.

Mr Jenkins gave some perfunctory directions to Moyles Farm, leaning over the counter and pointing out of the large window towards the outskirts of the village. While Sue stayed behind to pay for their items, Donny continued through the open doorway to see the village newcomer get into a large car, which contained someone else he had never seen before. As Sue caught up with him, Donny gave his assessment of the situation. 'There's something not right about this.' They watched the car pull out onto the B352 and he ordered. 'Give me your mobile phone.'

Sue could not understand what he was saying. 'Why, what's wrong with yours?'

'Mine doesn't have Ben Moyles' number on it but yours does.' Sue shot him a glare. 'Don't look at me like that. I know you've got his number. Now hand it over.'

Without saying anything further Sue handed her mobile to Donny who scanned the contact numbers before pressing the one that indicated their mutual acquaintance.

Meanwhile, at the farm Ben was in the process of wiping off some excess baked beans from inside the microwave. They had spilled over onto the glass turn-table while he was making lunch. Normally he would only have a sandwich but the bitterly cold weather had settled into a clear, windless winter February day, the sort of conditions that are deceptive and can catch farmworkers unaware when they are toiling outside. Every breath seemed to condense in the calm, crisp weather. Something warm inside was called for and baked beans fitted the bill. He had inadvertently set the timer on the microwave to five minutes instead of three and the extra simmering had caused the contents to spill over so he was cursing himself for creating unnecessary work. Once the job was finished he intended to get back to the maintenance shed and finish off the grain-grinding he had started when the phone call came in from the hospital, the day before.

When Ben first heard the ring-tone his thoughts were that it must be his father calling with news about Rich. He was surprised to see Sue Wallace's name come up on the screen as the source of the incoming call.

'Hello Sue. How are you doing. It's a surpr…'

Ben instantly recognised the voice interrupting his response. 'Never mind that now, just listen.' Ben's face was suddenly ashen with shock and he was puzzled by the contact from his former friend. Why was Donny Wallace calling him on his wife's phone? Ben's attention was on red alert.

'Someone has been asking about you in the village. They were talking to old-man Jenkins in the garage about where your farm is. Me and Sue were in there doing some shopping at the time and heard them talking. They're on their way to the farm now.'

There was a touch of anxiety in Ben's next questions. 'Who are they and what did they look like?'

'Oh, you'll have no trouble spotting them. One is a bloke with a strong tan, could be from the Middle East by the look of him. The other claimed to be your friend but he didn't look much like a friend to me. I've never seen either of them before. Anyway, didn't think you had any friends.'

Donny could not resist taking a dig, even under these circumstances but given the nature of the call, Ben was prepared to let it ride. 'Why are you telling me this?' Ben did not think he was calling out of pity.

'Been thinking about what you said the last time you were home. Reckon I still owe you, I guess.'

'Ok in that case, thanks Donny and ….'

The call ended abruptly; clearly there was a limit to Donny Wallace's level of guilt.

Ben stood in the kitchen of the farmhouse motionless, thinking about his next step and knowing that he had to be quick. Attempts had already been made to kill him while he was in France and he always knew it was only going to be a matter of time before someone found out he was not slain in the explosion at Puissance. That time had now arrived.

The first thing was to ensure he had some home defence so Ben went out to the boot of his car to retrieve the shotgun and cartridges his Dad had put there a couple of days earlier. However, he knew that would not be enough protection especially if there was more than one of them and Donny had no reason to lie on that particular issue. The next course of action was to ring Captain Jacques Durand and ask for help and advice. The detective was the only other person who knew everything about Ben's predicament. Sensing his fingers quivering with fear, Ben made a conscious effort to find the number from his contacts' list, deliberately slowing his movements in order to avoid the temptation to panic. He was relieved to hear the number ringing but frustrated when it went to straight to voicemail almost immediately. The only thing he could do was leave a message.

'Captain Durand. This is Ben Moyles. I need your help urgently. I fear that my life may be in imminent danger. Please send help to Moyles Farm in Hubbleton, Northumberland in the UK. URGENT!' A similar emergency 999 call to the UK police advised that the nearest patrol car was at least twenty minutes away and the exceptionally cold weather meant the police helicopter was grounded. Ben scampered upstairs to view the area from his bedroom window and saw a white SUV slow down on the road outside the farm before pulling away again. It could only mean one thing – it was too late to hide.

Apart from the shotgun Ben did have one major advantage: his knowledge of the farm. The inside of his mouth ran dry with fear, while his scientific training had taught him to think rationally under pressure. This was no time for distractions, Ben had to focus on the task in hand and act with precision. The situation in which he now found himself was going to be the biggest test of his life.

XI

After cruising past for about a mile, Zenib instructed his accomplice to turn around and then pause at the roadway entrance to Moyles Farm. Following a quick reconnoitre from the car they carried on and parked out of sight in a widening of the road, under a tree, where they waited. Thirty minutes later, Zenib gave the order. 'Right, let's do this.' It was the only instruction issued and one more than was necessary. The sun was beginning to set behind a distant hill and twilight had started to cast long shadows. Like approaching hyenas slouching and circling their prey the duo approached along the farm lane. Zenib stopped when the still air brought them into hearing distance. 'Listen .... that's a tractor or some machinery at work over there.' He pointed with a raised chin. 'C'mon, let's go over and find out who it is. You know what to do.'

Cautiously and silently, their stealth took the pair close to the maintenance shed where two tractor engines could be heard ticking over. The subordinate was directed to the wide entrance while Zenib slinked around the side of the building to the back. As Zenib disappeared from his line of sight, the accomplice peeked inside the shed and made a quick decision about his next move. There were two tractors and inside the cab of the Massey Ferguson was a driver who seemed to be operating some sort of grinding machine. His back offered an ideal target, facing away and presenting a clear shot. The assassin knowing he had not yet been spotted, raised the handgun and pointed its silencer directly at the target. A couple of thuds saw the two large snowflake holes appear in the glass of the cab and the figure fell over, slumped on top of the driver's steering wheel. Cautiously the killer crept closer to see the result of his work.

He did not notice Ben behind him crouched in a corner, hiding behind a bale of straw just inside the entrance. Ben rushed at the man from behind and as forcibly as he could pushed him headlong into the danger zone. The assassin fell forward onto a spinning, unprotected power take-off shaft and before he could assess what had happened his clothes became caught up in the gyrating rotary arm. This dragged him into the heart of the machine which whirred more slowly as the man's limbs were quickly detached from his screaming body. Ben watched on, almost with an ingratiating sickness of what he had just witnessed. The tractor engine stalled with the excess work being demanded as further flesh was dragged into the death area.

Zenib was startled and turned, looking towards the source of the blood curdling screams. Without thinking he ran towards the entrance and rushed in impulsively. There was now only one tractor engine switched on, with no driver in sight. As soon as he saw the human offal on the lightly-strawed floor, Zenib's face contorted in horror. The delay of lingering his eyes on the remains of his fellow assassin was long enough to allow Ben to spring up from his position inside the Deere's cab and power the tractor straight at the Arab. The hit-man did not get the chance to raise his gun because he was forced to dive sideways at lightning speed in order to avoid the front loader heading straight at him. It only just brushed past his flying body.

Ben was now in the John Deere racing at full speed along the side of the cattle shed, heading for the rear of the building to assess his next move. Zenib jumped to his feet, dusting off some straw from his expensive trousers. His look of rage followed the sound of the tractor through the walls until the engine noise changed at the back of the cattle shed. From high gear, the John Deere moved to neutral indicating it was now just ticking over and stationary. Zenib calculated that Ben Moyles was probably no longer inside the tractor cab. Suddenly the assassin realised that his target had nerve as well as brains and he would have to proceed with extreme caution.

Zenib cautiously exited the maintenance area and inched forward along the side of the cattle building, his reflexes at their peak. An empty polythene sack was on the ground in front of him spread out along his path. He was reluctant to avoid walking over it in case by stepping away from the side of the shed he exposed himself to a potential gunshot and he suspected a farmer's gun was already pointing in his direction. Too many thoughts were racing through his brain, all motivated by self-preservation. However, he was an experienced killer and in these situations he also had a default position. Given that the noise of the tractor engine would hide any sound of his footsteps he decided to stand on the polythene sack and continue to creep along the side of the shed hoping to remain unseen.

Suddenly, out of nowhere a dog came around the corner like an arrow, barking and snarling at Zenib. Archie jumped up at the assassin who raised one arm to protect his face and throat but his other sleeve was gripped by firmly clenched canine teeth. A huge, well aimed kick to the dog's under-belly produced a yelp that made the animal withdraw a couple of feet. In what seemed at first like a stand-off, Archie semi-circled around Zenib's feet trying to assess the right time to launch his next attack. However, calmly and efficiently the assassin pointed his weapon at Archie and discharged the gun. With a whimper and a repressed squeal, Archie slumped lifeless to the ground. '*Gotcha*!' thought Zenib, finally claiming his first victim.

Zenib then looked at his painful wrist and could feel some blood trickling down his arm. Instinctively he put his injured hand to his mouth and sucked hard, trying to ease the stinging at the point where Archie's teeth had left their mark. Zenib had now progressed a few feet further along the side of the building and his eyes were focussed on the end of the cattle shed. At any moment he was expecting someone to appear in his line of sight. Constantly swivelling his head back and fore he was not looking where he was placing his feet.

As soon as he stood on the sheet of polythene that had once held fertilizer, it subsided under his weight. With an instant *whoosh* he collapsed into a man-made sink hole as there was no support under the empty bag. Unsure of what was happening Zenib discharged his weapon and in panic he raised both arms to a complete vertical, before the gun was dropped into the mire. His mouth opened and his eyes widened as his body plummeted downwards into the centre of a hole while the edges of the polythene moved upward and wrapped around his lower legs. Within a second, the assassin's lower half disappeared into the morass.

While waiting for the arrival of the killers Ben had been busy. As well as ensuring the shotgun was loaded and ready he had switched-on the engines of both tractors after kicking-off the remnants of the Massey's power take-off shaft. Inside the cab he had placed some work-clothes, held upright by a pitchfork. From the back the resulting dummy could easily have been mistaken for a farm worker, especially in a stressful situation. Ben then paid a visit to the cattle shed where he removed two of the manhole covers over the access points to the cesspit and replaced them with a couple of the empty polythene sacks. These were the 'presents' that Rich had given him the day before. Ben had positioned them precisely and delicately so they could not support anybody's weight. Fortunately, the calm weather meant they would not be blown away by the wind. Thanks to Archie, Zenib had not paid any attention to where he was placing his feet and must have thought the second plastic sheet was simply an empty fertilizer sack lying on the ground. As soon as he stood on the polythene it collapsed under his weight, causing him to fall quickly and helplessly into the stench.

When Ben heard Zenib's call for help he re-appeared from behind the tractor where he was hiding and cautiously made his way to the manhole. There he was forced to raise his hand to his mouth to protect himself from the pangs of ammonia, and methane gases. For the first time Ben could then see the face of the man who had been trying to kill him. The would-be assassin looked like an Arab but as his face was so heavily covered in animal faeces it was hard to tell where he was from. The quicksand of excrement and surface pool of urine was already up to Zenib's neck by the time Ben was looking down on him. Each time Zenib reached upward with his arms or tensed his ribcage trying to get out the mess of stench, he was dragged lower into the mire. The killer was gasping for air as his lungs were being burnt by the overpowering gases. Unfortunately, as he opened his mouth it was quickly filled with the most disgusting of tastes.

Ben considered whether or not to drag Zenib out from his vile tomb and then looked further down the path where he could see Archie's body lying lifeless in a small pool of blood. Ben disappeared from Zenib's line of sight for a few moments and cradled his dead canine friend before he returned. With Zenib's calls for help becoming more desperate Ben reached forward with his arms and Zenib thought he was finally going to be saved from a foul death. However, with a loud clunk, Ben dropped the grid cover on top of the manhole, leaving Zenib calling 'No, no, no!' while consuming huge mouthfuls of cattle faeces assisted in its consumption by draining animal urine. The last Ben saw of his enemy was his nose and eyes hovering just above the surface of a mass of disgusting animal excrement.

XII

Ben switched on his phone and dialled 999 to find out the whereabouts of his so-called rescuers and if their arrival was imminent. The blue lights in the distance belonged to his tardy saviours, while a re-directed helicopter was also on its way, courtesy of Captain Durand's phone call to the relevant Whitehall department in London.

As he sat slumped on the ground next to Archie's body waiting for the officers to arrive, he examined his mobile to discover he had received six unanswered calls and four text messages, all from his father while his mobile had been switched off. He was just about to open the first text when the phone signalled an incoming call. It was his Dad.

'Hiya, Dad – how are things at the hospital.'

'Ah ..finally there you are. What have you been doing? Skiving I suppose. I've been trying to get hold of you all afternoon? Where the hell have you been?'

'Just had one or two jobs to do around the farm, that's all Dad. Anyway, enough about me, how is Rich?'

'It's good news son. The heart *is* a match for our Rich so they're going to operate straight away. They're just getting him ready for theatre. That surgeon from London has arrived and he's getting scrubbed up now. It's all systems go – good news or what!'

'I'll be there with you as soon as I can Dad. Just got one or two things to tie up first.'

'Well I wouldn't want to trouble you. Just get your backside along here double quick or you'll have me to answer to, ok?'

'Ok, Dad. If you see Rich send him my best.'

'Will do. See you soon son.'

While getting to his feet Ben could see the arrival of the first blue-and-yellow panelled police car with its flashing lights. Screeching close behind was a black-windowed van; its rear doors burst open as six armed policeman jumped out, spreading away from the vehicle in well-rehearsed choreography reminiscent of a human ant-run. They were pointing their weapons in what seemed like organised chaos and shouting 'Police!' just in case no-one knew who they were. The first two officers to reach Ben who was now on his feet, gave him new orders. 'Police, lie on the floor now! Arms out straight, nose to the ground.'

Even in the pathos of the moment, Ben was able to smile to himself. Clearly, these officers did not know the principal players and therefore were obliged to assume that everybody was their enemy. Anyone who was totally compliant had a chance of being viewed as a potential ally. As they approached, Ben was able to shout a response. 'My name is Dr Ben Moyles and this is my family's farm. The body that you can see belongs to a person who was sent here to kill me. Please phone Captain Jacques Durand of the French Police currently stationed in Geneva. He will verify who I am!'

Once a sense of order was established, one of the officers lifted his attached radio closer to his mouth and sent a coded message, presumably to a superior. A passenger door in the rear-most, unmarked police car opened and a suit stepped out just as an ambulance arrived, weaving its way in and out of the battle scene. In a casual manner the smartly dressed man was accompanied by two armed, uniformed officers. Eventually he reached the point where Ben was now standing. The man reached for a photograph inside his pocket and placed it alongside Ben's face for comparison. The gesture was not really necessary but it added to his self-importance. 'It's ok gentlemen. I don't think we need to protect ourselves from Dr Moyles. I believe we can treat him as one of ours.' With that the policemen returned their guns to their default positions.

The man introduced himself as Simpkinson a name too close for comfort to Ben's former dead boss. He said he was a representative of Her Majesty's Government but when asked by Ben which department he represented he responded evasively, 'I don't think we need to bother about that now.' Although the security services had turned up too late for a rescue, it was clear they were taking a lot of interest now. 'First thing we need to do for you Dr Moyles is to have you checked out by the medical people, then put you somewhere safe. Clearly, we have a lot of questions.'

Ben had come this far on his own and was not about to be mollycoddled now. 'Well, unless you intend to arrest me for something, I am now going to have a shower and then drive over to the Queen Elizabeth Infirmary to be with my father. My twin brother is about to undergo major surgery – and short of being locked up, nothing else will stop me. Right now my brother is being operated on for a heart transplant and as you can imagine, it is no little thing.'

Simpkinson did not respond at first but simply stared directly into Ben's eyes while considering his options. 'Ok Dr Moyles. This is what I am prepared to do. I will allow you to go to the hospital, accompanied by a couple of my armed officers and I will join you there later. I need to ask you a number of questions because as you say, events here today have been '*No little thing*'. I trust you will appreciate that we need to process this crime scene and assess the situation in a lot more detail. I spoke earlier to Captain Durand on a video link to France and he has filled me in with some of the details about what has happened in connection to the explosion at the Puissance complex over there and how it related to your situation. I have also been instructed at the highest possible level within Whitehall about what needs to happen next.

Given your current personal circumstances, I can cut you some slack. But you must also understand *my* responsibilities. Do we have a deal?'

Ben could see the proposal was logical and reasonable. 'Yes, we have a deal.' As Ben turned towards the farmhouse he added, 'By the way, you might want to examine the contents of the slurry pit. There's another body in there.' He did not see Simpkinson murmur an expletive under his breath.

While Ben returned to the farmhouse to shower and change, a large number of crime scene officers had seemingly arrived from nowhere. In white, plastic onesies they were pouring over the corpse in the maintenance shed with the contents of their silver tool boxes. As he soothed his body with warm soapy suds Ben leaned against the shower and allowed the hot water to cascade over his motionless body. There was still a lot to be concerned about but he was grateful just to be still alive. He had surprised himself with his calmness in an extremely dangerous situation.

There was one other pang of sadness that he would still have to explain to his Dad, if not tonight then certainly soon: it was Archie. The dog had been more than a working animal at Moyles Farm and had again surpassed himself by helping to keep Ben alive. He suspected that his brother might be more upset than his father about Archie's shooting. Graham had experienced life and death on the farm almost as a daily occurrence. It was probable that the old man would be more upset at the inconvenience of having to train another animal to the same level as Archie, although it was also possible that Ben was being too harsh in his assessment of his father's level of compassion. There was no doubt that in his list of working sheepdogs, Archie had been the best. Unfortunately, as an exhibit in a murder investigation the canine's body could not be recovered for burial until the officials gave their permission. It would have to wait, though Ben knew he would be laid to rest on the farm in an appropriate spot.

It was well into the evening before Ben was able to get to the hospital to be with his brother and father. The operation was already into its third hour. As he entered the family waiting area, Graham got to his feet and hugged his son. Ben spoke first: 'How is he doing Dad, any news yet?'

Graham did not see the need to wipe the extra moistening in his eye but it was clear he was stressed. 'No, a nurse has popped in a couple of times but that was just to see if I was ok. She didn't have any news about the operation. They reckon it'll take about eight hours and then probably a week in intensive care, depending on how things go.'

At that moment one of the armed officers briefly pushed open the door to inspect who was inside. This caused Graham some alarm so he wandered over to the entrance to see for himself what was going on. Standing astride the open doorway he asked with some fresh anxiety 'What the hell is all this? Why are armed police standing all around the place? What is going on?'

Ben tried his best to placate his father. 'Don't worry about it Dad. It's to do with that explosion in France but everything is ok. I'll tell you all about it after our Rich's operation.'

Graham noticed a better level of service and support after Ben arrived. Some junior member of the team wearing a nice blue suit kept popping in to ask if he could bring them anything. Neither member of the family was interested in who he was or why he was asking but they appreciated the coffee and sandwiches he brought for them. After a further two hours,

Simpkinson appeared and asked to speak to Ben in a room he had organised further down the corridor. Graham was overly stressed, 'Do you have to do that now. It's God knows what time in the early hours of the morning and you want to interrogate my son. Why don't you just f...'

Ben interrupted at just the right time. 'It's alright Dad, I'm going to have to talk to him at some point and it might as well be now. Far rather I get it over with while our Rich is in theatre than have to do it when he's coming round from his operation. Don't worry, I won't be long.'

Graham ultimately accepted the situation with a reluctant grunt of acknowledgement. Ben's expression told Simpkinson all he needed to know about having to leave his Dad on his own.

In the mocked-up interrogation room that had been used to investigate an old man's prostate during afternoon clinic, Simpkinson and Ben settled into uncomfortable chairs to cover the main events of what had happened on the farm. Ben told the whole story, holding nothing back. He informed the man from the Ministry how he had received a call from someone who he termed a friend (Donny would have been annoyed) that two men of foreign persuasion were looking for Moyles Farm. One of them had claimed to be an acquaintance but Ben's 'friend' had never seen him before and regarded him with suspicion.

Given what had happened to him in France, Ben told Simpkinson how he had reported his concerns to Captain Durand and then made a 999 call to the police in the UK. He had spotted a car pull up outside the lane and then viewed the men getting out when he went up to get a better look from his bedroom. Rather than hide he had decided to end the situation once and for all, mainly to protect his father and brother from further threats. Ben then chillingly described the events that led to one of the assailants being mangled in the tractors power take-off shaft. The other assailant who Ben assumed to be the leader was tricked into falling into a slurry pit, where he died an unpleasant death. Ben explained how this Arab had shot his dog, though he conveniently omitted to say that he could have saved him if he had wanted. Instead he preferred to relate that he replaced the slurry cover in order to contain the pungent gases and ensure no one else suffered the same fate. Ben asked if his body had been recovered yet and was informed that although it took a while to clear the slurry tank, his corpse had been located.

After listening to Ben's version of events Simpkinson seemed satisfied that he had a handle on the situation. 'Your assailants are known to various security services in a number of countries. This has indeed been a conspiracy on an international scale. I have also spoken to your friend Captain Durand who has been making progress at his end with investigations of his own. I can inform you of various developments which you may find interesting.

It would appear that Captain Durand was correct in his belief there was a money trail. Your former colleague Dr Thiroud was too fond of gambling for his own good and accumulated a lot of debt. In that regard he was helped out by the woman who I believe you know as Veronique Perrin.' Ben was now listening to the revelation of facts as if he was enduring a rite of passage. Each new disclosure was testing his basic belief system. 'Captain Durand's Swiss colleagues have been involved in tracing the source of the funds that were used to support Dr Thiroud and discovered links to a holding company based in the Seychelles. As you can appreciate, the Swiss know one or two things about banking.

When they explored further up the food chain they found that regular significant amounts of money, fifteen-thousand Swiss Francs in fact, were being deposited each month into the account of someone else I believe you know.' The obvious question to spring onto Ben's lips at that moment escaped him because he was too stunned to absorb what was happening. He sat and allowed the Government representative to continue. ' I believe you know him in his role as the Chief Executive of the Schtern Banking Group.' For a moment Ben could not follow what he was being told and had to make a conscious effort to emphasise the name of the fraudster yet to be disclosed.

Eventually Ben blurted out three questions, all requiring the same answer, 'Gaston Dubois? You mean Gaston, husband of Camille Dubois? Is that who you mean?'

'I'm afraid so. Unlike Thiroud it would appear as if Mr Dubois was doing it solely for the money. A nice little earner wouldn't you say. Presumably he was relaying everything about you and your work that he had gleaned either directly from Dr Thiroud or indirectly from his wife.'

'So *she* was not involved in anything untoward?' Ben was desperately hoping that his friend Camille was nothing more than an innocent participant in all of this subterfuge, then he received his answer.

'No. There is nothing at this moment in time to link Madame Camille Dubois to the money that was being paid to pass on information about you. In fact Captain Durand said she was physically sick when she was presented with the truth about what had been going on.'

'So she is innocent of everything?'

'As far as we know, yes.'

Ben would have preferred indisputable proof but at least this was the next best thing. He could not bring himself to believe that his friend could have betrayed him. Then again, he would not have believed the same of Gaston. In that moment, Ben remembered the occasion when Camille announced that she and Gaston were going away to stay for a weekend break at their second home in Innsbruck. She had told him that all of Gaston's bonuses had been used to pay for the expensive ski lodge. He wanted Camille to be innocent and the evidence seemed to be pointing in that direction.

Ben followed the thread being unravelled by Simpkinson. 'But what did Gaston do with the information. It would have been of no use to him. Was someone else involved?'

'Well the Swiss Fraud Squad traced the money that was paid to Monsieur Dubois to the same holding company in the Seychelles that had been used to pay-off Thiroud's gambling debts. That's where the trail became more difficult to follow but fortunately for us, and as I said before, the Swiss know one or two things about banking. Apparently the holding company is a consortium of other companies with a range of accounts in not just the Seychelles but also in American Samoa, Bahrain and Grenada.'

This was stunning news. 'That's quite a web of deceit.' It was the closest Ben got to admiring the unseen cunning.

'Yes it is – except all trails lead back to one source. A consortium of oil companies known as the AOPC based in Batar in the Middle East. Some of that money was also being syphoned off into a personal account. They were passing on funds to someone who was pulling the strings. It would have to been someone wielding a lot of power.'

Ben was now asking more questions. 'So do you know who that is?'

'Well that is really where the trail goes cold but there is one interesting development. There is a financial pathway which also leads into an oil company based in the USA but it simply ends at that point.'

'So are you saying that whoever was trying to suppress the development was trying to protect the interests of oil companies?'

'Yes. That is exactly what I am saying.'

'And it could be someone with links to not only countries in the Middle East but also in the USA?'

'It's possible but I don't think we'll ever be able to track that person down. They're too well protected. All I can say is that State intervention has been at the heart of all of this right from the start.'

'So who will be charged with what?'

'Well we can only potentially charge Monsieur Dubois with fraud if we can prove a link with the person at the heart of all of this. Unfortunately we do not have enough to charge him at this stage and it is doubtful that we ever will. His lawyers will simply claim that the money was freely given in appreciation of his work. Similarly we can't charge anyone with blackmailing Dr Thiroud because it is the same source. The money used to pay off his debts came from the same person. That was how he was forced to hand over secrets about not just you but Professor Thompkins. It was Professor Thompkins who was first identified as the target. It was only when your ideas were successfully put into practice that they realised they'd backed the wrong horse.'

'So that's why they tried so hard to find out where the safe house was? They even beat up Veronique to make it look more convincing. Are you also saying we may never know who has been behind this and who has been trying to silence me?'

'It looks like they got away with it but I wouldn't worry about them coming after you. It's the same with Thiroud's murderer. He or she was probably some low life junky paid a few Euros to stick a knife in his back and then disappear.'

'I've just realised – Christ! They could come after me again.'

They could – but I very much doubt it. You're under the protection of Her Majesty's Government. We will make sure your secrets are safe and once they are in the public domain, it's more likely that they'll try and get you on their payroll, not try and kill you.'

Ben rocked back on his chair and blew out his cheeks in recognition of the magnitude of what he had just been told. He had trusted Gaston and had even liked him but he had betrayed their friendship for money. Ben wasn't sure what he'd do if he ever saw him again. What about Camille? Was she in on it as well? Perhaps he would never know. Even if charges were brought against Gaston he would probably hire the best lawyers and get away with an innocent verdict. He could certainly afford to and as a banker he might even get a promotion for being so shrewd.

'I need time to take in all this. I feel safer now that those swine are dead and I'm back home. I must get all my data sorted and released as soon as possible and I don't think the farm is the best place for that anymore.'

Simpkinson offered some reassurance. 'Don't worry, we have somewhere safe for you. The British Government will look after you now.'

Realising how long he had been with Simpkinson, Ben needed to return to more pressing priorities. 'I have to get back in there to be with my father. He's already got one son to worry about, he doesn't need another one. Simpkinson closed the folder on the desk and responded, 'My men will take care of you for the next few days. I'll be in touch.' Both men stood and while shaking hands disingenuously on Ben's part, Simpkinson added, 'I hope it all goes well for your brother.' Ben could not summon enough goodwill to acknowledge the remark.

Ben returned to the family waiting room where his Dad was out of the chair and looking in desperate need of some sleep. That was not going to happen. 'Any news Dad?'

'Nothing yet son, but they must be coming to the end of it soon. I don't think our Rich has got enough strength in him to endure much more.'

Ben was playing the role of a comforting son. 'Don't worry on that score. Our Rich is as tough as old boots.'

Graham's mind had clearly been in overdrive while Ben was out of the room. 'Who was that chap you needed to talk to? What did he want, anyway?'

'Don't worry about that Dad, everything is fine. I'll tell you all about it some other time.'

An hour later the door opened and two medical staff still wearing scrubs entered the room. The consultant removed his surgical cap, failing to notice that his mask was dangling from one ear, until its movement reminded him to take it off altogether. Graham almost collapsed in relief when he saw the consultant's face break into a smile. The doctor placed his hand on the father's shoulder. 'It's gone well Mr Moyles. As well as we could have hoped.' Ben blew out his cheeks and patted his Dad's other shoulder. 'There's still a long way to go but the early signs are good.'

Graham could not wait. 'Where is he now? Can I see him?'

'Well I've come straight from the Operating Theatre and they were getting him ready for ICU so we can keep a close eye on him. I would suggest you get some rest. Richard is going to be out of it for a while yet and we do not expect him to wake up for at least another twelve hours. It would be my advice to use the time well and get some sleep. I believe there is a bed for you across the way in the family unit?'

Everything after the first sentence of what the Consultant had just said went over Graham's head. He was not concerned about his own welfare, only that of his son.

He went to shake the doctor's hand with all the vigour he could muster, laying his left hand on top of the other for good measure and compounding his thanks with genuine words of relief and appreciation. 'Thank you doctor. Thank you for what you have done. You have been marvellous. I can't thank you enough.'

'That's ok Mr Moyles. You'll see me again soon, I have no doubt.'

Finding themselves alone in the waiting room Ben and his Dad hugged each other as father and son, both releasing tears of relief. Ben was the first to offer words of comfort. 'He's made it Dad. Well done Rich, you little beauty!'

'I can't believe it son. It's going to change his whole life for the better. Come on we'd better go and see him.'

The atmosphere in the Intensive Care Unit was reverential, people only speaking in whispered tones, not daring to disturb sleeping patients. Graham had to identify himself to the nursing staff over the intercom before the door lock was released remotely, allowing them both to enter. Then the visiting pair were obliged to scrub their hands and put on protective masks and gowns to prevent the possibility of introducing any bacteria into the sterile environment. Rich was in a room on his own and when Graham saw him he gasped at his son's vulnerability. There seemed to be wires over the whole of his body, each one attached either to a catheter or an item of monitoring equipment, lighting up screens with flickering numbers and moving graphs in colours of orange, yellow and green. Graham scanned the monitors, hoping not to see red anywhere.

Rich was motionless, with a tube attached to the side of his mouth which Ben presumed was helping his brother to breathe. Ben and Graham looked at each other with expressions of sympathy for what the young man had already endured, knowing that further serious challenges still lay ahead. Ben whispered to his father, 'You go and have some sleep Dad. I'll sit with Rich.'

Graham was still the alpha male. 'I'm going nowhere. You go and use the bed and get some sleep. If I nod off in this chair that's good enough for me. You need to get some rest as well. There's the farm to see to tomorrow for starters. You have the bed and I'll stay here. Go on.'

The authority in his father's voice was something that Ben knew well enough. Rather than leave the courtesy bed unused, Ben left the ICU and crossed to the other side of the carpark to the Family Unit. There was no time to take stock of the day's events, it would have been too stressful. Instead, all Ben's reflexes were ordering him to cut out the world and he was soon fast asleep, in an attempt to re-energise for the following day.

The next morning saw Rich still unconscious and his father fast asleep in the chair beside his son's bed. Nurses on the early shift were doing their regular checks, ensuring all the monitor readings were recorded, all the drips replenished and all the patients were still alive. After going through the necessary procedures, Ben entered the ICU carrying two plastic cups of coffee and passed one to his father while looking at his brother's still body. A nurse entered to speak to them. 'It should be only one visitor in ICU. I know he's just had his operation but one of you should really leave before the Ward Sister comes in.'

Ben took advantage of the opportunity for some comfort. 'How's he doing nurse? Everything alright?'

'You'll really need to ask the doctor when he arrives later this morning. All I can tell you is that all his vital signs are strong and he's doing well.' This brought a smile to both family members as the nurse left them alone.

'I'd better go Dad. Joe and Eric Setherton are supposed to be coming to start work this morning. If they turn up before I get there they'll probably just turn back. I need to be there when they arrive.'

'Ok son, I've got my mobile with me and I'll ring if there's anything to report. See you later.'

With that farewell, Ben left his Dad alone to watch over his other son and he made his way to Moyles Farm, with the help of an armed escort.

XIII

In Geneva, the working day had already started. For Gaston Dubois it involved an important meeting with his lawyers to plan a strategy of damage limitation. As the Chief Executive of the Schtern Banking Group his office commanded a magnificent view over the beautiful city of Geneva with Lac Léman and the Swiss Alps providing a stunning backdrop. He was contemplating the lawyers' advice as he pondered how to extricate himself from the sticky situation that had developed. Basically they had told him to sit tight, the police could not prove anything untoward: he had done nothing wrong, only accepted gifts which were freely given. The bank had not been compromised in any way and guilt by association was not proof. Dubois may have known Dr Sebastian Thiroud but he was not complicit in his murder, he may have appointed Mademoiselle Veronique Perrin's to a senior personnel position but how was he supposed to know her references had been forged. It was not his responsibility to check every reference of every person he appointed to the bank. That was surely the job of the Human Resources Division.

The only thing he had done wrong and which could get him into trouble was to make an arrangement with a major account holder by the name of Adam Danyel Connolly. The deal was in response to an approach made by a mutual friend, namely Dr Sebastian Thiroud. Gaston was asked to name his price for agreeing to conspire against the Puissance project by passing on any information he had about Professor Ian Thompkins and his associates. This material could pertain to bank accounts and finance or to any details of a private nature as a result of their personal relationship. The mistake that Dubois had made was to sign a contract which sanitised this arrangement from 'AC' Connolly's perspective. As he gazed out of his top floor office's glorious panoramic window he contemplated the significance of that mistake. He could hardly expose Connolly as the person behind the whole conspiracy if he had a document indicating his own duplicity in the affair. Connolly had been clever enough to protect himself and Gaston Dubois would be risking a lot to go public in an effort to try and get off the hook. That was the dilemma he was contemplating as he watched a yellow tourist boat through his office window leaving the quayside and making its way towards Lausanne.

Gaston decided to take some further time to consider what to do next and told his personal assistant that he would be out of the office for the next hour. His intention was to walk along the shore of the Lake and try and think about his future plans. Leaving the office, Gaston walked past a maintenance worker who was cleaning the floor with a mop and bucket and he decided to take the man to task, 'Do you have to do that now? We're almost in the middle of a working day, for God's sake.'

'Sorry monsieur but I was told to come here because someone reported a spillage on the top floor. I shall not be long.'

Gaston entered the elevator and pressed zero for the ground floor about twelve storeys below. When the silver-coloured sliding doors closed, the lift began its journey. However, a switch engaged on a small panel hidden inside the cleaner's inside pocket activated a mini explosion which was enough to sever the cables controlling the speed of the elevator's descent. The result was catastrophic. The capsule containing its only passenger plummeted to the ground at a speed that no one could have survived. The impact was devastating and the outcome instantaneous. Gaston Dubois was dead.

While Captain Jacques Durand raced across the streets of Geneva to respond to an emergency at Schtern Towers, Ben Moyles was finishing his instructions to Joe and Eric Setherton on the farm before leaving them to begin their duties. On that particular day there were still a lot of restrictions imposed on the Setherton brothers' movements because the authorities had not yet finished with the Farm as a crime scene. However, Joe and Eric were not complaining; light duties were exactly the sort they preferred. While they saw to the animals' immediate needs Ben returned to the hospital to be at his brother's bedside.

A more lenient nurse was now on duty and the sympathetic smile pushing through her mask indicated that she did not seem strict enough to invoke the ICU's policy of one-patient-to-one-visitor as Ben walked past her in his protective gown and mouth cover. Graham did not see his son enter and jumped with a start when he was patted on the shoulder. 'Any developments?' whispered Ben, hoping for some good news.

Graham's tone was similarly hushed. 'Hi, son. Yeah… they are happy with him and have said that if he does not wake in the next hour or so, they might reduce his medication to bring him out of the coma.'

Ben peered over his brother as his head rested on the pillow. For a second, the sun was blocked and his movement produced a shadow over Rich's eyes. This seemed to unsettle the patient who began to blink before squinting in confusion. It was enough to get Graham Moyles out of his chair. 'Nurse, nurse … come quick. I think our Rich is coming round.'

He was right.

After sipping some cold water through a straw Rich began to regain consciousness. His painful soreness was eased by morphine but nobody was expecting him to suddenly jump up in bed. It was his first step along the long road to recovery.

XIV

'AC' Connolly was not used to waiting for other people but in this particular meeting he had the subservient role because the other attendee was a member of the Legislature of the United States. Senator Lenard Fitzimmons had held office in the American Congress for a number of years and had been a persistent target for lobbyists representing oil companies in the USA. They had on many previous occasions sought to influence the American Government by bringing pressure to bear on the Senator regarding the Country's energy policy. Fitzimmons was late to the meeting for good reason, he was attending another important gathering in a conference room of the Upper Chamber across the main esplanade which separated the respective buildings. The emergency issue under discussion was the impact that a new source of clean, sustainable energy would have on the American economy and particularly its coal, gas and oil industries. There was a clear threat to the market value of fossil fuels as a direct result of recently discovered scientific techniques.

Fitzimmons was in his early seventies, a silver-haired fox who was not easily intimidated. The arrogance of his long years in power gave him the confidence to speak plainly, a characteristic admired by many other politicians. He possessed eloquent public speaking skills and held the respect of most neutrals. Sometimes his bluntness was not always politically correct and it could get him into trouble with the Press. Connolly half-turned in his chair like a naughty schoolboy before getting to his feet when Fitzimmons entered the room. Before offering to shake hands with his guest, the politician immediately flicked a switch on the telephone console and instructed his personal assistant, 'No calls please, Alan – unless it's the President himself.' AC went to shake hands and was unsure whether the reason for 'Fitz' not responding was because he did not see the gesture or he just did not want to. In any event, the Senator settled into his seat and began their discussion.

'This is a bad business, AC. I thought you said you were going to sort it out. Well that didn't work!'

'Circumstances were not in our favour Senator. Things did not go according to plan due to misfortune and the inefficiency of my subordinates.' Connolly had decided that he would not talk about events directly, preferring to circumvent names and factual incidents which if spoken could be irrefutable in a court of law. The more ambiguous his references the more they were open to misinterpretation. He was not sure if their discussion was being recorded and he did not want any accusations being cited in front of a judge and jury. Like all politicians, AC would claim his words had simply being taken out of context if formally challenged. It was not difficult to see why events in Sergy had not affected his apparent integrity.

'Well whatever the reasons, I've got oil companies firing at me from every Godamn direction. They're as angry as hell and the apple cart has been well and truly turned over. Where are we with this mess in France or Switzerland of wherever the hell this Sergy place is supposed to be. Can any of that stink be traced back to us?' Connolly was slightly relieved that his superior was using the word 'us'.

'Not at all Senator. As far as everyone is concerned the conspiracy cannot be attributed to anyone or any company in the United States. On the contrary most of the investigation and media focus seems to be directed at countries in the Gulf especially Batar, where some of the money can be traced back to.'

Fitz expressed some relief. 'Well that's something I suppose. What about the 'sand jockeys' themselves they got anything to say about the sanctions we have imposed on them because of it.'

Connolly had spent a lot of time in the Middle East and although not a particular fan of political correctness, he did not like derogatory references to the people from that area. However, given the importance of the discussion at hand, he decided not to confront the issue. 'My bet Senator is that they will suffer a great deal of financial uncertainty, at least in the short term. Already stock values in the major oil companies have fallen significantly. The same is true of gas prices. If it continues there is no question it will only take a short period of time before it begins to affect the economies of Middle Eastern states.'

'So if this thing works and it looks like it damn-well could, the Arabs could go bust in the next few years while we go on and develop own energy source without having to trade with those people? All they could do is peddle the oil to each other until they go back to the Middle Ages where they belong?'

'That's right Senator. Meanwhile we have the inside track on accessing this new energy supply. Our friends in Europe will see to that.'

'You know that for a fact?' Connolly nodded his head as the Senator continued. 'So are you saying these Middle Eastern States could even take the rap for blowing up the scientists and we would come out of the swamp smelling like my wife's boudoir?'

'That's it exactly sir. All we would need to do is sow the seeds of doubt onto the world's political stage. If, for example a Senator who has the President's ear was to show him that Bureau investigations have traced the money trail from that explosion in France all the way to banks in Gulf State of Batar.....'

Fitzimmons was becoming agitated. 'We have that information?'

'Indeed we do Senator – and if the President was to repeat that to the media, or better still have our ambassador throw a tantrum at the United Nations Assembly about betrayal, then investment in the Middle East would begin to disappear. Our friends would come running to us to stand in the queue of investors trying to put their money into clean energy.'

Connolly's analysis of the situation was beginning to appeal to the experienced politician. 'The main thing is though, we have to act now, while all this stuff is going on. We can have a head start if we act quickly and go under the radar. If instead of pouring money into oil shares your investors in the oil business put their wealth into this new source of energy, we could cream off the crop as it grows. Instead of being oil billionaires our friends would be 'fusion' billionaires. Oil is exactly what it says it is, a fossil fuel. This clean stuff is the way forward and we can get in there first. All we need is money and power and that's where you come in Senator.'

Connolly's skill at being untraceable and unaccountable came to the fore. Instead of being blamed for Zenib's mess he was cleaning up in a way that not only got him out of trouble, he was also able to point the finger at the Middle Eastern States for a serious terrorist act that killed some of the world's most able scientists. His plan would allow America to get in bed with the Europeans in a way that would see the West dominate energy production over the next fifty years at least. Oil producing countries that were once poor would become poor again.

Fitzimmons brought the meeting to a conclusion. 'So how soon can you have this evidence in front of me. I don't want to sit in front of the President of the United States unless my gun is smoking.'

At this point, the master tactician knew he had won again. 'You can have all the evidence and data on your desk by the end of the day, along with computerised records on a flash drive, Senator.'

Fitzimmons' face lit up with relief at what he had been told. This was a plan for the future. They might even call it the 'Fitzimmons Plan' in years to come. This appealed immensely to the old man's ego. He stood and shook Connolly's hand with confident firmness. 'Thank you AC – good job.'

Connolly turned and raised his eyebrows as he left the room, the Senator failing to see his gesture of relief.

As soon as Fitzimmons was alone in his office he spoke into the intercom to his personal assistant once more. 'Alan, I want you to get me an appointment with the President at the first opportunity. Let him know that I have some vital information that I need to discuss with him. Tell him it is in the best interests of the United States that we meet.'

As he flicked the switch from green to red on his desk console, the Senator knew the world was about to undergo some major changes and the USA was going to stay on top of the pile. From the slim walnut case on his desk he took out one of his favourite Cohiba Siglo Cuban cigars and sat back into his leather chair. Purposefully he lit the tobacco and inhaled deeply to enjoy the indulgence. The Senator afforded himself a huge grin at the thought of the information he now had under his control, though his face was virtually obscured by the exhaled smoke escaping from his mouth.

PART FIVE

Everyone loved to be on the farm in the summer, especially when Nature did not ration the long sunny days. There was time to relish the beauty of the landscape because everything and everybody was less demanding. It had been six long months since that cold February when life changed for the members of the Moyle family. For once, the changes seemed to be for the better. Graham was either in the high pastures tendering the sheep or repairing the wall that was forever being knocked over in the winter winds. He did not mind constantly having to renovate the same wall, it was what he had always done and he was a man of simple pleasures and routines. Money had never meant much in his life.

Ben had demonstrated to the World that he had indeed been the brains behind the developments to find a source of clean, sustainable energy based around nuclear fusion. The data going back before the time of the explosion and the measures he had taken ensured that everything was authentic and could be proven. It still made him smile that the data from his laptops had been stored safely in a safety deposit box in Schtern Bank in Geneva. Little did his enemies know that what they were looking for had been under their noses all the time. Gaston Dubois had been guarding the very thing that ended up being the cause of his death.

Ben was up early on the farm, even rising before his Dad, he wanted to enjoy the sunrise and found sleep difficult since returning to normality. Life seemed too good to be true but slumber did not offer that haven of rest he had once enjoyed during days of innocence. Having spent two months in isolation under the protection of the British Secret Services preparing to release his knowledge to the world, he always had a lingering concern at the back of his mind. Nothing he did after the trauma of Puissance could erase the fact that he had killed two people. True, the killings had been necessary for his own self-preservation but the experience had changed him from being a wide-eyed, ambitious scientist into someone he found difficult to recognise. Ben had seen animal deaths many times on Moyles Farm and watched his Dad put creatures out of their misery but this had been different.

The days that he had once experienced running during a rising dawn in the countryside around Sergy were now a distant memory. Ben was out of condition, a consequence of too sedentary a lifestyle sitting in front of computer screens and behind a desk. Still, he had to start somewhere so putting on an old tracksuit and walking briskly out of the farm and into the beautiful landscape of the Cheviot Hills seemed like a good idea. He walked through the kitchen and into the rear porch of the farmhouse where he clicked his fingers at the curious face that had just reared up out of a basket.

'Come on boy, come on!' The six-month-old collie had not yet begun proper training and the early indicators suggested that he might not make it to sheepdog status. Pluto was a crazy dog and had not yet settled down. Graham had bought him to replace Archie, intending to train him up into a working sheepdog but this canine was nuts. Pluto had a long tongue that he allowed to hang loosely out of the corner of his mouth just like the Disney character. Rich had given the dog the same name because he always made him laugh, just like the cartoon canine. It was a wholly inappropriate label for a working sheepdog but given what Rich had been through neither Ben nor his Dad raised any objection.

Graham had been obliged to also invest in a ready-trained collie which he had bought from another farmer who lived on the Scottish side of the border. 'Hamish' was already schooled in handling sheep and only needed fine tuning before he was ready. In March, when the animals needed constant herding from one pasture to another the dog proved invaluable. Bonding with Hamish was work-related and he was kept in his own kennel out in the barn. It was a different home to the lair that had once belonged to Archie. That kennel had been burned not only as a mark of respect to the canine worker but also for practical reasons. Archie's scent on the kennel could have acted as a distraction for Hamish and delayed the time it took for the new canine to settle. Rich had chosen Pluto from a collection of pups during the early stages of his convalescence. The cute dog acted as a distraction from his recovery and allowed Rich to focus on something beyond his delicate condition.

Initially, Ben's twin brother spent ten days in hospital and then had to visit Cardiology as an out-patient every two weeks before the period was extended to a month. Around this time the family were hoping to lengthen the interlude to one or even two months as he was beginning to return to something resembling a normal life. There was a daily cocktail of tablets to consume but compared to what he had previously endured this was a minor inconvenience. Avoiding threats to infection on a farm was not easy but for Graham and Ben, nothing was too much trouble. They took it in turns to accompany Rich to the hospital for his regular check-ups. The Setherton boys were being employed virtually full-time on the farm because the organisation needed for medical appointments consumed time for Graham and Ben, taking them away from their normal daily duties.

Ben and Pluto bounded along the countryside taking in the fresh air and the beautiful scenery. Ben was alternating between throwing a ball and occasionally bending over to pick up a stick he found randomly lying on the ground. Pluto did not care what he brought back in his mouth, he was prepared to run after anything. The pair walked upward for about two miles before they came to the summit of the hill, where they stopped to take in the view. Ben sat on a protruding stone while Pluto lay at his feet, his surfeit of energy finally satisfied as his eyes began to close.

The tranquillity allowed Ben to think about the year's events and his mind revisited the unease he still felt about Gaston, who he had once considered a friend. His death had clearly been no accident but the only thing found on the top floor near the lift entrance had been a disused mop and a half-filled cleaning bucket containing soapy water. It came as no surprise to Captain Durand that the CCTV cameras on that floor had been disabled along with all those on the fire-escape stairwells, which almost certainly provided the escape route for the killer. The Chief Executive's death was reported in the Swiss press as a tragic accident. Gaston's demise also marked the end of the trail as far as finding anyone else complicit in the conspiracy was concerned. Gaston's wife, Camille had attempted to contact Ben via email and text, which he read. Her messages expressed regret at the turn of events and she attempted to explain how she knew nothing about Gaston's activities. However, Ben did not reply to any of her messages, there was no point. Whether she was guilty or innocent no longer mattered. Camille Dubois had no place in his life any more.

Ben did still keep in touch with Jacques Durand, who had finally been able to retire after a long and distinguished career. The police captain was unhappy about not being able to resolve his final few cases, which he concluded were all connected in some way. With typical Gallic acceptance he simply shrugged his shoulders and put it down to experience. On a visit to Geneva the two men had met to relish a couple of cognacs together and they enjoyed the social occasion significantly more than some of the formal situations they had endured. Jacques and his wife had moved to a comfortable house on the shores of Lake Geneva where the views acted as an antidote to some of the detective's more unpleasant memories.

Only once had Ben returned to Sergy in the last six months. That was to collect the remainder of his personal possessions and to attend the funeral of his old friend, Antoine Moreau. Ben's former neighbour never really recovered from his assault by undetected assailants, something which disturbed his equilibrium greatly. Following another fall in his apartment Antoine's calls for help after two days saw him admitted to the hospital in Sergy, where he died twenty-four hours later. Neither his sister nor his nephew attended the funeral and apart from two other people, there was no one else at the church service. The French authorities organised the funeral and Antoine's body was laid to rest in the cemetery in Sergy, on the edge of town.

Something in the sky above caught Ben's eye and he gathered sight of a kestrel hovering in the clear blueness above him. The bird appeared from nowhere and he surmised it must be targeting prey from its vantage point, no doubt sussing out the scene before descending onto an unsuspecting shrew. Just as it lowered, the kestrel swiftly flew off in a different direction, clearly spooked by something. A large buzzard majestically entered the scene and Ben watched a Darwinian drama unfold as the bigger bird's wingspan frightened away its smaller competitor. He fantasised that the newcomer might even have been a golden eagle although he doubted one would be that far south. The beauty of the unique scene comforted his rootless soul.

He looked down at the sleeping goon at his feet and smiled. There was a lot to be happy about these days. Fame had accompanied his world-changing discovery and as expected he was the toast of the international scientific community. The Nobel Prize nominations were due to be announced in Norway in September and it was no surprise that the name of Dr Ben Moyles was being heavily touted. Journalists followed his every movement when he was off the farm and several serious documentaries had been made about his life, cataloguing his humble beginnings from a remote area of Britain and his rise through the ranks of Puissance. Fortunately there was always Rich around to keep his brother's feet well and truly on the ground.

Big companies were lining up to invest in the commercial production of his power units. Sponsorship was not a problem and money was falling out of the sky in his direction. Although he had not spoken for a couple of months to his accountant, Ben was already a multi-millionaire, at least on paper. The plan was to have the majority of Western homes energised by the *Moyles Power Company* within the next twenty years and his personal purse would be expanded as a result. Perhaps that holiday the family had provisionally planned in order to watch a test match in the Caribbean would become a reality after all, particularly as he was spending some of his time out there. The small Caribbean island of Guadinique a former French protectorate, was the site for the new Centauri Project, the next stage of research in producing sustainable power. Alpha Centauri A and Alpha Centauri B are a binary pair of stars next in line in their closeness to Earth, after the Sun. Their name was the obvious choice after the Puissance site became redundant. Guadinque, independent since 1963 and formerly occupied by British troops was the ideal location for the next phase of international energy development. Its island geography made it easy to safeguard thanks to its position on the doorstep of the USA.

The security agencies had assured Ben that his life was no longer in danger, at least no more than any other wealthy international figure. Dr Moyles was now perceived as an asset to world development rather than a threat. The essence of his discovery was in the public domain for all countries developing their own power production to use to their advantage. Consultancy work across the globe was guaranteed.

Ben got up from his stony improvised seat and the sudden movement was like an electric shock to Pluto's system. The dog was on his feet in a flicker, instantly reverting to his highly-charged energised state, barking with excitement. 'Rich was right about you,' said Ben, 'You really are one stupid animal.' Pluto ignored the insult, preferring to retrieve the stick he had dropped nearby before dropping it at Ben's feet. His master obliged and threw the piece of wood with the superfluous instruction, 'Fetch boy.'

An hour later the duo arrived back at the farmhouse, where a coolish cooked breakfast was sitting on the kitchen table. Ben stared at the meal with some surprise, while his brother explained the reason for its presence.

'I didn't know where you had gone and made that for you earlier,' said Rich who was sitting in his father's favourite chair. The recovering patient was trying to prevent Pluto from running around his legs and jumping onto his lap. 'Me and Dad have had ours already. Where have you been anyway?'

'Just took Pluto out for a walk to get some exercise. I could certainly do with it. It's a beautiful morning out there.'

'Almost afternoon now. Just going to go into the lounge and watch a bit of the cricket. Fancy watching it with me? It's the second day of the first Ashes Test.'

'How are England doing anyway? Losing again, I suppose.'

'You guessed it. Another middle order collapse. The tail-enders are hanging on though. Think I'll go into the lounge and switch the telly on… Coming?'

'You go in and I'll just warm up this breakfast. I'll come in after I've eaten it. Looks nice, cheers bro.'

Twenty minutes later Ben walked into the lounge. 'Where's Pluto? he inquired, observing that the scene was more peaceful than expected.

'Had to put him out the back, he was getting too boisterous.'

'Tell me about it. He sure is one crazy dog. If he doesn't calm down soon the old man will be inserting some lead behind his ear.' The thought alarmed Rich, who regarded Pluto as his own pet. Ben realised what he had said after seeing the look of fear on his brother's face. 'Only kidding – Dad would never do that, don't worry.' Looking at the screen, something about the cricket match did not seem right to Ben. 'What's going on. Those are the England openers aren't they. I thought you said the middle-order had collapsed?'

'Yes these are recorded highlights from yesterday. Apparently there has been some overnight rain in London and since this is coming from Lords, there's a delay to play. There will be a wicket inspection at one o'clock.'

'Typical! It's glorious day up here but it's raining down South. It's usually the other way around. The world's gone mad.'

Rich's improving health sometimes caused his immaturity to bubble to the surface. 'At least they're not showing a repeat of that documentary featuring the well-known international figure, Dr Benjamin Moyles.

Oooh ... he's so clever ... what a man.' Ben threw a cushion at his brother, loving every second of the insult. Suddenly Rich had an idea of his own. 'Tell you what, let's have a game of schoolboy cricket. We've not played it in ages and I bet I can beat you easily now I'm feeling better!' Rich raised his arms in an Atlas bodybuilder pose.

'Ok we'll see. I'll go and get the book and pencils, I think I know where they are. You think of your team and I'll be back with mine.'

After a few minutes Ben returned with everything needed for the game. 'Ok who's in your team, bro?'

'Mine is the Silent Movies eleven. What about yours?'

'Mine is the Dead World Leaders eleven. Write your team members names into the book and then I'll do mine.'

Ten minutes later they were engrossed in their childhood game, laughing like two little boys at the ridiculous situations the roll of the pencils was producing. At that moment Graham returned to the farmhouse after returning from completing some never-ending repair work to a dry-brick wall in the lower pastures. He was attracted to the lounge by the sound of laughter and was curious to see what was going on. The two boys were so wrapped-up in their own world they did not see him enter.

'Ha-ha, that's out!' declared Rich. 'Come on, who's in next? I make that sixty-five for four.'

'Alright, alright ... I know what the score is.' Turning to the doorway Ben continued, 'Oh, hi Dad. Didn't see you there.' He returned to his game. ' Right, so next one in to bat is Mahatma Ghandi, who is facing the spin bowling of Buster Keaton.'

Rich brought his knees up to his waist in a gesture of enthusiastic fun. Graham turned away before offering a mild reprimand. 'Don't suppose you two have noticed that you're in here during the middle of the day with the light on.' His rebuke went unnoticed as the boys' father gazed at them with a look of immense pride. 'I suppose I'd better switch it off, somebody's got to save the electricity.' With that parting shot, Graham wandered into the kitchen with laughter ringing in his ears.